THE YEAR OF FOUR

A PHOEBE POPE NOVEL * BOOK 1

NYA JADE

DREAMWELL PUBLISHING

ISBN-10: 0998695904
ISBN-13: 9780998695907

Cover Design by Damonza
Illustrations © 2012 by Coby L. Cyr

Web: www.PhoebePope.com
Facebook: www.facebook.com/PhoebePopeBooks
Twitter: @TheNyaJade

For Al, my love.

"It is entirely possible that behind the perception of our senses worlds are hidden of which we are unaware."
—ALBERT EINSTEIN.

ONE

Phoebe was too far away to sense whether the boy had one heart or two. Through the maze of trees with clattering leaves, she could see him moving with purposeful speed. He was headed toward her destination—a brownstone chapel perched at the top of a small hill. Not knowing the boy's nature made Phoebe hesitate. Then came the sound of tower bells. Eight o'clock. There was no time to think of an alternate route. She was officially late for the Conversion.

A loud, echoing *crack* quickened Phoebe's pace as lightning slashed the indigo sky above her. She had barely reached the base of the hill when rain began pounding down. Clutching the camera that hung from the strap around her neck, she sprinted the final stretch, arriving breathless.

Phoebe wiped the rain from her face, and then entered the chapel. Inside, light from moon-facing windows cast a misty glow across the sanctuary, the air redolent with the smoke of a blazing fireplace. She glanced around the heart of the nondenominational Green Lane Academy. It seemed so ordinary, so quiet, even peaceful. Rows of pews with velvet cushions ran the width of the room. She moved between them, taking care to remain in the shadows. An irregular shape in a dark corner caught her eye and Phoebe could just barely make out the outline of the boy. He knelt with his head between his hands, his body huddled against a pew. Praying.

Phoebe paused several feet away and waited. After a moment she felt energy seeping from the boy's skin, raising the hairs on hers. Cold and electric, it meant one thing: the boy had only one heart. She couldn't risk him seeing what she had come there to do. That meant waiting. Just then, something stirred behind her.

With her hearts thudding, Phoebe spun around to face a girl who appeared to be around her age: sixteen, maybe seventeen. Her eyes stared expectantly at Phoebe from behind a severe pair of black-rimmed glasses.

"Thank God I'm not the only delinquent who's late," the girl said. "Christ, did I scare you?" she asked, clearly baffled as she took a hesitant step backward.

"No," Phoebe lied and lowered her fists.

The girl looked unconvinced. "Well, I didn't mean to. I figured you were aware of me."

"It's all good . . ." Warmth crept over Phoebe's skin. She blushed, embarrassed that she was only now sensing the physical energy of a fellow Shaper.

"I'm Hayley."

"Hi. I'm Phoebe."

As they shook hands, the boy grunted and shifted to the end of his pew.

"Come on, let's get warm," Hayley said.

Hayley moved toward the fireplace with short, graceful steps. Phoebe followed, feeling awkward in her limbs by comparison. At nearly six feet tall, she towered over her petite companion. They slid into a fireside pew.

Flames crackled toward a portrait of the Virgin Mary hanging high on the wall above it. Phoebe gazed at the oil painting briefly, and then turned sideways, facing Hayley, who had already removed her coat and spread it out next to her.

"So," she said. "Where's the entrance?"

Hayley gave a lazy shrug. "Dunno. My search got interrupted."

"Oh." Phoebe glanced quickly at the human boy. "Why'd you miss the escort?"

"Major hair crisis."

Phoebe raised an eyebrow. "Really?"

"A girl's gotta look good—just kidding," Hayley said, laughing. "My kid brothers stuck gum in my ponytail. I don't smell like peanut butter, do I?" She swept strands of her light-brown hair under her nose.

Phoebe shook her head. "Why? Another brotherly prank?"

"No. It's my mom's remedy for removing gum," Hayley said, examining the ends of her hair. "It takes forever, but it beats the hell outta chopping it out. So . . . why are you late?"

Phoebe absently ran her camera strap between her fingers. She was going to tell Hayley that she got distracted photographing the old farmhouses-turned-dorms dotting the campus, but she didn't get the opportunity. A sudden sound of footsteps on the creaking floor cut through the air and both girls snapped their heads to the right. The boy had risen to his feet. He crossed himself, shot them a look of silent fury, turned on his heel, and left the chapel.

"What was that about?" Phoebe muttered. Hayley rolled her eyes and shrugged as they both stared at the door the boy had closed behind him.

"Some prefer the sanctity of silence when in prayer." The room resonated with a man's reproach. Phoebe flinched. She looked to the front of the chapel where a hooded figure stepped out from the shadows of the altar.

A wrinkled hand rose from inside a burgundy cloak and beckoned them. "Well, what are you waiting for?" the man said. "Come."

Phoebe sprang to her feet. Suddenly conscious of her own hair, remembering what the rain had done to it, she tugged in vain at the knots. She scurried down the aisle, Hayley close at her heels, mumbling, "Forgive us Father—"

"I'm not a priest, lass," the man said, his eyes reflecting moonlight as he watched them mount the steps to the altar. "I'm Gabe, the custodian for this narthyx point."

"Nice to meet you, Gabe. I'm—"

"Phoebe."

"How'd you know?" Phoebe's eyes widened.

"I knew your father during his time here. I see you've inherited his incurable tardiness in addition to that famous hair of his," he said, softening his tone.

As a reflex, Phoebe ran a hand through the white streak in the front of her copper-colored locks. She had a sudden urge to cry, but she shoved it down. The pain of losing her father still remained fresh, no matter how many months rolled by. Hayley took one look at Phoebe's face and had the good grace to feign sudden interest in the racks of unlit candles behind them.

"You do him proud being here," Gabe said warmly.

"Thank you," Phoebe said quietly. "How do we find the ceremony?"

"Follow the moons to the Great Hall." Phoebe waited for some elaboration but none came. Gabe simply raised his chin toward the pulpit and chided, "Come, now, before you miss the whole thing."

The girls gathered behind the gently hunched man as he pushed against the pulpit. A reverberating series of clicks echoed from within the stone structure, and a moment later, it slid to the side, revealing a dark, square opening with a stairway leading down.

"Careful of your step," he said.

After thanking Gabe, Hayley slipped agilely by him and Phoebe into the passageway, disappearing into the blackness. Phoebe began to step cautiously into the stairwell when the sleeve of her sweater caught. She glanced up and saw that Gabe held her cuff between forefinger and thumb.

"If you need anything, lass," he said, dropping her arm, "anything at all, you know where to find me." Phoebe considered his narrow, lined face and saw the sincerity etched into his features. It seemed her father had meant something to this old man. She nodded. A guarded smile appeared on Gabe's face as he slid the base of the pulpit over the entrance.

Darkness swallowed Phoebe. The sound of Hayley's footsteps echoed around her. She pressed a finger to her temple and blinked rapidly. Soon her eyes adjusted to the dark and she could see Hayley's moving form. Phoebe followed her, careful to keep a steadying hand on the cold stone walls as they made several sharp turns. Having no sense of the depth of their descent unnerved her as the stairs continued to slope downwards into utter blackness. Just when she thought it would never end, Phoebe heard the merciful sound of Hayley opening a door.

Inches behind Hayley, Phoebe passed through the doorway and stopped short. The smooth walls of a circular room were inlaid with at least thirty black doors spaced five or so feet apart. Plaques in the center of each one told where each door led, as Phoebe saw ABOVE DINING HALL, ABOVE LIBRARY, and ABOVE CHAPEL on the door they'd just come through.

"The narthyx chamber," Hayley said reverently, running her fingers over the words, *"That which is Below is like that which is Above*—H. Trismegistus," written in gold letters on the wall. She looked around, an expression of awe spreading across her glowing face.

"So cool to finally see it," Phoebe said.

"Mm hmm," Hayley agreed, distractedly.

Phoebe couldn't help but grin as she continued reading the plaques. These were the secret passageways that connected the Campus Above with the Campus Below. The human students roamed their austere halls unaware that below their manicured grounds existed a prestigious school of an entirely different kind.

Two

They stepped through the door marked Below Courtyard and entered a gleaming white marble quadrangle. Phoebe turned in a slow circle. She felt entranced by the splendor of stone arches all around them, rising to meet upper corridors with balconies overlooking a large, central fountain and garden.

"This way!" Hayley called, pointing across the courtyard to an archway lined with golden images of the moon in its four major phases. They set off at a run and followed a trail of moons down hallways and around corners. Anticipation rattled Phoebe's chest. Her father had run down these very halls.

Moments later, at the trail's end, they came upon a tall muscled guard positioned outside a pair of mahogany doors. He watched their approach with narrowed eyes. Phoebe parted her lips to apologize for their lateness, but before she could speak, the guard grunted and released the iron bar lock. The massive doors swung inward and he waved them in with a flick of his wrist.

The instant Phoebe stepped into the Great Hall, the scent of sweet spices wafted into her nostrils. She stood still, trying to absorb the scene before her. A large, two-story dome glistened at the center of the cavernous room—a glass structure embellished with several golden images of a lion's head. Countless ornamental glass bottles ablaze with firelight formed a circle around the base of the dome, washing the room in warm light. Inside, long tables, garnished with white moon flowers, had been arranged in three rows in front of a wide stage. The festive tables were packed with hundreds of students whose backs faced Phoebe and Hayley.

Phoebe elbowed Hayley. "Amazing, huh?"

"Unreal," Hayley gushed. "Now what?"

"Over there." Phoebe nodded toward the only two empty seats at the last row of tables near the dome's entrance.

Hayley charged forward, pulling Phoebe along with her.

"Don't look," Hayley whispered, "but we're getting the evil eye."

"Crap." Phoebe cringed at the disapproving glare she got from some faculty members. *Great first impression*, she thought.

"Next," a commanding male baritone bellowed, as Phoebe and Hayley settled into their seats. "I call before you Xavier Reno."

Phoebe's eyes followed an elaborate marble staircase, one of a pair that spiraled upward to a balcony that was situated under the dome's ceiling and to the right side of the stage. There, a middle-aged man with a prominent aquiline nose and deep sunken eyes stood peering down at the crowd. He wore a purple toga that swathed him in silken waves. From her father's description, Phoebe knew at once that this man must be Professor Yori, Headmaster of the Campus Below.

Phoebe turned her attention to the stage where a male student draped in an ivory toga rose from a bench. After a nervous glance at a blond, heavyset girl next to him, also in a toga, who gave an encouraging smile, the boy moved forward, tugging up fistfuls of cloth to prevent tripping as he walked. He arrived at center stage, and cautiously picked up a luminous object from a round, gilded table.

Hayley gasped, shifting in her seat for a better view. "Utaviium," she said, faster than Phoebe could think it. And it was. Thin and cylindrical, Utaviium was a pale blue crystal enchanted to capture and hold a single bolt of lightning. It was beautiful to look at; both of the girls sat transfixed, focused on the frenetic light within the crystal.

"Xavier, show yourself!" Professor Yori declared.

In the moment of those words' utterance, several things happened at once. The boy's toga slipped to the floor. He smashed the Utaviium at his feet. A massive wave of energy rippled through the dome, and for an instant, Phoebe was blinded by the intensity of its accompanying light. When her vision recovered, a giant, red falcon stood where the boy had been.

Spreading his bejeweled fingers across the balcony's railing, Professor Yori spoke down to the majestic bird, "Son of Osiah, rise!" Phoebe watched a pair of iridescent wings unfold sleekly, wings that from tip to tip spanned the width of the stage. The falcon lifted and lowered them slowly. The students erupted with applause as he took silent flight, faltered for a moment, then shot upward to a long perch suspended from the dome's ceiling by gold chains. All heads peered up as, beating his wings inward to steady himself, the falcon took his place on the perch next to a silver eagle and a black hawk.

Phoebe glanced to her side. She saw Hayley's eyes ablaze with her own excitement. Never before had she seen the mind-thrilling spectacle of a first time Conversion. Goosebumps waltzed up her arms.

Professor Yori cleared his throat, reclaiming the crowd's attention.

"I now call Leslie Davis."

The blond girl who had been sitting next to Xavier strolled to center stage, grabbed another Utaviium, and bobbed a hasty curtsy.

"Show yourself," Professor Yori said again, with an equal measure of intensity. The girl shattered the Utaviium like Xavier had done, and Phoebe bit back a gasp as a jaguar with silver spotted gold fur appeared in her place and began to stalk the stage, tail whipping in the air.

"We welcome a daughter of Gavya!" the headmaster said. When thunderous applause filled the air, the massive cat exploded off the stage, joining a white leopard Phoebe hadn't noticed sitting on the floor between the stage and the crowd. She found the regal assurance of both animals spellbinding. And, although she wouldn't find out until the first full moon after her seventeenth birthday, Phoebe could not help longing to know what alternate Shape her second heart belonged to.

As Phoebe's mind wandered, so did her gaze, and she noticed for the first time the purple banners that hung the length of the Great Hall's back walls. Gold words embroidered into the center of each one read: VESUVIUS AD 79. Old and faded, the banners were a reminder of Pompeii, the ancient Roman city and ancestral homeland of Shapers that had once thrived before the eruption of Mount Vesuvius buried it under volcanic ash. The human world viewed the demise of Pompeii as a catastrophic act of nature. But every Shaper knew that Mount Vesuvius had been triggered by an act of war.

A collective movement of chairs scraping back pulled Phoebe's gaze away from the banners as the entire congregation rose to its feet. Moving slowly, a slight limp in his stride, Professor Yori descended one of the staircases. He removed a laurel wreath from his bald head and passed a hand over the interlocking branches and leaves. When he reached the bottommost stair, he was met by a couple of older students who assisted him with disrobing in a swift but careful manner. The voluminous toga unraveled, revealing that the headmaster wore a stately black suit underneath.

Once the two students had removed his rings, folded the toga between them and left the stage, Professor Yori said, "We have come to the conclusion of this full moon's Conversion. I congratulate all the newly converted on this important rite of passage. This includes those of you who Converted over the summer in the presence of your community leaders, family, and friends. Reaching the day your second Shape is awakened is a momentous event to celebrate so"—he raised the wreath in a sort of benediction—"blessings of Osiah and Gavya."

The students moved their right hands to their lips in unison, and then crossed both arms in an X over their chests—one fist placed over each heart.

"Welcome back, Cadets." Professor Yori gestured for them to be seated. "And a special welcome to our newest Hastati class. Your decision to train for the Shaper Intelligence Service is an admirable one, and a decision that I know was not made without long and careful thought. It is why we mark the beginning of the year with a grand Conversion Ceremony in the tradition of the Old Country. It reminds us of what we serve to protect. And now, as is our custom, the Principes class will swear in the new Hastati class."

Phoebe stood with her classmates as everyone in the middle row of tables rose and turned to face them. Together the second-years said, "We, the Principes class, candidates for advancement to Triarii class, bid you welcome."

"We are happy to be welcomed," Phoebe replied with her class, reciting the response they'd been given in their trainee handbook.

The Principes continued: "Please give your enrollment statement."

"We are here to gain physical toughness. Develop strength of character. And sharpen our mental acumen."

"Why do you fight?"

"Loyalty to each other. Service to the Royal Court. And in honor of Pompeii."

"And when called to the task?"

Phoebe's stomach lurched. Her palms suddenly felt clammy. With a shallow breath she answered timidly, "We will kill Vigos, no questions asked."

Then Phoebe shook hands with the Principes boy in front of her, who looked at her with concern. Embarrassed, she composed her face into a picture of calm. She pulled her hand from his grasp and sat slowly, caught up in the meaning of the oath. Doubt, sharp and unwanted, coiled in her stomach. What if she couldn't make her father's career her own?

"The start of a new moonester," Professor Yori said, "brings with it a few quick announcements. First, and of most importance, recent reports indicate a spike in Vigo activity in the area—" Gasps and murmurs broke out as every student turned to address his or her neighbor.

Professor Yori's whistle cut through the noise. The dome fell silent. Maintaining his composure, the headmaster looked out at the sea of students. "In the one hundred years of the Campus Below, Vigos have never once found the school. We remain perfectly cloaked by the presence of humans."

Phoebe knew that Professor Yori was right. Her father had once explained that because of the warm physical energy that radiated from Shapers, a gathering as large as a school would be a beacon for Vigos to track. Luckily, the presence of a greater mass of cold energy humans, like the Green Lane Academy population, could shield them. This truth failed to stop the shiver that swept through Phoebe.

The headmaster continued, "The concern is localized in Boston. There will be no trips into the greater city area or into the town of Dedham until further notice. Now," he continued, "on to the more administrative announcements. Hastati years, if you have not already done so, please make sure to finalize your course selections for both campuses by midnight tonight."

Phoebe frowned inwardly; she hadn't turned in her Above schedule yet. Shapers were required to take classes with the Green Lane Academy students because subjects such as mathematics, science, and English, needed for assimilation in the human world, were not taught at the Campus Below. Anxious about her double course load, Phoebe was still deciding which electives would require the least amount of work.

"And lastly," Professor Yori said, "the custodians would like you to know that the door in the narthyx chamber that leads to the Above library is closed for maintenance."

Just as Professor Yori began to dismiss the students, a thin, gray-haired woman hurried toward the stage, handed him a folder, and then bustled away. The headmaster reviewed the file briefly, a muscle twitching beneath his short graying beard. Looking up he said in a tight voice, "I would like to see Scott Roland, Lewis Baker, Mariko Higashi, and Phoebe Pope in my office tomorrow during the lunch hour." And as far away as Phoebe was from the headmaster, she could have sworn his eyes had flashed in her direction as he'd said it.

Hayley leaned close to Phoebe and whispered, "Is he talking about you?"

Phoebe nodded. "You think it's 'cause I was late?"

"Can't be," Hayley said, shaking her head. "I'd be on that list too."

Phoebe stared at Professor Yori, a nervous feeling brewing in her stomach. What could he possibly want?

"Go with Osiah and Gavya," he boomed and dismissed the crowd with a small bow.

Later, as the rest of the campus slept, Phoebe lay heartsick in the small grassy courtyard behind her dorm. Under a clear sky, she gazed at the brittle-looking moon, willing her body not to succumb to fatigue. If she did not sleep, the nightmare would not come. But Phoebe knew that, whether or not her eyes closed, the memory would still find a way in. Always.

She remembered rain hammering on the roof of the car as her father sped down a road lined by a wall of forest on either side. Behind them, the choral growl of the Vigos rose.

"Seat belt!" her father had shouted. His eyes were focused ahead, his jaw hard. Drawing the belt across her body, Phoebe stared in the side view mirror, seeing the moving shadows growing larger in the distance. Her panic soared.

"It's going to be okay." Her father stole a quick glance at her. "They can't chase us all night. I promise you."

Phoebe glanced at the speedometer and swallowed; the needle had pushed up past ninety. They turned a tight corner, and then, as her father had promised, the Vigos fell back, their growls receding into the drone of the rain. Phoebe saw triumph flash in her father's eyes mere seconds before the car hydroplaned, turning and turning as though it would never stop.

Even now, as she lay curled in on herself, her arms wrapped around her body, Phoebe could hear the explosion of the car smashing into the tree. She could taste the gagging heat of blood dripping down her throat as she crawled her way out of the tangled mass of glass, metal, and branches.

"Dad," Phoebe cried, stumbling over to the broken shape of her father lying nearby.

His eyes flickered up at her. "Honey," he said, his voice hoarse and urgent. "They heard the crash." He coughed raggedly, and blood ran from the corner of his mouth. "You've got to go." What her father was asking her to do rattled around in Phoebe's brain, failing to fully register even as her legs gave way underneath her. Her knees hit soggy earth, and, frantically eyeballing his injuries, she touched his face.

"You've already started heal—"

"I can't heal enough before they get here." His eyes slid to the darkness behind her, in the direction from which they'd come. Phoebe could hear them coming and the ground beneath her trembled with the vibrations of their advancing feet—Vigos drunk with the scent of a Shaper down. Phoebe felt intolerable pain at the thought of leaving her father. She wouldn't do it.

"I can get you out of here!" She took both of his wrists in her hands and began to pull with a determination that burned. Then something twisted inside her chest, hard and insistent. Phoebe recognized it immediately; her father was *pushing* emotion into her: courage and the will to survive.

As if he'd just slapped her across the face, Phoebe glared up at him, blinking. "Stop it—stop it!" Her voice broke. They both knew he needed every drop of those instincts for himself. Phoebe squeezed her eyes with the effort of *pushing* them back into him, but even in his dying moments, her father's ability was stronger than her own.

"Don't fight me on this one, kid." He ran a bloodied hand through her hair, his voice now just above a whisper. "You have to go. Please." Tears seeped into the blood on Phoebe's bruised face. "If they're distracted with me, they won't sense you." Her father looked at her with eyes that held love and the wildness of one last *push*. When he did, Phoebe felt his power crash though her with a force she couldn't fight. A burning need to survive controlled every part of her. She scrambled to her feet and ran.

Phoebe fled into the forest feeling none of the branches that clawed at her hair and scraped her arms and legs. A few hundred yards from the crash site, her skin flared hot from the physical energy of a nearby Vigo. Daring to look back, Phoebe staggered at the sight of the silver-striped black Tiger approaching her father, its fiery eyes burning bright. Large silver spikes ran down its heavily arched back to the tip of a tail that was poised to strike.

A scream caught in Phoebe's throat. None of the stories had adequately prepared her for this. The Vigo was huge. A lot bigger than she'd imagined. The beast roared in triumph. And an instant later, it morphed into a tall woman, who wore a dark jumpsuit, her blond hair as pale as early morning mist. Phoebe had barely absorbed the rapid transformation when a violent shiver pulsed through her, sharpening the instinct to flee. And she did.

Now, in the solitude of her dorm's courtyard, Phoebe listened as a breeze tickled wind chimes someone had hung on a branch above her. Her eyes stung with pent-in tears until she reluctantly began to sob. Her father was gone. Phoebe slid a hand underneath her shirt. She fingered the scar that arced across her stomach, and brushed the one that ran down the fold of her right shoulder with her thumb. Her other hand traveled behind her left ear, tracing that jagged scar along the back of her neck. Her body was a landscape of reminders.

❦ THREE

The next morning, Phoebe felt an energizing sense of peace, as though her dreaming mind had spread a balm over her aching hearts. By quarter to seven she'd showered, pulled on her Green Lane uniform, and taken photos of the sun pushing the navy of night below the horizon, all before anyone stirred in her dorm. A chill wind snaked its way into her coat. She put a hustle in her step, crunching leaves kissed with every hue of autumn under her feet.

Within minutes, Phoebe arrived at the red barn that housed the Green Lane dining hall. As she crossed the threshold, she felt a light tap on her right shoulder. Hayley stood behind her, smiling mischievously, with her hair pulled up into a neat twist.

"Doesn't anyone see the irony of us Shapers living on a campus that used to be a farm?" she whispered with a smirk.

"At least it's not a zoo," Phoebe retorted in a low voice.

Hayley laughed. "The pancakes are to die for. Come join me when you're done." She indicated a corner table that held a lone tray of food.

"Sure thing." Phoebe moved with the river of students around the many buffet stations, quickly loading her tray with more food than she could possibly eat, and arrived at Hayley's table to find her perusing a copy of the *Green Lane Gazette*.

"You won't believe this," Hayley said, looking over the top of the paper at Phoebe with a slight frown on her face.

Phoebe put down her tray and sat. "What?"

"It says here in this article that three particle physicists from Harvard were recently abducted outside their Boston homes," Hayley said. "Authorities have no leads." Phoebe paused as she reached for her scone. "They're saying," Hayley continued, dropping her voice, "that this comes at a time when there has been an escalation in unexplained criminal activity in the city."

Phoebe looked around them. They were two tables away from the nearest group of humans. Still, she whispered, "You think it has to do with Yori's announcement?"

Hayley nodded solemnly.

Phoebe's eyes narrowed as she broke her scone in half and began spreading a liberal amount of jam onto both pieces. "What would Vigos want with particle physicists?" she murmured.

"Hell if I know. But what I do know is that the ban on trips into Boston sucks." Hayley laid down the paper and heaved a dramatic sigh. "Coming here was supposed to be my great escape," she said, sounding defeated.

"From what?"

"Santa Claus, Indiana."

Phoebe jerked an eyebrow. "Santa Claus? As in Rudolph's fat boss?"

"The one and only," Hayley half laughed with such a distinct note of bitterness that Phoebe stared at her blankly, wondering how a town with a beloved namesake could be so bad. As though reading her mind, Hayley added, "You have no idea how boring it is there. Let me put it this way: Answering the thousands of 'Dear Santa' letters our post office gets from around the world during the holidays is the biggest event of the year."

"That sounds cute—"

"It's not cute," Hayley said in an almost indignant tone, "when you have to dress like an elf while doing it. Look at me"—she waved a hand over her body—"do I scream elf to you?"

Phoebe couldn't stifle a snort. "So you traded one small town for another?"

"Yeah. But at least Dedham has access to a legit city," Hayley said. She pointed a forkful of pancakes at Phoebe. "Where are you from?"

Before Phoebe could answer someone took a seat on the edge of their table. She and Hayley glanced up at a lanky girl with maple-colored skin and hair that fell in thick, ebony ringlets over her shoulders.

"Where ya been, roomie?" she said to Phoebe. "Didn't hear ya come in last night and I'm a light sleeper. Then when I woke up this morning, you were gone."

Phoebe had met her roommate Cynthia and her entire family the previous night when they arrived at the dorm chattering excitedly, with tons of luggage in tow. Cynthia's father had found it necessary to corner Phoebe and drone on about the family's school legacy, Cynthia's stellar junior high grades, and certain future as an Ivy Leaguer. Pushed beyond her endurance, Phoebe had grabbed her camera, politely excused herself, and slipped out to explore the campus.

"Hi Cynthia—"

"It's Cyn," Cynthia said, interrupting. "Remember?"

Phoebe forced a small smile. "When I got back you were fast asleep."

Cyn drew down her perfectly arched eyebrows in a disbelieving expression. Phoebe knew that Cyn wasn't wrong to doubt her. She had been lying awake in the dark when Phoebe had returned from the courtyard. Using her Shaper silent stealth, however, Phoebe had managed to slip into the room, undress, and crawl into bed unnoticed.

"What did you get into last night?" Cyn asked, still eying Phoebe with suspicion.

"Nothing much. Just wandered around taking photos."

"All night?" Cyn's eyebrows rose further.

"Then she was hangin' with me," Hayley jumped in.

Phoebe shot Hayley a grateful look and made a quick introduction. "Cynth—Cyn, this is Hayley. Hayley, Cyn."

Cyn turned her liquid brown eyes to Hayley, regarded her for a moment and then grinned broadly. "You're reading my article!" she said, stabbing the features section of Hayley's paper with a French-manicured finger. Phoebe confirmed this with a quick glance at the byline. "Crazy, isn't it? On the next page I talk about the millions of dollars worth of equipment that disappeared along with the physicists."

Phoebe and Hayley exchanged quick glances.

"Anyway," Cyn said, returning her attention to Phoebe. "I came to tell you that the *Gazette* is looking for a new features photographer. I told them you'd be perfect. The work you did for the paper at your old school was amazing!" Phoebe's surprise showed, and Cyn didn't miss it. Smiling brightly, she rolled her eyes, "I Googled you. With my endorsement, the job is yours if you want it." Cyn smoothed her pleated navy skirt and slid off the table. "Think about it, roomie." She sashayed off, throwing a "Nice to meet you, Hayley" over her shoulder as she went.

"Damn," Hayley said, staring at Cyn's retreating figure. "Why didn't I think of Googling my roommate, Maya Le—" The end of Hayley's sentence drowned in a sudden, earsplitting clamor of screams that erupted around them. Excitement sizzled through the room. Phoebe pressed herself back against her chair and stared with puzzlement at several groups of girls fairly quaking at their tables, looking as though they were about to pass out.

"Oh my God!" Hayley said in a pitch that had escalated a few unnatural octaves.

Phoebe returned her gaze to Hayley. "What?"

"I can't believe it's actually true." Hayley riffled diligently through her backpack, muttering something under her breath about the magazine being in there somewhere. "They said he might be going to a private school in the area, but I didn't believe it."

"Who said who'd be going where?"

"*Teen Hollywood Dish*," Hayley said, as though explaining the obvious. She threw her hands up. "I can't find my latest issue. But he's actually here," she said pointing, her eyes gleaming, "Colten Chase is here!"

That spun Phoebe in her chair. Her eyes followed Hayley's wavering hand to a table near the doorway and her jaw hung slack; it was him. When it came to pop culture, Phoebe rarely troubled herself with keeping up, preferring time spent behind her camera or in a book. Even so, she wasn't oblivious enough to not know Colten Chase, star of the *Taylor Hawk—Teen Agent* movies. He was practically the teen James Bond.

"Colten Chase is a student here?" Phoebe said incredulously, glancing back at Hayley whose eyes had glazed over.

"He's so hot," Hayley gushed. "And tall!"

Phoebe craned her neck to see more of Colten over the chaos of students elbowing each other out of the way just to stand close as he walked by. He had a tan-complexioned face lit by large, expressive eyes. Chestnut hair spilled over his collar, tossed in a fresh-out-of-bed manner that Phoebe knew most girls found appealing but she considered lazy. *What is wrong with using a comb*, she thought. Still, Phoebe couldn't deny that even when dressed in the plain uniform of gray slacks, a white button down shirt, and a navy tie, Colten was gorgeous beyond belief.

"I thought he was done with school," Phoebe said, peeling her eyes away from him.

Hayley, who seemed to have regained her composure said, "Well, according to *Dish*, he spent more time on movie sets last year than in the classroom and has to redo his senior year."

"But why here?"

"Why ask why? He's here and we're here. All is good! Anyway," she added with an air of authority, "I know Green Lane is a top-tier school and all but I'm sure he picked us since nothing exciting ever happens in small towns. Probably not worth it for the paparazzi to bug him here."

Hayley's theory was entirely lost on Phoebe, who wasn't taking in a word of it, but rather was surreptitiously stealing another glance at Colten. She was fascinated by the way his body moved with a certain confidence, almost grace, as he acknowledged those in his presence, shaking hands with engaged interest and signing autographs. Phoebe gathered that his was a well-practiced routine when it came to handling such adoration.

Colten's head suddenly swiveled in their direction, and his distressingly beautiful green eyes caught hold of Phoebe's. His gaze swept across her face; struck by its intensity, she looked away hurriedly, lowering her eyes to her tray. After giving herself a moment to recover, Phoebe chanced another glance. To her surprise, Colten was still staring at her, this time with a wide, dazzling smile that almost dared her not to blush. And blush Phoebe did, just as the bell rang and his eyes dropped from hers.

"What was that about?" Hayley asked with a pointed sidelong look.

"Hmm . . . ?" A dull ache throbbed behind Phoebe's eyes prompting her to massage small circles into the crease between her brows. "What was what about?"

"C'mon," Hayley said, "don't even try to pretend Colten Chase wasn't just checking you out."

As Hayley gathered up her newspaper and hoisted a backpack with a square *Hip Hop Life* patch on her shoulder, Phoebe cast around for a counter comment and managed, unconvincingly, "He was just looking in this general direction."

"Yeah, in the direction of those supermodel legs of yours!" Hayley waggled suggestive eyebrows behind her black-rimmed glasses.

At this, Phoebe laughed a dismissive, self-deprecating laugh and lowered her gaze. People often said that Phoebe was beautiful, with her storm-cloud eyes, and hair saturated with the red-gold brilliance of copper. At times Phoebe could see this. But mostly she only felt too tall, too thin, and completely awkward.

"I mean, do you see him?" Hayley continued. Phoebe looked up, embarrassed, wondering if Hayley had seen her furtive looks at Colten. "Over six feet of sexy is checking out your tower of sexy and you're being blasé about it."

Phoebe shrugged. "Someone that hot," she said, trying not to steal another look, "probably isn't that interesting." Phoebe knew it was an unfair generalization, but she'd seen enough celebrity interviews to know that many of the gorgeous ones got by on good-looks-octane and nothing else.

"Well I'm hot,"—Hayley shimmied her shoulders—"and very interesting."

Phoebe grinned at her in agreement. Hayley exuded charming energy with her olive skin, bright smile, and deep dimples. "You may be a little too hot," she said, laughing as Hayley shimmied some more. "Where's your first class?" Phoebe asked, changing the subject.

"Below. You?"

Phoebe reached into her backpack, pulled out some papers and consulted her schedule. "I'm up here."

Shaper schedules were staggered between the two campuses so that a third of the Green Lane population didn't mysteriously disappear all at once. And from what Phoebe understood, there were Shapers among the Green Lane administration who ensured that no eyebrows were raised where cadet movement was concerned. Free periods, placed at strategic times during the week, allowed cadets to slip Below. And whenever needed, some SIS classes met at night.

Hayley grabbed Phoebe's schedule, compared it to her own and frowned. "Looks like when you're up, I'm down—oh wait," she said as she thrust Phoebe's schedule back in her hands and pointed, "we have Bio Encryption and Tactical Bird Song together. Well, until then, my friend, I gotta go see about a walk-in refrigerator." Hayley double-winked at her mention of the kitchen narthyx point, and Phoebe winked back.

For a moment, Phoebe watched Hayley push through the kitchen doors and smiled. In the past, she'd had trouble with most of her friendships on account of her acute ability to sense emotions. Being keenly aware of everything your friends were feeling about you was as thoroughly exhausting as it was disappointing. More often than not, expressed sentiments in the vein of 'I'm happy for you . . . Of course you look great . . . You should totally ask him out . . .' came along with unexpressed waves of resentment or envy that Phoebe had trouble ignoring. As a result, Phoebe had eventually shied away from jumping into new friendships until she'd had an epiphany: she could use her ability to screen for fakers. Phoebe felt a strong twinge of guilt for having just probed Hayley's emotions, but it was quickly overpowered by the relief that settled over her as she realized that Hayley said what she meant.

Phoebe screwed up her eyes against the pounding that had become a blistering headache. Screening Hayley had required partially opening the mental gate she normally kept closed to block the stampede of strangers' emotions that came at her from all directions. She called them emotional intrusions, and Colten's arrival had driven them to a fever pitch that rocked her brain.

With her mental gate firmly closed, Phoebe stood up and risked a final glance in Colten's direction, but he was no longer there. Finding herself oddly disappointed, and paying little attention to those around her, Phoebe bumped into a boy and dropped her papers in surprise. She lowered herself to the ground but he was quicker, already retrieving her items by the time she met his onyx eyes.

"Sorry. Didn't see you," he apologized, taking a rapid peek at her top sheet before handing the stack over to her.

"My fault," Phoebe corrected, studying him as they rose in tandem. His dark eyebrows gave him a broodingly handsome look, and he stood tall with his thumbs hooked in the pockets of his pants, observing her. Phoebe couldn't help noticing a pattern of raised scars on the side of his neck as he shook his shaggy, raven hair from his eyes and said, "Interesting classes you got there. Is Understanding Vigos new to Green Lane? Didn't see it listed in my course guide."

Phoebe's throat tightened and her hearts hammered madly at the thought of what the boy's words potentially meant. She lowered her eyes to hastily confirm what he'd seen, wondering how she could possibly explain herself without putting the Shaper cadets at risk. In the same instant that a warm tingle washed over her skin registering the boy's physical energy as a Shaper, she heard him laugh. The dirty trick he'd played on her hit Phoebe a second before she lifted her eyes to find him gone.

After two morning classes Above, Phoebe spent the better part of the one free period where she wasn't scheduled Below, in the *Green Lane Gazette* staff room. Cyn had burst into delighted giggles when Phoebe accepted the position of features photographer after the meet and greet. As much as it pained Phoebe to have to both live and work with Cyn, she knew she needed an outlet. Photography pulled her into a part of her mind where the pain of losing her father did not slice her.

"And this," Cyn said, clipping a laminated card to Phoebe's white blouse pocket, "is your press pass. It's as legit as the one my mom has at the *Globe*." Cyn straightened Phoebe's badge, stepped back and smiled.

"You know, the *Gazette* is one of a few student papers that gets the same respect as the big—"

Phoebe raised a polite hand, cutting her off. "Thank you. This is great," she said, heading for the door and escaping another long-winded endorsement for the paper.

The morning had turned from dank and chilly to brisk and sunny, and Phoebe made her way outside, settling onto a bench bordering the courtyard that separated the schoolhouse from a multilevel library. She pulled her camera out of her backpack, and panned her surroundings. Two boys lay stretched out in the yellow-tipped blades of green grass, letting the brilliant midmorning sun bake them. One napped on his backpack while the other lay on hands laced behind his head, a baseball cap covering his face.

Phoebe leaned forward, elbows on knees, and brought her camera to her eye. She trained its lens on the boys and captured how the sun made long silhouettes of their sleeping bodies. Phoebe sat back against the bench, and casually scrolled through the images on her screen, discarding any she didn't care for. The sunlight on her face flickered into a cool shadow as a pleasant voice said, "So, you're one of the enemy, I see."

Phoebe jerked and looked up. She was floored to see Colten looming above her. Up close, he was even more breathtaking than she'd realized. The knot of his tie was half-undone, and his shirtsleeves were casually pulled up to his elbows, disclosing tanned, sculpted forearms. His long hair fluttered beneath a Green Lane cap he wore backward. He stared at Phoebe with inviting eyes and a sideways smile that kept her words jammed in her throat.

"Um," Phoebe started, finding her power of speech. "Hi Taylor—I mean—" Phoebe broke off, tongue-tied and mortified that she'd called Colten by his movie character name. Embarrassment rushed in and she stared down at her lap, as color drained from her face. She would have given anything to have the ground crack open and devour her at that moment.

Colten flashed his Hollywood smile. "It's a common mistake."

Phoebe caught something teasing in his tone, which made her cheeks flame so that she couldn't look up to meet his eyes. She played with the hem of her skirt, unsure of where to look. "What do you mean," she asked, speaking quietly, "when you say I'm one of the enemy?"

Colten sounded amused. "The press badge, the camera." And finally, when Phoebe gazed up at him with puzzled eyes, he added, "You know? Paparazzi. It seems a guy can't even enjoy the sun in peace."

At that, Phoebe peered behind Colten to the courtyard; only the boy napping on his backpack remained in the grass. Shock reached her face first and then comprehension bloomed. "I am so so sorry," she said quickly. "I had no idea I was shooting you. It was about the pattern of shadows . . . really." Phoebe glanced at Colten before looking back into her lap.

A grin eased across Colten's face. "May I?" he asked, gesturing at the bench. Phoebe nodded, hardly believing that Colten wanted to sit by her. *Does he want to talk? That can't be it*, she thought. *Maybe he wants to inspect the photos for himself.* Phoebe set her camera down at the end of the bench and slid her backpack to her feet, allowing room for him. Scrubbing her clammy palms on her skirt, she sat up straight as though she herself was about to be photographed. Colten slid in beside her, closer than he had to on the wide bench, his eyes never leaving her face.

"If you want," Phoebe said, clearing her throat unevenly, "I can delete those photos." Phoebe, who felt awkward and unsure around beautiful people (and they didn't get more beautiful than Colten Chase), hoped she didn't look as nervous as she sounded.

Colten shrugged, smiling. "Don't worry about it. I've been photographed doing much worse." He adjusted his body slightly to face her better, the weathered bench creaking as he did so, and Phoebe felt herself tugged by an invisible cord to do the same.

"So where are you from, Lady Paparazza?"

"San Francisco."

Colten threw his head back and chuckled. "Cali girl, huh? Man, have winters beat you up?"

"Not yet, but I can only imagine." Phoebe cringed at the thought. Already, the crispness of fall was proving to be no friend of hers.

"So this must be your first year," Colten said, sounding intrigued.

Phoebe nodded.

"Why boarding school out East?"

"My grandfather. He offered to foot the bill."

"And your folks just let you take off like that?"

Phoebe looked away from the question, her hands clenched on her lap. When she spoke, she kept her voice controlled. "It's just me and my grandfather," she said, eyes back on Colten's; she saw sympathy there, and braced for an apology.

Colten said, "I'm sorry if I—" just as Phoebe said, "Don't worry about it." Phoebe wanted to nip the discussion in the bud. She didn't want to get into the accident. And telling someone that her mother had walked out on Phoebe and her father days after her birth tended to be a conversation killer. "Not everyone is cut out to be a parent," she'd once heard her grandfather say.

Colten turned his face away from her, his mind suddenly somewhere else. Unable to read his expression, Phoebe stared down at the black loafers, which somehow made her size ten feet look much smaller than they were. At that moment, three girls exited the library, glanced in their direction, and giggled behind their hands. Phoebe heard the gossip in their whispers but chose not to focus on the words. *It's not worth the energy*, she thought. Though Shapers could hear and see across distances, expanding the reach of these senses required effort when in human form. Most kept them restricted to a more normal range.

Phoebe took a long breath and broke what had become an awkward silence.

"Your turn to tell me something," she said, her words stumbling over each other.

Colten removed his cap and rumpled his hair. "What about?"

"You."

"I'm really not that interesting," he said.

Phoebe nearly giggled, remembering what she'd told Hayley earlier. To cover her reaction, she let a skeptical expression take over her face while Colten chuckled and added dryly, "I'm sure you can find information to the contrary with any Internet search."

"Well then give me a head start," Phoebe pressed mildly. "What brings you here?"

"Work. The next movie in my *Taylor Hawk* series picks up in the city where the last one ended." Phoebe offered a blank look. "You know, Boston," Colten added.

Phoebe shook her head. "No, I don't know. Didn't see it."

"Ouch," he said, bringing a hand to his chest for effect. "Have you seen any of them?"

"Just the previews. No offense," she hurriedly added.

Colten grinned, stretching his long legs out in front of him. "None taken. The honesty is kinda refreshing. If I had to guess," he said, sparing the courtyard a glimpse before meeting Phoebe with eyes that sent her stomach into free fall, "I'd say you're less fast chases and explosions and more indie romance."

Phoebe bit her lip to stop a grin. "Nice try," she said.

"I'm wrong?" Colten seemed a bit discombobulated by this.

How could he presume to be right? Phoebe thought. Then it occurred to her that most girls probably went along with anything Colten said—it was kind of hard not to when looking into his enthralling eyes.

Phoebe toyed with her hands awkwardly. "I like period romance movies like *Sense and Sensibility* and *Emma*," she said. "And I do like fast chases and explosions. I just, um, like them to involve spaceships . . . " Phoebe briefly looked at Colten, gauging his reaction. She worried that maybe she shouldn't have let her inner geek out of its cage.

"A Jane Austen lovin' space nerd, huh?" Colten said. He sounded both surprised and amused and didn't bother hiding it. "So what are some of your favorite flicks starring little green men?"

Phoebe laughed, but before she could answer, a sudden feeling of disorientation washed over her and she grasped the back of the bench to steady herself.

Colten's concern was instant. "Are you okay?" His narrowed eyes searched her face.

"I'm fine," Phoebe said at once, striving to keep her eyes from his. *What was that?*

"You sure?"

Phoebe nodded and quickly changed the subject. "So once you're done with the Boston shoot," she said, "will you make up the rest of your senior year someplace else?" She forced a smile.

Colten raised an eyebrow a fraction, tilting his head. It was clear she had thrown him with that bit of knowledge. Then, a grin played on his lips. "We'll see," he said mysteriously. The bell rang, startling Phoebe out of the moment. She shot to her feet and scooped her backpack up from the ground, remembering that she was due at a meeting with Professor Yori. Without pause, or even a backward glance, she headed toward the schoolhouse, cutting across the courtyard as Colten said something in her wake. If he showed offense at her abrupt departure, Phoebe didn't catch it. She was already shoving through the glass double doors of the schoolhouse.

It wasn't until she was nearing the narthyx point that she registered what Colten had called to her as she fled: "See you around, Phoebe Pope." Phoebe stopped abruptly in her tracks, confounded by the fact that Colten had known her name. She hadn't introduced herself.

# FOUR

The anteroom to the headmaster's office was furnished simply, with a trestle desk across from two high-backed wooden chairs. Behind the desk sat a curly-haired woman with a faintly lined, elongated face. She looked up when Phoebe entered, her black eyes sparkling.

"Cadet Pope?" she asked as she rose from her chair. Phoebe nodded, brushing back her hair self-consciously, fearing it looked miserably disheveled from her mad dash through the Below courtyard.

"Right this way." The woman pushed heavy oak doors that opened into a larger room. Phoebe's eyes flicked around, taking in the décor. The headmaster had furnished his office with ornately framed paintings of Pompeii, beautifully bound books on mahogany shelves, and a few pairs of crossed diamond-bladed daggers hanging on the walls. An unusual antique silver clock was perched on the wide desk: instead of numbers around its edges, it had engravings of the moon's phases. And at that moment, the black metal hands pointed to a full moon.

"Great. We're all here," Professor Yori said, drawing Phoebe's attention to him. He was, as before, impeccably dressed in a blue tailored military-style coat with bronze buttons running from its high collar down to the hem. He strode toward Phoebe with a pronounced limp that she hadn't noticed in the Great Hall, his arms spread in welcome. "Thank you, Hanna," he said to the older woman. Hanna bowed her head and withdrew from the room, pulling the doors shut.

"Come, come," Professor Yori said, taking Phoebe kindly by the arm and moving her deeper into the office at a brisk pace. "Let me introduce you to the others." Professor Yori led Phoebe to one of two armchairs next to a maroon sofa where three students sat staring at her. "These Hastati-year cadets are Mariko, Lewis, and Scott," he said, gesturing to each person in turn as he spoke.

Phoebe offered an amiable wave to the assembled company. Mariko, an Asian girl with beautifully shaped lips and braided black hair, sat twirling a long strand around a finger, her dark eyes coolly appraising Phoebe. Next to her, Lewis was a thin black boy, his eyes brown under gold-flecked dreadlocks. Phoebe watched him with interest as he absently knuckle-walked a quarter in his left hand. And leaning back in the sofa with his hands folded behind his head, sat the raven-haired boy from the dining hall.

"You," Phoebe gasped before she could stop herself. Scott's mouth twitched into a hint of a smile that she could tell was making fun of her.

"I see you two are already acquainted," Professor Yori said, looking between Phoebe and Scott.

"We bumped into each other earlier," Scott said.

Phoebe reddened slightly.

"Please take a seat, Cadet Pope," Professor Yori said, returning to his desk with a Shaper-characteristic swiftness in spite of his limp. Phoebe sank comfortably into the overstuffed armchair and deposited her backpack on the floor.

"This is a unique year for us," Professor Yori said. "It's the first time there have been four Hyphas in any incoming Hastati class. We've never had more than one or two here, if any at all."

Phoebe sat perfectly still, her lips parting in utter shock. Stealing a look sideways, she could see the others begin to eye each other with newfound curiosity. Professor Yori leaned back in his chair, looking from one to the next of the students before him, absorbing their reactions.

Phoebe understood the headmaster's fascination. There weren't many Hyphas in Shaper communities. The offspring of Shaper-human mating, Hyphas were not markedly different from their Shaper peers, except for a physical energy that ran a tad bit cooler due to human genes. Their race, however, was still somewhat of an enigma since not all Shaper-human unions produced children.

"The SIS curriculum is extremely rigorous," the headmaster continued. "It's not enough to want to serve. Daily academic excellence is a requirement for all would-be-agents, and unfortunately, those who fail to keep up are asked to leave. You all are starting with a bit of a handicap—"

Mariko interrupted looking alarmed. "What handicap?—Sir."

"Well, because of your"—the headmaster paused as though carefully measuring his next word—"unique upbringing, you haven't been taught the basics of wielding the element of Osiah, our sky patron." Professor Yori flicked the fingers of his right hand as though trying to swat at a fly, and the room was filled with a gust of wind that disappeared as fast as it had come. "Or that of Gavya, our earth patroness," he said, placing a paperweight in his palm. Phoebe sat forward, leaning her chin into her hand, watching as the wooden block disintegrated into dust before her eyes. "With that in mind, we've created a program to help you bridge this gap—to make sure you're up to speed by the time you encounter courses like Tactical Air Control and Elemental Breaching in your Principes year."

Professor Yori brushed the remains of the paperweight into a waste bin and no one said anything. They all knew what he'd meant by 'unique upbringing.' Shaper-human unions were a delicate subject. In centuries past, Shapers had lived openly among humans until Vigos began to use human informants as a tactical strategy. Those who remained unmoved by offers of money had been tortured to disclose the whereabouts of Shaper families. With that information, Vigos had killed Shapers at a startling rate. During a period some called the Great Erase, Shapers worked to convince humans that preternatural abilities, like shape-shifting, existed only in their imagination. Humans had been kept in the dark ever since. Now, like their Shaper parent, Hyphas were also bound by this secrecy. Their supernatural nature had to be kept from their human parent. And, as a result, the fundamentals of elemental magic taught to children born into households with two Shaper parents could not be taught in Shaper-human ones.

"If I may say, sir," Scott said, bringing his hands to his side and leaning over his knees, "it sounds like you're putting us in some sort of 'special ed' program."

"Not at all, Cadet," Professor Yori said at once, his tone firm. He raised a hand to his face and slowly rubbed his beard. "Think of it as academic boot camp with top notch mentors to guide you."

"Is this in addition to our other classes, sir?" Phoebe asked, tapping the edge of her seat with her fingers. She was already finding her two course loads daunting.

"I'm afraid so," Professor Yori said to a collective groan. "We don't want you falling behind in your other studies. You will meet as a foursome early in the morning for this additional training—"

From the door, Hanna cleared her throat delicately, interrupting him. "They're here," she said.

Professor Yori's whole bearing seemed to change then; he straightened his back, adjusted his collar, and when he stood he dusted invisible lint off of his coat. "Show them in, Hanna," he said, moving from behind his desk to the center of the room.

Hanna vanished and a moment later, entering the office with enviable grace, were three of the most beautiful women Phoebe had ever seen. The tallest of the trio, a streaky blond, possessed a delicate-boned fragility intensified by her ivory tinged complexion. Another was mocha-skinned with an angular face framed by long, springy, black hair. The third, a darker blond, wore her hair in two thick waist-length braids that hung down her back. Her skin was dusted with freckles. Their lean frames were clad in form-fitting white jackets over skin-tight black pants and tall black boots; their hoods swept behind their necks. They stood at silent attention, fixing a watchful gaze on the assemblage.

Metal clanked against wood; Lewis's coin had dropped to the floor. He sat staring at the women as though part of his brain had just dissolved. Scott moved from his relaxed slouch and cocked his head to the side in clear interest.

"Allow me to introduce you to your mentors," Professor Yori said, an odd inflection in his voice. "This is Yelena and Afua." The blond and black woman bowed respectively, "and Deborah-Anna." The braided mentor gave a curt nod.

"Please make yourselves comfortable." Professor Yori indicated the extra chairs Hanna had brought in behind the women, but they remained standing.

Yelena spoke with a slight Russian accent, her tone formal. "We are fine. Thank you."

"Very well," Professor Yori said, making his way back to his desk. A strange moment of silence followed, broken only by Lewis, who said, "Sir, can we start today?" His dopey smile had grown.

Mariko snorted, and her eyes slid to Lewis's face, her eyebrows drawing down. "My, aren't we a bit eager."

"Hey man," Lewis said, his tone defensive. "I've been waiting a long time for the freedom to mess around with what we can do."

"Yup. That's the reason," Mariko muttered.

Phoebe bit down on her involuntary urge to laugh, not wanting Mariko's glare on her next. She had to admit, though, that Lewis probably couldn't help himself. In the presence of these women, any male could lose his senses and any female, her self-confidence.

Professor Yori perched himself on the edge of his desk facing his students, and smiled. "We'll give your instructors the weekend to settle in from their long journey, and have you start Monday."

Long journey? Phoebe thought. Her eyes had wandered curiously to the stunning company, their expressions inscrutable, standing impossibly straight and composed. To her shame, Phoebe found herself tempted to probe and confirm that these women were not as devoid of emotion as she imagined them to be.

"We hate to end your meeting," Afua said abruptly, her voice commanding. "But I believe we have things to discuss."

Professor Yori nodded. "Yes, yes, of course. Your sessions, Cadets, will take place Monday and Thursday mornings at seven in the study hall wing." He brought his hands together and stood. "Let's say our goodbyes then," he said briskly. He escorted Phoebe, Mariko, Scott, and Lewis to the door and held it open for them. None of the Hyphas spoke as they exited the office. Just before the door closed behind them, Phoebe thought she saw something like unease replace the smile on Professor Yori's face.

"I guess it would have killed them to throw one hot guy into the mentor mix," Mariko said sardonically once they'd started down the empty hallway.

Lewis laughed louder than the comment warranted, and pointed at himself and Scott, saying, "Lucky for you, we're easy on the eyes." That earned him a fist bump from Scott.

Mariko harrumphed. Then, looking directly at Phoebe, she said dryly, "See you in drool camp. I'll bring the mop to clean up after these two, if you bring the rain coats." Phoebe had barely cracked a smile before Mariko turned and marched down the central stairway to the lower halls. Lewis followed at her heels, tossing and catching his coin in his left hand, filling Mariko's ears with the unwelcome banter of his conversation.

"And then there were two," Scott said. He stood at Phoebe's shoulder, a smirk planted on his face. "By the way, you know this morning was all in good fun, right?"

"You nearly gave me a double heart attack!" Phoebe said.

"In my defense," Scott said, humor ringing in his voice. "You shouldn't have had your Below schedule out in the open up there. It's like Vegas: what happens Below stays Below."

Scott was right and Phoebe knew it; plus, she couldn't help smiling at his poorly feigned look of remorse. They descended a few staircases, stepped into the courtyard, and then, quite abruptly, Phoebe stopped. She brought a hand to her neck, feeling for the camera strap that wasn't there.

"What?" Scott's brow furrowed in confusion.

Phoebe didn't answer. She rummaged through her backpack, straining to remember when she'd last had it. *The foot of my armchair*, she thought, just as the bell rang. Propelled by a desperate need to locate her prized possession, Phoebe doubled back to the headmaster's office, leaving behind a befuddled Scott, who stood in the courtyard with his mouth half open. She burst into the anteroom, finding Hanna gone and Professor Yori's concerned voice carrying through the walls. Phoebe paused, her hand uncertain on his doorknob.

"—they're behind those abductions?" Phoebe expanded her range of hearing as Professor Yori added, "You're sure on this intel?"

"BIRs are always vetted," answered Yelena's Russian voice. She sounded mildly affronted.

"BIRs?" Professor Yori said.

"Blackcoat Intelligence Reports," Yelena said. "Our sources leave no doubt that Boston Vigo packs are involved."

Phoebe wasn't quite sure she'd heard correctly. Were these women Blackcoats? The Shaper equivalent of the Secret Service, Blackcoats handled the personal security of members of the governing Royal Court. Only seven of the twelve royal families had escaped Pompeii and the Blackcoats concerned themselves with eliminating Vigo threats to the Crowns.

"What does any of this have to do with my students?" Professor Yori said, sounding concerned and confused. "Why the need to protect them in particular?"

Phoebe's body clenched at the word "protect," and for a moment she felt like she was out of breath. *Were they in danger?*

"Are you familiar with the Year of Four, Professor?" Afua said.

There was a moment of silence. Then Professor Yori spoke with an uncertain edge to his voice. "I thought that was just a—"

Someone walked into the room behind Phoebe.

"Are we eavesdropping on matters that don't concern us?" said a voice, crisp with distaste. Phoebe turned around. A woman stood resplendent in a navy skirt suit, her straight black hair bobbed to her chin. In one hand she held a potted white orchid, while the other clutched a thin briefcase. Lips set in a hard line, she stared at Phoebe with piercing black eyes.

"No, ma'am." Phoebe swallowed. "I—I was just—"

"You were just leaving."

Phoebe lowered her eyes. "Yes Professor—"

"Montclaire," the woman finished for her. "Just Montclaire."

Phoebe nodded, feeling her face get hot with shame.

Montclaire moved her gaze over Phoebe as though inspecting every molecule of her being. "And you are?" she asked.

"Phoebe."

"Phoebe what? I imagine you weren't picked up from some street corner."

"Phoebe Pope."

Montclaire arched her eyebrow at this, making a reappraisal. "I see. Well I hope for your sake you are a better student than you are a liar, Cadet Pope." She waved a hand at the door. "Go. Now."

Phoebe left, hurrying out of the anteroom, trying to sort out what she'd just overheard. If these women were indeed Blackcoats, she could not imagine why they'd spend their time mentoring. Weren't they needed for more important matters? She also hoped to both Osiah and Gavya that she never crossed paths with Montclaire again. As for her camera, she'd have to return for it another time.

"You're a Hypha?" Hayley gaped at Phoebe, astonished. Since Professor Elmore had yet to arrive for Bio Encryption, Phoebe had just finished telling Hayley what had happened in her meeting. She'd left out the part about the mentors possibly being Blackcoats; she still didn't know what to make of it. "I've never met a Hypha before," Hayley breathed, clearly fascinated. "Now I want to inappropriately poke you and see how you tick."

Phoebe grinned and rolled her eyes.

"You can inappropriately poke me anytime," said a husky voice behind them.

Phoebe and Hayley turned simultaneously to see Scott sitting with a wicked grin firmly in place.

Hayley giggled and flushed.

"They're collecting names for Full Moon on the Field tonight, ladies," Scott said, brandishing a blue sheet of paper. Grinning, he flicked it gently onto the table between them.

Hayley asked playfully, "Will you be there? . . ."

"Scott," Scott said. "Scott Roland." He twitched a wink and added, "I'll be there if I can expect to see you."

Hayley flushed some more. Phoebe's exaggerated eye roll did not go unnoticed by Scott who sat back and crossed his arms, a bigger smile playing around his lips. "You too, Pope. Sign up and pass it forward."

"We're so in," Hayley mouthed to Phoebe, giddy, and wrote both of their names down on the sheet. She elbowed Phoebe. "What's your cell number?"

Phoebe rattled off her number.

"They're gonna text us the location of the game," Hayley explained.

"Game?"

"According to this," Hayley said, passing the sheet forward, "Full Moon on the Field is a midnight game of Shaper Soccer. It's tradition for the second-years to invite first-years to play."

Phoebe began to open her mouth to say that she was extremely allergic to any sport involving fast moving balls, but closed it when a stubble-chinned man with fluffy white hair came scurrying into the class carrying a cardboard box filled with colorful leaves.

"The autumn leaf," Professor Elmore began speaking immediately with a deep voice that belied his thin, short stature. "You don't think twice about it when you crunch it beneath your feet. Why would you," he said smiling, as he swept among them, dropping leaves on desks, "when trees shed millions each year? But it's precisely this fact that makes them perfect for hiding messages in plain sight."

Professor Elmore reached the front of the room, plucked a green leaf from a potted plant on his desk, and turned to face the class. "Our magic," he said, running a finger over the leaf, "allows me to do in here what nature does to leaves in the fall."

Phoebe watched closely, as with each pass of Professor Elmore's finger, the color of the leaf slowly changed from green to orange, then yellow. Hayley caught Phoebe's eye and they exchanged looks with raised eyebrows. Around them, other cadets were doing the same.

"What I've done is force the breakdown of chlorophyll. For those of you staring at me with blank expressions, it would behoove you to review the basics of photosynthesis. Now, if I take things a bit further"—he pinched sections of his leaf between a finger and thumb—"I'm left with this: a leaf in the advanced stages of rot and decay." Professor Elmore thrust the leaf in the air for everyone to see the pattern of black spots that now covered it.

"What if I told you all that this leaf, like the ones on your desks, has been coded with your homework assignment?" Murmurs of interest bubbled around the room at this, and everyone began to examine their own leaves closely. "It's a season-dependent strategy, but SIS agents leave messages for each other with patterns of dots made to look like naturally occurring decomposition."

Professor Elmore, who had fully captured the class's attention, continued his lecture with gusto. By the end of the period, Phoebe was one of only two students to successfully use a Decomp Pen—a flat-tipped writing implement used to create decomposition—to code her name onto a maple leaf.

Phoebe carried her feeling of accomplishment into Tactical Bird Song, a class she'd been looking forward to since it had been a favorite of her father's. She was smiling to herself when she entered the classroom, but stopped in her tracks, stunned by the opalescent hawk circling above her, whistling loudly. No sooner had the whole class settled into their seats and taken out their notebooks, than the large bird swooped down over their heads. Many ducked, and the room tittered with nervous confusion. The hawk landed gracefully at the front of the room and abruptly converted into a voluptuous, tawny-haired woman. Professor Koon.

"Who can tell me what I was whistling to y'all?" she asked, her voice bubbly. She pulled her faculty robe tight around her shoulders. When the class offered her nothing but blank looks she laughed. "Well, of course you have no clue." She ran a hand through her hair. "If you did, you wouldn't be here now, would you?"

After a short pause during which Professor Koon retrieved a microphone stand from a closet and placed it in the middle of the room, she said, "I explained through my whistle that Tactical Bird Song is the study of how to use simple notes to convey complex messages. Anything from messages between lovers,"—she gave a theatrical wink that generated laughs—"to messages conveying distress. Now," she said, attaching a wireless mic to the stand, "I hope y'all have warmed up those voices!"

Phoebe groaned inwardly. She hated her singing voice.

"Did I miss anything important?" Hayley said breathlessly, slipping into the seat Phoebe had saved for her.

Phoebe shook her head. "How'd it go with Elmore?"

"He said not to stress. That I'd figure out the Decomp Pen soon enough," she said, sounding unconvinced. "Hey . . . what's with the mic?"

"You're just in time to sing for us, Cadet Corman," Professor Koon chirped. "C'mon up!" Hayley went very pink and shot Phoebe a questioning glance. "Don't worry, Cadet Pope will be joining you. We work in pairs in this class."

Great, Phoebe thought as she reluctantly got up and followed Hayley to the front of the room.

Hayley lowered the mic stand a bit to prevent her from standing on her toes. Phoebe fidgeted with her hands as they waited under the stare of their class.

"I'd like for you to repeat these four notes that mean, 'Welcome to your first year.'" When Professor Koon sang, her voice was rich and deep, with the kind of delicate warm tones that stole air from a listener's lungs. The class could only stare in wonder.

Hayley broke the awed silence. "So is it an instant fail if your voice sucks?" she asked, very serious. Everyone but Hayley laughed. "What?" she asked, looking around, a defensive edge in her voice. "It's a legit question."

"It's not a singing competition, dear," Professor Koon answered kindly. "Think of it more like vocal Morse code. The notes don't have to be beautiful, just accurate." Whispers of relief swept through the entire room and Phoebe felt the knot inside her stomach begin to loosen. At Professor Koon's encouraging nod, she cleared her throat, opened her mouth, and released four shaky notes.

At the end of the day, Phoebe met Hayley at the lockers where they stored their SIS textbooks before making their way above ground.

Outside, the sky blazed with the retreating rays of a setting sun. Tall grass swayed at their feet, and Phoebe couldn't help but stare at the clusters of leaves on the ground.

Hayley noticed right away. "Oh my God, I've totally been doing that since BioE," she squealed. "That eccentric skinny man's got me convinced we're crunching through valuable intel!"

Phoebe laughed and then frowned at her cloudy breath hanging in the air; she'd forgotten her coat in her locker. She crossed her arms over her chest and slid her hands under her armpits for warmth. "I've been meaning to ask," she said to Hayley as they marched down a sloping trail toward the girls' dormitories. "What's up with the glasses?"

"It's my Clark Kent look."

Phoebe cracked up.

"What?" Hayley said, trying but failing to hold her straight face. "It's an extra touch to sell my human cover. Also works for sexy librarian, don'tcha think?"

Phoebe shivered while she laughed, hugging herself tighter for extra warmth.

"What about you?" Hayley said once Phoebe had recovered her breath.

"What about me?"

"Is that really natural?" Hayley's gaze traveled to Phoebe's bangs.

"Yup."

"Ever tried to dye it to match the rest of your hair? I'm not saying it's hideous or anything," she quickly added. "Just curious."

"Yup," Phoebe said, tugging at the thick lock of white hair. "Nothing works."

"Over the counter stuff?"

Phoebe nodded. "Even wasted hundreds of dollars at salons."

"Really?" Hayley considered Phoebe for a moment. "In that case, I think it makes a BBS."

"A what?"

"A bold beauty statement—movie star alert!" Hayley hissed. "Oh my God! Oh my God!" In the distance Phoebe could see Colten walking toward them, a black jacket clinging snugly to his chest, backpack slung over his right shoulder.

"Just be cool," Hayley whispered, pushing back flyaway strands of hair that had broken free of her elegant twist. "We'll just stroll by and take a whiff of that sexy air around him."

At that precise moment, Colten raised his hand in a casual wave. "You're a hard person to find, Phoebe Pope," he called out. A smile spread on his face that was so beautiful it radiated across the distance to them.

At that, Hayley gave Phoebe's arm a sharp tug, whispering, "He's been looking for—wait a sec." She stopped dead in her tracks, comprehension dawning. "He knows your name?"

"Yeah. But I don't know how," Phoebe said through chattering teeth. Excitement swept over her; she was surprised by how much it pleased her to know Colten had been trying to find her. She watched his purposeful strides as he closed the yards between them.

"There's a story? I can't believe you've been sitting on something like this!"

"I kinda forgot," Phoebe admitted sheepishly. And she had. Between navigating the confusing network of hallways Below and trying to understand the conversation she'd overheard, thoughts of Colten had been driven from her mind.

"Are you kidding me right now?" Hayley lowered her voice further, her words coming in a rush. "Homework you forget. You don't forget living proof that God is a woman with a fantastic eye for detail in—" Hayley couldn't finish her sentence, swallowing her words as Colten stepped up to them.

"Hi ladies," he said. Phoebe shivered involuntarily at the sound of his silken voice.

Hayley let out a chuckle, speaking before Phoebe could. "Um"—she batted her eyelashes up at him—"hi yourself."

When she did speak, Phoebe was surprised to hear her voice come out as a whisper. "Colten, Hayley. Hayley, Colten." As Hayley struggled for a moment to maintain her composure, Phoebe added, "Hayley's a big fan—"

"—of your body—I mean your body of work," Hayley said, snapping out of her stupor, mortified.

Without missing a beat Colten said, "It's a relief to hear that. I give up a lot of carbs for this body."

Stunned, Phoebe measured his expression and smiled, realizing he'd made a self-deprecating joke. The same thought seemed to have struck Hayley who raised relieved eyes to his face.

Colten directed his attention to Phoebe, his mesmerizing smile radiating mild amusement. "I think I have something you might want." He unzipped his backpack and removed her camera.

Phoebe gasped, the memory of having placed it on the bench rushing back to her.

"You left it when you ran away from me earlier."

Hayley choked on a cough and Phoebe understood the meaning of the sound: *we're talking about this later.*

"Thanks. I've been looking for that—I owe you." When Phoebe reached her hand out to claim her camera, Colten's fingers brushed against hers in the exchange. Her breath shortened. She pretended not to notice the subtle tilt of Colten's head or the curious gleam in his eyes as he made note of her reaction.

Hayley looked between them and announced suddenly, "I've got to go see to something." And just like that, she scampered down the hill, abandoning Phoebe to Colten's company.

Colten's eyes stayed on Phoebe's face. "Your friend's funny."

Phoebe murmured her agreement, staring after Hayley with a glare she hoped burned "traitor" through her back. Turning her eyes to Colten she said, "I'm sorry about earlier. I was late for a meeting with Headmaster"—she paused searching her brain for the name of the Above Headmaster—"Baker," she remembered, relieved.

"Nothing serious, I hope."

Phoebe blushed at what sounded like true concern in his tone. "No. Nothing like that." She lowered her eyes, surprised to find that she'd been unconsciously walking with Colten in the direction of the dorms. They strolled along a path that wound under the canopy of cloud-spearing trees with small ground security lamps dotting the way. A wind carrying the scent of potential rain blew, and, shivering, Phoebe raised her chin to the quickly darkening sky.

Feigning nonchalance, she asked, "So how did you know my name, anyway?"

Colten stopped walking and his expression became unreadable. "You're cold," he said firmly, not answering her question. "Take my coat." Before Phoebe could even begin to decline the offer, Colten had shrugged himself out of the coat. He draped it around her shoulders.

Phoebe half-smiled awkwardly, feeling completely out of her element; Colten's concern for her well-being took an unexpected hold of her, making her happier than she cared to admit.

"Thanks." She slipped her arms into the sleeves that were hanging limp at her sides. The coat was soft and warm against her skin with a strong smell that made her think of cinnamon rolls and firewood. Phoebe zipped it up, inhaling its smoky-sweet scent.

"It looks good on you." He closed the gap between them and straightened the crooked collar, looking rather pleased with himself.

Phoebe found Colten's nearness intoxicating. Thinking came with difficulty.

"I'll give it back when we get to Cedar House," she said, biting down on her bottom lip as a grin spread across Colten's face. "Or I can give it to you before—I mean, you don't have to walk me all the way," she quickly added.

"I don't mind," he said. "It would be tragic to watch you freeze to death just feet from your dorm."

Phoebe dropped her gaze to the dirt path, secretly pleased.

"So," Colten said, as they continued walking. "How'd your first day go?"

"Good. Yours?"

"It had its high points," he said. Phoebe could hear the smile in his voice.

"Like?"

"For starters," Colten said. "The front office told me I don't have to repeat calculus. And then, there was meeting you. . . ."

Phoebe flushed from the roots of her hair down to her tips of her toes. Her pulse quickened. *Did he really mean that,* she thought. *Or is he this charming with all girls?* Without meaning to, she stole a sideways peek at Colten and made the mistake of catching his gaze. He seemed entertained by her apparent embarrassment. Phoebe looked away, gathering her thoughts. Was Colten toying with her or was he being genuine? She decided right then to read him.

She opened her mental gate a bit. A rush of animated emotions spun her head. Too many to belong to just Colten. Phoebe closed her mental gate, not understanding where the heightened emotional output was coming from.

"Is everything okay?" Colten asked.

Phoebe didn't hear the question. She flicked her eyes around and found the source. It was her dorm. Through the lounge window, she saw a mass of girls watching them.

Colten saw them too. His eyes were alight with humor.

"I guess we have spectators," he said.

Phoebe eyed the growing crowd. "I'm sure they're just for you." She was trying to hide it, but having an audience made her uncomfortable. Phoebe's hair lifted in a sudden breeze, swirling around her face and shoulders. Quite unexpectedly, and rather absently, Colten reached out a hand, grabbing wild strands of hair with the intent of sweeping them behind her ear. Phoebe stiffened, and just like that, as though it had suddenly occurred to him what he was doing, Colten's hand fell away and he stepped back from her.

"Have a good night," Phoebe said, running off.

"You too," Colten said to her back, sounding perplexed.

Phoebe knew with utter certainty that Colten must be convinced that she had a compulsive inability to say goodbye like a normal person. She hadn't meant to ruin the mood. She just didn't want Colten's fingers to brush against her scars.

"No," Phoebe whispered.

"I get no details?" Hayley asked incredulously. "None at all?"

It was past curfew, and they were huddled together making their way to the meeting point for the game. The sky was velvet black with stars in place, illuminating the campus grounds before them.

"Not after how you abandoned me."

"Oh, please." Hayley smiled teasingly. "Any normal person would be thanking me for the alone time. He obviously wanted alone time."

"Then I'm happily abnormal."

Hayley gave up. "You'll forgive me at some point and I'll get the scoop then."

Phoebe held back a smile. Then, she said mockingly, "'I'm a fan of your body—?'"

"Not another word about that," Hayley said aghast, cutting her off. "Not one of my finest moments. I'll admit that. But damn that boy for making my brain go all mush." And with that they giggled like idiots, trying their best to keep their volume low.

The girls walked past a chain of small ponds along the southern end of the campus and in the darkness came upon a group gathered at the forest's edge. Phoebe scanned the crowd. Lewis was there and so was Mariko. They stood side by side speaking, an expression of adoration etched plain as day on Lewis's face. Some distance behind them, Scott, who sported a Ghana World Cup soccer jersey, had just finished saying something to make the girl next to him laugh. He flashed a bright smile when he caught Phoebe's eye.

A voice spoke, high and clear. "Listen up, pre-cons," a burly sandy-haired boy said, using the nickname for first year students still waiting to convert. He hopped onto a nearby boulder and peered down at everyone. Next to him, another boy, small and thin, zipped up a windbreaker. "I'm Sam, and this here is Paul," Sam continued. "And we're your captains for tonight's game." All the students gathered up before them. "For you newbies who aren't familiar with the rules of our brand of soccer, here's a quick rundown. It's like human soccer, except we have two games playing at the same time on the same field. There's a ground team and an air team. Those of us who convert into birds play above those who are land bound," Sam explained, looking into more than a few confused faces.

Paul cut in. "Two teams means two balls, folks. The ground team plays with a regular soccer ball. Air team plays with this smaller silver one." Phoebe watched as Paul spun a ball the size of a baseball on top of a finger. "Like soccer, each side has eleven players. For us, six of those players belong to the ground team and the other five play in the air."

"The goalie has a tougher job," Sam said, taking over, "because he or she has to prevent two balls from entering the goal. When a ground player scores, it's one point. When the air team scores, it's a three point gain."

"What! That's not fair," a boy yelled from the back.

Sam smirked. "Yes it is, 'cause those guys have to work harder for it. If anyone on an air team drops the ball, they're out of the game. If they touch the ground, even if it's just the tip of a wing, they're out. All right, that's all."

Paul reached for a tree behind him. He pushed his palms against the trunk and the tree slid sideways, as though gliding through butter. "You thinking what I'm thinking?" Hayley said, standing on her tiptoes for a better view. She and Phoebe watched as Paul moved more trees to reveal a dirt trail that cut a path through the forest to a clearing ahead.

"That you can't wait to be able to do that?" Phoebe said awe-struck.

"Actually, I was thinking magic makes even the scrawniest guy look hot, but that works too." Much to Hayley's horror and Phoebe's amusement, Paul turned and smiled in their direction right before yelling, "Let's play ball!"

They entered a clearing floodlit by a moon that hung just above the trees. Goal posts were quickly put into place amid a rustle of eager voices and low catcalls, while the group was swiftly divided between the two captains, with Phoebe and Hayley ending up on opposing sides.

"Okay blue team, I know everyone wants the action of running around," Phoebe heard Sam say as she joined the huddle around him. "But, I need a volunteer for goalie."

"I'll do it," Phoebe said immediately, happy for a job that didn't involve running. For no reason she understood, her feet tended to twist when in motion. The idea of two balls coming at her at once wasn't appealing either, but it was the lesser of two potentially embarrassing evils.

Sam turned to smile at her. "Way to be there for the team, pre-con." Phoebe smiled back. "All right air team," Sam said, rounding to face a cluster of players to his right. "Give 'em hell up there!" With that, Phoebe saw short bursts of pulsating light as five of her teammates seamlessly transformed into splendid falcons and hawks, and took flight as a group, hovering just above them. Phoebe took a breath, braced herself, and headed over to her goal.

A boy dressed in a referee's jersey walked into the center of the clearing. He cleared his throat and addressed the group. "Welcome to

Full Moon on the Field," he said. "Blue team and red team, I want a clean game." A whistle blew and the game sprang into action.

Phoebe found herself staring in utter shock from the goal. No matter how many times she rubbed her eyes, the scene unfolding before her was hard to believe. Paul had become a white leopard and charged after Lewis, who was skillfully dribbling the ball toward the other side's goal. Watching a leopard run down a human on any ordinary day would be a frightful sight, but in the strangeness of the current situation, Phoebe felt only excitement. Her hearts swelled with the pride that came from absorbing the beauty and power in the changing forms around her.

Phoebe saw Lewis make a swift pass to a blue team jaguar who snapped the ball ten feet from the left corner with its bronze head to score the first goal. Mariko, who was goalie for the red team, stomped in frustration.

"One to zero for blue!" the referee yelled.

Phoebe focused hard on the game, trying to keep track of who was turning into what Shape. She ran a nervous hand over her face, feeling the moisture of beading sweat. Ten feet above her, the whirling activity of the air game kept her on doubly high alert. With her attention fixed on the silver ball passing rapidly from one set of talons to another, Phoebe nearly missed the approaching jaguar. The silver-spotted cat swung its tail, firing the ground ball hard toward her. Phoebe dove across the goal, barely managing to block the ball that ricocheted off her back.

"Gosh darn it!" a girl said after shedding her Shape. Phoebe stood dazed, recognizing her as Leslie from the Conversion Ceremony.

A rush of excitement charged the game with more intensity. Hayley kicked the ball hard from center field to a lanky teammate who melted into a lion. He stopped the ball with his tail and whipped it to Scott, who swiftly maneuvered it toward Phoebe. From the corner of her eye Phoebe saw a falcon simultaneously swooping down at her with the silver ball in its beak. Releasing the ball, the falcon swung at it with its large crimson wing, sending it sailing above Phoebe's head. In a split second decision, Phoebe launched herself at the incoming silver ball. She blocked its entry while Scott's ground attack resulted in a goal.

A whistle blew. "One all!"

"Nice call on blocking Xavier!" Sam shouted, dashing by Phoebe. With the game on the opposite end of the field, Phoebe watched as a radiant indigo hawk took a steep racing dive toward Mariko. In an attempt to avoid Mariko's swinging arms, the bird's wing swept the ground.

"Wing foul. Blue team player out!" the referee's voice rang.

The game continued its dizzying speed with both sides taking the lead a number of times and each air team losing members to dropped balls.

From her goal, Phoebe watched as a red team falcon zigzagged toward her, ball in its gold talons. She blinked and the bird dove. As she reached up to block the ball, an arrow came flying suddenly out of the trees, piercing the bird through the chest. Phoebe saw, as though in slow motion, the bird transform into a curly-haired girl, plummet from the sky and hit the ground with a sickening thud. She landed a foot from where Phoebe stood shaking. Phoebe lowered her eyes. The blood pulsing from the wound flowed down the girl's chest, forming a scarlet pool at Phoebe's feet.

For what felt like a long, breath-stealing second, nothing happened. And then pandemonium swept over the clearing. Screams split the night air, which was heavy with the scent of fear. Many students scattered. Others froze in hysterics.

"Get the pre-cons out of here!" Sam yelled, prompting older students to herd groups of sobbing first-years down the path out of the forest, while the remaining Principes cadets assumed attack stances: palms facing out, nervous eyes darting everywhere.

Phoebe had barely managed to kneel beside the girl when two boys rushed to join her. One immediately said, his voice hoarse, "Osiah and Gavya, it went through a heart. . . ."

Phoebe didn't hear the rest of the exchange between the boys. She'd doubled over in painful distress. Gut-stabbing panic surged wildly inside her, and she tried to smother it. Intense emotion often disconnected Phoebe from her sense of control, causing her to accidentally *push* her feelings into anyone around her. Phoebe couldn't let that happen. Not here. Not now. Even as she fought to contain herself, Phoebe felt the panic crushing its way out, *pushing* into the few students left in the clearing. Immediately charged with a heightened sense of panic, they all ran, climbing over brambles and twisted roots in their effort to flee the forest.

Alone now, frightened and sick with the horror of what she'd done, Phoebe stared into the girl's dirt-stained face. She shook at the sight of the arrow embedded in her heaving chest. Phoebe's senses felt scrambled. Tears streamed down her cheeks. She pressed her hands around the wound to staunch the bleeding, trying to imagine who had struck this girl and why. A thought flew into Phoebe's mind as the conversation she'd overheard came back to her. Her hearts thudded. Was this the danger the headmaster and the mentors had been discussing? As Phoebe listened to the girl's labored breathing, she could almost picture her father, and she shivered violently at the memory.

"It's going to be okay," Phoebe said, trying to *push* what calm she could into the girl to ease some of her fear. The girl gazed up with wide eyes that begged Phoebe not to leave. "I'm not going anywhere," Phoebe promised, her own memories pressing against her hearts. "Help is on—" A horribly familiar burn coursed through Phoebe's skin, choking off her words. The girl let out a ragged cry that told Phoebe plainly that her skin scalded as well. A heavy breath, and then a low rumbling growl sounded through the trees. When Phoebe lifted her head to stare into the blackness of the forest before her, the huge, fire-orange eyes of a Vigo stared back.

❦ FIVE

The Vigo emerged from the shadows. Silver-striped black fur wrinkled around its eyes as they narrowed on Phoebe's face. The razor-sharp spikes jutting out of its back glinted like thin, steel cones in the waning moonlight. Phoebe saw that they were barbed. A paralysis gripped her. Her trance only broke when the Vigo charged, yellowed teeth snapping, viscous saliva flying from its jaw. She threw herself in front of the wounded girl and flung up her arms to shield her own face.

Phoebe felt the scorching heat of the Vigo's mouth before its jaws closed in an iron grip around her arm. Teeth sunk against bone. She screamed through the explosion of pain. For a few frightening seconds Phoebe could think of nothing as the heavy beast dragged her toward the woods. Sharp rocks tore through her sweatpants and scraped against her legs. In a flash of clarity, she realized how critical these next moments were to her survival. Reaching down with her free hand, Phoebe picked up a fallen branch and struck at the Vigo's flared nostrils. It had no effect. She stabbed at its eyes. The Vigo only pulled harder and Phoebe felt the searing pain of her shoulder starting to separate from its socket.

A menacing growl sounded in the darkness behind Phoebe. It rumbled in her bones. Another Vigo, slightly smaller than the first, broke through the trees into the clearing, filling the edge of her vision. In the middle of the forest, far from help that didn't appear to be on its way, Phoebe realized with fluttering hearts that things had gone from bad to impossibly worse. A bolt of fear ripped through her, and abruptly, her arm fell from the Vigo's jaw. It hung limp at her side, as blood ran in rivulets across the dry grass.

Breathing through her savage pain, Phoebe watched in terror as the two Vigos circled each other slowly. She hardly dared to move when both Tigers curled their lips back and lowered thick, corkscrew-shaped canines. Then, to her shock, the smaller Vigo pinned the large one to the ground, its claws deep in the stunned beast's throat. The large Vigo twisted free with lithe, swift movements and struck a massive blow across the smaller one's muzzle with a mighty front paw. Blood, thick like oil, splattered in all directions. At a speed Phoebe could hardly believe, the Tigers hurtled their muscled bulk at each other, slashing, snarling, their clashing spikes ringing with an awful clangor. Roars of beastly fury drenched Phoebe in cold terror as the earth beneath her shook.

Collision after collision, they fought tirelessly. Then, the larger Vigo hooked a claw through the air and missed its opponent's throat. Unable to stop its momentum by digging its hind paws into the ground, the large cat skidded and crashed against a pine tree. It sprang back to its feet, furious. But it stood absolutely still, transfixed and glaring, as if it were momentarily hypnotized by the presence of the antagonist, who bared its teeth and growled. A low savage rumble.

As Phoebe watched in bafflement, the larger Vigo rapidly twisted its ears one hundred and eighty degrees so that the backs were facing front, lowered its tail to the ground, and squeezed its eyes into slits. It bowed its massive head slightly and then turned and fled. Everything around Phoebe grew still as the remaining Vigo faced her. Its burning eyes glared at hers down the length of its bleeding muzzle. She saw the fire within them flicker just before the Vigo sped off, becoming a ghost in the darkest part of the forest.

Phoebe's thoughts tangled as she fought to make sense of what had just happened. Were they coming back? Had the smaller Vigo been . . . defending her? There was little sense in that last thought, Phoebe knew, but she couldn't get her head around any other reasoning for how it had behaved. Perhaps the two Vigos were simply competitors, but that didn't explain why the smaller Vigo hadn't tried to attack her. Phoebe knew her thinking was foggy, and must be descending toward unconsciousness, for no Vigo would ever stop a Shaper kill.

Phoebe dragged herself back to the wounded girl, slowly and painfully, somehow managing not to faint. She grabbed hold of the girl's hand and held it in a firm grip. Delirious with pain, Phoebe fought off the blurriness invading her vision. Moments passed, and then, just as Phoebe was drifting off, someone gently pried her hands from the girl's, grabbed Phoebe under her armpits, and pulled her to the side.

"Everything is going to be okay, lass," a man's voice said quietly. Phoebe raised hazy eyes to see Gabe. His hood was down, revealing closely cropped white hair. He smiled reassuringly at her, and then, whipping a small syringe from under his cloak, he pushed the needle into her wound. Phoebe screamed in pain until nausea choked her throat. She vomited and gaped at Gabe, wild-eyed.

"That's a good reaction to have," Gabe said, gently wiping at her sweaty brow with a damp cloth. "It means the Vigo venom hasn't had time to do its worst yet."

The sound of thundering footsteps and beating wings halted Phoebe's attempt at a reply. Leopards, jaguars, and lions exploded into the clearing. Above them, eagles carrying stretchers descended cautiously to the ground. A whirl of activity erupted, with bodies clustered and throbbing all around Phoebe, voices shouting instructions above her, and strong hands moving her onto a stretcher.

"Only Phoebe was bitten," she dimly heard Gabe saying to someone nearby who muttered an inaudible response. "Yes, I gave her the shot," he added.

Phoebe rolled onto her side and saw Afua with a dagger ready in her fist. The diamond blade flashed in the moonlight. A second later, body secured to the stretcher by thick straps, Phoebe felt a warm pulsing wind and a lightness take her over as she was lifted upward into the night sky. Fatigue ushered her into unconsciousness.

In her dream, Phoebe remembered the first time she'd made her father cry on purpose. A thick swirl of fog pressed against the kitchen windows where she sat at a table with him on a day they were denied their spectacular view of the Golden Gate Bridge.

"Well done," he'd said, while tears spilled from his blood-shot eyes.

Phoebe stared at her father, unable to speak. It was hard to reconcile the pride she felt in accomplishing her task with the horror of seeing what her power had done: the strongest man she knew had been reduced to a sobbing infant.

Opening up her senses to him had stunned her. Once she began, the connection had come instantly, his emotions gnawing at her in a way that was immediately overwhelming, a veritable floodgate. He taught her to see them as glowing keys on a piano, keys that she could tickle lightly or *push* hard. She reminded herself that it was a gift, but as she took hold of her father's emotions and played his mood like a sonata, she had to witness him feeling something he would otherwise not. She had found it traumatic.

"How did it feel?" she asked timidly. "When I *pushed*?" It had been her father's idea for her to practice on him. And it had been his idea for her to start with sadness.

Her father took her hands in his and kissed them. "At first it feels like bad indigestion."

Phoebe giggled in spite of herself. "That's silly," she said. "It's your mind I *push*."

"Yes, but I think whatever you do up here"—her father tapped a finger to his head—"floods the chest and then takes over."

Phoebe thought about that for a moment. "So can all Shapers do it—?"

"No," her father said at once, cutting her off with such an aggressive tone that Phoebe was unsettled and even a little afraid. "No," he repeated, his tone much softer. "This has to be our secret—"

he broke off, overcome by another wave of tears. Phoebe couldn't handle watching him come apart anymore and quickly looked for the key that played happiness. Her father, seeing in her eyes what she planned to do, shook his head.

"It's okay to let me sit with this sadness," he said. "Next time we'll work on other ones. I promise."

And they did work on other emotions, but often returned to sadness. Phoebe eventually came to realize that her father did so when he needed an excuse to cry. She discovered this one day by accident when she'd stumbled on him gazing at an old picture of her mother. Shortly thereafter, he'd asked her if she wanted to try her *pushing*. Breathing deep, she always agreed, and always they'd start with sadness. Many unanswered questions surrounded her mother's abandonment. She and her father had never really discussed it, but Phoebe knew one thing for sure: her father still held her mother in his hearts. So she continued to give him his moments of sadness, even when she discovered that her ability came with a drawback; for every emotion she *pushed*, a piece of it lingered within her for a short time afterward. Phoebe would sit with her father and wrap her arms around his trembling torso and share in his grief for the woman she didn't know.

As Phoebe's dreams began to flicker and fade, her mind grabbed the tendrils of a distant memory and held on desperately. It was the day her father had made her promise never to reveal her ability. It was also the day he'd given her his camera. Phoebe knew how much her father loved that camera, as he would often take her to his outdoor photo shoots, always explaining the importance of capturing light. "Great light can transform an image," he'd say. Between her excitement over the gift and the sound of the ocean crashing on the shore, Phoebe almost didn't hear her father's surprising apology as they walked along San Francisco's Ocean Beach.

"I need to apologize to you, Phoebe," he had said as she hung the camera from her neck and gazed down at it reverently.

Phoebe raised her eyes to him, surprised by this. "For what? This is the best gift I ever—"

"For using your ability for my own personal gain."

Phoebe said nothing.

Her father stopped walking and dug his bare toes into the coarse sand. "Your mother leaving, was a very difficult thing for me," he said, his voice catching. "But I knew that I had to remain strong for you and so I buried the grief so deep within me that I almost forgot it was there. . . . I've been using our sessions and your ability to *push* emotion to help me access that grief."

Phoebe was shocked speechless. It wasn't what her father had said that astounded her, because she'd figured that piece out on her own, it was his admission of it. And at that moment, with her mental gate open, Phoebe felt her father's shame and torment.

He continued. "I sensed what it was doing to you, Phoebe,"—he paused for a moment to collect himself—"and I knew it was my fault but still I ignored it. And you suffered in silence."

This was true. Phoebe had become increasingly consumed by the sadness that plagued her father; she'd lost her appetite, lost weight, and slept uneasily; all things she hadn't realized that her father had noticed, even in his fog. And yes, it had taken a toll on her, but Phoebe had believed what she'd been doing was important. She was helping her father.

"You have to promise me," he said, extremely seriously, "never to reveal your ability to anyone. What you can do is powerful, and it can be abused." He looked away and gazed tearfully at the water. "I love you and even I couldn't help taking advantage of your gift. Think of what some people would do if they had you under their control. With this secret, trust only yourself."

Feeling her father's fear for her swell, Phoebe nodded.

"Why did she leave?" Phoebe was shocked to hear the words that fell abruptly from her mouth. Many times she'd thought of asking her father that question. And many times she'd failed to put it into words.

"It's complicated, Phoebe."

Phoebe knew that her father didn't want to talk about it, but she pushed the issue anyway.

"Try me."

He looked at her with surprise and then looked away. "Sometimes you can't help who you love, sweetheart, no matter who they are. . . ."

Phoebe stared at her father as he stared at the ocean. They both knew, of course, that he hadn't answered her question. And Phoebe had an uneasy feeling that he might never answer it. But she let it go, because at that moment a rich purple-blood-orange sun was setting, and Phoebe, pulled by a need to remember that light, raised the camera to her eye and captured it. And that was the beginning of how she would come to deal with unanswered questions, one photograph at a time.

Six

When Phoebe awoke, an intense soreness hit her first. Then urgent voices whispering nearby slowly registered. Raising her head slightly, careful to look as though she were still asleep, she glanced about the unfamiliar room through the slits of her eyes. Next to a table covered with flower-filled vases, Phoebe could see Professor Yori speaking with a cloaked figure.

"—no, unfortunately there's no one for us to contact," Professor Yori said. When Phoebe chanced opening up her eyes a bit more, the cloaked figure came into better view. It was Gabe.

"I thought there was a grandfather," Gabe said, his voice low.

"Yes, there is. But he's on her maternal side," Professor Yori said. "The school must act as her guardian in Shaper matters." He glanced over at the bed, and Phoebe kept still. "We have a few moments until she starts coming to," he said, returning his gaze to Gabe. "Give me your assessment."

Gabe spoke quickly. "The game was too close to the Campus Above's perimeter sensors. By the time the system picked up on the presence of Vigo physical energy, the Vigos were much closer to the students than we were."

The headmaster sighed, leaned forward, and picked up a mug from the table. "We've had students sneaking off to play this game for years without one incident. Now, this will be seen as incompetence on my part for turning a blind eye to the tradition."

"I doubt you'll be judged harshly, sir," Gabe said sympathetically. "As you said, there have been no prior incidents."

Professor Yori said nothing. He brought his mug to his lips and drank deeply. "Unfortunately, our visitors won't see it that way." After a moment's pause, he added, "Is it possible to extend our Eye to the perimeter?"

"Yes, but it will take time to cover the acreage and—"

"Make it happen. Have your custodians work in shifts if you have to."

Phoebe heard the door open and close with a slight creak. She let her mind wander, images flickering before her eyes like confetti: Hayley's dimpled grin, Colten's eyes, a picture of the sky she had captured with her camera a few days before, the girl with an arrow protruding from her chest, the Vigo's jaws. . . . About fifteen minutes later, after allowing what she felt was a good amount of time to pass so that the headmaster wouldn't think that she'd overheard the conversation, Phoebe stretched and opened her eyes fully. With a stab of honest shock, she saw that Professor Yori now stood by her bed. Close up, she could see that he wore a black robe open over a navy suit. Everything about his face looked tired; it was as though sleep had escaped him for days.

"Sorry to alarm you," he said, peering down at her. "I've been waiting for you to come to. I wanted a moment for us to speak before the meeting."

Phoebe squinted at him, yawning. "Where am I? What meeting?"

"You're in a suite in the Pre-Con Clinic," he said, answering only one of her questions.

The Pre-Con Clinic. It was one of many wings of the city-like Campus Below that Phoebe had not been to yet, but she had heard plenty. She took a quick glance about the suite, a sizable room home to two leather sofas and a round table set with six chairs. It seemed absurdly plush for what amounted to a hospital room, and despite the room's inviting décor, she felt a wave of nervousness.

The headmaster sat in the bedside armchair, his right leg at an awkward angle. He regarded Phoebe over the rim of his mug, studying her rather intently. Then his face softened. "How are you feeling?"

"Like I slammed into a truck." Despite her exhaustion, Phoebe sat up clumsily against the headboard. Arm still aching where the Vigo had bit her, Phoebe peeled back the layers of bandages to assess the damage. The wound was tender to the touch, but her skin had knitted back together, leaving raised scars only at the individual teeth marks. She counted ten of them. Large square marks interspersed with smaller round ones.

"All I need is a pen to play connect the dots," Phoebe said, laughing humorlessly while flexing her fingers to make sure she could still feel them.

Now gazing directly at his right leg, Professor Yori said, "It's a shame the injuries we incur prior to Conversion never entirely heal. But"—he looked up—"Osiah and Gavya willing, yours will come very close."

Phoebe rubbed her arm gingerly; these new scars were nothing compared to the ones she already had. Even so, she bemoaned the fact that pre-con Shapers had limited access to their supernatural powers—especially the regenerative ones. It was a peculiar limbo. And she felt like a half-charged battery waiting for the catalyst of Conversion to reach full capacity.

Professor Yori's heavy sigh interrupted Phoebe's thoughts. "You do realize that we cannot inform your grandfather about this," he said, echoing what Phoebe had overheard earlier.

Phoebe nodded. "Even if you could," she said with a fond smile, "you'd have a hard time finding him. His last postcard said he's birdwatching somewhere in Argentina." Shortly after she'd decided to go to boarding school, her grandfather, a retired cardiologist, announced that he'd signed up for a yearlong birdwatching trip. Neither of them had acknowledged it at the time, but they both knew that he didn't want to be stuck in an empty house, mourning their loss alone.

"Ah yes," Professor Yori said. "I understand he's become a world traveler." He sipped from his mug, his eyes becoming serious. "You were truly lucky to survive such a vicious attack, Cadet Pope," he said.

At once, an unpleasant thought slithered through Phoebe's mind and took hold. Her mouth went dry. "Did the other girl not make it?"

Professor Yori managed a small smile. "Katie Banks will be okay. They successfully removed the arrow at the Aviary Clinic. It did pierce a heart so she will need to spend the rest of the moonester at home to fully recover, but she should be fine. These flowers," he said, indicating the table behind him, "are from her family. They send their heartfelt thanks to you."

Phoebe's stomach lurched at that. "I don't deserve them." The words spilled out before she could stop them.

"I see," Professor Yori said, setting his mug on a side table. He brought the tips of his thick fingers together under his chin and considered her. "And may I ask why not?"

Because there were others who would have stayed to help if I hadn't pushed them to leave, Phoebe thought to say. *Because I'm a coward who would have run if I hadn't froze.*

"Bravery," Professor Yori said, sparing Phoebe from answering, "means different things to different people. That's actually what I wanted to talk to you about. No doubt, the entire campus is aware of what happened and the part you played in Cadet Banks's survival.

"Naturally there will be questions and there will be adulation but at the end of the day, it is important to remember that, for you, it was also a traumatic experience. Unfortunately, in the quest for sensational information, people tend to forget that fact." He paused for a moment, his eyes straying to the flowers. "With this in mind, I've taken the liberty of excusing you from all classes today. And as far as your instructors Above are concerned, you have come down with the stomach flu."

No sooner had those words left his mouth than the door opened and the three mentors appeared, their black faculty robes rustling over the stone floor as they glided in; Scott, Lewis, and Mariko trailed in their wake.

"Way to make us look bad by playing hero," Scott said. He pushed his hair off his face to wink at Phoebe from across the room.

Lewis, who was standing behind Scott, took a rolled up comic book from under his arm, and hit him with it. "Not cool, my man," he said to Scott who winced dramatically.

Mariko stalked over to Phoebe's side, but not before giving Scott a reproving look. "Are you okay?" she asked, her wide concerned eyes riveted on Phoebe's arm.

"I'm fine," Phoebe said. "It looks worse than it feels."

Unconvinced, Mariko shuddered.

"Good to see that you all got the message to meet here," Professor Yori said, rising to his feet. "Please, sit." He motioned them to the assortment of furniture. Still scowling at Scott, Mariko sank into the chair beside Lewis. Scott perched on the arm of a sofa. The mentors remained standing as before.

Afua, her springy black curls pulled back into a high ponytail, spoke first. "Have you briefed her?" she asked Professor Yori who shook his head.

"I figured you'd prefer to address them as a group." The headmaster sat back down heavily.

A palpable tension circulated in the room. Something in Professor Yori's eyes bothered Phoebe, and then, without warning, she had a burning urge to read him. She bit the inside of her cheek as she let down her mental shield enough to sense his feelings; anxiety knotted all around him. But before Phoebe could begin to guess at a possible reason, Afua's dark eyes locked onto hers with such intensity that Phoebe drew a breath.

"If you could, please give us your account of what happened," Afua asked.

With everyone's eyes fixed upon her, Phoebe's face flooded with color. She took a ragged breath. Attempting to speak without emotion, she told them how the first Vigo had charged at her and Katie, how the second one had appeared soon after and fought with the first, who fled. As she spoke, Mariko, Lewis, and Scott listened intently, fear and interest gripping their faces simultaneously.

When Phoebe finished, Afua pushed up her sleeves and crossed her arms over her chest, not removing her flashing eyes from Phoebe's face. Phoebe was distracted by several black lines tattooed around Afua's right wrist like bracelets. Perhaps it was a trick of the light, but to Phoebe, it looked as if the lines were glowing.

"What she's saying confirms an S and D triad," Afua said finally, anger creeping into her voice. She looked at Yelena and Deborah-Anna who both nodded. Professor Yori emitted a brief strangled noise and Phoebe guessed that whatever Afua had just said had come as an unpleasant shock to him.

"A what?" Lewis said, his expression cycling through fear, curiosity, and dread.

"A Search and Destroy triad," Afua said to Lewis matter-of-factly. "Your curriculum will cover this next moonester, but Vigos hunt in threes. There's a Tracker, who is usually the team leader; a Sniper, which shot Katie down; and the third is the Closer who goes in for the kill. What you described"—Afua returned her attention to Phoebe—"was the Tracker sensing rescue coming and jumping in to have the Closer cut their losses."

Phoebe couldn't help feeling that there had been something more to the interaction between the two Vigos. She opened her mouth to say as much, but then thought better of it, catching Afua's raised eyebrows. Instead she asked, "Why are you telling us this? I mean—why all four of us Hyphas, in particular?"

Professor Yori glanced briefly at Afua, an understanding passing between them. The headmaster scrubbed a hand over his face, and then spoke with less confidence than Phoebe had ever heard from him. "I've called this meeting to let you all know that they"—he gestured vaguely to the mentors and looked away despondently—"are Blackcoats and—"

"Blackcoats?" Lewis interrupted, his face slack with awe. "As in the Royal Security Corps?"

Afua nodded. "I'm a combat specialist and team lead. Deborah-Anna handles technology and Yelena, intelligence."

Mariko paled. "I was only kidding when I wrote on my ShaperCity page that Princess Carol could stand to lose ten pounds," she blurted. "I meant no offense to the Royal Court."

Lewis and Scott barely stifled chuckles at that.

"We Blackcoats do not concern ourselves with the contents of your social networking profiles," Afua said.

Suddenly, and with an accusatory bite to his tone Scott said to Professor Yori, "So if you lied to us about them being mentors does that mean we don't really need any extra help?"

"Careful, Cadet," Afua said warningly. There was such a ferocity in her gaze that Scott had to avert his eyes as he bowed his head in apology.

Professor Yori waved Afua down. "Your need for mentoring is a fact." He sounded even more tired. "But instead of having our professors do it, the Blackcoats agreed to mentor you as visiting scholars. It's a convincing way for them to be here undercover and not raise any alarm with the faculty or the student body."

Mariko shot forward in her chair. "Alarm about what?"

The Blackcoats exchanged meaningful looks. At Afua's deferential nod, Deborah-Anna reached a hand inside her robes and produced a small gray box. She flipped open the lid and removed a handful of small, silver C-shaped clips.

"Before we talk further," Deborah-Anna said, passing the clips around, "we would like you all to wear these."

Lewis turned the clip in his hand. "What is it?"

"A new piece of Blackcoat technology called Privaque. Please clip them to your uniforms."

"What does it do?" Phoebe asked.

Deborah-Anna swept her two thick braids behind her. "It's an active noise cancellation device that interferes with speech sound waves," she explained. "Only those in your immediate company will hear you. Given that we are in a community with elastic senses, we need to take this measure to safeguard against eavesdropping."

"We have reason to believe," Afua said, once everyone had received a Privaque, "that you four may have been the specific targets of last night's attack."

Phoebe's eyes scanned the other Hyphas; their faces displayed a horror that mirrored her own. "Are you sure? I mean . . . why us?" she said, her voice little more than a whisper.

Lewis, who had become visibly undone, echoed, "W-why us?" He dug into his pockets, retrieved a coin and proceeded to knuckle-walk it across his hand at an alarming speed.

"According to intel,"—all eyes snapped to Yelena, who had remained silent until then—"Vigos have become aware of a prophecy that alleges:

'Four to Convert under the same moon,

Shapers by blood born from a non-Shaper womb.

In one will awaken the power to wield more

than the earth and the air.

In the Year of Four,

all Vigos beware.'"

Yelena moved from her place against a wall and walked over to stand by Afua, her long hair fluttering around her face. "We believe that a Vigo by the name of Alexori has sanctioned a hit to eliminate the prophesied threats—"

"Hold on," Professor Yori's voice rose in aggravation, cutting Yelena off. "You did not inform me that this involved the New England Padrone." His grip on his mug began to shake.

Phoebe found herself feeling chilled. It was only because she'd done the recommended summer reading for her Understanding Vigos class that she understood the headmaster's reaction. And judging by the expressions on the faces of the other Hyphas, they too had read up on Vigo political hierarchy. Italian for "master," the Padrone was a Vigo that even Vigos feared. The ruthless head of all Vigos in a geographic territory, he set Alpha guidelines for pack leadership and resolved inter-pack disputes.

"We've only just received that piece of intel ourselves," Afua said.

The headmaster's mood was clearly not assuaged by her concession.

"But what does the prophecy even mean?" Mariko said, her voice close to trembling, her hands gripping the arms of her chair as she stared at the Blackcoats.

Deborah-Anna spoke for the trio. "We believe it means that at the time of Conversion, one of you four will come into a power of considerable strength that you can wield to help defeat Vigos."

"What kind of a power?" Phoebe asked slowly. Given her secret ability, she'd been trying not to think it could be her.

"It's unclear if this is even—" Deborah-Anna started.

"It's purely speculation at this point," Afua said speaking over Deborah-Anna, her eyes flashing a warning in the brunette's direction, "but it will most likely be something you wield with your palms like our earth and air powers. We won't know until you convert."

Phoebe was careful not to release a relieved breath.

"Even if we believe the prophecy," Scott said, speaking respectfully. "Aren't there other pre-con Hyphas around?"

Yelena took over. "Yes, but not four born to human females on the same day."

"December 14th?" Phoebe blurted.

Scott nodded, his tone dry as gravel. "December 14th."

Mariko went rigid. Lewis sank lower in his seat, clenching and unclenching his hand around his comic book.

"How does the Padrone even know about the prophecy?" Phoebe asked abruptly, trying to quell the fountain of panic that threatened to burst through her. "How does he even know who we are?"

"We've told you all we can at this juncture," Afua said, a note of finality in her voice. "Just know that our unit's mandate is to protect the four of you until this Vigo threat is fully investigated and handled."

"And in the meantime?" Lewis said. "What's to stop the Vigos from just grabbing us while we're Above?"

"Assuming we are correct about their motivation, it is unlikely that they will try again now that they know there are Blackcoats on campus. But should they attempt—"

"—but they got to us at the game," Lewis pressed.

"Unfortunately," Afua said, with a stiffness in her tone, and shifting her gaze to Professor Yori. "We were not made aware that there would be such an event."

At these words, Professor Yori sputtered in outrage. "Had we informed the Hyphas of the potential threat to them in a more timely manner, as I had suggested," he said, a vein in his bald head beginning to pulse, "they would not have even been at the game in the first place. Let me remind you that—"

But they wouldn't get to hear the headmaster's reprimand, because just then the door opened and a nurse walked in holding a handful of folded clothes Phoebe recognized as her own. The nurse's head was down and she was humming, clearly in a world of her own, until she reached the first couch, saw Scott's legs dangling over its arm, and jumped, clutching her chest.

"Why heavens of Osiah and Gavya!" she said, taking steadying breaths. "You scared me. So sorry to intrude, but I didn't hear a peep from this room and figured Phoebe was still sleeping."

All Professor Yori's fury seemed to fade at seeing the woman's fright. He almost looked grateful for the interruption.

"It's okay, Mary," he said lightly as if a heavy cloud of tension didn't hover over the room. "We should be getting to the rest of our day." He pulled a pocket watch from inside his robe and peered down at it while Mary hurried over to Phoebe, deposited the clothes at the foot of her bed and then scurried from the room.

"As I was saying," Professor Yori said rising to his feet as the door snapped shut, "we should be on our way."

"Before we disperse," Afua said, as Mariko, Lewis, and Scott stood. "I must insist that you speak to no one about the information imparted to you today. We Blackcoats are only here as a precaution, and with the entire Campus Below already feeling the shock of the attack, we cannot have rumors spreading about a matter still under investigation." Afua looked to the headmaster for support.

"That's right," Professor Yori said with a forced cheerfulness. "Think of this as your first official experience with information containment."

Professor Yori held the door open and Phoebe watched as everyone but Afua exited the room. At the headmaster's questioning gaze Afua said, "I'd like to ask Cadet Pope a few more questions." Professor Yori moved toward a chair amiably, but Afua added firmly, "I'd like to do so alone."

The headmaster appeared distinctly rankled. "Why?"

"Because I'd like to." Afua's lips became a thin line.

"By all means," Professor Yori said with a hint of resignation and smoothed the front of his robes before giving Afua a stiff nod and striding toward the door. He paused, hand on the knob, and glanced back at Phoebe. "Be sure to get plenty of rest this weekend."

Phoebe inhaled and sat straight against the headboard. She struggled to control her nerves. What more could the Blackcoat want from her?

"Please feel free to help yourself to some flowers," Phoebe joked nervously, after the door had closed behind the headmaster.

"You doubt my assessment of what happened out there," Afua said, dismissing Phoebe's comment. She moved around the table of flowers, pausing a moment to read one of the cards. "Why?" Phoebe jerked an eyebrow, but before she could ask what had given Afua that impression, the Blackcoat answered, "You had a telling look. So, please, enlighten me."

Phoebe glanced down at her arm before meeting Afua's eyes again. Sometime during the meeting, the thing that had been nagging her at the back of her mind had come to the forefront. She chose her words carefully. "My memory's a bit hazy—" Phoebe swallowed hard. "But it seemed like the first Vigo was surprised to see the second one."

"How so?"

"After they fought, it backed away in a strange way—eyes slit, tail down, ears—"

"Ears twisted?" Afua said.

Phoebe nodded. She must have given Afua a particularly confused look because the Blackcoat said, "All Tigers have white spots on the backside of their ears. It's a sign of submission when the spots are twisted to face an aggressor. Vigos do that when they relinquish a kill to a Tiger that's not a member of their pack."

"So there was more than one triad at the game?" Phoebe said, guessing.

"Perhaps." Afua crossed over to the bedside and Phoebe struggled to keep her composure. The Blackcoat had an aura about her that seethed with power. She had a raw intensity that had even staggered a decorated former SIS agent like Professor Yori. Indicating Phoebe's right arm, Afua said, "May I?"

Phoebe nodded and extended her arm, her hand visibly shaking. Afua examined the wound in silence. She narrowed her eyes. "Your scar pattern is inconsistent with a kill bite," she said.

Though Afua's face remained inscrutable, Phoebe had picked up a note of shock, even astonishment in her voice.

"What do you mean?" she asked.

"These"—Afua ran a finger along the tender scars—"were made by incisors only. They would be sandwiched between two larger marks had the canines been lowered during the bite." Phoebe shuddered; canines delivered the venom that was lethal to Shapers.

"Alexori issued a catch not a kill command," Afua said, mainly to herself. Then, to Phoebe, "It seems, for reasons we need to find out, the Padrone wants to extract you Hyphas alive."

That possibility did very little to make Phoebe any less terrified.

Afua released Phoebe's arm. "Hazy or not, Cadet, the smallest detail can be crucial to an investigation. You'll need to learn to speak up when you know something."

Phoebe met Afua's eyes, surprised. "Yes, ma'am."

Afua gave a curt nod and swept out of the room.

Alone, Phoebe released the tension her body had been holding. She kicked her covers aside, swung her legs over the edge of the bed, and gazed dully at her toes. Everything she'd heard finally began to crash down upon her in full force. It didn't seem fair. Vigos killed her father and now they wanted her too. Alive or dead, she wasn't sure which would be worse. A chill crept into her bones. Phoebe picked up the clothes the nurse had laid on the bed: sweatpants, t-shirt, hooded sweatshirt—all with the scent of the previous night laundered away. If only soap and bleach could do the same for the thoughts in her mind. Phoebe scrambled into her clothes, pulled her hoodie over her tangled mass of hair and left the clinic. Before she could really try to shove her memory of the attack aside and attempt to resume her life, strange as it had suddenly become, Phoebe had one important stop she needed to make first.

❧ SEVEN

In the daytime, the chapel was quite gorgeous. Sunlight splintered through stained glass windows, casting patterns of jewel-bright colors against otherwise pale walls. Phoebe moved in and out of the blinding light as she walked down the aisle, her hands deep in her sweatshirt pockets. She had called out a few times for Gabe when she first entered the heavy doors with no response from the old custodian.

Ascending the short flight of steps to the altar, Phoebe circled the pulpit, noticing for the first time the small images of moons carved into the stone. Now that she thought about it, every narthyx point she'd used so far had similar markings. She had turned to leave when Phoebe noticed a door on the back wall standing slightly ajar and caught a glimpse of light inside that seemed to be rippling.

"Hello?" she said, walking toward the back wall. "Gabe?" As Phoebe reached for the handle, a sudden gust of wind slammed the door shut, making her jump backward. She turned and looked carefully in all directions. The tall form of Gabe swept down the aisle toward the pulpit and she heard his voice call out sharply, "That is a restricted room!"

Phoebe lowered her hood, and Gabe's somewhat hard expression relaxed when he took in her face. "Phoebe," he said, blue eyes glittering. "It's nice to see you up and about, lass, but you shouldn't be snooping around."

Phoebe went red with shame. "The door was open"—Gabe frowned—"and I thought it was your office," Phoebe said, swallowing a lump in her throat. Gabe strode up the steps to the altar, pulling a set of keys from his robes, and locked the door before saying to Phoebe, "This way to my office."

Phoebe followed him two doors down to a small room with wood paneled walls, a desk, and two well-worn armchairs. Gabe closed the door and turned to look at Phoebe.

"Please sit," he said. "Care for some tea?" Phoebe shook her head and backed into a chair while Gabe grabbed a thermos from his desk and poured its steaming liquid into a mug. "How's the arm?"

"Fine." Her arm wasn't exactly fine; it still throbbed a bit, but it was nothing he needed to concern himself with.

Gabe's face brightened. "I'm glad to hear that."

"That's why I'm here," Phoebe said. "I wanted to thank you for giving me that shot." Even though Phoebe now knew it hadn't been a kill bite, no one had known that at the time. She was immensely grateful to Gabe for having been there with the antidote.

Gabe furrowed his brow, sinking into a chair across from Phoebe's. "We custodians are trained first responders," he said. "I only regret not getting there sooner. It was a brave thing you did, staying with that girl."

Preferring not to respond to that comment, Phoebe twisted her hands in her lap. She scanned the quaint office, her eyes lingering on his sparsely decorated desk. Next to a clock adorned with moon faces, sat a red, wood-framed picture of a girl astride a motorcycle. Her shoulder-length black hair looked windblown and wild. Phoebe gazed at the girl's smiling face with interest.

"That's my daughter Becka back when she was just a bit older than you are now," Gabe said, answering Phoebe's unspoken question.

"Does she live nearby?"

Gabe, whose face had gone somber at the question, rose from the chair and approached the desk. He picked up the picture and held it up to the light. "She used to be close enough for me to see her every day," he said, his eyes pained.

"Where did she move to?"

"She didn't." After a long pause, the custodian choked on his next words. "Vigos took her from me."

Phoebe dropped her eyes, horrified. "I'm—I'm so sorry for your loss. I didn't know." She brought her elbows to her knees and bowed her head into her hands, for suddenly her entire body ached. Thoughts of her father raced through her mind, and she inhaled deeply to stop the moisture in her eyes from pooling into tears.

Gabe put the picture down, gave Phoebe a melancholy smile, and returned to his seat. "You know as well as anyone that people mean no harm when asking about our loved ones," he said softly. "I appreciate your asking."

There was a knock on the door, and a male student with tousled sandy hair entered. He nodded at Phoebe once, then handed Gabe a folded note. "I'm afraid," Gabe said, reading the note and crushing it in his hand, "that I have to cut your visit short. I'm needed elsewhere." Gabe walked Phoebe to the door and rested a hand on her shoulder. "I hope you'll be by again now that you know where my office is," he said.

Phoebe nodded and left Gabe's office. The custodian possessed a gentleness about him that she liked. And as much as she was sorry for his loss, she couldn't help taking some small comfort in knowing that there was someone nearby who really understood what it meant to have a Vigo take a loved one away.

Phoebe didn't know exactly how long she'd been following the winding stone trail that took her farther and farther away from the campus buildings, but when the scent of damp earth filled her nostrils, she wasn't surprised to see where she'd ended up. For as long as Phoebe could remember, she'd had a sort of unconscious compulsion to seek out bodies of water in times of disquiet. Tilting her head to one side, she stared at the imposing building before her. The Green Lane boathouse and its stately stone and brick had a majestic presence on the shore of the campus lake.

Phoebe entered the ground level, noting its stone floor unusually patterned with manhole-sized black and silver polka dots, and marched up spiral stairs to a spacious clubroom. Fancy glass doors led to a balcony that overlooked the lake, and Phoebe soon found herself there, leaning over the railing. It was a rare day when she didn't take a picture of something, so when the sinking sun's rays reflected against the water's surface like diamonds scattered on black glass, Phoebe felt her neck itch for the weight of the camera she didn't have on hand. Darkness came quickly thereafter, and with it, a cold mist that blew over the lake. The chill penetrated Phoebe's layers, finally prompting her to leave.

Phoebe stepped back from the railing just as a boy's voice said, "Hope I didn't keep you waiting too long, Gorgeous."

Startled, she jumped, finding herself face-to-face with an even more surprised-looking Scott who had paused in midstride.

"Well, this is embarrassing," he said, scrubbing a hand over the side of his neck. "I thought you were—"

"—someone else," Phoebe finished for him. "Don't worry I won't be in your way. I was just leaving, anyway." She took a couple steps forward but Scott blocked her way.

"Wait," he said, as she tried to sidestep him. "I'm glad I've run into you. I've been looking for you," he added hastily, seeing the look on her face.

Phoebe tilted her head as she took in Scott's appearance. He wore a Brazil soccer jacket over a pair of dark jeans. Scott watched Phoebe curiously, and she realized that her scrutiny could easily be construed as her checking him out.

"Well," Phoebe said, dropping her gaze. "You've found me."

"I want to apologize for what I said earlier—about you making us look bad," Scott said, rushing his words as though he thought Phoebe would leave if he didn't make his point fast. "I mean . . . we're all in this together." He pushed his hands deep into the pockets of his jeans and kicked the ground.

Phoebe shrugged, looked briefly up at the stars and said, "Actually, I thought you were joking. I mean, I'm sure you were just trying to lighten up the situation."

"No," Scott said. "I'm an ass." That earned him a look of surprise. "But once you get to know me"—he met Phoebe's eyes and grinned—"you'll see that I'm at least a charming one."

Phoebe couldn't help but laugh, and it felt rather good. Relaxing a bit, she backed up several steps, stopping when she came up against the railing's metal balusters. She then turned to face the lake. "'Charming ass' is an oxymoron," she said in all seriousness.

"Yes it is," Scott mused. "That's what makes me a conflicted guy," he said with a short, self-deprecating laugh. Phoebe snickered a bit more, which seemed to please Scott who leaned on the railing beside her. "Care for a smoke?" He patted his jacket pocket and pulled out a pack of cigarettes.

"No, thanks; I'm good," Phoebe said, watching him shake one out for himself.

Scott tapped the cigarette against his bottom lip and gave her an amused look. "You know it won't kill you, right?"

Phoebe smiled, but said nothing. Thanks to the wonder of Shaper genetics, she knew, any lung damage caused by smoking would be minimal. But she'd tried smoking once—an experience that had involved coughing and near vomiting—and it was something she didn't care to relive.

"So, what are you doing up here?" Scott held a lighter beneath his cigarette, cupping his hands around the flame to protect it from a sudden breeze. "Hiding from your fans?"

Phoebe glanced up at him and narrowed her eyes. "What's that supposed to mean?"

"You don't know?" Scott's tone held a hint of surprise. "You're all anyone's talking about Below. Folks want a glimpse of the girl who fought off two Vigos while protecting a fellow cadet—"

Phoebe interrupted him, exasperated. "That's not what happened!"

"Hey man"—Scott held up his hands in a defensive gesture as he blew a stream of smoke toward the lake—"I'm just reporting what I hear."

"Sorry," sighed Phoebe, realizing how harsh her tone had been. But she hated attention, and she could barely stand the thought of people giving it to her based on a misunderstanding. Phoebe stared thoughtfully at the moon over the lake. Perhaps Scott was exaggerating to get a rise out of her.

"So they think you're a badass," Scott said, dragging Phoebe from her thoughts. "Let 'em. There are worse reps to have. But"—he leaned closer to her—"if you need help keeping love-struck stalkers away, I've got your back."

At that, Phoebe snorted. Scott had choked a bit on a drag when saying "love-struck stalkers," making it that much sillier. "I think I'll be okay," she said.

"Scott?" said a girl's sunny voice at the same time Phoebe felt the skin-tingle of cold energy.

Phoebe and Scott looked up together and both stared at a tall brunette dressed in a gray fur-lined coat, who stepped onto the balcony. She wore an eager smile, which vanished the instant she noticed Phoebe. She looked alternately at both of them, giving Phoebe the are-you-a-threat once-over.

"I think 'Gorgeous' just arrived," Phoebe muttered teasingly, but only so Scott could hear her. Then, realizing her presence created an awkward situation, Phoebe gathered herself and started to leave. In the quickest of movements, Scott caught her hand.

"We cool, Pope?" he said in a whisper. He dropped his cigarette and crushed it under his foot. Phoebe stared at him, not expecting to see his face take on the nervous look he now wore. When she nodded in answer, Phoebe could have sworn she'd heard Scott release a relieved breath. It gave her a sense that he wasn't as cocky as he came across. Scott let go of her hand just as the girl reached them. Pulling her hood over her head, Phoebe left Scott to the task of explaining himself.

When Phoebe finally pushed open her dorm room door, she found Cyn sitting on the edge of their small sofa, pulling a pair of furry black boots over black jeans.

"God, you look awful," Cyn said by way of greeting. "That stomach flu must have worked a number on you—you're not contagious, are you?"

Phoebe stood confused for a moment, then, remembering Professor Yori had said that officials Above would be told that she'd had the stomach flu, said, "No, I'm all good."

Phoebe padded across the hardwood floor to her side of the room, sank down onto her bed, and hugged a pillow. Cyn fixed her with a gaze—one that was mildly suspicious at first. She began to frown and then stopped when she became aware of what her features were doing.

Cyn said, her tone all business, "Two things you should know. First, someone dropped a bag of—um dead leaves for you." When she stood and crossed to her desk, Phoebe saw that Cyn was wearing an obnoxiously bright pink shirt underneath her denim jacket. Written across the chest in a large stylized font were the letters CC.

"Do your friends think it's funny to send you trash?" Cyn extended a small paper bag to Phoebe who took it with a curious smirk and didn't respond. Instead, her eyes zeroed in on a large maple leaf pinned to the bag's handle. Phoebe bit back a grin when she saw that the leaf had been coded with a message. It read:

"Had class code 'Get Well' messages to you. Tell me how they did. Rest up. Prof. Elmore."

Phoebe peered into the bag and saw a good stack of leaves in various stages of coded decay. Only the weight of Cyn's stare kept her from pulling them out to read.

"So what's the other thing I should know?" Phoebe asked cheerfully, putting the bag aside.

Cyn looked between Phoebe and the bag as if waiting for Phoebe to explain its significance. When Phoebe didn't, she said with a hint of annoyance in her voice, "I'm writing a seven-part feature on important Green Lane graduates in the arts and this,"—she handed Phoebe a sheet of paper—"is the schedule for when the alumni will be on campus for you to shoot portraits. Since you missed today's meeting, I thought I'd be a great roommate and bring you your assignment."

"Thanks." Phoebe ran her eyes down the list and raised an eyebrow. "Don Beil, the first chair violinist for the Boston Symphony, went to Green Lane?"

"Yup," Cyn said proudly as though they were related. "And I got him to agree to be a part of this feature. By the way, he can only meet at the crack of dawn. That's not going to be a problem, is it?"

Phoebe shook her head. "There are only six names on this list. I thought you said . . ."

The skin between Cyn's eyes creased. "The last person I have in mind isn't technically an alum yet and is proving difficult to land, but I—"

Before Cyn could finish, someone knocked on the door and she pranced over to answer it.

"You sexy beast!" came an excited voice from the hallway. "You ready?"

"Almost." Cyn stepped back, and a slim girl Phoebe knew by sight but couldn't remember where from, sauntered in. Medium height, she wore the same pink shirt as Cyn's over a pair of black chinos. The girl gave Cyn a hug and then her eyes flicked to Phoebe.

"Karli, this is Phoebe," Cyn said, running over to her mirrored closet to apply a layer of lip gloss.

Phoebe said, "Hi," smiled and waited for Karli to respond in kind, but she didn't. Instead her eyes roamed, taking in the space around Phoebe as though assessing her very existence. Phoebe smoothed her comforter self-consciously under Karli's appraising stare. She knew that her and Cyn's sides couldn't be more different. Cyn's walls hung with shiny, metal framed pictures of her and her friends—that's why Phoebe recognized Karli—and her bed was set with a nest of colorful pillows. Only three things hung on Phoebe's wall: autographed posters of her two favorite bands, Vampire Weekend and Adele, and a landscape print by Robert Doisneau.

Karli's eyes lingered at Phoebe's desk for longer than necessary, and Phoebe made a face trying to figure out what among her possessions—dictionaries, notebooks, and cameras—could possibly hold Karli's attention like that.

"So what do you think of our shirts, Phoebe?" Cyn said, stepping away from her mirror and breaking the silence she seemed oblivious to.

"What does CC mean?" Phoebe asked.

"Karli got permission to start a new club," she said excitedly. "And the CC stands for—"

"Colten's Cuties!" both girls said at the same time before breaking into a fit of giggles.

Phoebe covered a reflexive snort with a cough and quickly said, "So it's a fan club?"

"Sort of, since we meet to discuss all things Colten Chase," Cyn said.

"But not just trivia," Karli said, having caught Phoebe's unimpressed expression. "Important things, too. For example, he's big on environmental issues and tonight we're brainstorming ways our group can raise money and awareness for his causes."

"Want to come?" Cyn asked.

"I'm sure Phoebe has better things to do with her time than be silly with us," Karli said, an unwelcome tenor plain in her voice.

Phoebe waved them away. "I have a steamy date with the library," she lied as coolly as she could.

"Oh—could you do me a favor while you're there?" Cyn said.

Phoebe bit back a groan. It looked like she had no choice now but to actually go to the library. She'd been hoping to sneak in a quick photo shoot. "What's the favor?"

"The *Gazette's* past issues are in the basement of the library and I need an old article for some research," Cyn said. "It would be great if you could photocopy it for me."

Phoebe wanted to say that she couldn't believe it wasn't all online yet, but instead said, "Sure," hoping it would get her out the door faster.

"Thanks!" Cyn wrote something quickly on a Post-it note and handed it to Phoebe on her way out.

The moment the door shut behind Cyn and Karli, Phoebe reached for her cell, fell back, and stretched herself across her twin bed. She closed her eyes for a moment, but opened them again when she caught Karli's voice say bitterly, "—didn't tell me your roommate was the girl Colten walked to the dorm."

"She was?" Cyn said, clearly surprised. "I wasn't here . . ."

Phoebe sat upright with a start. She glanced over at her desk, suddenly realizing what Karli had been fixated on. Colten's jacket hung on the back of her swivel chair. Phoebe crossed to her desk, reached for the jacket, brought it to her face, and inhaled. The scent she remembered still clung to it. Phoebe sat down and began to twirl in her chair, smiling at the thought that had just popped into her head: the jacket gave her a reason to find Colten Chase. But that would have to wait. Right now, she had to deliver on her favor to Cyn. Phoebe sent Hayley a text message asking her to meet her at the Above library. Seconds later, her phone buzzed with Hayley's response: "Sure."

Phoebe was curled up in an armchair in a far back corner of the library, her nose behind a book, when Hayley arrived dressed in a tracksuit. Her hair was tucked into a baseball cap that had "Jay-Z" written across it.

"Sorry I'm late, I—are you reading a dictionary?" Hayley said.

Phoebe flashed a shameless smile, closed the book and stretched out her legs. "I love words," she said simply. It was true. A love she'd shared with her father, Phoebe had often accompanied him on excursions to rare book stores in search of antique dictionaries.

"You're in touch with your inner dork; I like that," Hayley said, smiling. She dropped her tiny frame into a leather chair next to Phoebe, her expression becoming serious. "Listen, I'm sorry I didn't come to see you earlier, but I can't stand hospitals and clinics." Hayley paused, looking embarrassed, then began removing several books and papers from her backpack. "I know it's silly, but they make me really uncomfortable."

"Don't worry about it," Phoebe said. "Really, it's ok," she added, noticing the deep flush creeping up Hayley's face.

"I smuggled this in for you," Hayley said, casting a careful eye around them before handing Phoebe the plastic container she'd just pulled from the bottom of her bag.

"What is it?"

"Cookies," Hayley said, smiling sheepishly. "I've been worried about you, and when I worry, I bake. Hope you like peanut butter."

Phoebe was at a loss for words for a moment, then said, "Wow . . . this is . . . thanks." She opened the container, grabbed a cookie and sank her teeth into it, savoring its buttery goodness. Then, without warning, and without knowing what triggered them, tears began to roll down her cheeks and drop off her chin.

Hayley stared at Phoebe with alarm. "Christ, you hate them. I—"

"No, no," Phoebe broke in, almost laughing at Hayley's pained expression. Wiping at her streaming eyes, she said, "The cookie's great. I'm just a mess right now, sorry."

It wasn't until that moment that Phoebe realized she hadn't allowed herself enough of an emotional response to everything that had happened the night before; she was embarrassed to have Hayley witness it.

The shock faded slowly from Hayley's face. She tilted forward and placed a hand on Phoebe's knee. "Are you kidding me right now?" she said, trying to smile. "After what you've been through, what are you apologizing for?"

Phoebe puffed out her cheeks and widened her eyes, trying to keep a rein on her volatile emotions; the last thing she wanted was to *push* her weird cocktail of frustration and sadness into Hayley. One girl crying in the library garnered a few looks, but two sobbing helplessly would be a scene.

"Want to talk about it?" Hayley asked. "I'm good for just listening if that's what you need."

Phoebe wanted to tell somebody what was going on more than anything, but the Blackcoats had asked for discretion. Nevertheless, after years of never being able to talk about her ability, the idea of having to carry the burden of yet another secret was proving to be too much. If her father were around, she could draw strength from him. But he wasn't. Phoebe's instincts told her that confiding in Hayley was worth the risk. Right now, though, she felt too drained to even think about it, much less talk about it.

"Another time, okay?" Phoebe said, wiping at the last of her tears with the back of her hand.

"Yeah, for sure. . . . You know what you need?" Hayley said, more to herself than to Phoebe, "A Spa Sunday."

"Ice cream?" Phoebe said, confused.

Hayley laughed. "I mean the day of the week." She scooted forward in her chair. "I'm talking nails, hydrating masks, the whole lot. It's something my mom and I used to do every Sunday night to take a break from the four males we live with. I figured I'd keep it going here. But if you're not up for it," Hayley added quickly, "that's plenty okay too." She looked a little nervous to have so blatantly outed her girly side.

Phoebe waved a hand as if swatting at Hayley's words. "Sounds great. Count me in," she said, giving Hayley a grateful smile.

Hayley smiled, then checked her watch and groaned, "I'm going to be late for physical fitness," she said. "Having night classes Below sucks." In Hayley's mad scramble to grab her things, a few of her books slipped from the table to the floor. Phoebe stretched out a hand to help and that's when she saw the magazine. Lying next to Hayley's dropped calculus book was the latest issue of *Dish* with a caption on the cover that read: "Are Colten Chase and Tanya Brown getting serious?"

Phoebe picked it up. The cover showed Colten kissing an olive-skinned, brunette girl who embodied the definition of glamour. They looked nauseatingly beautiful together and envy surged through Phoebe with a force that filled her with shame. Hayley snatched the magazine out of her hands, saying, "You weren't supposed to see that."

"Why not?" Phoebe demanded. Her tone came out harsher than she'd intended and softening it, she added, "It's none of my business who Colten Chase kisses."

Hayley paused, narrowing her eyes. "C'mon, let's be honest. You like the guy."

"The entire female population on this campus likes the guy."

"True. But you're the only one I've seen him pay any real attention to. Anyway," she said, rolling up the magazine and waving it lazily. "It's the *Dish*. They're always printing garbage."

"Then why do you read it?"

"'Cause I'm not above entertaining garbage." Hayley grabbed her backpack and on her way out called over her shoulder, "Don't you dare brood over that cover!"

Phoebe watched Hayley go, thinking that she didn't have anything to brood over, whether that cover was fake or not. Colten was free to kiss whomever he wanted, even if it drove her to inexplicable distraction. She leaned back against her chair and shoved her hands into her sweatshirt pockets. It was only then, when she felt the sticky end of Cyn's Post-it note on her fingers, that she remembered the favor she'd promised. Happy for something else to focus on, Phoebe made her way to the basement.

The cold room was dimly lit and smelled of old forgotten manuscripts, must, and pulp. Phoebe moved between the rows of lofty metallic shelves, her fingers sliding across the folder spines. Near the end of a long aisle, she located the section dedicated to the *Gazette* and scanned faded labels for the year Cyn had requested.

Phoebe was up on her toes pulling down a thick, dusty folder when the hairs along the back of her neck rose, giving her the uneasy sense of being watched. It was only paranoia after the attack that had her in this jumpy state, she told herself. But then she heard footsteps, and from the corner of her eye, caught a fast movement between the stacks. A spasm of fear seized Phoebe, and with the folder held against her chest, she edged further down the aisle, her steps hastening into a light sprint.

"Hayley?" she called out, wondering if her friend had forgotten something and come down to look for her. But she promptly discarded that theory, remembering she hadn't told Hayley about her errand. Phoebe quickly maneuvered her way through the stacks. Her eyes darted from side to side and she listened for footsteps. In the same second the glow of an exit sign came into view, she felt a hand touch the back of her shoulder. Phoebe whirled around, swinging her arms with such a force that she slammed the folder into a shadowy figure before dropping it to run.

"Wow. I wasn't expecting you to be that strong," a familiar voice said, stopping Phoebe in mid retreat. She slowly turned around to find an astonished-looking Colten lying flat on his back, his baseball cap at his side. Her immediate impulse to go to him was halted by the horrified realization of what had just happened; for a moment, she froze. Then she snapped out of it, mortified.

"Oh my God," Phoebe said, running back to Colten. She could feel her face burn with color and was grateful to the dimness for providing some cover. "I am so sorry!"

Colten lifted himself onto his elbows and reached for his baseball cap. "Remind me to hire you as a bodyguard the next time I need one," he said, his mouth curving into a grin.

"I thought—I thought—" Phoebe's voice broke off. Truth be told, she didn't know what she thought. Right now she loved the way Colten's eyes crinkled when he smiled. She extended a hand for Colten to grip and helped him to his feet. They stood facing each other, his large hands warm on hers. Phoebe didn't pull away, finding the touch of Colten's fingers comforting. She almost didn't feel him running them over the puckered skin of her bite marks or notice the dark expression creeping over his face as he did so.

Phoebe felt her breathing stop and withdrew her hand. "What are you doing down here?" she said, hoping to distract him from asking any questions about the strange marks. She wondered if her scar had triggered a bad memory for him.

Colten's lips twisted into a wry grimace. "I study down here."

Phoebe looked at him, eyebrows half cocked. "Really?"

"Yeah. I've been avoiding some junior high girls who seem to find all the places I go to study," he said. "When I heard footsteps in the stacks, I thought they'd found me here. I got up to check it out and saw it was you."

Phoebe looked around. "Where is there to study down here?"

"Come on, I'll show you."

Colten bent down to retrieve the *Gazette* folder and handed it to Phoebe. "Your weapon of choice, Madam," he smirked.

Phoebe rolled her eyes and followed him to a corner of the basement where a single study carrel stood against the wall. She momentarily thought it odd that a carrel would stand on its own, but then she saw the faint carving of a moon on its side and understood. This was the library narthyx point. Phoebe let her eyes wander, her expression preoccupied.

"Is something wrong?" Colten asked, studying her curiously.

Phoebe blinked at him. "Huh?—No." She realized suddenly that she'd expected to see a custodian nearby and then remembered the first day announcement that the library narthyx point was closed for maintenance. "I'm studying upstairs," she blurted, filling the awkward pause. "If you don't want to study alone—not that there's anything wrong with that—I study alone all the time, but—"

"Is this an invite to join you?" Colten seemed to be fighting a smile.

Phoebe nodded without meeting his eyes.

"Well, now that I know you're capable of protecting me from dangerous junior high girls," Colten said chuckling, "I'll have to take you up on that offer."

Phoebe snuck a look at him as he collected his things. He was dressed in faded blue jeans and a gray crew neck sweater unzipped to reveal a white t-shirt that hugged his torso. She caught herself musing how much better he looked in non-uniform clothes.

Phoebe became aware of Colten staring at her. She looked up. His face was a mask of amusement. "You really weren't kidding about being a space nerd, huh?" he said.

"Huh?"

Colten's eyes flashed down to Phoebe's sweatshirt.

That's when she realized that she was wearing her, "Space Camp Junior Cadet" hoodie. "Oh," she laughed lightly. "It was a joke gift from my grandfather."

"So you're not a space warrior in training?" Colten shook his head in mock disappointment.

Phoebe tugged on the oversized garment and laughed. She could only imagine how beat up she must look, but she could do nothing about it now.

"Shall we?" Colten asked. Phoebe nodded. Together they stepped out of the stacks and headed up the stairs to the main floor. Acutely aware of the curious eyes that marked their movement as soon as they emerged from the stairwell, Phoebe tried her best to act comfortable around Colten. She gave him a quick sideways glance and stopped dead in her tracks.

"Oh my God, your face!" she said. In the light of the main floor, she could now see a deep bruise running along Colten's jaw line. She raised a hand, without thinking, to touch his face, but Colten moved his head out of her reach.

He rubbed his jaw dismissively. "It's from a fight—"

"What?" she asked, incredulously.

"I took a swift kick to the jaw when working with my stunt trainer," Colten explained. "Occupational hazard when you do your own action stunts."

Phoebe's sigh of relief came out a bit louder than she meant, and Colten, looking her over, considered her a moment, and then tipped his head back and laughed.

"You thought you did this to me?" Colten could barely contain his amusement. "You're strong but not that strong."

Phoebe let him enjoy his laugh. *If he only knew,* she thought. Just then, the lights began to flash, signaling library closing time.

"So much for studying together," Colten said. Phoebe thought she'd detected something like disappointment in his tone, but she wasn't sure. It seemed more likely that she was projecting her own feelings.

Phoebe gathered up her things and Colten waited for her. When they opened the library door, a gust of damp cold air met them outside. A layer of dense steel-colored clouds seemed to stretch endlessly across the dark sky, and only a faint glimmer of starlight managed to filter through. Phoebe and Colten stood a few feet from the bench where they'd first met, Colten the very picture of calm, and Phoebe's nerves raging a war against her stomach that thankfully only she could hear.

"I'd offer to walk you to your dorm," Colten said, "but there are only so many times a guy can handle a beautiful girl running away from him before he starts to acquire a complex."

Phoebe was speechless for a moment. She felt a liquid warmth spreading inside, hearing Colten call her beautiful; she could almost forgive him for bringing up her abrupt exits.

"How 'bout I drive you instead?" he said to her surprise, and then added with a grin, "It's a more contained situation."

Phoebe felt her breath come more quickly. Her mind raced with the excitement of being alone with Colten in his car.

There was a pause in which Colten smiled at Phoebe's inability to speak. "I swear my car is clean," he said. "No dirty smelly gym socks on the floor."

Phoebe smiled, opened her mouth to accept the ride, and then snapped it shut without uttering a word. Colten's comment about his gym socks had jostled something in her mind: she was dirty. Sure, her clothes had been laundered but she hadn't showered since before the game. She could almost feel a filmy layer of dirt, oil, and sweat suffocating her pores. Why she hadn't thought to take a shower when she'd returned to the dorm was beyond her. *Stupid, stupid, stupid,* Phoebe thought.

"Thanks . . ." Phoebe began slowly, her voice a bit higher than usual. "But I'm okay to walk." The idea of her body odor seeping into Colten's car, his private space, was too embarrassing a thought to entertain.

"You sure?"

"Yeah. The cold air will wake me up for a long night of homework." She couldn't quite mask the sound of vague disappointment in her own voice.

After staring at her for a moment, openly confused, Colten tipped the bill of his baseball cap forward with a flourish and said, "As you wish."

Phoebe waved goodbye. She hadn't even gone two feet when the sky split open and raindrops the size of pebbles began to patter down on her head. She turned to look at Colten, who tilted his head skyward and laughed as though sharing an inside joke with the weather.

Grinning widely, Colten said, "The offer to drive you still stands."

The rain began to fall more heavily, and Colten, as if fearing they both stood a good chance of drowning if he waited any longer for Phoebe's response, grabbed her hand and towed her after him. Phoebe looked down at her cold wet hand in his. The touch of his warmer skin shot a charge through every nerve in her body. Her senses were in overdrive. Phoebe felt like she could drown in giddiness. She'd been in desperate need of a shower and mother nature—bless her—had promptly delivered.

The run to the brightly lit parking lot drenched them both, and Phoebe's hair clung to the sides of her face.

"This is your car?" she said, blinking her eyes in the rain.

Smiling, Colten walked around the hood of the car to the passenger's side and opened the door for Phoebe. "Not what you were expecting?" he said.

"No," she admitted. Colten's car was a shiny black Smart Car with silver trim. Phoebe folded herself in and relaxed against the bucket seat, acclimating to the foreign smallness of the car's interior.

Colten climbed in behind the wheel and started the engine before Phoebe even had her seat belt on. "Were you expecting something a bit more movie star?" The Smart Car curved out of the parking lot and headed down the main campus road in the direction of the dorms, headlights illuminating the flurrying rain.

I was expecting something a bit bigger, Phoebe thought, but she wasn't going to tell him that. "Actually," she said, having a sudden brilliant thought. "When you think about it, your choice of a Smart Car is very movie star-like."

"How do you figure?"

"You celebs are known to show your allegiance to causes, and since you're all about the environment, it makes sense that you'd want to be seen in a vehicle that is considered green."

Colten gave Phoebe a sideways glance. "You've been doing a background check on me." It wasn't a question.

Phoebe opened her mouth to say, "No, I didn't Google you. I got that piece of trivia from this girl, Karli," but thought better of it. "Sort of," she said vaguely. Phoebe watched a grin stretch across Colten's lips.

"As long as it's just the good stuff," he said.

"It is, if you count the new cover of *Dish* as good stuff." Phoebe had spoken without thinking, and immediately felt a pang of regret. She didn't want him to think she was a jealous-type or caught up in the media hype—especially since she normally didn't even read that stuff. And especially since they had only spoken a handful of times. But if she were being honest, part of her was curious what Colten had to say about it. And when he said nothing, Phoebe, feeling awkward, gazed pointedly out of her window, watching the campus buildings slip by. As they rode in silence, Phoebe could feel Colten's deep breathing. She didn't need to tap into his emotions to know that she'd upset him. She could sense it in the tension in his body. She grabbed one of Hayley's cookies from her backpack and began to chew it slowly— uneasy situations called for emergency baked goods. Not wanting to appear rude, Phoebe offered Colton a cookie, which he declined. The silence continued.

"Did the picture bother you?" Colten said at last, his voice half an octave lower than normal. They were parked behind her dorm, and he'd turned off the car. Nothing but the sound of rain hammering on the rooftop filled the silence between his question and her answer.

"Would it matter if it had?" Phoebe said evasively, trying to inject a note of playfulness into her voice, and instead leaking her anticipation.

"Yes, it would," Colten said, drumming his fingers on the steering wheel, "because I'd hate for you to believe everything you see in the magazines and read online about me."

"Fair enough," Phoebe said softly. She decided to drop the subject.

"Tanya is my co-star in the new movie," Colten continued, speaking through tight lips. "And that photo is a still shot from one of our love scenes. It was leaked to the press by the studio."

"The studio? Why would they do that?"

"Marketing. It's good for the movie if folks think the co-stars are together. The execs want people talking about it and writing about it, especially when there's a premiere around the corner. . . ."

"You must have tough skin to put up with all that," Phoebe said, her voice barely audible.

Colten shrugged. "I see it as part of the job description. Wanted," he said, affecting a supervisory voice, "someone who can fax, answer phones, and sometimes date a co-worker when needed to boost company profits."

Phoebe laughed lightly, relieved that the somber mood appeared to have broken. Colten's ability to mock his lifestyle impressed her. Capitalizing on his joke's effect, Colten then proceeded to entertain Phoebe with his top ten list of outlandish rumors about himself as the rain stopped.

"I think my all-time favorite," he said getting to the top of his list, "was the one that claimed I was secretly dating a mother and daughter pair and that they were both pregnant with my babies."

Before Phoebe could properly react to that, Colten had jumped out of the car and was at her door, opening it for her. "I'm sorry," he said, peering down at her. "I've kept you out past curfew."

Phoebe glanced at the dorm and saw that Colten was right: most of the bedroom lights were out. As Phoebe went to step out of the car, a wave of disorientation suddenly spread through her and she half-stumbled out. Instantly, Colten caught hold of her. As he steadied her balance with a firm grip of her shoulders, he bent his head to hers, touching her forehead lightly with his chin.

"Thanks," Phoebe said. Her preoccupation with her strange dizziness distracted her from the fact that she and Colten stood a breath's space apart.

Colten stepped back from Phoebe, his eyes appraising. "Are you okay?"

"I'm fine," Phoebe answered immediately.

He gave her a skeptical look. "I think I should walk you to the door."

Phoebe, nodding her head, took a determined step forward and tripped just as she was saying, "If you don't mind."

"Let me help." Colten took Phoebe's arm.

"Okay," she muttered sheepishly.

Feet still wobbly, Phoebe found herself relying on Colten's support as they walked toward the dorm; she loathed the fact that he was distinctly amused.

"Just so we're clear," she said with some vigor. "This is not a damsel in distress moment."

"Of course not," he said, then unexpectedly added, "have lunch with me—"

"Yes!" Phoebe said with an involuntary note of eagerness that surprised her. She bit her lip and added, casually, "When? Tomorrow?"

Colten chuckled. "I wish. I have to be in New York over the weekend. Monday?"

Phoebe nodded.

"Great. It's a date," he said, breaking into a smile. "Have a great weekend."

"You too." Phoebe's voice came out in a whisper.

Colten waited at the bottom of the steps until Phoebe opened the door and slipped inside. Through the door's fanlight, she watched his car disappear into the slick darkness and slowly became aware of one fact; her attraction to Colten Chase had just become a major, major distraction. *It's a date*, she repeated to herself. An overwhelming sense of giddiness kept Phoebe up all night.

❦ Eight

"Aren't they the cutest rugrats you've ever seen?" Hayley gushed as Phoebe stared at a large bulletin board that had been completely papered with photos of three young boys making ridiculous faces.

"Yeah," Phoebe said. "I'd forgive them if they put gum in my hair."

Hayley giggled in response, her dimples deepening.

"Hold on." Phoebe took a closer look at the pictures. "Are they triplets?"

"Yup."

"Wow. How old are they?"

"Seven." Hayley moved to stand next to Phoebe. She rolled down the sleeves of her blue tunic shirt. "They made that collage for me so I wouldn't miss them too much, but it only makes me miss them more. That's Harper, Henry, and Harvey," she said, pointing to each cherubic face in turn.

When Phoebe whirled to give Hayley a disbelieving look, her petite friend said, "Oh, I'm dead serious. My folks are Harold and Helen"—she indicated a framed picture on her desk—"so you can guess why they thought giving us all H names would be cute."

"What are your middle names?"

"We don't have any. Mom says it keeps the monogramming simple," Hayley added with a laugh.

Phoebe found that Hayley's family pictures were beginning to make her unhappy. She felt a wave of all too familiar longing. Phoebe gave the boys one last look, then slid her gaze to the wall above Hayley's desk, which was decorated with magazine cut-outs, posters, framed t-shirts, and drawings of hip-hop stars. She stared at the faces. Only a few looked familiar to her.

"My roommate Maya thinks my shrine is over the top," Hayley said, admiring her wall with a wide grin. "But that's only part of it. You should see the one I have at home." Phoebe cocked her head to one side, trying to picture it. "What do you listen to?"

"Mostly indie acts," Phoebe said, naming a few while helping Hayley clean up the ingredients they'd used in making their avocado face masks: honey, molasses, orange juice. All things Phoebe would never have thought to put on her face.

"How long do we have to let the mask dry again?" she asked, tossing avocado peels into a trash bin.

"Half an hour," Hayley said, drawing her light-brown hair up into a bun. Phoebe wiggled her nose uncomfortably. "Trust me, this mask is good for the soul. We can do our nails while we wait."

Hayley reached under her bed and pulled out a large, silver storage case with PROPERTY OF MISS TEEN SPENCER COUNTY stenciled in pink on its sides.

"You're a pageant girl?" Wide-eyed, Phoebe sank onto one of Hayley's two large beanbag chairs.

Hayley gave a slow dimpled grin. "Former pageant girl," she said, hauling the case toward Phoebe and settling herself onto the beanbag next to her. "For some reason my mom got exponentially more girly with the birth of my kid brothers. Pageants were one of her many let's-be-girly-together ideas."

Hayley flipped open the case and pulled out its four interior shelves. For a moment Phoebe stared with her mouth open; she'd never seen such a vast collection of nail polish before. "How many pageants were you in?"

Hayley shook a scarlet red nail polish bottle before setting it down on its shelf and choosing another one. "Too many, but—" As she began, the door slammed open and both girls jumped as though scalded. Blue drops of polish splashed onto Hayley's foot.

"What the hell!" she yelled.

A pretty, dark-haired girl with a pixie cut entered. She had a dusting of freckles across the bridge of her nose.

"You scared the crap out of us, Maya," Hayley said, reaching into her case for a bottle of nail polish remover. "What's the emergency?"

Maya gave a sheepish smile. "Sorry. I keep forgetting our door has no weight to it—Hey," she said, looking at Phoebe. "You're in my French class, right?"

"Yes," Phoebe said, smiling back.

"If you're ever looking for a study partner let me know," she offered before saying to Hayley, "I followed your recipe but I can't tell if my dough is rising properly. Could you double check for me?"

"Did your yeast bubble before you mixed it in?" Hayley said.

Maya scrunched her nose. "Yeast?"

Hayley stared at Maya with frank eyes. "That's not good," she said, standing.

While Hayley followed Maya out, Phoebe crossed to the window and unlocked its latch to let a crisp breeze brush against her cheek. She could taste the threat of rain lurking in the air. Phoebe liked Hayley's dorm. Unlike the renovated farmhouse she lived in, Hayley's residence was a modern glass and brick building. Her third floor room overlooked a garden of low, flowering shrubs that ringed a giant oak tree with thick branches, like longing arms, that reached to touch her windowpane. Phoebe was still standing by the window, staring at the creamy moon that tinted the blackness outside, when Hayley returned saying, "It wasn't a complete disaster."

Phoebe turned. "What happened?"

"She thought the yeast was optional," Hayley explained. "So instead of fluffy bread rolls, she now has bread sticks."

After they'd settled back onto their beanbags and selected their nail polishes, Phoebe asked, "So what was your talent?"

Hayley laughed. "You're still on this pageant thing?"

"You're the only Beauty-Queen-soon-to-be-spy I know."

"Queen's a big stretch," Hayley said, resting her chin on her knees while painting her toes a bright blue. "I started with ballet—my mom's idea—but got bored with it and switched to hip-hop."

Phoebe was impressed. "Wow. I wish I were coordinated enough to dance."

"Not dance. Freestyle."

"What? Really?" Phoebe said, a look of disbelief on her face.

Hayley laughed. "Yeah. I'm a tiny little white girl so folks weren't ever expecting me to drop rhymes. I won five pageants with that act. Even gave myself a moniker: Lil' Blueprint." At Phoebe's questioning look, Hayley explained. "Lil' for obvious reasons and Blueprint after my favorite Jay-Z album."

"So . . . you still got it?" Phoebe wiggled her eyebrows, expectantly.

Hayley's face lit up. "Do I still got it? Hell yeah!"

Phoebe began chanting like an obsessed fan. "Lil' Blueprint! Lil' Blueprint!"

"Hell yeah!" Hayley said, jumping to her feet. "This is Lil' Blueprint representin' all the short ladies out there," she began.

"I'm four feet eleven always gotta hem up my jeans / But I'm big fun like Mardi Gras in New Orleans / I like my gangstas polished like young DeNiro an' Pacino / I can reach the top shelf liquor, thanks for askin' me tho' / You see height ain't power, and should you forget / Like grain pound into flour, might be the worst beatin' you get / I got moves to remove haters, yeah I'm that pistol quick / Have you believin' King Kong slayed ya an' not some ninety pound chick."

And then Hayley did a few pirouettes coupled with elegant leaps before she collapsed laughing onto her beanbag.

Phoebe could only stare; her mask had hardened and she couldn't move her face muscles. "In case you can't tell," she said, bringing her hands to her cheeks. "This is me giving you a look of awe right now."

Hayley laughed until she could barely catch her breath. After rinsing off their masks a little later, Hayley said to Phoebe, expectantly, "Well?"

"Well what?"

"Was I right about that mask being good for your soul?"

Phoebe slumped back down to the floor. The dark mood she'd been fighting all night had managed to crush the joy of Hayley's company. Phoebe looked around; she did not want Hayley to see a change in her eyes. "My soul's feeling good," she said so cheerfully her voice broke.

"It didn't work, did it?" Hayley said at once.

Quickly, Phoebe brought a hand to her cheeks. "It did. My skin feels great."

"I'm talking about Spa Sunday. It's not taking your mind off things, is it?" she said, her eyes straying to Phoebe's slightly exposed bite marks.

Phoebe, already feeling terrible, felt even worse as she took in Hayley's disappointed face. "This was—is great. . . ." Phoebe was spared the trouble of attempting a smile by Hayley waving a hand in front of her face to dismiss Phoebe's apologetic demeanor; then she deposited herself cross-legged in front of her and said, "Can I see it?"

Phoebe nodded and pulled up her sleeve.

Hayley whistled in her breath. There was a long silence in which she just stared. "Does it still hurt?" When Phoebe shook her head, Hayley allowed her fingers to gently trail over the puckered skin and said, "I still can't believe they found the campus."

Unable to contain herself, Phoebe blurted, "They think they came for me and these three other cadets." Hayley paled and Phoebe gasped at her own unbidden disclosure. "You can't tell anyone this. Anyone," Phoebe stressed. Now that it was out, she wanted, needed to talk about it.

While a speechless Hayley nodded vigorously, Phoebe grabbed her backpack. She felt inside for her Privaque and pulled it out.

"What's that?" Hayley asked, watching as Phoebe attached the silver clip to her shirt.

Phoebe exhaled, then said, "It's a Privaque."

"A what?"

Back on her beanbag, Phoebe took a deep breath, then explained all about the Privaque and the Blackcoat meeting she'd had the morning after the attack.

"Christ," said Hayley, rigid, blinking rapidly in shock after Phoebe finished. She drew her knees to her chest and rocked herself back and forth for a moment. "And they couldn't say which one of you it's about?"

Phoebe shook her head.

Hayley stared at her hip-hop shrine, thinking. And by the expression working its way across her face, Phoebe could tell that Hayley knew something.

"Well, it turns out that my dad isn't crazy after all," Hayley said finally. Those were not the words Phoebe expected.

"Huh?"

"My dad," Hayley said, inching her beanbag closer, "is what most folks call a conspiracy nut. For years he's been saying that there are secrets— prophecies—that the Royal Court doesn't want us to know about. He thinks they've been skillfully covered up by the higher-ups by referring to them as stories and myths until everyone basically feels silly even talking about them in a serious tone of voice.

"He recently started reading some new blog that talks about that sort of stuff, and it's been driving my mom nuts how obsessed he is with it. But I actually think I've heard him go off about the Year of Four before. . . ."

Phoebe looked at Hayley nervously. "You can't tell him about this. Please." For a moment, she felt a jolt of panic, and began to reconsider her decision to trust Hayley so quickly.

"Of course not," Hayley said automatically. "The last thing I need is for him to feel vindicated and talk my ear off. Wow, Blackcoats on campus . . ." her voice trailed off as she considered the weight of that. "Are they super rigid and intense?"

Phoebe nodded vigorously, thinking of Afua.

"Do you know why they're called Blackcoats, by the way?"

"No," Phoebe said, realizing for the first time that she hadn't even considered it.

"My dad says it's because way back in the day, when they killed a Vigo, they presented the Royal Court with its black coat. Crazy huh?"

"Completely." Phoebe stretched her legs out and found herself staring at the textured ceiling as they eased into a long silence. The quiet suited her fine; she was finally content in the relief of having confided in Hayley. The din of dorm activity out in the halls provided a lulling soundtrack.

"By the way," Hayley said, after a few minutes. "Don't think for one second you're getting away with not telling me about your car ride with Colten."

Phoebe sat up in surprise. "How'd you know?"

"I overheard two girls talking about some redhead they saw getting into his car Friday night. What business do I have becoming a spy if I can't figure that out," Hayley said with a deadly serious drawn face, at which Phoebe gave a loud snort of laughter.

"Tell me everything!" Hayley commanded.

Phoebe stretched her legs out and began her story.

Less than a minute into it, Hayley cut her off, howling with laughter. "You hit—hit him?" she said, gasping for air and tearing up. "Talk about knocking him off his feet!"

"God." Phoebe raked fingers through her hair. "I felt so bad. I still feel bad."

"Yeah, yeah," Hayley said, wiping at a rogue tear. "Go on."

"We had an awkward moment and I blurted that he should study with me."

"Ballsy. I like it."

Phoebe grinned. "When we got upstairs it was closing time. He waited for me to get my stuff and then offered to drive me home." Phoebe fiddled with her fingers before confessing sheepishly, "I sort of turned him down—at first."

Out of nowhere, a wet face cloth hit Phoebe in the chin and she blinked, shocked. There was a moment of confusion until Phoebe's eyes fell on Hayley's outstretched hands.

Phoebe said, disbelief coloring her tone, "Did you just—?"

"Yes." Hayley's smile was wicked, unrepentant. "I did that on behalf of every girl who would die for a ride from Colten Chase! Oooh," she said, waggling a finger at Phoebe and starting to get worked up. "It was that stupid *Dish* cover, wasn't it?"

"No!" Phoebe said, feeling defensive. "It was 'cause I hadn't showered in two days."

Hayley rolled her eyes. "Doesn't matter if it'd been a week. You get in the car and roll the windows down!" The dramatic craziness in Hayley's voice was clear. Phoebe laughed and continued her story.

"Anyway," she said. "He walked me to the door and asked me to have lunch with him—"

Hayley's high pitch squeal cut Phoebe off. "He asked you out?!" she said, thumping the sides of her beanbag with her fists. "You're officially the luckiest girl on this campus. Scratch that. The world!"

NINE

When Monday morning arrived with cold winds and even colder rain, Phoebe was more than happy to be Below. She met Mariko, Lewis, and Scott for their first academic boot camp in a classroom that had been arranged with four tables, each set with balloon-filled baskets and several stainless steel bowls that contained what appeared to be dirt.

"Didn't know we were having a party," Scott said, picking up a balloon and flicking it to Lewis who slapped it back.

Both Yelena and Deborah-Anna walked into the class then, and without preamble, Yelena's Russian lilt filled the room. "Please take your seats."

As they sat, Deborah-Anna handed each of them a small bottle filled with pills. "Take one of these before we get started," she said. "And continue to take one daily to help support your burgeoning elemental power."

Phoebe glanced down at the bottle. It was labeled: "Chewable MultiEarthamins."

"I've never heard of these," Mariko said, shrugging out of her Green Lane navy blazer. She twisted off her bottle cap and shook a greenish brown pill into her hand.

Lewis was the first to take one, and Phoebe watched, intrigued, as his face twisted in distaste as he chewed. "It tastes like dirt," he said, brushing a few dreadlocks out of his face.

Phoebe laughed until the taste of the pill in her mouth began to register. Lewis was right. Dirt.

"Once you come into your full elemental powers, your training at the Campus Below will teach you to use them beyond what average Shapers can accomplish," Yelena said, pacing up and down, her hazel eyes fixed unblinkingly on them. "But, like the headmaster said, you haven't had a chance to exercise what little powers you do have. So today we start with the basics of air control."

"With balloons?" Mariko asked.

Ignoring Mariko's skeptical expression, Yelena continued. "If you leave a balloon alone it deflates over time because air permeates through its pores. Today you'll practice using your powers to speed up deflation by drawing the air out."

Yelena grabbed a white balloon from Phoebe's basket, balanced it in her palm, and the group watched as the balloon shriveled into nothing within seconds. Then, just as quickly, it re-inflated again. "Pushing air back in is a lesson for another time. Now, pick up a balloon and begin."

Phoebe raised a tentative hand. "How exactly do we do it?"

"Visualize"—Yelena tapped a finger to her head—"connecting to the air in the balloon. You will feel a tingle in your palms when it is working."

Phoebe picked up a balloon, turning it over in both hands, contemplating it seriously. It had absolutely no effect. Yelena had made it look easy, but it wasn't; all she'd managed to do in ten minutes was give herself a headache from sheer concentration.

Beside Phoebe, Lewis was off to a great start with two balloons already deflated. Mariko leaned toward him, impressed with the ease at which this new skill came to Lewis. The moment Lewis saw Mariko flash him a rare smile, he accidentally burst the balloon in his hand with a loud *pop*, and Mariko immediately resumed her studious expression.

Phoebe peered to her right in time to see Scott pinch the end of his balloon and poke the end of an unraveled paper clip through it. Amazingly, none of the Blackcoats seemed to catch this. Phoebe stared at him, disbelief coloring her face. For a moment their eyes met, and Scott winked and jerked his head toward Phoebe's own full basket, then returned his attention to his now shriveling balloon.

After half an hour of focused concentration with no luck, Phoebe was happy to hear that they were moving on to the next task.

"The three bowls in front of you contain the main soil types: sand, silt, and clay," Deborah-Anna said, moving from her position by the wall. "Before you can begin to manipulate living things like trees or inanimate objects made from earth materials, you have to connect with the basic foundation: soil." As she spoke, she dipped her finger in a bowl of sand. When she lifted it, a thin column of sand suspended in the air, as though magnetically attracted to Deborah-Anna's fingers. "Immerse your hands in each bowl and try to feel the connection."

Phoebe's fingertips had just started tingling in her bowl of sand when next to her Scott pushed his chair back in frustration.

"Is there a problem, Cadet?" Yelena asked, folding her arms.

"This"—Scott gestured at the balloons and the bowls—"is a waste of time. Vigos have put a price on our heads and we're here playing child's games. You should be teaching us to fight. Physically. You're Blackcoats, after all—"

A loud whooshing sound swallowed the rest of Scott's sentence as an explosion of wind filled the room, blasting the balloons from the tables, and smashing the bowls to the floor with a metallic clatter. Scott flew across the room and slammed violently against the back wall, pinned a foot above the ground by a gray mist that encased his entire body. Phoebe drew in a shuddering breath and brushed away the sand that had gotten into her eyes and mouth. She had never seen anyone thrown so fast. Mariko and Lewis sat perfectly still, stunned at the sight of Yelena; silvery vapors hung in the air over her hands, and her expression radiated lethal anger.

"When you cheat by piercing balloons, Cadet, you waste my time," Yelena said, her accent thicker under duress. She moved her hands as if passing an invisible ball between her palms, and Scott's body mimicked the back and forth motion.

"Vigos have superhuman strength and agility that is superior to our own. Harnessing our power over the elements is our only tactical advantage. If you do not learn basic control, you will not be able to fight them!"

"Stand down, Yelena," Deborah-Anna said, finally intervening. "I believe"—Deborah-Anna's eyes turned to Scott—"Cadet Roland has gotten the point." She spoke calmly as though Scott had merely been made to sit in the corner. "Isn't that right, Cadet?"

"Yes, ma'am," Scott said from his misty cocoon, sounding remorseful, if not feeble.

Yelena, whose mood did not seem improved by this, lowered her hands. The silver vapors disappeared and Scott crumpled down to the floor, his eyes still shocked and uniform disheveled. The bell rang just as he got to his feet and began inspecting himself for injuries. After reminding them to take their MultiEarthamins daily, Deborah-Anna dismissed the class with the exception of Scott. Phoebe took one step outside of the classroom and glanced back cautiously. Yelena handed Scott a broom, indicating the sand, clay, and silt that was everywhere.

When Phoebe walked into her Understanding Vigos class, whispers broke out at every table and heads turned. After several cadets had shot her awe-filled glances, Phoebe remembered what Scott had said about her newfound fame. Apparently, the weekend had done nothing to diminish the aura of mystique around the attack. She made for a seat at the rear of the class, and began pulling books out of her bag to avoid catching anyone's eye.

A few moments later, Phoebe felt a hand clap her on the shoulder and a girl say in a perky voice, "I just wanted to let you know I think you rock."

Soon seats were abandoned as people rushed toward Phoebe, reaching out hands. Phoebe didn't know what to say. She felt her cheeks burning from everyone staring at her.

"Unbelievable," a boy said, grabbing her hand between both of his and pumping it hard.

"I can't imagine two Vigos at once."

"You're such a bad ass."

One cadet asked, "Was there a lot of blood—" just as Scott, who had slipped onto the seat next to Phoebe, said with feigned adoration and a cocky tilt of his head, "Can I have your autograph?"

"That's enough!" A woman's voice rang across the room. Phoebe looked over her shoulder. A berobed Montclaire stood in the doorway. She swept the room with such an intense glare that an instant rush of movement erupted as the students hustled back to their seats.

Montclaire raised her voice above the clamor, "Yes, we have a resident hero, and yes, that is quite exciting, but show-and-tell is now over." Hearing the word "hero" bothered Phoebe, but she shoved her discomfort aside and continued watching Montclaire's movements, confused. According to her schedule, a Professor Jones taught this class.

"I am Montclaire. Not Professor Montclaire or Mrs. Montclaire. Just Montclaire. Professor Jones is out for an undetermined amount of time tending to a family matter, and I will be filling in for her," she said, arriving at the front of the room. Montclaire crossed behind the desk and began rummaging through a drawer for something. Scott leaned in toward Phoebe and whispered, "Wasn't I right about your fans? I can still offer my protection services if you want." His eyes glittered with humor.

Phoebe play-slugged Scott's arm. "How are you even here already?" she said under her breath, glancing up at the clock on the wall. "Shouldn't you still be cleaning?"

"I've got some serious broom skills, Pope," Scott said, running a hand over the scars on his neck. Phoebe turned her skeptical look at him, and he explained, "My mom's a wood turner. As a kid I earned extra cash sweeping her workshop. That clean up job back there was nothing compared to her mess. And can you believe," Scott said, knitting his brow in frustration,

"Yelena wasn't impressed with my speed? She took it as cockiness. Now I'm stuck doing campus clean up jobs at her beck and call."

Phoebe looked quickly back to Montclaire who was now searching through shelves in a side closet, then asked in a low voice, "Why'd you provoke her like that?"

"How was I supposed to know she'd go mental?" Scott said, opening a notebook. "I was just trying to make a point."

"So was she."

Scott leaned back in his chair. "Yeah, point taken: Blondie is unstable—"

Montclaire's voice suddenly rose, cutting Scott off. "We're all set now," she said, waving a touch screen remote control in her hand. "In this class, you will study all things Vigo: their physiology, their political hierarchy, and their socialization. All of this is important for the analysis and dissemination of intelligence information," she said crisply. "You need to understand the capabilities and limitations of the enemy in order to plan and act accordingly. So, let's meet the star of our class."

Montclaire pressed a button on the remote and a low buzz sounded from the front of the room; two center floor panels slid back into the wall. A rectangular glass tank rose slowly and smoothly from the large opening. When it had fully emerged, a horrified silence fell.

Phoebe stiffened. Next to her, Scott let out a long, soft whistle. "That's sick and twisted," he said quietly.

It is, thought Phoebe, staring ahead. An enormous Tiger stood on the tank's floor in a mid-stride pose Phoebe was quite sure must be the work of a skilled taxidermist. Its sharp, barbed spikes looked tarnished, yet not any less dangerous. Large empty eyes seemed to take each of them in, all in turn, as if it were determining who to sink its yellowed corkscrew canines into first.

"I think I'm going to be sick," said the girl seated on the other side of Scott, moments before her body went limp. Scott, reacting rapidly, grabbed the girl around the waist, and lay her gently on the ground. Montclaire called for silence over the outbreak of chattering from the class.

"Good show of reflexes, Cadet," she said, smiling her approval at Scott. "Now, if you would, please carry the young lady to the hospital wing."

Scott picked up the ashen-faced girl and pulled one of her arms around his shoulders, but not before leaning into Phoebe and whispering, "If this is too much too soon, fake a faint to get out of it." He wore a rare serious expression.

Phoebe read concern in Scott's eyes. "I'm okay," she mouthed, surprised, her gaze briefly straying to a plaque at the top of the tank that read VIGO MALE. Scott's eyes widened as they fell on the white-knuckled grip Phoebe held on the edge of her seat, which wobbled slightly from her fingers' tension. He gave her a look that seemed to convey, *if you say so*, and carried the girl off.

"You must have strong constitutions if you plan on fighting Vigos one day," Montclaire was saying. Phoebe shook herself to attention, and focused on the gaunt woman who moved in a slow circle around the tank, taking stock of the beast inside. "If this dead Vigo is affecting you"— she tapped the tank with an index finger—"then allow me to sign your dismissal papers and send you off to another career."

At that, Phoebe and her fellow cadets uncoiled their slumped postures, raised their chins and gave Montclaire their rapt attention. The threat in Montclaire's demeanor had been clear; she wasn't bluffing, and the air seethed with nervous tension. No one wanted to be sent home. The shame of it would be too great.

"Now—I understand you had summer reading, so let's see what you've managed to retain." She tapped the remote against her right leg and continued to circle the tank. "What are the four fundamental differences between us and our guest?"

A mousey-looking girl said, "He can't wield elemental power."

"Correct. And?"

"He doesn't change back to his human form when killed."

"That is correct," Montclaire said. "But that fact isn't one of the fundamental differences."

"He only has one functioning heart," a cadet contributed from the back. "The second one is a vestigial organ."

"Correct," Montclaire said. "We will discuss this fact further when we get to physiology. What else?"

"He had a limitless lifespan," said another cadet.

"Correct," Montclaire said. She pushed another button on her remote, sending a red pointer beam at the tank. "In this one's case," she said. "A diamond-tipped arrow shot cleanly through here"—the beam hovered over where his heart should be—"brought him to his end."

Everyone stared in awed silence. Diamonds were the only substance hard enough to kill a Vigo. Weapons fashioned from this precious stone killed by piercing a Vigo's solid heart or slicing through neck muscle and titanium bone for a clean decapitation. Phoebe had never seen any such weapons until she'd laid eyes on the daggers hanging on the wall in the Headmaster's office. Now she began to wonder what the arrows looked like, or how they'd feel in her hand.

"We're down to the last and most fundamental difference," Montclaire said, rounding Phoebe's desk. "What is it, Cadet Pope?"

Phoebe's body went rigid and she thought quickly. "We're born, not made."

"And how are they made?" asked Montclaire, who hadn't moved, clearly intending for Phoebe to answer the question.

Phoebe tensed up even more. Montclaire's words from their first encounter challenged her. *I hope for your sake you are a better student than you are a liar.*

"When a Vigo feeds on human energy, the venom contained in the bite can initiate a musculoskeletal change," Phoebe said. "Not all victims turn—a natural selection process keeps the Vigo population in check. But some do." Phoebe knew that last part was right out of the text book; reciting things verbatim was something she did when nervous.

Montclaire cocked her head as if considering the answer, then stepped back from Phoebe's desk and addressed the class. "Technically, Cadet Pope's answer is correct, but it's missing a bit of detail. What is the human energy she's referring to? Someone please show me that your education Above counts for something."

"Mitochondria," a pig-tailed girl sitting up front answered. "They're the organelles that provide cellular energy in humans. Vigos use it to power their morphing and heal their wounds. They call it mito for short."

"Precisely the kind of answer I was looking for," Montclaire said approvingly. "Mito has an exothermic reaction with Vigo blood, releasing heat that we're especially sensitive to. That is why the presence of a Vigo is heralded by the fiery burn of our skin."

Phoebe shuddered as if the words "fiery burn" had singed her entire skin all over again.

A boy with a gelled mohawk spoke. "Can we feel this burn from a Vigo in its human form?"

"Good question. Can we?" Montclaire turned the question over to the class. When no one answered she responded, "Mito is considered dormant when a Vigo is in its human form. But, because it is present in the bloodstream, we still feel a bit of a burn when they're nearby. It's just not as searing hot the way it is when an exothermic reaction powers morphing."

And with that, the bell rang for the end of the class. It couldn't have been a more welcome sound to Phoebe who was looking forward to her lunch date with Colten. Grabbing her backpack, Phoebe darted out of her seat toward the door, but a footstep shy of the threshold, Montclaire's ringing voice called out.

"A moment please, Cadet Pope."

Phoebe turned. By the time the last student had left the room, Montclaire had walked over to Phoebe, pausing just a foot away from her. The instructor wore a searching expression. When she spoke, her breath smelled of mint and coffee.

"I know I'm not the first to say this, but what you did, staying with Cadet Banks, was brave," she said coolly. "You definitely have the makings of a fine agent."

Phoebe was a bit staggered by Montclaire's statement, particularly after Montclaire had judged her so harshly at their first meeting. She nevertheless forced herself to look directly at her instructor and tried to keep her expression inscrutable. "Thank you, ma'am," she said softly.

"I was wondering," Montclaire said, her gaze suddenly intense, "if you would tell me what they've told you about the motivation behind the attack? Was it random or were you targeted?"

Phoebe startled at the question. "They?"

"Yes, they," Montclaire replied, her eyes glinting with a kind of dark amusement. She folded her arms over her chest, and waited.

Phoebe shifted about, then spoke slowly as though choosing each word carefully. "I think it's probably better for Professor Yori to answer your question," she said, looking over at the Vigo—anywhere but at Montclaire. "It's not my place to talk about it. Ma'am."

Montclaire's eyebrows crept up at this. "I see," she said, smiling coldly. As they stared at each other, a growing silence between them, Phoebe felt her stomach drop uneasily. In a way, she felt like a hypocrite because she'd told Hayley everything. But somehow that felt different: Hayley was a friend and she needed the support of a friend. Montclaire, on the other hand, was faculty, and if Professor Yori had wanted her to know anything, she'd be informed.

Montclaire eyed her for a moment longer, then pointed her remote at the tank, initiating the Vigo's descent into the ground. "Since we have nothing more to discuss . . ." Montclaire started as Phoebe took a step back from her, "You should know that they protect the interest of the Royal Court, not yours."

Phoebe paused for a moment as that sank in, and then left as quickly as she could without breaking into a run, her hearts thumping wildly. Phoebe slowed her pace and allowed her mind to go over her exchange with Montclaire. How did she know that there were Blackcoats on campus? How was it even possible when Professor Yori had said none of the faculty had been informed? Had Montclaire eavesdropped on the Blackcoat conversation after sending Phoebe out of the anteroom? Whatever the case, it was clear to Phoebe that she had crossed some sort of line with Montclaire, though she didn't know what else she could have done.

She stopped and focused on the painting that spanned the hallway walls. It helped to calm her mind. Overflowing barrels of wine, food laden tables, musicians, and dancing children: the hand-painted mural depicted a Conversion Ceremony in the vibrant streets of ancient Pompeii. Phoebe reached out a finger to touch the astonishingly glorious art when she remembered, with a thrilling jolt, her lunch with Colten. She plunged down the hallway, cut across the courtyard, and disappeared into the narthyx chamber.

❧ TEN

bove ground, birds chirped their afternoon song, a melodious duet with the distant chapel bells. Mist had settled over the campus like damp, white silk tossed aside by a careless wind. Phoebe, who could barely see the sun behind a stretch of clouds, was happy to step into the barn where cold didn't bite at every inch of her exposed skin.

She scanned the crowded dining hall and spotted Colten in the middle of the room, sitting on the edge of a table, surrounded by a gaggle of girls. Noticing Phoebe's approach, Colten's face went from detached to radiant. He smiled at her, said his goodbyes politely and firmly, and then extricated himself from the adoring group. Phoebe watched him cut a path toward her through clusters of ogling girls, narrowly dodging a few arms that shot out to touch him.

Phoebe chuckled and waited for Colten to reach her. Nervous, she twisted her camera strap around her fingers. Her smile slipped slightly when she caught the glare of the girls Colten had left behind, eyeing her with something more than curiosity. And then, just as Phoebe switched her attention back to Colten's approach, she heard her name being spoken with a note of disgust. Phoebe's skin tightened defensively as she reflexively tuned in to what the girls were saying.

"—I'm sure that's her," she heard a girl say. "She's a new sophomore. Phoebe Pope."

Another girl snickered. "Too bad she's not so Pope-like."

"What? What have you heard?"

"My friend caught her at the boathouse with this guy. At night. Let's just say—"

Phoebe could vaguely hear Colten saying her name, but the girls still held her attention.

"Hey there," she heard him say again, much closer this time. She finally turned her focus to him. Phoebe forbade herself to dwell on what she'd heard, instead filing it away to brood over later. She was having lunch with Colten, and she was beginning to notice that although she was acutely aware of his fame, something about him eased her tension.

"Hey," she said quickly, finding herself under Colten's appraisal. "Sorry I'm late."

"No problem." Colten examined Phoebe more closely and cocked his head to one side, "Wanna leave the fishbowl and go somewhere else for lunch?"

Phoebe looked up, surprise competing with relief on her face. "Where else is there to eat?"

"You'll see," Colten said mysteriously. "You game?"

Phoebe nodded. In a barely perceptible movement, Colten placed a hand on the small of Phoebe's back, ushering her toward the door. The touch was unexpected and shot a jolt of electricity up her spine. She spared a moment to memorize it. For a fleeting second, Phoebe let her mind wonder how that would translate to the effect Colten's lips could have, and then promptly mentally kicked herself.

They set off together in the direction of the open campus fields, their arms sometimes brushing and sending tingles up Phoebe's neck. She wondered if perhaps electric shock treatment from Colten's company could help keep her mind from her problems. She rather liked the idea of that: Colten therapy.

"How do you do it?" Phoebe asked breathily, breaking the silence of their walk.

"Do what?"

"Deal with your life being a constant fishbowl. Everyone always wanting to look at you, be with you?"

"Is that true? Everyone?" Colten peered sideways at Phoebe and grinned as what he was really asking her slowly dawned on her.

Phoebe didn't look at him when she answered. "I agreed to lunch, didn't I?" she said mockingly and he laughed, a sound Phoebe found distractingly sweet.

Colten nudged her arm playfully with an elbow, and Phoebe felt a sudden inexplicable need to touch him. She nudged him back, clenching her hand to keep it under her command.

"You get used to the madness eventually," Colten said, lightly. The sun caught the gold highlights in his hair, brightening his features. "After a while it just becomes a buzzing in the background."

"I can't imagine living in the public eye like that," Phoebe said. "To have no privacy, no secrets—"

"I have my secrets," Colten cut in. And giving Phoebe a penetrating stare, he added, "We all have our secrets."

Phoebe took a discreet breath at that; those words rang truer for her than Colten could possibly realize. She frowned at the thought that he could never imagine the things happening in her other world; it would make his hair curl.

Her thoughts were interrupted by the sound of a car horn blaring. Quite suddenly, Colten seized her upper arm and yanked her to the side. Phoebe looked around, surprised to see that they had been walking along the campus's main road; she'd been too absorbed in their conversation to notice where Colten had been steering them.

A moment later, a vintage white VW Beetle cruised to a stop beside them. The driver's window slid down, and Karli stuck her head out smiling, eyes on Colten, ignoring Phoebe entirely.

"I have room if you want to head off campus for lunch," she said, in a tone of voice that implied the invitation was meant only for Colten.

"Thanks, but we already have plans," Colten said smoothly.

Phoebe's hearts jolted. He'd said "we." It was then that Phoebe realized Colten hadn't let go of her arm, something Karli's eyes had just made a quick jealous note of.

Phoebe felt suddenly emboldened. "Maybe next time?" she said sweetly, not wanting to give Karli the satisfaction of making her feel invisible.

Karli narrowed her eyes slightly, but continued as though Phoebe hadn't spoken. "We're still on for Friday night, right Colten?" Karli smiled suggestively at Colten and Phoebe couldn't help but search his face to see if it was having the desired effect. She found him unreadable.

"Yes," Colten said politely, tipping his baseball cap at Karli.

A triumphant smirk curled her lips. "Great," she said. She then turned to Phoebe, smiling broadly. "Nice to see you again, Phoebe," she said in saintly voice. Karli honked and waved, and as she sped off, Phoebe finally noticed the two other girls in the car. They were all laughing.

The pressure of Colten's grip loosened and Phoebe's hand slipped free. She stroked where he had held her, feeling the lingering warmth of his touch and fought the urge to ask him about his Friday night plans with Karli. It was none of her business.

As they resumed walking, Colten fought to stifle a grin, then gave up and chortled openly.

Phoebe cut a sideways glance at him. "What's so funny?"

"I'm surprised your eyes didn't spin out of their sockets each time Karli spoke," he said, using an index finger to draw a circle around her face. "Is there a reason you don't like her?"

Phoebe was flustered. She didn't like how Colten's searching eyes made her feel transparent. She worked on arranging her face in a more even expression and refrained from saying, "I find her club blatantly opportunistic." Instead she said, "I don't know her enough to have an opinion of her."

Colten glanced at her, and then looked at the path ahead. "Okay," he said, in a tone that conveyed he didn't quite believe her. "I just thought," he continued, "that I'd get your opinion before I met with her and her group on Friday. We're discussing some event they want to throw to raise funds for a charity I'm involved in."

Phoebe said nothing to this. She only swallowed, feeling both relief and regret in equal measure. She wished she'd conveyed her thoughts more frankly.

The path they were on had just gotten steeper and Phoebe could see a rectangular building some distance away. She was about to ask if that was their destination when Colten said abruptly, "I don't make you uncomfortable, do I?"

The question threw Phoebe off guard. Colten watched as she twisted her hands and bit down on her lower lip.

"No," she said. "Well—I mean, I'm as comfortable as someone can be around a . . ." She let the rest go unsaid.

He frowned, considered her words and then pulled his mouth to one side with a slightly forlorn look. "You're going to have to start seeing me as just Colten," he said firmly.

That's easy for you to say, Phoebe thought but said, "Well, nice to meet you, Just Colten." She extended a hand to him in jest. "I'm Just Phoebe."

Colten laughed and took her hand in both of his. "That's something I can get used to," he said, rubbing the inside of her wrist with his thumbs. "Just Colten and Phoebe."

Colten and Phoebe. Phoebe turned it over in her head and absorbed an accompanying flicker of warmth and an unexpected swirl of butterflies in her stomach.

"We're here," he said, releasing her hand.

Phoebe's eyes widened. Colten had brought her to a greenhouse. She didn't even know that Green Lane had one. Behind them, the cluster of buildings that made up the school was barely visible and Phoebe realized that in her campus exploration to date, she had yet to wander out this far. The large building was rectangular and steeply roofed. Through its glass walls, Phoebe could see aisles of greenery and bright flowers that rose from the ground climbing upward toward the sky beyond.

Phoebe looked between Colten and the building. "We're eating here?" she whispered hopefully.

"Come, I'll show you." He took her hand again as though it was the most natural thing to do and pulled her through the door he held open for her.

Immediately Phoebe's nostrils were filled with a collision of scents so rich and complex that she felt she could taste each one. Beside her, Colten chuckled at her absorbed expression.

"Maybe you should join my class," he said.

"What class?"

"I'm taking an elective in sustainable farming," Colten answered. "I'm learning how to nurture vegetables and keep them alive."

Phoebe was impressed. "Show me your stuff."

Colten steered Phoebe by the straps of her backpack and moved her playfully through the many rows, coming to a stop in front of an aisle of vegetables.

"Which ones are yours?" Phoebe asked, bending to read the names written on empty seed packets that had been stuck in the dirt.

"These." Colten pointed to vines at the end of a row of tomatoes.

Phoebe stared and struggled to keep her composure, but she couldn't stop herself. She bent over in a fit of laughter that even bringing both of her hands to her mouth failed to stifle.

"I'm sorry but—" Phoebe gasped. She could hardly breathe for laughing so hard. "But these are some sad, sad tomatoes." Ordinarily Phoebe would have found a gracious way to be tactful, but where every other vine had round vibrant tomatoes, Colten's were withered and looked like they were suffering from severe sun burn. There was no getting around the clear contrast.

"I'm glad you're not in my class," Colten said, feigning hurt feelings.

Phoebe opened her mouth to say something, but no words came. Instead she was overcome with another fit of giggles.

"All right, all right. Enough already," Colten said.

Phoebe didn't know what had come over her exactly, but she felt a huge rush of relief to see that Colten Chase was not perfect at everything he did. Maybe she could actually think of him as "Just Colten."

"Time to grab some lunch."

"I've never even heard of this place," Phoebe said as they walked to the southern end of the greenhouse where a sign overhead said GARDEN CAFÉ.

"On Wednesdays and Fridays they harvest some of the vegetables and offer an organic salad bar with a soup of the day," Colten explained. "It's all they serve, though. I hope that's okay."

"It's perfect," Phoebe said. "I'm a vegetarian." Not eating the flesh of another animal was the Shaper way; it seemed only natural to honor the fact that they took an animal Shape. A half-smile crossed Colten's face as they entered the small café.

"What?" Phoebe demanded.

"It's nice to learn something significant about you," he answered.

They moved through the salad bar and sat down at a picnic table to eat.

"What else can I learn about you?" he said, his voice low and husky.

Phoebe remembered what Colten had said the first time that they'd met and smiled. "To quote someone famous," she said, "'I'm really not that interesting'."

A flicker of a smile. "Touché." Colten propped both elbows on the table, resting his chin in his hands and his eyes on Phoebe's face. "Then tell me three uninteresting things about you," he pressed.

"Why three?"

Colten shrugged. "Arbitrary number."

"Okay." Phoebe shrugged and started counting them off her fingers as she spoke. "I like dictionaries—the older the better—'cause I have a big crush on words."

Colten caught her gaze. "Lucky words."

Phoebe's traitorous face responded with a flush, but she lowered her eyes and barreled on before her words escaped her. "One of my favorite places to hang out is a camera store in San Francisco called Gassers and . . . um . . . and I like being near water."

"Tell me one more thing—"

"By my count, that was three," Phoebe said, looking up at him. "Your turn."

"Yes, but now I want to know something unexpected. Something that no one would guess by just looking at you."

In her mind, Phoebe muttered, *I have two hearts and at some point my second heart will awaken an ancient shape-shifter magic within me.* Out loud she said confidently, "I can hot wire any old car in under two minutes."

"Really?" Colten gave her a disbelieving look that quickly turned to genuine admiration.

Phoebe shrugged as if it weren't a big deal. "Yeah." It was a skill she'd picked up because her father constantly lost his keys and had refused to pay for roadside assistance.

"You're right. . . . I would never have guessed that. So do you carry tools with you and go around boosting random old cars for fun then?" he said teasingly.

"I do carry tools with me," Phoebe said, her expression serious.

Colten jerked an eyebrow. "Really?"

"Really," Phoebe said, tapping her backpack. Having her tools on her was habit. "Your turn," she said, seeing another question forming on Colten's lips. "Three random things about you."

Colten rubbed his chin, making a show of thinking. "I play the accordion," he said.

"Really?" Phoebe searched his face for any signs that he might be kidding. "That's such an old person's instrument."

"Funny you say that," he said, his eyes lighting up. "I learned how to play from an old man. Ol' Billy Jones down in the Bayou." His voice had taken on a southern accent. "He was one of the extras on set when I was down there filming."

"You any good?"

"Let's put it this way," Colten said, speaking in a very confident tone. "I play the accordion as well as I nurture tomatoes."

A loud snort slipped out of Phoebe. She slapped a hand over her mouth as a few more followed. Embarrassed, she quickly said, "Okay, on to fact number two."

"I'm allergic to gluten," Colten said.

"That sucks. Isn't it in everything?"

Colten shrugged. "Pretty much. But it's forced me to learn how to cook—I think that counts as my third fact."

"What?"

"The fact that I'm a great cook."

"Isn't that a matter of opinion?" Phoebe said, teasing.

Colten arched a brow. "Guess I'll have to prove it to you sometime," he promised.

"In that case, it counts," Phoebe said.

"Good," Colten said. His green eyes showed a glint of satisfaction. "Now, back to you—"

"Not so fast!" Phoebe said. "You're forgetting the important bonus question: Something no one would guess by looking at you."

Colten leaned back, his teeth gleaming bright in his smile.

"Well?" Phoebe faked an impatient expression and picked up her glass. Just as she took a long sip of soda, Colten said, "I sleep naked."

Phoebe spewed her drink. It splashed onto her plate, and dribbled down her chin, staining her blouse, but she was too stunned to care. Colten laughed so hard his shoulders shook. Phoebe paled at once. She could feel people looking around at her.

"It seems," Colten said, when he could speak again, "it's easy to get a rise out of you."

Phoebe looked at Colten who was now watching her with barely restrained amusement. She scowled, all the while biting her inner cheek against the stream of salacious thoughts his disclosure pumped through her mind. Thoughts that heated her body. Her pulse raced.

Colten leaned forward and dangled a napkin in front of Phoebe's face.

"Thanks," she mumbled.

They fell into a silence then, and Phoebe found herself wanting to open her mental gate to read Colten's feelings. Being with him made her insecurity flare. And knowing the exact nature of his feelings could potentially soothe that flame down to embers. But she couldn't shake the idea that it wouldn't be fair in this getting-to-know-you dance that they were in—her side having such an advantage. She refrained, hastily.

"Back to you," Colten said. His eyes flickered to the camera Phoebe had set on the table. "Why photography?"

"I don't like the idea of moments being forgotten," Phoebe said. "Capturing them allows me to return to the feelings they generated when I first saw them."

"A personal archive of life moments."

"Yes." That was exactly how she saw it.

Colten stared at her with tentative, curious eyes. "How do you feel right now?"

Phoebe swallowed, not sure what Colten was getting at. She prayed that the flush spreading across her chest wasn't making any vertical movement as well.

"What do you mean?" she asked.

He leaned toward her. "This very moment. How do you feel? Say the first thing that comes to your mind."

"Flummoxed," Phoebe blubbered, instantly regretting her word choice when she said it. *Really?* she thought. *Couldn't go for flustered?*

Colten held his hand out. "Give me your camera, word girl."

Phoebe squinted at him in confusion, but picked up her camera and handed it to him. In a move that was as fast as it was unexpected, Colten moved to sit next to Phoebe, slid his arm around her and drew her close. Phoebe was breathless, her mind spun. Her nose filled with his smoky cinnamon scent, reminding her of the jacket she still had to return. Extending his arm out to hold the camera away from them, Colten took a couple of pictures.

"Now," he said, leaning back and placing the camera on the bench between them, "when you want to feel flummoxed again, you can take a look at those pictures."

Phoebe stared at him blankly as he grinned back at her, her brain trying to reengage itself. She didn't have the heart to tell Colten, that because she didn't own a simple point-and-click camera, his pictures would most likely be unfocused. "Um," she said, zipping open her backpack and removing his jacket. "I've been meaning to give this back to you. Sorry I kept it a while."

"I wasn't worried. It was in good hands," Colten said, taking it from her and slipping it on. A cell phone rang and Phoebe knew it wasn't hers.

"Do you have to take that?" she asked.

Colten glanced down at his watch and shook his head. "It's Nicole," he said, and quickly added, "she's my manager, calling to make sure I don't miss the flight that I'm about to miss."

"Where are you going?" Phoebe asked a bit too quickly. She bit her lower lip, worried that the disappointment she felt had colored her tone.

"L.A. for a few days. I have an audition and some other business," he said. "Can I make a request?"

Phoebe hesitated for a moment, "What?"

"If I land the part, would you be my study partner? You know, help me with my lines?"

"Why me? I don't know anything about . . ." Phoebe's voice dropped off as she cursed her knee-jerk reaction.

Colten interlaced his hands behind his head and looked at her as though she were missing an obvious point. "Just say yes, Phoebe," he said standing, his voice soft. For a fleeting moment his face was unexpectedly shy. "It's a cheap excuse to spend more time with you."

Phoebe blinked up at Colten. He stood with his back to the glass wall where sunlight pushing through the clouds haloed his tall frame. Her cheeks burned and she struggled to think clearly. "What if you don't get the part?" The minute those words left her mouth, she couldn't believe she'd said that. It was official, she thought, she was clearly mental.

"If you say yes, I'll make sure to get the part." Colten's cocky smirk returned, and for a moment, Phoebe wondered if she'd really seen a nervous look flicker over his face. She found herself wishing that this— whatever they were engaging in—wasn't so easy for him.

Phoebe took a breath. "Yes."

"Great," he said quickly, and bent forward to grip her shoulder in a gentle squeeze. "I hate to leave you, but I have a flight to catch."

Phoebe felt her entire body begin to unwind as she watched Colten disappear through the greenhouse. She picked up her camera and looked at the pictures he'd taken of the two of them. As she'd expected, they were semi-blurred images. But she couldn't miss that his was an easy expression while her face screamed girl-caught-in-an-overwhelming-moment. Still, "flummoxed" had been the wrong word to describe how she felt around Colten. Or maybe she needed more than one word. One of the correct terms was certainly "happy," pure and simple. Phoebe found herself wanting nothing more than for Colten to land that part.

❦ Eleven

Without Colten to distract her, Phoebe began to obsess about what she'd heard those girls say in the cafeteria. Even more so, she was brooding over the feelings she'd allowed herself to sample from each girl as they'd glowered at her in turn: bitterness and envy. Both with sharp edges and fangs. There was no doubt in her mind that it was her time spent with Colten that drew those emotions out. On some level, she empathized. But to call her unPope-like and imply that she was some kind of slut was going a bit far.

Before long, Phoebe found herself in a deserted hallway she didn't recognize. The network of hallways in the Campus Below was still confusing to her, and in her preoccupation she'd taken a wrong turn. As she walked, she looked at the portraits along the walls. Gold-framed images of SIS agents of legend shown in both their human and animal forms. Phoebe was just changing direction when a door with the words FACULTY LOUNGE embossed across it swung open at the end of the hallway. Deborah-Anna and Montclaire walked out, talking rapidly in low voices, both looking extremely agitated.

An impulse of curiosity made Phoebe slip behind a nearby support pillar at the very moment Montclaire's eyes wandered the length of the hallway. Phoebe, working to quiet the sound of her hearts thumping in her ears, concentrated on stretching her range of hearing.

"My point," Montclaire said, snapping her eyes back to Deborah-Anna, "is that I would consider it a professional courtesy if you brought me into the loop—made use of my expertise."

The two women had stopped walking and Deborah-Anna stood almost at attention.

"I don't want to be rude," Deborah-Anna started. "But—"

"Blackcoats aren't rude, we're direct," Montclaire said bluntly. "So be direct."

"It goes without question that I think highly of your innovations in the field of intelligence," Deborah-Anna said. "But as I understand it, your condition—"

All of a sudden, Phoebe couldn't hear anything more. Confused, she peered around the pillar in time to see Deborah-Anna's hand moving from the Privaque she'd just pinned to her robes. Phoebe continued watching the women, frustrated that she couldn't attempt to read their lips without exposing herself. But from what she could see of Montclaire's expression, the substitute professor was far from pleased with the words coming from Deborah-Anna's mouth. Her dark eyes narrowed and she folded her arms with a sharp twist of her shoulders. The women stood in a silent impasse, and before Phoebe could begin to think of what to make of it, a stream of chatter erupted from a small group of cadets entering the hallway. A few of them glanced at the women curiously and they backed away from each other slightly, composing their features and easing their rigid postures.

Phoebe held her breath, waiting for the group to pass her pillar so that she could slip among them and hopefully disappear undetected.

Deborah-Anna and Montclaire gave each other cordial nods just as Phoebe began casually walking alongside a pig-tailed girl who eyed her with suspicion, then returned to the conversation she'd been having with a friend.

Phoebe hardly knew what to think as she broke away from the loquacious group further down the hall. Montclaire, a Blackcoat? *Of course*, Phoebe thought as she recalled what Montclaire had said to her after class: "Would you tell me what *they've* told you about the motivation behind the attack?"

Montclaire had not mentioned the word Blackcoat. And clearly, Montclaire didn't need to talk to the headmaster as Phoebe had evasively suggested. Phoebe shook her head in embarrassed understanding; *Montclaire had already been aware of the presence of her own kind.*

A few more distracted wrong turns later, when Phoebe rounded the corner to Tactical Bird Song, she heard someone calling her name behind her; slowing her pace, she peered over her shoulder. Hayley, looking flushed, came rushing into sight.

"I have something to tell you," both girls said at the same time, as Hayley caught up to Phoebe.

They laughed.

"You first," Hayley said.

In a low whisper, Phoebe told Hayley what she'd overheard between Montclaire and Deborah-Anna.

"If she is one of them, that's strange they're leaving her out," Hayley said in a hushed voice. Then, with a frown added, "I'll tell you what her condition is: she's hardcore mean. That whole shock and awe thing with the Vigo-in-a-tank caused a couple of cadets in my section to puke and she made them clean it up in front of everyone."

"Wow. That sucks," Phoebe replied, thinking of the girl who had fainted in her class.

They came upon their classroom and found that students had gathered outside of the door reading a bright note that had been pinned to it. A few students exchanged high fives and rushed past them exclaiming "Free period!"

"What does it say?" asked Hayley, who couldn't see the note over the crowd. "Did she leave us homework?"

Phoebe read: "A last minute conflict requires me to cancel class. We will make up the hour this evening at a Pre-Con Practicum I'm holding in the Floating Gymnasium. It's located on the lower level of the Athletic Wing. Meet at eight o'clock. Be prompt. Professor Koon."

"What the hell is a Floating Gymnasium?" Hayley asked.

"You're asking the Hypha girl?" Phoebe said mock-incredulously.

Hayley laughed. "Right." She turned and asked the girl behind her who shrugged in answer. "Guess we'll have to wait and see."

"What did you have to tell me?" Phoebe asked, as they left the classroom.

"It's more something I have to show you," she said with excitement.

"You have it on you?"

"We gotta go online." Hayley grabbed Phoebe's arm and hurried her through the semi-crowded hallway, arriving at the library just as someone behind them yelled, "Hey Pope!"

Phoebe paused, her hand on the glass door she'd just opened.

"Scott, right?" Hayley asked, dropping her voice and nodding toward the boy making his way toward them.

"Yeah," Phoebe said.

"As much as I want to know what that prophecy hottie wants, I better go snag us a computer," Hayley said under her breath, stepping under Phoebe's arm and into the library.

"How was the rest of Montscare's class?" Scott asked when he reached Phoebe.

"Montscare?"

"Yeah, just made that up," Scott said, hanging his head, his dark hair falling into his eyes. "Stupid, right?" He tugged on the knot of his navy tie.

Grinning in spite of herself, Phoebe said, "It's appropriate. So what's up?"

"Just ran into Mariko," Scott said. "She wants to use this free period for a hang. I'm supposed to bring you."

"Where?"

"The graveyard."

Phoebe jerked an eyebrow. "Isn't that a bit too foreboding?"

"That's what I said," Scott said grinning. "But it's just a Shaper nickname for what the Above folks call the field behind the old windmill."

"Oh," Phoebe said, looking into the library. "Let me finish up with Hayley and we'll—"

"It's just us." Scott gave her a meaningful look. "So we can talk freely," he added. "See you there?"

Phoebe nodded.

Scott strode back down the hall, hands in his pants pocket, whistling tunelessly while Phoebe hurried to find Hayley.

The Below library was always crowded because it was the main place that Shapers could go to openly do Shaper homework, meet in study groups to discuss upcoming tests, and use the private virtual network that only Shapers could access. Phoebe turned along the aisles of books and located a wall of computers at the back. Hayley had parked herself at the far end of the student-packed row.

"Are you on ShaperCity?" Hayley said when Phoebe pulled up a chair next to her. Phoebe shook her head. "Oh, you've got to get a profile. Even my mom has one. She just posted pictures from her attempt at having Spa Sunday with my brothers." Hayley pointed at the computer screen.

Phoebe pinched her nose to keep from laughing. "Is that—?"

"Yup," Hayley said shaking her head. "Avocado on every body part. Look,"—Hayley switched to the next picture—"Harper has it coming out of his ears. They're seven. What was she thinking?"

"That she misses you, Tinkerbell," Phoebe said with a smirk.

Hayley stared at Phoebe, shocked. "How did you—?"

Phoebe indicated the photo caption that said: "Spa Sunday's not the same without you, Tinkerbell."

"Argh!" Hayley said. "This is why it's a bad idea to 'friend' your parents on these sites!"

Phoebe shook with silent laughter. "Your secret's safe with me . . . Tinkerbell."

"Zip it!" Hayley closed the browser and opened a new one. "So you know how I told you that my dad reads some conspiracy blog?" she said changing the subject.

"Yeah."

"Well, it's run by some guy named Liam Corten," Hayley explained. "My dad said that the blog was inactive for awhile and then two new posts went up this week." Immediately Phoebe felt her nerves rising, and Hayley, sensing it, said, "Don't worry, I didn't tell him anything about you or what's going on. He actually didn't even ask me why I wanted to know. He was too excited that for once someone in his family cared to listen to his crazy talk."

Hayley drew an expectant breath and typed in the URL. Soon the words, *Circle of Awareness* flashed on the screen. The girls inclined their heads together and read the first entry.

Blackcoats in the air
Posted by **Liam Corten** on September 15th at **3:00 AM**

> It has been a long time. I know. But sometimes digging for the truth takes time and I am now back reporting all that I know. You may recall that earlier this month, Harvard scientists were kidnapped and their multi-million dollar equipment stolen. Shortly thereafter, Blackcoats were dispatched to the Boston area, all signs pointing to Vigo activity that is deemed a possible threat to the Royal Court. What could it be, you wonder? You can trust the Court to keep it hushed up. But don't worry, I am keeping tabs. When I know, you will know.

Posted in: mystery

Phoebe and Hayley exchanged glances and scrolled to the post written two days later.

The Four are real
Posted by **Liam Corten** on September 17th at **1:18 AM**

I have it on good authority that what has the Blackcoats chasing after their tails is the fact that Vigos are aware of the Year of Four prophecy. Yes, a *prophecy*—those things the Court simply dismisses as the mutterings of insane soothsayers. I ask you this: If it is merely insane talk then why seek out the potential Four in question and protect them? Yes folks, the *Four* are currently under Blackcoat protection in an undisclosed location. I believe that this sends a message that this prophecy is indeed true. At least true enough for Vigos to want to destroy the Four and the Royal Court to want to protect them.

Posted in: prophecies

"Listen," Hayley said, seeing color slowly drain from Phoebe's face. "We should take this blog with a grain of salt. At the end of the day, this guy could just be a nutter that keeps other nutters like my dad entertained."

"And if he isn't?" Phoebe said, finding herself a bit more convinced of Corten's information. "It's pretty eerily on point, don't you think?"

Hayley shrugged dismissively. "For your sake, let's hope he's on the lunatic side of crazy."

"I guess—hey what's the Exile Conspiracy?" Phoebe asked, her eyes latching onto a link seconds before Hayley closed the web page.

"Ugh. I don't even want to go there," Hayley said, swiveling in her chair. "My dad goes off on that enough."

"So what is it?"

Hayley sighed with an air of boredom. "In a nutshell. Some folks think there's an alternate truth to the Tiger clan getting kicked out of Pompeii." She rolled her eyes. "Something other than King Vigo losing his mind and damning his entire clan. . . ."

Phoebe's eyes widened, her mind straying to recall history. A number of centuries ago, Tigers were counted among the Shaper clans until their exile on the eve of King Vigo's execution. According to lore, the Tiger monarch convinced his clan to give into their wild predatory instinct—something that was subjugated by law—promising it would unleash stores of untapped power that would make them the envy of all Shapers. In his power-hungry madness, he led a clandestine hunt for humans beyond the walls of Pompeii. A hunt that triggered an insatiable blood lust—later discovered to be mito lust. Soon, however, a plague tore through the clan, degenerating their second heart, stripping them of their elemental powers, disfiguring their magical shape and turning their golden coats soot-black. Although many believed the plague was judgment from Osiah and Gavya intended to punish only the Tigers, the Royal Court ordered the clan's exile for fear that it would spread. King Vigo's trial for breaking royal edict and inciting a tragic massacre was swift. His execution was even swifter. Some say his clan's vows of revenge were heard long after the gates of Pompeii were locked behind them.

"How did it go, anyway?" Hayley asked.

Phoebe's attention jumped back to the present. "Hmm?" she said, betraying her wandering mind.

A flicker of annoyance passed over Hayley's face. "Tell me about your lunch date!" she said, her eyes demanding. "Where did you go 'cause I certainly didn't see you in the dining hall."

A smile lit Phoebe's face only to be eclipsed by a frown. "Crap!"

"What?"

"Scott," she said, suddenly remembering. "I'm supposed to be somewhere right now. I'll tell you about lunch later."

"Uh-uh, missy!" Hayley said, her voice rising. "You can't leave me hanging. Was it good?"

"No." Phoebe pushed back from the table and chuckled softly at Hayley's sharp frown. "It was great!"

"Ooh I want details!" Hayley squealed, drawing a scathing look from the portly librarian, who had just walked past them. Lowering her voice, Hayley said, "Give me something to chew on."

Straight-faced, Phoebe said, "He sleeps naked."

Hayley opened her mouth, and then closed it, mute with shock. Phoebe left the library laughing helplessly. Even Hayley had no words for that.

❦ TWELVE

The path to the old windmill took Phoebe over a bridge that crossed a dry creek and dumped her on the north end of the campus, an area long since abandoned by landscapers. She was a few hundred yards away from the moss-covered stone structure, when she stopped in confusion; it was a graveyard of sorts. Antiquated farm equipment lay in clusters behind the structure—combines, hay plows, tractors, and others she couldn't identify. In the center of these rusting relics stood an old wooden playground set. It was around this that Phoebe saw the other Hyphas were hanging out.

Mariko hung by her feet from the precarious-looking monkey bars, her uniform skirt falling over her shoulders to reveal the pink gym shorts she wore underneath. Lewis sat atop a shelled out tractor, his dreadlocks flowing to his shoulders, his torso bent over an acoustic guitar. And Scott, who had an unlit cigarette dangling from the corner of his mouth, was bouncing a soccer ball on his knee as he balanced on one leg.

"You're just in time to hear Bob Marley over here play us another tune," Scott said sarcastically to Phoebe who made a beeline for the only unbroken swing on the playground set.

Lewis had been playing only a few seconds. He looked up and furrowed his brows. "Only black-guy-with-dreads-playing-a-guitar you could come up with, my man?"

"Whoa dude," Scott said raising his lighter to his cigarette while keeping his ball bouncing, "I meant no offense."

While Lewis returned to strumming his tune, Mariko jumped down from the monkey bars and said, "In Broom Boy's defense"—she brushed her hands off on her skirt—"Bob is the most famous dreadlocked musician of all time."

"Exactly!—wait a minute," Scott said slowly, casting a frowning look at Mariko. "Broom Boy? Really? Think that's funny?"

"I could go either way. . . ." Mariko said evasively, but the snarky look she gave him as she climbed to the top of the spiral slide was answer enough.

Phoebe didn't know whether to laugh and she hid a betraying smile by bringing her camera up to her face and taking a few pictures of Lewis while he fingered the frets of his guitar. He chuckled and said, "Marley's iconic, but y'all should broaden your horizons. Get hip to folks like my man, Michael Franti and his band—"

"Spearhead," completed Phoebe, resting her camera on her lap and sharing a smile with Lewis. "They're from my hometown."

"Frisco girl, huh?" Lewis said. Phoebe nodded. "Cool. Ever see 'em play live?"

"Couple of times with my father. . . ." Phoebe let her voice trail, coiled her free arm around the swing's chain and then finished quietly, "My father was a fan." She stared pensively at the ground, effectively stopping the next question from leaving Lewis's lips. Phoebe did not know how long she'd been gazing at the wood chips beneath her feet before Mariko said, "No pity party is complete without booze." She looked up. Mariko, who had slid to the bottom of the slide, extracted a silver flask from her backpack.

"Pity party?" Phoebe asked, looking around at the others. "Is that what this hang is about?"

"Last I checked, all of us were on an endangered Hyphas list, so yeah," Mariko said, bringing the flask to her lips. When she raised the flask inquiringly, both Phoebe and Lewis shook their heads.

Mariko merely shrugged and walked the flask over to Scott who had paused his foot mechanics. He took a big swig and promptly choked on it.

"What the hell is that?" he said wheezing, his eyes watering fast.

"My dad calls it weapons-grade sake," Mariko said, thumping Scott on the back. "It's not the watered down crap you get at restaurants."

"You don't say." Recovered, Scott placed the soccer ball on top of his left foot, flicked it up and caught it on his chest; he let the ball roll down and began a steady bounce from one knee to the other.

Mariko, who had snagged the flask back, drew even deeper than before. Both Scott and Lewis stared at her, impressed.

"So," Mariko said, walking over to the seesaw and taking a seat on the non-splintered end. "I think we should discuss the fact that we have Blackcoat protection. Who else finds it strange?"

Lewis stopped his strumming and stared at her. "What do you mean?"

"She means why the Royal Security Corps? Why not give us SIS agents?" Scott said, expertly bouncing his ball from knee to arm to foot.

"Exactly," Mariko said. "Vigo threats are constant. That's why we have SIS. So why does our situation call for the Blackcoats? It's like bringing a tank to a BB gun fight."

"That's a stretch, don't you think?" Lewis said, pausing to re-tune a string.

"You know what I mean," Mariko said, her voice unable to hide her irritation.

"I think I get why they're here," Phoebe said, speaking up and meeting Mariko's questioning stare. "If there's a chance that the prophecy is true and one of us can defeat Vigos, it makes sense that the Royal Court would have an interest in it."

"I'm with Pope on that." Scott glanced over at Phoebe, then back at Mariko whose attention had strayed to the fraying ends of her braids. "The Crowns are protecting a potential weapon."

Mariko looked up. "But that's what's weird. When you hear a prophecy don't you think nursery rhymes or campfire storyteller?"

"Your point?" Scott said, bringing his ball to a rest beneath his foot.

"That is my point. A big deal is being made about something we normally take about as seriously as the tooth fairy."

"That didn't stop you from freaking out when the Blackcoats first told us about it, did it?" Scott said.

Mariko was silent, but subjected Scott to a long, hard look that Phoebe was beginning to believe was trademarked.

"Ultimately, whether the prophecy is true or not doesn't change the fact that a Padrone has a contract out on us," Phoebe said, clenching the chain of the swing more tightly to keep her hands from shaking. "We're in danger either way."

A brief silence followed. Then, Lewis zipped his guitar into its black carrying case and said, "I think the prophecy is true. And I think the Blackcoats know what the power is."

"Don't you think they would've told us if they knew?" Phoebe said.

Lewis looked around as though waiting for someone to approach. Seemingly satisfied that no one was around, he said, "They wouldn't tell us. Not if it's the ability to wield one of the missing elements."

Phoebe and Mariko stared at Lewis. Scott had frozen with his cigarette halfway to his mouth.

At their dubious expressions, Lewis said, "Hey man, don't give me that 'it's taboo' look. I'm only speculating, not coveting."

"Impossible," Mariko said, blinking, her voice slightly higher.

"Is it?" Scott said, lighting his new cigarette. "Think about it. . . . The idea of Shaper-human offspring was once considered impossible"—he indicated the four of them—"but then here we are."

Phoebe stared, still unable to speak. Since antiquity, Shapers had only been able to wield the two elements. And it was utterly forbidden to covet the missing elements because of the pivotal role that desire had played in the Exile. Many believed that the Tiger monarch's madness sprung from his desire to wield them, a desire that had him convinced that consuming human blood (an unforgivable sin) was the answer to unlocking such powers within a Shaper.

"Well, if I were a Vigo," Lewis said, pulling his dreadlocks back into a ponytail. "I'd want to kill whatever Shaper had control over fire."

Lewis's soft-spoken words hit Phoebe hard. "Oh my God," she whispered, then raised her voice. "Maybe that is it." Other than diamond-tipped weapons, the only other sure way to end a Vigo's life was by incineration. If Shapers could wield fire, it would be a game changer. *And it really has nothing to do with my ability*, Phoebe thought, her shoulders sagging with relief.

"Not you too." Mariko glanced disapprovingly at Phoebe, who shrugged. "Look, if that were true, then one of us would already have pre-con signs of it."

"Anyone hiding pyro tricks?" Scott said, joking.

Lewis turned to Mariko. "You're right," he said, reluctantly. "But could you imagine it?" He mimed shooting power from his palms. "A stream of flames shot right at a Vigo and then it's bye bye cousin—"

"Don't say that!" Mariko yelled, cutting off a startled Lewis. "Don't you freakin' say that!" She hopped off the seesaw, snatched her backpack from the ground, and bolted.

Utterly bewildered, Phoebe, Scott, and Lewis stared after Mariko as she ran, her braids bouncing about her. The sound of tolling chapel bells broke the stunned silence and Phoebe got to her feet.

"I have a photo assignment to get to," she said slowly. As Phoebe shouldered her bag, Scott crossed over to Lewis and offered him a cigarette; when she caught his eye, he winked.

"What did I say?" Lewis moaned, looking worriedly from Scott to Phoebe.

"Who the hell knows what that was about," Scott said. "I wouldn't sweat it." He fished his lighter from his jacket pocket. "Besides, even if none of us end up wielding fire, the fact that Vigos think we might be able to is reason enough for them to want us dead."

"Yeah, I guess," Lewis said, noncommittally. Then, as he and Scott lit up, Phoebe turned to leave, thinking over what Scott had said and wondering about Mariko's outburst.

Up ahead, the sinking afternoon sun veiled the horizon of campus buildings with a delicate, shimmering fabric of ocher and crimson light. Long shadows inched stealthily across Mariko who'd stopped walking at the sound of Phoebe's approaching footsteps.

"I'm not a freak, you know," Mariko said.

"Of course not," Phoebe said automatically. She stopped momentarily when she reached Mariko. "You don't have to explain."

Phoebe kept moving toward the main campus. They walked side by side in silence for several long seconds before Mariko said abruptly, "One afternoon when I was ten, I was home alone after school and sensed a Vigo in my backyard. Everything was locked up, but I knew it was only a matter of time before she got in."

The hairs stood on the back of Phoebe's neck. "Did she?"

"No."

Phoebe exhaled with Mariko.

"But later that night," Mariko continued, hugging her backpack to her chest. "My dad found a note pinned to the back door that said, 'Too bad we couldn't play today, cousin.' My dad moved our family that week," she said, adding in a dark whisper, "When I hear one of our own use that word it sets me off—those monsters are not our family!"

But technically, they were family. Phoebe had even heard that Vigos sometimes used "cousin" when torturing Shapers as a reminder of this. Many Shapers believed that humans, on a subconscious level, had retained the memory of this shared ancestry: in biology, humans had grouped tigers with lions, jaguars, and leopards (the four great cats) in the genus Panthera—genus being the Latin term for family.

"I didn't tell you that story so you could feel sorry for me," Mariko said, jerking Phoebe out of her thoughts.

"Yeah—I mean no, of course not," Phoebe said quickly.

"And don't go telling the guys either," Mariko said. "It's probably good for Lewis to think I'm a freak. Maybe it will cure him of his puppy love thing."

She sped off before Phoebe could utter a reply.

🍁 THIRTEEN

Later that evening, Phoebe rushed, half-stumbling, down the stone steps on the north end of the athletic wing that led to the floating gym. She was late for the Pre-con Practicum. Her session with opera singer Collette Nole had taken much longer than necessary due to the famed diva demanding to see each photo Phoebe took to make sure it was "always only of her good side"—a process that star-struck Cyn had been happy to oblige. Now Phoebe was arriving at a large anteroom to find her classmates already crowded around Professor Koon who stood stoically in front of a huge black door. A sign above the door read: NO PRE-CONS ALLOWED PAST THIS POINT WITHOUT THE PRESENCE OF AIR GUARDS.

"Now that we're all present," Professor Koon said, smiling at Phoebe who wormed guiltily through the small crowd to where Hayley stood, "we can get started with tonight's practicum. One of the exciting parts of your Conversion Day is becoming a son or daughter of Osiah or Gavya. Let's see by a show of hands how many of you will be children of Gavya?"

Phoebe looked around as five of her cadetmates, including Hayley, raised their hands. However, Phoebe noticed, that Hayley seemed more nervous than confident.

"The rest of you," Professor Koon said, smiling, "belong to Osiah, just like I do. Don't expect that to win you any special treatment!" Phoebe and Lewis exchanged a she-forgot-about-us glance while Professor Koon waited for the laughter to settle before continuing.

She said, "Now, as infants, you spend a good amount of time crawling on all fours, so those of you transitioning into children of Gavya will not experience as big of a shock where movement is concerned. Osiah's line is a different matter altogether, and because of this we use the floating gym to pre-expose you all to the sensation of flight. This allows for a bit of a head start."

A few people gasped excitedly at that.

"Yes, it's exciting," Professor Koon continued, "especially for those of you who will be land bound. You get an opportunity to experience flight in this special intro session which is just about body floating. However, the future sessions that cover specific flight control techniques are reserved for the birds among us. Now," Professor Koon said, speaking over the sound of disappointed grumbling, "everyone please grab a wingsuit." She pointed to a wall where thirty or so blue jumpsuits hung from hooks in a row. "They are arranged from small to extra large so find your size and put it on quickly. Once our air guards arrive we'll be ready to start!"

With that, everyone sauntered over to the wingsuits, eager to begin.

"Are they supposed to be loose or fitted?" said one girl, who couldn't decide between the two options she held in her hands.

"I don't think it's a fashion show," Mariko answered slyly. The girl scowled at Mariko and went with the smaller sized suit.

"Please take your shoes off," Professor Koon said as she walked around helping people who were having trouble getting into their suits.

Phoebe glanced down at her body after zipping herself into a medium wingsuit. "We look like flying squirrels," she remarked, spreading her arms and legs out. Made from a light and comfortable parachute-like cloth, the suit had material under the arms that connected the wrists and hips, and more material between the legs making walking quite awkward.

"You're so right," Hayley laughed, flapping her arms. And then, "You're lucky that you get to take the advanced sessions."

"I'm not so sure," Phoebe said.

"Why wouldn't you? You're one of the birdies!" Hayley laughed, but stopped at seeing an uncomfortable expression work its way across Phoebe's face. "What's the matter?"

"I'm a Hypha."

"Oh, crap," Hayley said. "Your mom's human." She quickly added, "I didn't mean that in a bad way."

"I know."

They both left it at that. They didn't need to discuss that among Shapers there was no bigger moment than your Conversion day; the day a Shaper child inherited his or her mother's animal form. Growing up, Phoebe had loved hearing her father tell the story of his big day. But the apprehension in his eyes was never lost on her: shape-shifting magic was passed from mother to child. Her mother was human. He'd worried about what that meant for her on Conversion day. And she worried, too.

Just as Hayley gave Phoebe's hand a reassuring squeeze, several older athletic-looking students came running down the steps to the anteroom, much to Professor Koon's very apparent relief. Phoebe counted fifteen of them. It seemed as if there was one guard per student in the class.

"Great, our air guards are here!" she exclaimed, opening the door behind her and ushering the class through to the next room. Phoebe was immediately surprised to feel grassy earth cool beneath her bare feet. She stopped short, and behind her, Hayley bumped into her back.

"What the—?" Hayley said, echoing Phoebe's exact thoughts. Phoebe turned in a slow circle. So did several of her classmates, everyone wearing similar looks of awe. The room, which seemed to stretch a hundred yards in each direction, was filled with spruce, maple, and birch trees. Phoebe inhaled the sharp, earthy tang of leaves, root, and bark.

A few reddish-brown leaves fluttered down from the canopy above them, and Phoebe opened her hand, letting them land in her palms. She didn't know how it was possible, but they were standing in an autumn forest. Phoebe studied the leaves in her hand and Professor Koon said, "We prefer for you to experience flight in nature. These trees have been enchanted with earth magic in order to grow here. Now, they won't reach the great heights that they would if they were Above, but it serves our purposes fine."

A boy with curly brown hair and a curious grin raised his hand and asked, "What are all these holes in the ground between the grass?" He sank to his knees in the grass, pulling at the blades and spreading them apart with his hands.

Professor Koon smiled broadly. "The entire floor of this gym is a vent," she explained. "When I turn on the wind, air will come shooting up through those holes in a vertical column providing the lift you need to take off."

Phoebe was struck with a sudden intense nervousness, and Hayley, she saw, looked equally uneasy.

"Not to worry," Professor Koon said reassuringly, "It's all perfectly safe. And for anyone thinking these trees will be pulled from their roots' anchors by the wind, they won't. They've been enchanted to handle the highest of wind speeds."

"Before we can start, though, I need a volunteer. A wingsuit model if you will." Professor Koon looked around. And then when no one raised a hand, she gestured to an embarrassed-looking Scott, who was instructed to lie on the ground for a demonstration on how to use the wingsuit.

Everyone stopped their murmuring conversations to watch with rapt attention.

Professor Koon bent over Scott's body and began to arrange his limbs. "To float the body higher, spread your arms and legs to open the material flaps. And then when you want to float down, fold your elbows and knees up like this."

Phoebe couldn't help chuckling. In the current position Professor Koon had Scott in, he looked like a criminal that had been forced to lie on the ground and surrender.

"You are not to float above the tops of the trees," Professor Koon warned, helping Scott to his feet. Scott dusted off his wingsuit and slumped to the back of the group. "The air guards and I will be up there with you to help if you have any problems, but the key is not to panic."

Professor Koon turned to the fifteen students who had been waiting patiently behind her, their backs resting against a wall. At her nod, they converted into falcons and hawks, lifted into the air, and scattered themselves around the various trees in the gym. From their perches, they peered down at everyone staring up at them.

"When the air comes on," Professor Koon said, "lean in, spread your arms, and let the rest happen!" She hurried over to a wall panel by the door and pushed a series of buttons. And without another word, she herself converted into a hawk and rose to the top of a spruce.

Phoebe noticed a fifteen second countdown on the panel, and she and Hayley exchanged uncertain glances. Then the air blasted on with a roar. Phoebe closed her eyes, tilted forward, and threw out her arms, hoping for the best. She quickly lifted up five feet, then twenty, the air whipping at her face. At the feel of adrenaline rocketing through her, Phoebe opened her eyes and blinked down at the grassy floor that had dropped away. All around her, classmates were shooting upward through the gym and more than a few times, Phoebe heard the thud of people colliding into one another as some students got off to a less than smooth start.

It took Phoebe a moment to get the hang of floating on air. But once she did, she found the freedom of it exhilarating and began to picture what it might be like to be a daughter of Osiah. She let herself go a bit higher. Suddenly, Lewis zoomed dangerously close to her and she had to slacken her elbows and knees, ducking under him just in time to avoid a collision. Above her, Lewis shouted something that sounded like a gargled "sorry", his voice greatly distorted by the force of the wind.

Phoebe began to float up again and had just spotted Hayley hovering at a nearby oak when a high pitched tinny clanging suddenly erupted, echoing around the gym. Through the alarm, a prerecorded voice said repeatedly, "This is a Vigo drill. Proceed to the courtyard exits."

The air guards dove toward the ground and circled there as though preparing. A split second later, Phoebe knew why. The blowing air cut off and Phoebe, along with others around her, began plummeting downward. Voices shrieked and arms went flailing. Phoebe landed lopsidedly on the back of a falcon who carried her to the ground and shook her off gently.

Staggering a bit as she tried to catch her balance, Phoebe watched as the other air guards quickly and efficiently rescued the rest of her classmates.

"Leave your shoes behind! Keep your suits on! If this were the real thing you wouldn't have time to change," said Professor Koon, who had returned to her human form. She repeated this refrain several times as all of her students landed. When the last of the frazzled-looking teens had reached solid ground and all of the air guards had returned to their human shape, Professor Koon sped everyone out of the floating gym. Stumbling in their wingsuits, they followed her through the athletic wing and into the hallway, joining several other teachers, each with their own line of students trailing in their wake.

"This scene is crazy," Hayley said, shuffling alongside Phoebe as the group turned a corner toward the courtyard. Phoebe, who was trying to keep her mind focused on not tripping over her feet in her awkward new attire, simply nodded her agreement.

They entered the courtyard, which seemed almost filled to capacity. From balconies, custodians shouted instructions over everyone's head, reminding the faculty which exits belonged to which class year. Doors Phoebe had never noticed before slid open between the walls on the east side of the courtyard revealing dark passageways that meandered and disappeared behind them.

Through the madness, Phoebe noticed a sweaty male teacher take a swig of something from a flask. When he caught her staring, she quickly looked away and from the corner of her eye saw a girl faint and get thrown over the shoulder of a male classmate, and Montclaire hurrying against the grain of traffic as though heading toward the narthyx chamber. But it all happened so fast that Phoebe wasn't certain about what she'd seen. In fact, she was so busy absorbing the scene that she didn't realize she had stopped moving until she was swept by the tide of her class pushing her forward as Professor Koon called over her shoulder, "The Hastati class exit is the last one on the right. Please move quickly!"

Cold air rolled over them as they marched swiftly along the narrow sloping passageway. Nobody said a word, but anticipation charged the air like a jolt of adrenaline. They hadn't been walking for more than two minutes when the door snapped shut behind them, a jarring sound that caused some people to break into a run. The end of the passageway widened into a round area big enough for everyone to gather, and they faced a pair of staircases that rose steeply out of sight.

"Say your name as you climb so that I can mark you off my roster," Professor Koon said. "And when you get to the top, please remain as a group."

Students began disappearing in twos, calling out their names as they went. When Phoebe's turn came, she spoke her name, moving as quickly as she could. She clambered up the stairs, until finally, she poked her head through a large round opening at the top. Hayley extended a hand and helped Phoebe take the last steps into the new room.

Phoebe cast an eye around the minimally lit space and saw the shadowy bodies of students emerging from several other holes in the ground. She gave a light gasp as she recognized the place: they were in the Green Lane boathouse. What she'd simply dismissed before as an odd floor pattern of very large polka dots were actually the manhole covers for the Campus Below's emergency exits.

Next to her, Hayley whispered, "I hope they make this quick, 'cause I need to find a bathroom!" The black and silver covers slid back into place one by one, until finally all of the students had surfaced.

The first floor of the boathouse was now jam-packed with hundreds of Shapers. All shivering. And all wondering what was going on. Just then, a voice rang out across the space and Professor Yori came striding into sight, flanked by Gabe and the Blackcoats. They stopped up front, their eyes roving nimbly over the assembled crowd. Gabe glanced down at his watch, stepped closer to the headmaster and whispered something in his ear. Professor Yori nodded and then cleared his throat. A hush descended on the boathouse.

"Ten minutes and fifty-two seconds," he said. "That is how long it took everyone to evacuate. And that is five minutes and fifty-two seconds too long." He paused, and when he spoke again he sounded deadly serious. "Had this not been a drill, there would have been many casualties."

Phoebe shuddered as the headmaster continued. "It has been a long time since we've had one of these drills, but in light of recent events, it was deemed necessary. Let's strive for better efficiency next time. The goal," he said, his tone still serious, "is to seal all exits five minutes after the alarms sound in order to trap the enemy inside." Professor Yori paused to let that last point sink in. Then, bringing his hands together he said with a forced jollity, "We are pretty much at the end of your class hour, so unless your professors think otherwise, I see no need for you to return to your lessons."

His statement generated a few yelps of glee.

"Let's not all rush out of here at the same time and draw attention to ourselves," Professor Yori continued. "We shall leave by class. Hastati-year first."

Phoebe and Hayley hurriedly slipped out of their wingsuits and balled them up in their hands in preparation for their exit.

Professor Yori gave a small nod. "Go with Osiah and Gavya. You are dismissed."

 # FOURTEEN

After the chaos of the Vigo drill, Phoebe returned to her dorm to find a young uniformed man leaving a note at her door.

"Can I help you?" she fought back a note of concern in her tone.

The man turned. On his shirt Phoebe read, "Concierge Courier: Your Packages, Our Discretion"

"Phoebe Pope?" he asked.

"Yes."

"Please sign here." He handed her a package and a clipboard. Phoebe glanced down at the label on the box and felt her stomach flip; it was from Chase. Quickly, she signed for it and returned the clipboard to the man who smiled sheepishly, "Mind telling me where I can find the library? Got packages to pick up and this is my first day on the job." He showed Phoebe his map, scratching his head. "This is one confusing campus."

Phoebe gave the man easy directions, then entered her room and shut the door behind her. She dashed for her bed. Sitting cross-legged with the box on her lap, Phoebe tore it open, expectantly. Inside she found a veritable mound of tissue paper courtesy of someone who had been overzealous with the packaging. Phoebe dug through it to find a tomato-shaped pillow underneath. At first she was confused, but then came comprehension. Phoebe broke into little fits of laughter and pulled the pillow out. Upon further inspection, she saw that one side of the pillow had a smiley face embossed on it while the other was embroidered with the words *Not A Sad Tomato*.

Phoebe completely lost track of time as she lay curled around her new pillow thinking of the boy who made her forget about the chaos around her whenever they were together. She wondered if it was possible that her seedling of a crush was starting to grow quickly. Though it scared her a little to admit it, the answer was yes. A happy tomato yes.

Phoebe woke with a start to the sound of pounding on her door. She heard Cyn groan and hoped that she would answer it, but when she didn't, and the pounding continued, Phoebe swung her feet over the bed and planted them on the cold floor. *So much for Cyn's claim of being a light sleeper,* Phoebe thought as she stared at her bedside clock. 2:00 a.m. She had a photo assignment in four hours.

Fully prepared to yell at the person still knocking, Phoebe yanked open the door in frustration and then froze. There stood Yelena, dressed all in black and peering at her in a way that told Phoebe that something was wrong. Phoebe barely had time to wonder what was going on before Yelena said, "I need you to come with me now." She shrugged out of her coat and handed it to Phoebe.

Not daring to ask if she could change out of her pajamas first, Phoebe pulled on the coat and followed the Blackcoat out of her dorm. A few minutes later, Phoebe entered the chapel, yawning and shivering. She felt confused and a bit overwhelmed, and she had no idea why they were there. But as they hurried up the altar steps and walked toward the restricted door, Phoebe felt her body go suddenly numb. Was she about to get in trouble for almost entering the other day? Had someone other than Gabe seen her? She tried not to take betraying deep breaths as Yelena knocked on the door, which promptly swung open.

Phoebe entered slowly and stopped, hugging her arms around her. She took in the scene. Where there should be four walls, there were instead floor-to-ceiling screens flashing a stream of changing images. All around her, students and faculty could be seen going about their lives in the Campus Above, moving in and out of different frames.

"Good morning, Phoebe," said a voice on her right. Phoebe turned her head. A subdued-looking Professor Yori stared back at her from a corner. Phoebe's eyes strayed past the headmaster to where Professor Koon sat heaped in a chair, her head in her hands, a box of tissues at her feet.

"Forgive the hour," Professor Yori said. "But we have a matter that we need you to help us with." He walked up to her, folded his arms, and stared at the screens.

"What is this place?" Phoebe asked, a tremor in her voice.

"This is the Eye," he said. "For security purposes we have cameras set up at every narthyx entrance to the Campus Below as well as inside the access passageways and the Below courtyard. This is where all of those video feeds are monitored, allowing the custodians to direct you students Below without exposure to humans."

Phoebe stared in stunned silence. She'd been wondering how Shaper movement between the two campuses operated so smoothly.

"Can I ask . . ." Phoebe started tentatively. "Can I ask why I'm here?"

Yelena spoke. "If you could bring up that screen for us again," she said, speaking to someone over Phoebe's shoulder. Phoebe turned. She had not noticed Gabe sitting demurely in a chair in the back of the room. A remote control was in his hands. Their eyes met briefly and then he looked away, pointing the remote at the screens.

The images flashing on the four screens disappeared, replaced by a single picture that filled them all. Phoebe stared wide-eyed. In the Below courtyard students were all rushing forward, with the exception of one who stood looking in the opposite direction, a concentrated frown on her face. That student was Phoebe.

Yelena fixed a watchful eye on Phoebe. "Can you tell us what made you stop here?"

Panic filled Phoebe. She wanted to please her mentors and teachers, or at least assuage the deep concern they wore on their faces, but felt unsettled. "I don't remember," she said finally, and seeing the expression on Yelena's face added, "I really don't. There was so much going on and I—"

The door opened and Afua entered looking even more serious than usual. She looked from Phoebe to the screens and back.

"Did she remember anything?" she asked, keeping her gaze on Phoebe while addressing Yelena.

"No, not yet," Yelena said.

Afua then tilted her head toward where Professor Koon still sat hunched over. "And this is the instructor who saw them last?"

Saw them last? Phoebe found herself feeling that something was terribly wrong.

"Yes. This is Kat Koon," Professor Yori answered, frowning at Afua. Although he had spoken politely, Phoebe hadn't missed the defensive fire in his voice. For some reason, the headmaster needed to be protective of Koon.

Professor Koon straightened up and wiped at her eyes. She looked pale and haggard, her tawny hair flat.

"Walk me through what happened with your class during the drill, Professor," Afua said.

Professor Koon spoke to the floor. She explained everything from when the alarms sounded to how she had evacuated the class according to protocol.

"—and so when the last student climbed up to the boathouse and I hadn't checked those two off my roster, I thought they were just being typical kids who took advantage of a chaotic situation and skipped out on things," she finished in a choked voice. "I didn't know they'd been kidnapped!" Professor Koon buried her face in her hands and sobbed some more.

Phoebe felt as though someone had taken a bat to her knees. Quickly, she looked to Professor Yori. "Who's been kidnapped?"

Afua started to say something, but stopped at the expression on Professor Yori's face. "This is still my school . . . at least it is for now and so I will tell her," he said firmly. He turned to Phoebe. "We've been unable to find Cadets Higashi or Baker since the drill and we believe that they've been taken."

"Are you sure?" Phoebe said, her voice just above a whisper, wild fear pumping through her limbs. "Couldn't they have just gone off somewhere like Professor Koon was saying? I know that Lewis has a crush on Mariko, so maybe—"

Afua cut her off. "We've looked everywhere there is to look."

Phoebe's mouth went dry. "And Scott? Where's he?"

"Thankfully, like you, he's fine," Professor Yori said. "Deborah-Anna is standing guard at his dorm as we speak. We spoke with him earlier and he hadn't seen anything out of the ordinary either."

Phoebe felt shivery. "So Vigos," she said, "got into the school?"

"No," Afua said, confidently. "None of the sensors bordering the Above campus picked up on Vigo physical energy. It is our assessment that someone took advantage of the drill and—" Afua said with a matter-of-fact sort of tone, until Professor Yori interrupted, "With all respect, I cannot allow you to insinuate that one of my teachers would willfully cause harm to a student. Some of these men and women are respected former SIS agents who continue to serve the Royal Court by molding the minds of future agents."

"With equal respect," Afua said, her expression remaining hard. "Given that only faculty members were aware of when the drill was happening, and that some of them, as you've pointed out, are former agents, it follows that they possess the expertise to pull something like this off. Does it not?"

Sweat broke out on Professor Yori's bald head. He glanced at Professor Koon who had reached down for another piece of tissue, then looked back at Afua. When he spoke, he did so slowly, "I suppose you raise a valid point." Then, with painful resignation, "Is everyone else accounted for?"

"Yes," Afua said. "But we expected that. Whoever it is knows they still have two targets to go." The headmaster's frown deepened. "There will be a few more Blackcoats arriving by morning," Afua continued. "I would like for you to call a meeting so that we can apprise your staff of who we really are."

"Why in Osiah and Gavya would you do that?" Professor Yori said fiercely. "I thought the whole point of your parading around as mentors was to avoid any form of panic."

"Panic is both an enemy and a friend, Professor," Afua said firmly. "With the disclosure, I'm counting on it being the latter." At the headmaster's raised eyebrow Afua explained, "It's a psychological play. The unexpected presence of the Royal Security Corp on campus will instill a sense of panic in your traitor. An agent of your accomplishments should know that guilty people behave differently when they believe their capture is possible or even imminent. Mistakes will be made. After our announcement we will start monitoring your staff more closely."

The headmaster's eyes burned above his tightly set mouth. Phoebe watched as fatigue rushed in to overtake his look of frustration. She opened her mental gate to read his emotions. They were familiar to her since she'd read them once before. Of the strong ones she could feel— frustration, anger, despair—panic was the strongest.

Professor Yori spoke blandly, seemingly resigned to the suggested course of action. "I'll arrange a meeting for the lunch hour, but right now" —Professor Yori raised a hand to Phoebe, who had been forgotten in the exchange—"Cadet Pope should be escorted back to her dorm. And if you'll excuse me, I've got the Shaper parent of both our missing Hyphas to call."

"I'd like to be on those calls," Afua said in a tone that got no objections from the headmaster.

"Kat," he said, looking over at Professor Koon, "how about you come with me? You should get some rest."

Minutes later, Yelena returned with Phoebe to her dorm. It was still the early hours of dawn. All was quiet. The building was pearled with morning dew. After seeing to it that Phoebe entered her room, Yelena went outside to keep guard. Phoebe slid under her covers, but didn't sleep. She grabbed her tomato pillow and held it to her chest. Even thoughts of Colten couldn't ease her troubled mind. What was it that she wasn't remembering? Phoebe closed her eyes. For a fraction of a second she thought she'd remembered something important but dismissed it. The memory had been of a male teacher drinking from a flask. Hardly a security threat. As fatigue wove its way through Phoebe's body, three things turned over in her head: someone had taken Mariko and Lewis; she and Scott were next; and, above all else, she needed to be at that faculty meeting. If anyone could figure out who was behind the kidnappings, she could, by reading everyone's emotions. Now the only question was, how would she get in?

🍁 FIFTEEN

The minor notes of a violin melody floated up to Phoebe as she leaned over the boathouse balcony railing, her camera at eye level. Below her, on the lake, a silver-haired man sat in a boat, his wooden instrument tucked under his chin, drawing a bow back and forth across the strings with even, measured strokes. Mist rose around him in thin, layered sheets, cut into strips by the early morning sunlight piercing through, providing an almost mystical setting for Phoebe's photo shoot.

When a body leaned next to Phoebe, she didn't need to cast a sideways glance to know who it was. She'd seen Scott standing at the shore, throwing rocks into the lake. Their eyes had met through her lens and they had stared at each other for a moment, the strain of the previous night apparent to both of them.

"Hope I didn't keep you waiting too long, Gorgeous," Scott said, chuckling without humor as Phoebe slowly lowered her camera and looked at him. Up close she saw that his eyes were bloodshot, his demeanor weary. "For whatever reason, Pope, being near water helps to relieve my mind and right now—"

"It's all jammed up," Phoebe finished.

Scott nodded wearily and lit a cigarette. "Who's the old man?"

"First chair violinist for the Boston Symphony," Phoebe said. "He rowed crew here and I thought pairing the 'now' and the 'then' would make an interesting photo."

"I don't know how you do it, Pope," Scott said, exhaling a stream of smoke and watching her closely as she changed lenses.

"Do what?" she said airily, most of her attention focused on her subject and camera's mechanisms.

Scott didn't answer at once; he'd turned to gaze out at the lake. "Function," he said quietly. "How can you even do this assignment when . . ." Scott didn't have to finish his thought.

"Because I need to keep busy!" Phoebe said, her voice suddenly tremulous. Her hands shook so much her camera jostled. "I can't just sit here wondering if they're dead!"

To Phoebe's surprise, Scott pulled her into a one-armed hug that warmed her right down to her toes. "I'm scared too, Pope" he said. "I'm more spooked than I've ever been in my life. Stayed up all night thinking it could have been me. . . ."

"I know," Phoebe said in a muffled voice, closing her eyes, then opening them when she realized that the music from the lake had stopped. She stepped out from under Scott's arm and waved down to the violinist who stared up at her, a mild frown on his face.

"Are we all done, young lady?" he called out to her politely.

"Yes. Sorry! I'll be right down."

After thanking the violinist and seeing him off, Phoebe walked with Scott in the general direction of the dining hall.

"So he was crazy enough to agree to play in the lake, but not quite crazy enough to use his own violin," Scott said smirking and indicating the black GREEN LANE MUSIC case Phoebe had tucked under her arm.

Phoebe gave a halfhearted laugh. "No. He wasn't going to risk his Stradivarius." After a minute or so of silence, Phoebe said slowly, "Do you want to talk about it?"

Scott pressed a finger to his right temple. "I'm kinda spent for the moment. I got nothing left." He stopped walking. "In fact, I think I'm going to skip breakfast and—" Scott broke off, his gaze having wandered behind them. "And, it looks like they called for reinforcements."

Phoebe glanced over her shoulder. Two guys, dressed in Green Lane uniforms were walking a measured distance behind them. Although they did look almost young enough to pass for students, their serious yet graceful demeanor was all Blackcoat.

Scott gave a brief, hollow laugh. "I guess Mariko's request for hot male mentors was heard after all."

"Ha. That's right . . ." Phoebe trailed off, her mind going back in time.

"Listen, Pope," said Scott seriously, already walking away from her. "I'm tired now, but come find me later if you want to talk."

Phoebe nodded absently, watching as one of the new Blackcoats turned to follow Scott.

Over the course of breakfast, a group of girls roved around the dining hall distributing green fliers. From where she sat, Phoebe could see that hers was the only table not to receive one. Before she could think twice about it, an aproned Hayley appeared at her side, her arms streaked in flour, her hair restrained by a hairnet.

"Oh, thank Osiah and Gavya you're okay," Hayley said in an emotional whisper, looking tearful.

"What's the matter?" Phoebe said, suddenly alarmed.

Hayley wiped her hands on her apron and sat down hard. "Which two were taken?" she said.

"How do you—" Phoebe quickly fished out her Privaque. "How do you know?"

"Liam," Hayley said, breathlessly. Then, in a rush of words, "I checked the blog after grabbing my shoes from the floating gym, and it was all about The Four. I've been going nuts all morning. You weren't picking up your phone. You weren't in your room. And when Cyn said she hadn't seen you in a while, I looked everywhere I could think to look for you. I practically begged the kitchen folks to let me help them bake so I wouldn't lose it. . . ."

When Hayley paused for a breath, Phoebe said, "Wait, what did the blog say?"

"Why weren't you answering your phone?" Hayley asked, as if she hadn't heard Phoebe.

"I didn't take it with me to my photo shoot—"

Hayley took a napkin from the table and blew her nose loudly into it.

"So what did Liam say?" Phoebe pressed.

"He said that he had it on good authority that two of the four prophecy targets had been kidnapped last night. And that the Blackcoats were no closer to solving how the kidnapping had happened right under their whiskers—so who was it?"

Phoebe made Hayley take a few calming breaths, then quietly filled her in on everything that had happened the night before, finishing with the theory of a traitor.

Hayley looked at Phoebe, unconvinced. "A traitor?" She shook her head fervently. "Loyalty is in our DNA."

Phoebe shrugged. "The Blackcoats are convinced of it."

"And you still don't remember what you might have been looking at?"

Phoebe shook her head morosely.

Hayley pushed her glasses up the bridge of her nose, grabbed a glass of water from Phoebe's tray, and glanced around the dining hall, thinking. Midway through a sip, she choked and shot to her feet. "Colten—coming this way," she hissed.

"What?" Phoebe said puzzled. "He's out of town for the next few days for—" she broke off spotting him herself. Colten was not in uniform. He wore a leather coat zipped over a pair of dark jeans. His blazing eyes searched the room and found Phoebe. He gazed at her for a moment, and then moved quickly toward her.

"There's no way I'm letting him see me like this," Hayley said, raising her flour-covered hands. "We'll talk more in class." And head down, she scurried off toward the kitchen as Colten, who didn't seem to notice Hayley fleeing, arrived at the table.

Colten pulled out a chair, spun it around, and straddled it in one seamless motion. "How are you?" he said. The seriousness of his voice startled Phoebe. His features held tension that she couldn't interpret.

"I'm good," Phoebe said slowly. "How are you? Why are you here?" She saw his eyes begin to narrow and she brought a hand to her mouth. "You didn't get the part?"

Colten's mood shifted then, all of the tension gone from his face. "Oh, I got it," he said with a smirk. "I had a big incentive to get it, remember?"

"Congrats." Phoebe looked at him, confused; the humor in the set of Colten's mouth did not extend to his eyes. Again she wanted to read his emotions, but she stopped herself. Whatever had him on edge was a private matter; she wouldn't trespass.

"Sorry . . . I just thought you'd be gone for the next few days."

Colten reached out a hand and tousled Phoebe's hair. "Not happy to see me?" he asked playfully. *On the contrary,* Phoebe thought. Given what had just happened, she was more than happy to see Colten. She thought again how he had a way of repelling the madness of her other life even as it threatened to devour her. His company brought comfort, a gentleness that washed over her.

Phoebe ran a hand through her hair, searching for any scar-concealing strands that Colten may have unknowingly moved out of place. She wondered if she would one day get to a point where she could wear her hair in a retro ponytail like she used to, before the accident.

"I am happy to see you," Phoebe said, smiling and poking him lightly in the chest. "I'm just surprised to see you."

"The audition ended up just being a formality, and afterward I decided all other business could wait." Colten held her gaze and smiled, this one drifting to his eyes. "So we're still on with the line coaching, right?"

"Sure. When would you like to start?"

"Lunch?" Colten looked hopeful.

Phoebe shook her head. "Can't. I have a meeting but—"

"How about tonight, co-study hour?" he said quickly with an intensity she didn't expect.

Phoebe felt her hearts hammering. Co-study was the only two-hour stretch of time where members of the opposite sex were allowed in each other's dorm rooms. "Sure," she said, trying not to sound too excited. "If you don't mind my roommate, we can meet—"

"—in my room," Colten said. "No roommate. No problem."

Now Phoebe's hearts were practically spluttering, her mind glossing over the concept of having no roommate and fixating on the idea of her being alone with Colten in his bedroom.

"Okay," she said softly. Phoebe had begun to grin foolishly, and to avoid Colten's eyes while she tried to rein it in, she let her gaze wander about the dining room. What she saw next promptly yanked the grin from her face. To their right, Karli was cutting a path through the crowd toward the table, holding a stack of green fliers to her chest.

Irked at the thought of being made to feel invisible again in front of Colten, Phoebe reached for her tray and said, "I should go. I have some photos to drop off at the *Gazette* before class."

"But I haven't told you my room number yet," Colten said with a tilt of his head.

At that precise moment, Karli, who had arrived in time to catch what Colten had said, looked at Phoebe, bewildered and more than a little annoyed.

Momentarily forgetting Karli, Phoebe asked, "Oh, right. What is it?"

"Room 205. Clay House," Karli said, breathlessly, looking flustered as she dropped her stack of fliers on the table with a dull thud.

Colten clenched his jaw and kept his eyes on Phoebe. "That's right."

"So Colten," Karli said brightly. "I—"

"One second." Colten's annoyed tone cut Karli off. He took out a ballpoint pen from the pocket of his leather jacket, wrote down a number on a napkin and handed it to Phoebe. "Call me if anything comes up," he said, smiling.

"Sure," Phoebe said, trying to appear casual. "See you later—Oh," she said, a flush rising in her cheeks. "Thanks for the present."

Colten leaned back in his chair and grinned. "Hope it's getting great use."

"It is." Phoebe's flush deepened. She gathered up her belongings and gave Karli a polite nod of acknowledgment, a hint of triumph in her expression. Karli didn't smile back. Phoebe couldn't help noticing that her mood was further improved by the disbelieving look on Karli's perfectly made up face.

On her way out of the dining hall, Phoebe picked up one of the green fliers that had been dropped. Printed on it was a picture of the planet Earth as a disco ball. Beneath this, scripted words said:

Come be Green at the Fall Enviroball.

Sponsored by Colten's Cuties.

Proceeds to benefit Today's Climate Tomorrow

A favorite charity of our very own environmentally friendly star!

Phoebe wondered which annoyed her more: Karli's abuse of Colten's Cuties as a tool to get to Colten, or the fact that Fall Enviroball was actually a clever idea. The thought that had been haunting her returned; she had been deliberately skipped in the delivery of fliers. Phoebe crumpled the glossy sheet of paper and focused on her upcoming study date with Colten. But even in her renewed anticipation, questions about Colten began to coalesce in a small part of Phoebe's mind. Why had he been so agitated when he'd first arrived? If he'd landed the part and business in L.A. was fine, then why the moody demeanor? And his immediate concern about her. . . . It was almost as if Colten had some eerie sixth sense that something had happened. Phoebe ran a hand through her hair. Maybe she was underestimating how frazzled she looked from last night's chaos. She shook it all off. After all, she was consciously choosing not to read Colten's emotions. But emotional reading wasn't the same as mind reading. *Perhaps that's my problem*, Phoebe thought. *I'm always reading too much into things*.

 SIXTEEN

"I need you to help me with something," Phoebe said to Hayley as they plopped into seats in the back of Tactical Bird Song. She'd spent her morning classes barely hearing her lectures, brainstorming possible ways to access the faculty meeting that was happening in the next hour, but to no avail. Perhaps with Hayley's help, an idea would come to mind.

"What I want to know is why you even want to be there?" Hayley said.

With a twinge of guilt, Phoebe said in a low voice, "Just want to see if there's anything the mentors haven't been telling us Hyphas." It bothered Phoebe that she couldn't be entirely truthful with Hayley about what she intended to do once inside, but there was no way she could say, *You know how someone's trying to kill me? Well I'm hoping to use my ability to read emotions to figure out who here is helping them.*

Hayley thought for a moment. "Can't you just hang in the hallway and stretch your eavesdropping range?"

Phoebe shook her head. "Privaques, remember?"

"Right. Forgot. Well, we need a plan then," Hayley said, and before she could say more, a tired-looking Professor Koon came rushing into the room, her hair matted to one side as though she'd just woken up. Phoebe didn't need to read her emotions to know that the woman was still shaken from the previous night.

Professor Koon spoke, her tone uncharacteristically flat, "I've been listening to the homework recordings you turned in,"—she waved a small digital recorder in her hand—"and so far the problem I'm hearing from some of you is an issue with the note order in your whistle patterns."

"For example," she said, reaching the front of the class. "When question number five asked you to whistle a pattern for: 'Help, I'm injured in the north east side of the forest.'" She paused and looked around with a raised eyebrow. "Someone, who shall remain nameless, whistled this pattern on his recording."

Professor Koon pressed play on the digital recorder and a short melodious whistle filled the air. At once, a few people in the class burst into laughter.

"Anyone care to translate?"

"Help, I'm injured and I need a girlfriend, stat!" a boy said from the back.

"Suffice it to say," Professor Koon said, "that will not get you rescued." More laughter. "It's all funny now, folks," Professor Koon continued. "But some of the best laid plans can be easily ruined if a key communication is just one note off."

A light went on in Phoebe's head as Professor Koon asked the class to pair off to practice translating the instructions she would shortly be giving them.

Tugging at Hayley's sleeve, Phoebe bowed her head and whispered, "I think we should hustle out of here after class and try and beat the teachers to the lounge. You can be the hallway look out while I find a place to hide.

We can use bird calls to communicate any problems," she said, finishing just as Professor Koon converted to a hawk, perched herself on top of the table, and whistled her first pattern to the class.

Hayley sat still for a moment, considering. "I like it. But what if there's someone in the lounge when we get there?"

Phoebe hadn't thought of that. She shrugged. "I guess we'll have to wing it."

Hayley giggled. "You said 'wing it,'" she said, giggling again.

Phoebe bit her lip to keep from busting out laughing. She and Hayley put their heads together and began translating Professor Koon's note patterns as well as discussing ones that they could use later. Thirty minutes into the lesson an urgent thought came to Phoebe and she poked Hayley in the arm.

"Ouch," Hayley hissed.

"Sorry," Phoebe said. "Didn't mean to poke so hard but we've got a problem."

"What?"

"We can't use bird calls. The profs will understand what we're saying."

"Crap. You're right." Hayley's eyes narrowed in thought. "Eighties tunes," she said.

"Huh?"

"We'll assign meaning to some random tunes. It will serve the same purpose."

"Let's go with Madonna," Phoebe suggested. Hayley grinned her agreement and began writing a list.

The low whistled notes of Madonna's "Material Girl" told Phoebe to stay put because the coast was not clear. She was leaning against the wall next to a portrait of a distinguished SIS graduate from 1977, nervously looking up and down the hallway. Hayley came strolling out of the faculty lounge shaking her head. "There's only one professor in there and he's parked in front of a big food platter stuffing his face," she said. "I tried to distract him so you could slip in, but he kicked me out."

Phoebe let out an anxious breath. She and Hayley had pushed their way through teeming hallways to arrive at the faculty lounge in good time, hoping against all hope that they would find it empty.

"Well, he won't be alone for long," Phoebe said. She cast a wary eye around. A few male students emerged from a nearby study room, laughing loudly among themselves as they walked past Phoebe and Hayley. A couple of them gave the girls a second glance.

Thinking, Hayley watched the group disappear down the hall. "If we could only get him to—I have a plan!" she exclaimed. And to Phoebe's astonishment, she took off at a run. "Wait here," Hayley called over her shoulder.

Hayley came back two minutes later, out of breath, but looking pleased with herself.

"So what's the plan?" Phoebe asked eagerly.

Hayley, who kept glancing anxiously in the direction from which she'd just come, said, "You'll see." Suddenly, she nudged Phoebe. "Here they are."

"Here who are?"

"Your way in," Hayley said, smiling conspiratorially at Phoebe who looked around uncertainly. Sprinting up the hallway were two boys, both with wide grins plastered across their faces. Phoebe recognized the one carrying a soccer ball under his arm; he was the red team captain from the Full Moon on the Field game—the scrawny boy Hayley had called sexy. His much shorter, extremely freckled companion seemed to smile especially widely at Phoebe.

"You know what to do, right Paul?" Hayley said to the team captain once they'd reached them.

Paul's lips curled. "We're on it. And you'll make good on your part?" He looked from Hayley to Phoebe. Phoebe smiled and tried to look as though she knew what was going on.

"Yeah, yeah we're all good," Hayley said, quickly. "Let's get this show going."

Phoebe was thoroughly confused, but allowed herself to be swept away by Hayley. "We can watch from here," Hayley said, motioning Phoebe into an empty room across the hall from the faculty lounge. There, they stood still, watching the boys through a crack between the door's edge and the paneled frame.

Suddenly, a burst of light and energy filled the hall. The two boys had converted into leopards, one a shade of silver with gold spots and the other white. They began whipping the ball back and forth between them when the faculty lounge door swung open and a rotund man with a bald spot in the middle of an otherwise thick head of black hair, stormed out.

"No conversion allowed in the hallways!" he said, waggling a hand in which he held a half-eaten sandwich. The boys immediately returned to their human forms and gazed at their feet, both grinning guiltily. Glancing from his watch to the boys, the professor looked conflicted. "You second-year cadets should know better," he said taking a bite from his sandwich. "Come with me. If I let this go unpunished, you'll never take this rule seriously." They marched off behind the professor, and when they passed the room where Phoebe and Hayley stood hidden, the shorter boy looked over his shoulder and winked.

Phoebe stared at Hayley, completely nonplussed. "You got them in trouble?" Phoebe knew that converting in the halls, if caught, was worth a weekend or two of detention.

Hayley looked guiltily at Phoebe and shrugged her shoulders. "They were glad to do it."

A thought struck Phoebe. "What did you promise them?"

"I said that we would be their dates to that Enviroball everyone's talking about."

It took Phoebe a moment to process what Hayley had done. "What?"

"Hey," Hayley said, opening the classroom door to confirm that the hallway was still empty. "When I said I had a plan, I didn't guarantee that you'd like it. Now get in there."

Phoebe knew she didn't have time to dwell on Hayley's methods and hurried into the lounge while Hayley stood watch outside the door. Inside, Phoebe saw that the room contained sofas, chairs, and many unusually large cushions scattered about the floor. Several silver perches hung down from exposed rafters, and Phoebe found herself distracted by the arrangement of the lounge.

When Hayley's whistled "Holiday" echoed in the hallway telling Phoebe that professors were approaching, she frantically began looking for someplace to hide. She opened a coat closet, finding it too stuffed to fit another coat, let alone a person. Hayley's whistle came again with the message that teachers were halfway to the door. Panic stirred in Phoebe chest, and that's when she saw it.

At the back of the lounge, an unusual wood-slat storage bench stood flush against the wall. Long and tall, its slats were spaced far enough apart to conceal someone while giving them a view of the room. Phoebe hurried over to the bench, lifted the lid, and crouched into a space that was bigger than she'd imagined it to be. She had barely pulled the top down when the door opened.

Hearts pounding, Phoebe watched as teachers slowly filed in. A few immediately converted into their bird form and flew up to the overhead perches. Phoebe saw Montclaire enter with Professor Elmore who took leave of their conversation and melted into a navy jaguar and curled himself on a floor cushion. Others stood against walls or settled themselves on the various chairs. It suddenly occurred to Phoebe that her bench was a seat when a wire-thin male professor began backing his bony bottom toward it, coming dangerously close to sitting. Thankfully, after noting the distance from the bench to the rest of the teachers, the man changed his mind.

As Phoebe breathed a sigh of relief, Professor Yori strode through the door with Afua, Deborah-Anna, and Yelena just behind him.

"Afternoon," Professor Yori said grimly. He stared up and around at the assembled crowd and a hush fell over the faculty. "By now, you have all read the daily email informing you of student absences. And you have probably noticed that no reason was listed for Mariko Higashi and Lewis Baker." Phoebe found herself drawing a breath along with the headmaster. "It saddens me to inform you that they were kidnapped during last night's Vigo drill."

At first a protracted silence hovered as the headmaster's words sank in. Then, those who had converted returned to their human forms, voices tumbling over one another as everyone tried to speak at once. Phoebe opened her mental gate then, and began skimming through emotions, searching for anything suspicious. Not surprising, the teachers were fearful, horrified, sad, and on edge. And then Phoebe began sensing the faintest trace of something darker as well, but the feeling was too low for her to pinpoint its exact location.

"Please, please," Professor Yori said, raising both hands in a calming gesture. "Let's try and settle down. We will try to get to all of your questions—"

"We?" Professor Elmore said, interrupting.

Professor Yori glanced over at Afua, Yelena, and Deborah-Anna. "These women," he said, "that you've come to know as our visiting scholars . . . are Blackcoats. At this point, I defer to them for the rest of this meeting."

Gasps of astonishment erupted. Phoebe was struck by a growing emotion that she couldn't ignore. It was hard, angry, and vengeful. Phoebe tried to hone in on the person behind the hatred as Deborah-Anna distributed Privaque clips among the faculty and explained its purpose.

"I want to first assure you," Afua started, "that the school will not shut down in the face of this Vigo threat. All teaching and activities must carry on."

"Is this connected to the soccer game attack?" one teacher asked, starting a frenzy of questions.

The Blackcoats talked of the prophecy, Alexori, and the ongoing investigation to an increasingly agitated crowd. Soon Phoebe's head began to hurt from the strain of reading that many emotions at once. The experience of it was overwhelming, but she had expected that. The most she'd ever tried before was two at a time, and even then it had been tiring. Determined to make the best of it, Phoebe tried to keep herself open and filter through this field of volatile emotions. Her father had told her that in time she'd grow to be able to shoulder more, and there was no time like the present to test her ability. When talk turned to whether or not to inform the student body about the kidnappings, Afua immediately snapped at the group, "It should go without saying that discretion is paramount."

A wiry man with graying sideburns argued back, "Wouldn't informing them allow for vigilance as they move about both campuses?"

"That vigilance needs to come from you all. We don't want to induce panic and confusion—that would be even more dangerous," Afua said.

"Besides, Loren," Professor Yori said, stepping in. "Fear from the soccer attack has only just faded from their minds and to tell them about the kidnapping would bring it all up again."

When Afua ended the meeting by saying, "We're following a strong lead in these kidnappings and will keep you apprised," Phoebe was struck, suddenly, by a powerful spike of hatred. She immediately latched onto it and followed its strong vibration like a route on a map. Her father had taught her that in interpersonal relationships, emotions formed a web of connector lines between people. What you felt about someone created an emotional link between you, which grew stronger or weakened as your feelings changed. Phoebe's hearts quickened as she traced the hatred directed at the Blackcoats back to the faculty member who had released it. . . .

Phoebe almost couldn't breathe as Professor Yori dismissed the group and the faculty slowly began to leave the room. She felt sick. She saw now, with a certainty, that the Blackcoats had been right; a traitor moved among them at the Campus Below. And she knew who it was. The question now was how could she make anyone believe her when she couldn't tell them how she knew? On Hayley's "Lucky Star" whistle that the hallway was clear, Phoebe quickly slipped out of the bench, and walked out the lounge door, bracing herself for what she had to do.

❦ SEVENTEEN

"This one says, 'happy to see you'," Hayley said holding up the loose gray sweater Phoebe had chosen. "And these ones"—she thrust two V-necks at Phoebe—"say 'aren't you happy to see me'. You gotta advertise your assets!"

Phoebe snorted, and then saw that Hayley was serious. "It's just study hour," she said nervously.

"And you want him to study you. All hour."

Phoebe rolled her eyes.

It had been difficult for Phoebe to tell Hayley that her time in the faculty lounge had yielded no new information. Hoping to absolve herself of the sin of omission, Phoebe had told Hayley about her co-study date with Colten. Now Phoebe focused on the two sweaters Hayley had selected for the occasion, and pointed.

An hour later, Phoebe made her way to Clay House feeling comfortably pretty in a blue cashmere sweater over a pair of khaki cargo pants, all of the tangles brushed out of her hair. It was only now, as she stood staring at Colten's door, that Phoebe sensed the presence of the male Blackcoat behind her. Her face burned at the thought of having no privacy. She turned to face him. The Blackcoat looked upon Phoebe with knowing eyes and then faded into the shadows of an alcove.

Once he was out of view, Phoebe exhaled. Her mind was overloaded and she had no trouble admitting to herself that this time with Colten was something she needed. She hesitated at the door, and then knocked. It swung open immediately, catching Phoebe off guard.

Colten, dressed casual in a soft gray t-shirt and black sweatpants, still looked utterly handsome. Laughter shone in the vibrant green eyes that held Phoebe's gaze as she took a startled breath and said softly, "Hi."

"Hi. Come on in." Colten took hold of Phoebe's hands and pulled her into his room. He closed the door behind them and instantly Phoebe felt the unwelcome swell of insecurity. She tried to push it away, but it was hard when she could feel Colten watching her attentively.

"Wow. Must be nice to get sweet perks," Phoebe said, noticing the small, beige-tiled kitchen tucked in a corner.

"This is usually a faculty studio," Colten said behind her. "The guy who used to live here got married and needed more space."

Phoebe could feel Colten's eyes on her. She walked around surveying the rest of the place so that he wouldn't see her nervousness. The room was spacious, yet painfully minimalist with no thought given to any form of personal decoration. A red duvet-covered bed was set against the windowed wall, and a rectangular coffee table, doubling as a receptacle for books and his baseball cap, stood in the middle of the room as the only real decorative piece of furniture.

"I guess you weren't planning to stay long when you moved in," Phoebe said, joking.

He smiled, continuing to track her movement in the room. "I keep most of my things at my suite."

Phoebe raised an eyebrow. "Suite? This is a suite."

Colten laughed. "The studio got me a place in a hotel downtown for the Boston shoot. It's mine for the year so I make use of it."

"Why even stay here then?" Phoebe said.

"It's closer to the action," he said, grinning.

Phoebe suddenly noticed that there was nowhere to sit other than the bed. Following her gaze, Colten's grin widened.

"I haven't entertained anyone up here yet," he said, chuckling. He walked over to his coffee table, picked up his baseball cap, and put it on. "I can clear these books if you don't mind sitting here."

"Is this how you get girls into your bed, by having no other seating alternative?" Phoebe asked with wide unassuming eyes, secretly not believing her own daring.

Colten laughed, but Phoebe could see that he was also a bit taken aback. "I never thought of it that way, but it is a good plan. I'll have to remember that for when the next girl comes over," he said, sounding cocky but with a feigned innocent look that made it charming.

Phoebe narrowed her eyes, making a sour face at him, and tried her best to fight the smile tugging at her closed lips. She was feeling much more at ease now.

"I can turn the bed into a futon if you'd like," he said with a sincere smile.

"It's okay. I'm fine with sitting on your bed," she said casually.

His eyes roamed her face trying to interpret her expression. She tried to keep it unreadable.

"Okay, then," he said, equally casual. "Take a seat."

Colten's duvet was so thick that it practically swallowed Phoebe's body whole when she hoisted herself onto his bed. She let herself fall back with her feet dangling just at the edge of the wooden frame. Phoebe stared at the ceiling half expecting—or maybe hoping—to feel the bed sag under Colten's weight. When it didn't after a moment, she sat up flushed. Seated on the coffee table across from her, Colten watched her with a mix of amusement and fascination. He smiled, "I'm glad you're here."

"Me too," she said, almost in a whisper. Phoebe retracted her outstretched legs one at a time and scrambled her body backward until she felt her back meet the wall. She sat with the duvet pooled around her and studied Colten. His body seemed at ease but his eyes had an intense gleam to them. Nervous, Phoebe absentmindedly wrung her fingers in the softness of the duvet.

"So . . . will this new movie conflict with the one you're shooting now in Boston?"

"No," Colton said. "The director agreed to work around my *Taylor Hawk* schedule."

"What's the name of this new movie?"

"*Courting Caroline*," Colten said, standing. He walked over to his backpack and pulled two thick binders out. He handed one to her and returned to his seat.

Phoebe smiled mockingly. "That doesn't sound very Taylor Hawk-guns-blazing to me."

"It isn't," he said with a smirk.

"Why the departure?"

"Something about the story drew me to it, and"—he paused and smiled mischievously at her—"I thought I'd take a stab at a movie that you would actually go see."

Phoebe felt the flush crawling up her neck quickly spread to her face. She'd almost forgotten that she'd confessed to never having seen a *Taylor Hawk* movie. She lowered her eyes, her fingers playing with the edges of the script. "What's it about?" she quickly asked, avoiding his eyes.

"It's a period piece set in London about two people falling in love under false pretenses," he said. Phoebe looked up in time to catch Colten's ardent gaze. "The girl is born into wealth and expected to marry the same, but all the suitors in her parents' circle are pretentious and boring. She decides to dress down like a common girl and slip into town to find Mr. Right.

"Meanwhile the groundskeeper's son, who has loved her from afar for years, decides to spend what little money he has to buy the best suit he can get to pass himself off as a suitor. She crashes into him in town on a night she has snuck out. There are sparks between them as they exchange apologies and—"

"But doesn't she know who he is, being the groundskeeper's son?" Phoebe interrupted.

Colten shook his head, smiling. "She doesn't recognize him because she's never paid attention to him. So she's surprised to meet a wealthy man who is down to earth and even more surprised that he would be taken by a girl with no social standing."

Phoebe was intrigued. "What happens?"

"You'll have to help me with the script to find out." Phoebe made a face and Colten chuckled. "Be happy you're getting a sneak preview!" Then, his face suddenly became serious. "What do you think about all that anyway?"

"About what?"

"Do you think it's possible for two people to fall in love even if there are lies between them?" He looked past her unseeingly and Phoebe found herself grateful for that; her body had stiffened and she hoped he hadn't noticed. Half her existence was a secret.

She said finally, "I guess it depends on the situation."

Colten's eyes snapped back to Phoebe's. "Like how?"

"Well, if one person doesn't want the other person to know that they snore, that's minor."

Colten laughed darkly. "And what do you consider major?"

"I guess if someone's hiding that they're an axe murderer, that's major." Phoebe tried to laugh, watching Colten closely. And when he said nothing, she said stupidly, "You're not an axe murderer, are you?"

"Why?" Colten raised an eyebrow, looking at her curiously. "You're not falling for me, are you?" Phoebe made an involuntary choking sound and stared down at the script she'd been squeezing. Her mind was screaming, *Yes, I could be falling for you. Quite easily and quite foolishly, seeing that I barely know you.* But Phoebe knew that to even consider admitting that to someone who could have his pick of any girl would be a careless move with her hearts.

In the time it had taken Phoebe to have that thought, the silence had grown awkward. She fumbled for something to say and was rescued by a knock on the door. A shaggy-haired guy poked his head into the room and gave Colten a wide grin. Phoebe recognized him as a young math teacher, Kwady Parker, who had come to Green Lane straight out of college and was popular among the students Above.

"Just doing my rounds to make sure my co-stud visitors are where they're supposed to be," he said. He looked over at Phoebe and then glanced down at the clipboard in his hands. "Ms. Pope, I take it?"

"Yes," Phoebe squeaked, feeling as if she'd been busted for some wrongdoing.

"Good." Turning his eyes to Colten he said, "I'm sure I can count on you to make sure the lady leaves at the appropriate time?"

Colten nodded and then Mr. Parker was gone.

Phoebe tapped a finger against the script and said, "We should start since they don't give us much time."

"I just autographed a couple things for Parker's girlfriend's niece," Colten said. He squeezed the bill of his baseball cap and grinned. "If we go a bit past the two hour limit . . . I'm sure it will be okay."

Lucky for you, Phoebe thought, knowing very well there was a Blackcoat waiting out in the hall who wouldn't be as flexible.

After hesitating for a moment, Colten made his way over to the bed and sat down, situating his body the farthest away from Phoebe that it could get. "You'll be reading the part of Caroline," he said. "And we'll start on page seventy five."

Phoebe quickly turned the pages, happy to not be looking at Colten. "Why there?"

"It's the first scene we're filming."

Phoebe cleared her throat and began to read out loud. "Busy downtown street, London. Night—"

"You don't have to read that part. That's the scene heading."

Phoebe started over, finding the place where Caroline started to speak. Clearing her throat again, she said, "'Why don't you ever speak of your family, Richard?'"

"'Because there is nothing original about them. They live in a large estate in the North and content themselves with keeping up with their social calendar. I find it all quite a bore, actually.'"

Phoebe laughed. "Sorry," she said quickly and then carried on. "'Do you find yourself in London for business then?'"

"'Yes, the business of finding a wife. I was sent to call on Lady Appleton. Do you know of her?'"

Phoebe laughed again.

"What?" Colten said, breaking character.

"It's just funny because obviously he knows that she knows of Lady Appleton since she is Lady Appleton."

"Yes. That's the point," Colten said, nudging her leg teasingly with his.

"I promise not to laugh again," Phoebe said, laughing. "It's just listening to you speak with a British accent is—um—cute."

Colten smiled and pointed at the script.

Phoebe continued. "'Yes, I do know of Lady Appleton. I hear she's quite the delight.'"

"'Surely you are being kind. Ladies in such circles tend to concern themselves with their figure, their social standing, and whether the man they marry can keep them clothed in the latest lace from Paris.'"

"'That is a broad generalization on your part, if I may say so, sir. Don't judge the Lady until you have spent quality time in her company!'" Phoebe found herself getting into her role, taking on the prim and proper attitude she imagined for Caroline.

"'But to meet her, could mean fulfilling my obligation to marry when I so much prefer your company.'"

As the first hour of their study time rolled into the second, and the story of Richard and Caroline progressed, Phoebe found herself fully absorbed in it. In the time she'd been pretending to be Caroline and navigating through Caroline's conflicts, she had not thought once about her own current life situation.

"It's your line," Colten said, prompting Phoebe.

"Right. Sorry." Phoebe lowered her eyes to the script. They were almost at the end. "'You seem unlike yourself tonight, Richard. Are you not well?'" Phoebe continued.

"'There is a truth about me that I need to tell you.'"

"'It is interesting you say that, for there are truths that I, too, need to tell you,'" Phoebe said. "'And I insist on speaking first, for I fear mine is a deception of the worst kind.'"

Colten was suddenly on his feet. "'My love,'" he said, grabbing Phoebe's hand and pulling her off the bed, causing her to almost drop the script. He gazed into her eyes in a way that made her breath catch. "'I implore you to let me speak first for it is I who is of the worst kind.'"

Phoebe collected herself, cleared her throat and continued. "'Just know that whatever it is, you have my heart.'"

"'Do I?'" Colten moved closer to Phoebe, lowered his head and whispered in her ear. "'Do I really have your hearts?'"

Phoebe felt the color drain out of her. Could she have really heard Colten say "hearts?" *That's ridiculous; there was no way* . . . Perhaps in this moment, when her mind was jumbled by the lack of space between her body and his, she'd misunderstood the word he'd spoken. Phoebe bit her bottom lip, took a deep breath, and then asked faintly, "What did you say?"

Colten did not reply. Instead he pressed his body hard against Phoebe's and backed her against the wall. All thoughts were immediately lost as, bracing his hands on either side of her head, Colten leaned his forehead against Phoebe's and gazed into her eyes with enough heat to warm a small winter town. Phoebe, who was in danger of losing control of her knees, said the first thing that came to her mind and immediately regretted it: "Is this what the script calls for?"

There was a small beat before Colten dropped his arms and pulled away, his eyes conflicted. "I'm sorry. I forgot myself." His expression was strangely dark and he swore under his breath as though he had committed some serious transgression. He removed his baseball cap and ran a lazy hand through his hair before putting it back on.

Phoebe was thankful for the space. It allowed her to recover her breath. And feeling like the growing silence required something to fill it with, could only come up with, "Um, no problem." But in truth, it was a problem. She had imagined this moment several different ways in her mind, but now as she stared at Colten who was now staring at her with a distant expression from the edge of his bed, she knew she had ruined it. She felt her body getting hot again, and she knew it was from the sheer humiliation of acting like a prude in front of Colten. If painless spontaneous combustion was possible at that moment, she would have welcomed it as a quick exit strategy. She hoped against all hope that he couldn't see the rapidly rising flush.

Phoebe felt the need to say something, so she said, "How do you do it?"

"Do what?" he said, sounding detached.

"Kiss people you don't know?" Phoebe kept her back pressed against the wall.

"It's just part of the job—I get paid to kiss beautiful girls," Colten said nonchalantly. "But there's nothing romantic about it," he added quickly.

"I couldn't do it." Phoebe avoided his gaze, surprised by a sudden jealousy stirring within her at the thought of Colten kissing other girls, but then pushed it aside knowing perfectly well she had just ruined her own opportunity.

Colten surveyed her with curious eyes. "Why is that?"

"I can't kiss just anyone," Phoebe said, squeezing the script in her hands. "If I'm going to have someone's mouth on mine, I need to know that I like the things that come out of it: thoughts, opinions, ideas. And that takes a little time. . . ." Could she sound any more like a prude? She swore at herself internally, already dreading recounting this speech to Hayley later.

Colten absorbed the sight of Phoebe standing motionless. He opened his mouth to say something when a voice in the hallway called for the end of co-study. Phoebe decided then and there that she should leave before she felt even more out of her depth. She placed the script on the coffee table and turned for the door.

"What are you doing a week from Wednesday night?" Colten asked abruptly, standing.

"Nothing."

"Great. You can be my date for my movie premiere then."

Phoebe stared at him and Colten began to slowly chuckle at the stunned expression on her face. Just then a voice in the hall yelled, "Now folks, visitors out!"

"Well?" Colten asked.

Phoebe watched a grin stretch across Colten's face and knew that it was in response to the idiot smile she now had on hers. Of course, she wanted to go with him to his premiere. What normal girl in her right mind wouldn't? But then the unbidden thought of the Blackcoat waiting outside to escort her to her dorm brought Phoebe back to her senses; she was a prisoner of her Shaper life. The Blackcoats would never allow her to step outside the campus gates in the midst of the crisis.

Phoebe closed her eyes and tried to think of the best way she could tell Colten that she wouldn't be able to go. All she could manage was a muffled, "I can't."

Across from her, Colten wore an expression that hovered somewhere between confusion and disappointment. "Can't or don't want to?" he said, scuffing the floor with his bare feet.

Phoebe's voice came out a bit hoarse. "Can't." She lowered her eyes, and said it again, even softer. "Can't." Phoebe desperately wished she could have a normal life, or alternately, any kind of life that would allow her to do something like attend a movie premiere with the world's biggest teen movie star. But that wasn't possible, and suddenly, filled with the silence of the moment, the room felt crowded.

As hard as it was for Phoebe to believe, Colten looked genuinely let down, which made her feel that much worse. He shrugged his shoulders and pulled his baseball cap low over his face, obscuring his eyes. "I thought it was worth asking," he said distantly.

There were so many things Phoebe was feeling at that moment that she couldn't say out loud. And she hated how Colten could be connected to her life but at the same time be disconnected from it. Frantically, she searched her brain for something else she could say. Something that might prevent Colten from thinking that she had no interest in him.

"I'm a minor," she blurted.

Colten looked up. "Huh?"

Phoebe cleared her throat to give her time to gather her thoughts. "Green Lane policy requires parents or legal guardians to consent to off campus field trips. The um"—Phoebe cleared her throat again—"premiere would count as a 'field trip'."

Colten spoke, confusion in his voice. "And you don't think your grandfather would approve?"

Phoebe paused, surprised that Colten had remembered that it was just her and her grandfather; she'd mentioned it a while ago. "He'd approve." She smiled to lighten the mood. "It's just that he's on an around-the-world trip and getting in touch is hard."

Colten eyed her silently and Phoebe couldn't discern from his expression whether or not he believed her. As a Green Lane student, her excuse was valid. But it was her Shaper life that dictated everything.

"Well, my manager wants all premiere details confirmed soon," Colten said finally as Phoebe opened the door. "So if you reach him in the next day or so let me know . . ."

Phoebe wished Colten hadn't sounded so hopeful. It only made closing the door and walking away that much harder.

# Eighteen

Skylights set in a vaulted ceiling drenched the photo studio in a soft, buttery radiance, throwing dancing light beams upon portraits hung around the spacious room. Phoebe was sitting on a stool, in front of a faux ocean backdrop, staring at the black shelves that covered a cement textured wall. It was filled with an assortment of equipment: lenses, digital flash cards, props, tripods, monopods. She idly fingered her cell phone screen, contemplating what she wanted to use in this morning's assignment.

Phoebe's phone buzzed. She glanced down at the all-caps text and grinned. It said:

"WHERE THE HELL ARE YOU?"

It was quickly followed by:

"DID YOU GET MY TEXT LAST NIGHT???"

Phoebe sighed and punched in Hayley's number. She did not doubt that Hayley was exploding for want of details about her co-study date with Colten. She'd avoided discussing her debacle long enough.

"You said what?!" Hayley's voice blared, minutes into their conversation.

"I knew you were going to react this way," Phoebe said, swiveling on the stool.

"Is that why you ignored my texts last night—wait," Hayley said, interrupting herself. "Is that why you're not at breakfast? You're avoiding me?"

Phoebe indulged in a guilty grin. It wasn't only her pint-sized friend she'd been avoiding this morning. Colton was also on her 'must avoid' list. She hadn't recovered from the awkward end to their night. "I'm shooting an assignment soon," Phoebe said truthfully.

"You're my girl and all," Hayley continued. "And I say this from a place of deep love. But you're truly demented!"

Phoebe took mild offense. "Ouch," she said, her feeling ringing clear in her tone.

"Relax," Hayley said at once. "I said it came from a place of love. Look, I'm just frustrated for you. I mean, the hottest hottie tries to kiss you and you go with, 'Is this what the script—'"

Phoebe groaned. "You don't have to repeat it!"

"Oh, it bears repeating," Hayley said playfully. "In fact, I think I'll text you those words once a day. As far as I'm concerned, he's sending you all the signals and you just . . ." Hayley trailed off as if she'd taken a big bite of something.

Phoebe played with the pleats in her blue skirt, absorbing what Hayley had said. Then she mumbled, "Haven't you considered that this could just be a game for him?"

"What do you mean?"

"I mean, he's Colten Chase. I could just be the girl-of-the-moment. Something to amuse him until he gets bored," Phoebe said, finally expressing her pent-up reservations about Colten. "It's hard to figure out if he's being genuine or if he's being—"

"Smooth Mr. Hollywood?" Hayley finished.

"Exactly. Why bother getting emotionally invested just for him to get bored?"

Hayley gave a dramatic sigh as if everything she'd been arguing up to this point had just been negated by Phoebe's concern.

Phoebe glanced up at a wall clock and hopped to her feet. She placed the phone on the stool and put it on speaker. "How nice of you to actually care about his intentions," Hayley's tinny voice said. "If it were me, I'd jump the guy's bones for some serious bragging rights!"

"Seriously?" Phoebe said, arranging light stands around a red velvet armchair she'd placed in the middle of the room.

Hayley giggled helplessly. "Who am I kidding?" she said. "I'd analyze the hell out of it, too."

Phoebe released a breath, relieved. She flicked a switch on the wall and watched as the skylights darkened, blocking out the sun.

"Are you Phoebe Pope?"

Phoebe spun toward the voice. A gray-haired black man stood before her, leaning on a gold-knobbed cane and dressed in a pinstriped suit that made him look as if he were from nobility.

"Yes," Phoebe answered, praying that Hayley had heard the man's tenor voice and had the good sense to hold her tongue. "Nice to meet you, Mr. Goulde."

Delicate wrinkles framed the man's kind eyes as he smiled. "I'm a bit early, dear," he said warmly, as if reading Phoebe's mind. "But at my age, I try to give myself enough of a head start to get places on time." He laughed and took an arthritic step into the studio. Phoebe rushed forward to assist him. He waved her off, saying, "I'll manage fine. Just show me where to go."

As the famed, Julliard-trained pianist walked over to the plush armchair, Phoebe excused herself and made a swift return to the stool. She took her phone off speaker.

"I gotta go," she said to Hayley in a rushed whisper.

"Okay. See you in—"

"Oh," Phoebe quickly added. "Remind me to tell you about Colten's premiere."

Hayley's voice shot up to its highest octave. "What about it?"

Watching Mr. Goulde ease himself slowly into the chair, Phoebe said, "He invited me to go, but—"

Hayley cut her off with a deafening squeal that Phoebe immediately silenced by hanging up. She could only imagine Hayley hyperventilating in the dining hall. It was too bad that she'd have to break the sobering news to her later.

Headmaster Yori was quiet, frowning slightly from behind his desk. Phoebe had just informed him of her suspicion of the traitor's identity, and now she sat nervous, gripping her hands tightly in her lap.

"May I ask how you've come to this conclusion?" Professor Yori said, curiosity in his cautious voice. He leaned forward expectantly.

Phoebe shifted uncomfortably in her chair. "It's just a gut feeling I have," she said, watching his eyebrows lift. *Gut feeling?* That sounded ridiculous, even to her. But keeping that promise to her father was important to her, almost as though it was a way for her to hold on to him. "Also," Phoebe added, fumbling for supporting information. "I think she knew that there were Blackcoats on campus before Afua told the faculty. She all but asked me after the attack. And I saw her have some kind of argument with Deborah-Anna."

"Ah, I see." Professor Yori brought his hands together and sank back in his chair, and Phoebe could tell he was deep in thought. "I know that this must be a stressful and confusing time for you, Cadet Pope," he said, sighing heavily. "And it doesn't help that the notion of a traitor amongst us has been put in your head. But I'm sure you see how difficult it would be for me take your gut feeling and your other ideas outside of this room. Especially in the absence of proof . . ." he let his voice trail, picked up a water pitcher from his desk, and walked over to his book shelf.

"Not to mention that Montclaire is a highly decorated Blackcoat sworn to a lifetime of loyalty—"

"But she hasn't been brought into the loop," Phoebe said, almost at once.

"That's because retired Blackcoats are not brought into active cases."

"Well—maybe—" Phoebe said, grasping for words. "Maybe it's because she's retired."

"Is there a point you're trying to make, Cadet?" Professor Yori said, with a slight challenge in his voice.

Phoebe reddened. She wasn't making any sense. What was her point? "Maybe now her loyalty isn't as—"

"—strong?" Professor Yori finished. He watered a lovely white orchid plant that sat on his shelf and went back to his desk. "Blackcoats sacrifice a lot in the name of loyalty. When chosen for the service of the Crowns they relinquish their family name, using only their first names—Montclaire, Afua. . . . They do this to protect loved ones so that if they are ever caught, Vigos can't round up their family and use them as leverage or bargaining chips. As Vigos are well known to do. . . ." Phoebe gaped at Professor Yori. "So you see, Cadet," he said, his voice suddenly severe, "I know for a fact that Montclaire's loyalty is immutable. It transcends work, love, . . . and unless you can give me proof stronger than that. . . ." He rose to his feet and Phoebe, who understood this to mean that their meeting was over, did the same.

A thought hit Phoebe just as Professor Yori opened his door. "Sir, Montclaire is still relatively young. Is there a reason why she retired so early?"

"Said she found a new calling to teach others what she knows," Professor Yori said. "And when Professor Jones abruptly left town, Montclaire was available to teach her class." From the look on the headmaster's face, it felt to Phoebe that there was something that he was not saying. But brushing that aside, she headed for her next class, wishing she had never opened her mouth. Had she really thought he would simply take her word for it?

In the week after the kidnappings, Phoebe and Scott continued to meet the Blackcoats for their academic boot camp sessions. But with no Mariko frowning at a puppy-eyed Lewis, the atmosphere—which had never been upbeat to begin with—was even more subdued. It didn't help that Phoebe showed no significant progress, managing only to deflate one balloon, which, when compared with Scott's zero, was a success.

When Phoebe walked in for a new Thursday session, she found Scott hunched over the table, the hood of his USA soccer jersey pulled over his head.

"Hey. You awake?" she said, poking him in the shoulder.

"I am now," Scott groaned.

"Late night?" Phoebe said, shrugging out of her wool overcoat.

"You could say that," he said, turning his head. Phoebe saw that there were rings underneath his eyes.

"Well, snap out of it, Cadet!" she said, imitating Yelena's accent.

Scott laughed and leaned back in his chair. "So . . . Pope," he said, lowering his hood and surveying her with interest. "You and Colten Chase, huh?" His words hung between them, his tone neither question nor statement.

Phoebe narrowed her eyes at him. "Where's that coming from?"

Scott shrugged. "I hear things and I'm a bit surprised. You don't strike me as a celebrity chaser."

"I'm not," Phoebe snapped. "We hang out."

"Hey man," Scott said, picking up a balloon from his basket and spinning it on a finger. "I'm not trying to push any buttons." Then, softening his tone, "Just be careful, okay?"

"What's that supposed to mean?" Phoebe knotted her fingers together.

"Look," Scott said, leaning closer to her, his tone serious now. "A guy like that can get any girl he wants and—"

Phoebe tensed, her face a crimson-tinged mask. "I'm not good enough?"

"You're too good for him, Pope." Scott drummed his fingers on the table. "Look. You're my main girl and I just don't want to see you get hurt." The sincerity in his voice calmed Phoebe.

"I appreciate the concern," she said, relaxing her features. "But I'm all good."

"I have a one toe policy, by the way," Scott said.

Phoebe made a face. "What's that?"

Scott spoke, his voice low. "That pretty boy steps one toe out of line and I'll bring him a world of hurt—"

"Hey now," Phoebe said, laughing. "How 'bout we discuss your love life for a . . ." she let her voice trail as Afua swept into the room with Yelena and Deborah-Anna.

"Cadet Pope," Afua said. "Today you're with me."

Phoebe stood and exchanged confused glances with Scott.

"And me?" Scott asked.

Yelena said, "You stay here and focus on deflating balloons."

As Phoebe left the room, she could see Scott staring after them with a look that mingled curiosity and irritation.

Phoebe followed Afua to the athletic wing. They entered a long paneled hallway with only two doors, one on either side of them. Lighted signs above the door frames identified the rooms as Combat I and Combat II. Afua led Phoebe into Combat II—the only one without a red "in use" light on.

Phoebe's mouth fell open as she took in the large, hexagonal-shaped room whose walls were made of honeycomb shelves bearing diamond-tipped weapons—knives, daggers, arrows, throwing stars—all glittering so brightly, they washed the hardwood floor with multicolored light. As though in a trance, Phoebe began to walk toward them when Afua's voice stopped her.

"Those are for you to wear," the Blackcoat said, indicating a set of clothes on a steel table next to a long, thin duffel bag. She then pointed Phoebe in the direction of an adjacent changing room. Phoebe removed her uniform, dressed quickly, and returned to the main floor wearing a brown linen short-sleeve top and pants similar to those Afua now had on.

"I suggest you stretch your muscles before we begin," Afua said. She removed four javelin-like sticks from the duffel bag. Beautifully carved, two were adorned with a spiral yellow pattern while the others were red.

Bending to stretch her hamstrings, Phoebe eyed Afua nervously. "What are we doing?"

"You and I are fighting."

Phoebe jerked her head up, unsure if Afua was serious. But at the sight of Afua placing two of the sticks at her feet, Phoebe knew that she was.

Phoebe shivered. She had never in her life been in a physical fight and the thought of her first one being with a Blackcoat, even a Blackcoat hired to protect her, was frightening. Phoebe waited for an explanation as to why she and Afua were fighting, and when none came, she said, "We're fighting with these?"

"Yes. We'll be engaging in Zulu Stick Fighting," Afua said, walking across to the table to grab the remaining two sticks. "It's an ancient martial art form that is mainly ceremonial today, but it was once used in warfare training for sharpening offensive and defensive skills." Phoebe's eyes remained riveted on Afua who expertly maneuvered the sticks with her hands as if in a swift, fluid dance with an invisible opponent. "I use it as a warm up exercise for my unit." *Great*, Phoebe thought, *what they use for warm up would most likely kill me.* Afua gradually became a blur of furious movement, with her final steps landing her squarely in front of Phoebe, who sat in a split stretch, mouth agape.

"Pick up your red stick with your right hand," Afua instructed. Phoebe did as she was told and stood up. Afua continued. "This is your offensive weapon called the Induku. You use it to strike your opponent." Afua demonstrated by simulating striking jabs at Phoebe who flinched back.

"This one, the Ubhoko," Afua said, pointing to the yellow stick that Phoebe picked up, "is for defense. You hold it in your left hand. Practiced wrist movements will help you use it to block your opponent's attacks.

"The bottom tips of these sticks are usually sharp, and in real battle can be used to severely injure your opponent. For our purposes, so that you don't accidentally impale yourself, I've dulled the ends."

Phoebe spared a moment to feel the bottom of her sticks, confirming this fact. She sighed in resigned embarrassment; it was true, she probably would hurt herself.

Afua stepped into the area of combat—a large black circle in the center of the room—and beckoned Phoebe to follow.

"I'm not sure I can do this," Phoebe said, nervously entering the ring.

Ignoring the comment, Afua bowed and assumed a menacing attack stance. "It's kill or be killed," she said. "Ready?"

Phoebe wasn't ready. *Who was ever ready for a guaranteed beating?* But she knew whether she liked it or not, this fight was happening. Forcing herself to take a breath, she bowed, then said, "I guess I'm re—" A sharp pain shooting up Phoebe's right bicep cut her off; Afua had struck with cobra speed.

Afua narrowed her eyes at Phoebe, an expression completely devoid of sympathy. Phoebe bit back her pain. Determined to save face, she charged forward. Afua pivoted to the left with balletic grace, her swift counterstrike hitting Phoebe on the hip. Tears welled into Phoebe's eyes.

Afua shifted her weight between her feet and considered Phoebe for a moment. "It has come to my attention," she said. "That you have been invited to Colten Chase's movie premiere in Boston."

Phoebe didn't have time to be surprised by Afua's comment; she was busy ducking a fast strike. "Yes," she said, "but how do you know this?"

"Your guard informed me," Afua said. "He heard the young man ask you."

Phoebe frowned. She couldn't believe that her time with Colton had been under that much surveillance. In what way was co-study a security risk?

"Don't worry," Phoebe said, trying to mask her annoyance. "I told him that I couldn't go."

"We want you to go."

"What?" Phoebe stopped dead, completely thrown, and one of Afua's blows disabled her knees. Dazed, Phoebe teetered on the spot and dropped to the ground in a heap of long limbs.

"In battle, never stop moving," Afua said. "Get up."

Phoebe staggered shakily to her feet and grimaced from the weight she'd put on her knees. "I don't understand," she said. Unable to keep the shock out of her voice, "Why would you want me to go? I thought I was supposed to be lying low."

Once again, Afua attacked, and this time Phoebe swiveled sharply, escaping the offensive stab.

"Nice dodge. Let's see more moves like that," Afua said before answering Phoebe's question. "Your attending the event presents an opportunity for us to set up a sting operation to flush out our traitor. We believe that he or she has gone quiet because of our increased security Below.

"Our allowing you to attend such a public event will send the message that we've slackened our guard. If our instincts are correct, the traitor will inform their Vigo contact about the event in advance. If any Vigo attempts to take you, they'll be surprised by our presence and back off. Our plan is to track them in their retreat to Alexori and the others."

"Won't the traitor sense a trap?"

"The success of any sting operation lies in its believability," Afua said. "People have observed you spending time with Mr. Chase, so your invitation to attend his function will not come as a surprise."

Phoebe continued dodging Afua's attacks with limited success as she turned those words over in her mind. She knew that she was in danger already, but her decision to go would potentially put Colten at risk as well. She wasn't sure she could stomach that.

As though reading her mind, Afua said, "You and Mr. Chase would be protected at all times by a team of agents who will be walking the carpet, moving about the street crowd and the bleacher fans."

Phoebe began to feel real panic as she began to picture the layout of such an event. There was too much ground to cover, too many opportunities for things to go very wrong. She hadn't even considered how ideal the setting of an event like a movie premiere was for a kidnapping. Even with all of the cameras whirling, there were so many people, so many nooks and crannies.

Afua added, "Don't forget that we always feel Vigos before we see them, so—do more than just retreat from me," Afua said, abruptly going off topic. "Keep your Induku horizontal and extend your arm in front of you to protect yourself from my blows."

Following the instructions, Phoebe blocked Afua's next move, their sticks meeting mid-air with a loud crack. A look of victory lit Phoebe's face, but it was short-lived as Afua's stick whistled past her cheek and struck her shoulder like a gong. Phoebe grunted from the impact but remained upright.

"Never get cocky," Afua warned. "No one ever remembers the great moves you make during a fight. They only remember the outcome. Frivolous emotions can give your opponent an advantage over you."

Phoebe took Afua's criticism in stride. "What," she panted, attempting a weak jab at her instructor, "does Professor Yori think?"

Afua stared Phoebe down, sticks stretched out, contemplating her next move. "He hasn't been made aware of the operation," she said, her tone a shade softer as she twisted powerfully to a new spot in the ring, letting a quick strike from Phoebe slice air. Afua nodded at Phoebe approvingly, then added, "And he won't be."

"You think he's the traitor?" Phoebe asked, shocked. The possibility had never even occurred to her.

"At this point, we're not ruling anyone out."

Phoebe considered this for a moment, then asked, "How would the traitor even know I was going?"

"Faculty do pick up on student gossip, for one," Afua said, the faintest tinge of amusement coloring her words. "And second, there's a daily email with a list of student absences. Because you would need the afternoon off to prepare for the event, we would include you on that list along with the reason for your absence. He or she would have all day to contemplate making their move."

Considering this, Phoebe sucked in a deep breath. Afua misinterpreted it as fatigue.

"Power through it," Afua said, pausing momentarily, an action that allowed Phoebe to land a blow on her shoulder. Afua didn't flinch. "Well done," she said. "Use all distractions to your benefit."

Phoebe bit down on a smile. *Never get cocky*, Afua had said. Just then, the bell rang. Exhausted, Phoebe crumpled limply to the ground, her chest heaving. Afua immediately stood over Phoebe, her expression hard, her Induku pointed at Phoebe's face.

"The bell doesn't mean we're finished, Cadet."

Phoebe's eyes beetled at the sight of the sharp point on Afua's weapon hovering above her. "I thought you said the ends were dull!" she gasped.

"The ends of your sticks are dull. Mine are warrior sharp. You should have noticed that earlier. Notice everything to determine your advantages and disadvantages."

Phoebe swallowed.

Afua extended a hand, helping Phoebe to her feet. "Think about what I've presented to you. It's a lot to ask, but at this juncture it is the best way we can think of to find Cadets Higashi and Baker."

Phoebe understood now. The Blackcoats were running out of options. The more time went by, the less likely that Mariko and Lewis would be found alive . . . if they weren't dead already. Something tightened in Phoebe's chest. It was strong and unyielding. Her body burned with it. It was a need to feel empowered at a time when she mostly felt powerless.

"I'll do it," she said, her voice wavering slightly.

Afua nodded, and for a moment, Phoebe thought she saw a smile twitch on the Blackcoat's lips. "I'll inform the others," Afua said. "You and I will continue to train like this up until the night of the event." Catching the look on Phoebe's face, Afua calmly added, "We don't anticipate you needing to defend yourself, but knowing how gives you a head start. It will also give me an opportunity to run you through the plan as we put it together."

Afua's explanation put Phoebe's hearts in her throat, but she bobbed her head in agreement. "Okay," she said, trying to sound strong. She trusted the Blackcoat. Phoebe found herself thinking of Lewis' velvet singing voice and picturing Mariko's snarky smile. She would do whatever was necessary to ensure a successful sting.

After she and Phoebe exchanged bows, Afua bent to return the sticks to the duffel bag. On her way to the changing room, Phoebe stopped with a sudden thought. Turning, she said quietly, "There's just a small problem with the plan. I already told Colten no." In fact it was more than a small problem. After the way their co-study date ended, Phoebe wasn't sure if Colten still needed a date. Yes, she'd left things vaguely open ended, but his deadline had passed and she doubted that he or his manager were waiting around for her. The premiere was an important part of his job. They'd probably already secured someone else to accompany him.

Afua studied Phoebe for a moment. "Look at your body," she said. "Do you see any cuts?"

Phoebe peered down her long frame, and looked up with an expression of vague confusion. "No. Actually, I don't." She had some impressive red welts but no cuts.

"You just prevented a Blackcoat from drawing blood from you in your first fight," Afua noted, in a tone that said that although she'd been lenient, she was still impressed. "I'm sure you can find a way to get that boy to re-invite you to his premiere."

Later, as she shuffled through the hallway, Scott caught up to Phoebe and fell into stride beside her.

"So what was that about, Pope?" he said with a sideways glance.

"She had me fight her," Phoebe said tiredly, cringing and rubbing a sore spot just above her left elbow.

Scott halted, much to the annoyance of cadets rushing to get into class on both sides of them. One kid almost slammed into the wall trying to evade Scott and glared at him on his way by. "That was my idea, remember?" he said, frowning.

"I know," Phoebe said, twisting her lips in a commiserating half-smile. It felt odd and unsettling to not be able to confide in Scott about Hypha-related plots and plans. They really needed each other's support—especially now. "I'm sure she'll get to you," she said with middling conviction as she steered them in the direction of the lockers. "But in the meantime, I can show you some moves. If you want, I mean." Phoebe grinned at Scott and wiggled her eyebrows conspiratorially.

"Doubt they'll get to me," Scott said, sourly. "I'm back in Yelena's doghouse. . . ." He scuffed one sneaker against the floor.

"Why?"

Scott shoved his hands in his pants pocket. "I might have been a bit short with her when she wouldn't tell me where you went. . . ."

Phoebe gave Scott a sidelong look. "You know what?" she said, a grin forming slowly on her lips. "I'm beginning to think you have a crush on her."

"What? Yelena?—No!" Scott scowled.

Phoebe laughed. "I think you provoke her for the attention."

"End of discussion, Pope," Scott said, unable to mask his embarrassment with an annoyed tone.

"Fine. Fine. So how about it?" Phoebe said, glancing at a clock on the wall. "Meet me at the athletic wing in five minutes?"

"Can't," Scott said. "I have to report to Yelena—"

"Oh, Yelena," Phoebe said, smirking.

Scott ignored her and began walking backward in the opposite direction, head down. "She's standing guard while I polish trophies and some other crap as punishment. Rain check?"

As Phoebe nodded, Scott took off running, and Phoebe continued to the end of the hallway, wincing with every movement. Two thoughts ran through her mind as she stood staring into her locker. The first was that every inch of her body had been massacred by Afua. And the second was that somehow she'd essentially signed up to be Vigo bait. Was she crazy? Phoebe raised an arm that screamed with pain and reached for her bottle of Earthamins. She chewed a pill, thinking the awful taste would be worth it if along with its elemental benefits the Earthamin would soothe her aches.

When Phoebe shoved her locker door shut, she jumped at the sight of Montclaire leaning against the neighboring one, watching her.

"Jumpy, aren't we, Cadet Pope?" Montclaire asked with a thin-lipped smile.

Phoebe cleared her throat. "You just caught me by surprise, ma'am," she said.

Montclaire smiled wider, her eyes boring into Phoebe's. "It seems that I can say the same about you," she said brightly. She stood straight, tucked a few strands of her dark, bluntly cut hair behind an ear and crossed her arms. "I have a question I want you to answer, Cadet."

"Okay," Phoebe said in a nervous voice. Something about Montclaire's penetrating stare made her feel feverish with dread.

"In the swearing-in oath, when the Principes asked your class the question, 'Why do you fight' what was the answer?"

Phoebe heard flirtatious laughter close by. She turned her head slightly to a tall boy and a stout girl who were walking with their arms around each other; they glanced curiously at Phoebe and Montclaire as they passed by.

"I believe I asked you a question," Montclaire said, the shrillness of her voice reclaiming Phoebe's gaze.

"Yes, sorry, ma'am," Phoebe said, immediately. "Loyalty to each other. Service to the Royal Court. And in honor of Pompeii."

"I see," Montclaire said, with a slightly satisfied expression when Phoebe had finished. "Now, let me show you something." Phoebe watched as Montclaire rolled her right robe sleeve up to the elbow, revealing several iridescent black lines tattooed around her wrist similar to the ones Phoebe had seen on Afua.

"Royal ink," she said. "That's what makes these tattoos glow like that. And when it goes on it burns the same way the presence of a Vigo burns, so that you never forget. . . ." Her slender fingers traced a ring that was particularly thick. "Each ring represents a member of my Blackcoat unit lost in battle with Vigos. Good people I've respected and had the privilege of serving with . . . good people who were loyal to me and to whom I remain loyal because loyalty, Cadet," Montclaire said, "is paramount. That's why it comes before 'Service to the Royal Court' and 'In honor of Pompeii'. Without it, what do the other statements matter—?" she broke off, allowing the sound of the start-of-class bell that was now ringing to stop. And then, pulling down her sleeve Montclaire said, "It seems that our show-and-tell is now over."

Phoebe's insides squeezed with nerves. Montclaire knew.

Montclaire started to leave, but then she paused and considered Phoebe a moment longer. "How's your class presentation on Vigo markings coming along?" she asked.

"Great," she said, trying to stop her bottom lip from twitching.

"Good," Montclaire said. "I have a strong feeling that you will be kicking off our Presentation Week." Her dark eyes shone with wicked excitement at the thought.

With that, Montclaire turned and swept out of sight. Phoebe couldn't find her breath. Montclaire had all but blatantly stated that she knew about Phoebe's accusation against her. But Phoebe couldn't see how Montclaire could know, not when Professor Yori had made it clear that he would keep it to himself. Or was Afua right? Was there a chance that even the headmaster could not be trusted?

🍁 NINETEEN

"On the one hand, I'm glad you get to go to the premiere," Hayley said with a note of concern in her voice. "But on the other hand—" she left the rest unsaid and continued to rummage zealously through her stack of mail.

"Well. I don't know if he still wants to take me, even." Phoebe fidgeted with the postcard in her hand. It was from her grandfather who was now somewhere in Nepal.

During Bio Encryption, Phoebe had brought Hayley up to speed on the latest. She'd described her fighting session with Afua and explained how her going to the premiere would be instrumental in the Blackcoats' sting. Hayley seemed at a loss, unable to dismiss either her excitement or deep concern about the coming event.

Now back Above, they were sitting on the steps of the schoolhouse; Hayley was keeping Phoebe company as she waited for Broadway producer Stephanie Labrill, the next photo subject for Cyn's feature. Outside, the air was frigid, but warmth could be found in coveted patches of sun. Phoebe leaned back, soaking in the light that poured down on them, watching Hayley attempt to tear thick tape off the top of a small box.

"Grr," Hayley said. "Could my mom make this any harder to open?"

Phoebe sat up and pulled a mini tool kit out of the side pocket of her backpack. "Try this," she said, handing Hayley a flat head screwdriver.

Hayley's eyes widened in surprise. "Should I even ask why you have a tool kit on you?"

"For my many criminal activities," Phoebe quipped.

Hayley laughed and slid the screwdriver through the tape. "Oh man," she said, looking at the framed photograph she'd pulled from her box.

"What?" Phoebe said.

"Little Harper lost his first tooth," Hayley cried. "Those little runts are starting to lose their teeth and I'm missing it."

Phoebe scooted closer to Hayley whose face had taken on a sullen expression. "Aw, that's cute," she said, staring down at the gap-toothed grin of a freckled-faced boy who shared his sister's dimples.

"Ain't it?" Hayley sighed heavily, kissed the photo, and returned it to the box that Phoebe saw contained several bottles of nail polish. "I know what you're thinking," Hayley said, catching Phoebe's look. "I don't need any more nail polish. But my mom says I should try this brand. It's vegan."

"Vegan? Nail polish?"

"Yeah, chemical and animal product free—hey, let's do the next Spa Sunday in your room. We can go over dress options for the premiere."

"I haven't even thought about dresses. Or where I'd get something nice enough for an event like that," Phoebe said, attentively watching the cars that came in and out of the front parking lot, keeping an eye out for her guest. "For all I know, Colten's already asked someone else—"

"Doesn't matter," Hayley said with a hint of glee. "The mission you chose to accept was to get re-invited!"

"That's kinda hard when the mark hasn't been around."

Phoebe hadn't seen Colten since their co-study date. And given how that had ended on an awkward note, she found herself thinking his absence might just be intentional, and on account of her. He'd always seemed to make a point of inserting himself wherever she was before. She hadn't realized how much effort that must have taken on their gigantic campus until now.

"I know where Colten is," Hayley said guiltily.

Phoebe looked at Hayley, surprised. "Where?"

"According to my intel—*Dish* Mobile," Hayley said, shaking her cell phone, "he's doing a press junket with his co-star Tanya Brown. They're in New York."

"Oh." Phoebe's shoulders fell. She grabbed her screwdriver from Hayley's pile of mail and returned it to her kit.

"Don't you 'Oh' me," Hayley said. "He told you it's a fake relationship. Give me your phone."

"Why? I don't want *Dish* Mobile."

"Just give it to me."

Phoebe fished her phone from her bag, tossed it to Hayley, all the while eyeing her suspiciously. Hayley began punching away at Phoebe's keypad with one hand and raised the other, stopping Phoebe from releasing any words from her open mouth. A second later, Phoebe's phone vibrated and Hayley stuck out her tongue and said, "You're all set for the premiere."

Phoebe's eyes narrowed and Hayley tossed her phone back to her. Hayley giggled, "Colten says he's glad it worked out."

Phoebe gazed at Hayley, disbelievingly. She glanced down at her phone, read the message, and looked back at Hayley. Then laughter bubbled from her chest and before she knew it, it had claimed her breath.

Hayley laughed too, but clearly out of relief.

"I thought you were going to kill me!" she said mock-gritting her teeth.

Phoebe had seriously considered it. But then she'd been struck by the realization that less than thirty words had saved her from hours of agonizing. Phoebe had been contemplating a variety of ways to approach Colten, what tone to take, a clever way to come off playful and inviting without it seeming like a total departure from their last interaction.

Instead, Phoebe stared down at her phone again and read:

Phoebe: "Hey. Turns out I can go to the premiere after all. Still need a date?"

Colten: "Yes. Glad it works out. Thank your grandfather. See U soon."

Four or five reads later, Phoebe still couldn't figure out how his incredibly simple response could elicit such butterflies in her stomach. A black town car pulled up, looking as if it transported somebody important. Phoebe jumped to her feet and smoothed her uniform.

Hayley sat up, tilting her head with curiosity. "By the way," she said. "What did he mean by 'Thank your grandfather'?"

"Long story," Phoebe said. As she hoisted her backpack on her shoulder, her phone buzzed again. Phoebe glanced down at it. A wide grin took over her face.

"Ooh is that him again?" Hayley asked, standing. "What's he saying now?"

Phoebe showed her the text.

"He's offering to cook you dinner as a thank you?" Hayley said, snatching the phone to read the message again. "Unbelievable!"

Phoebe peeled her phone out of Hayley's hands. "You're assuming he's any good."

"Whatever. While I'm stuck with caf' food you'll be dining à la Chase," Hayley said with a dramatic huff. "You so owe me!"

Phoebe held up a hand to wave away Hayley's comment. "Let's call it even since I didn't kill you for that stunt you pulled." She ran to greet the ginger-blond woman exiting the car and held out her hand, biting back a giddy rush of exhilaration. "Mission" or not, she was going to a movie premiere with a guy she was completely crazy about—a guy who wanted to cook for her—and he just happened to be Colten Chase.

🍁 TWENTY

Phoebe could feel the unease coiling through the room as she and her cadetmates watched the broad, bushy blond-haired boy up front change his slides. It was the start of Presentation Week, and true to her word, Montclaire had slated Phoebe to present on day one. She tried to calm her mounting nerves as she listened to the boy who had volunteered to go first. Phoebe knew his eagerness had spared her from that fate.

"The Vigo tongue," the boy was saying, moving his laser pointer along the purple-pink organ pictured on his slide, "can extend to a length that allows it to wrap around a grown man's neck. It has hundreds of tiny harpoon-like needles embedded in each taste bud. When feeding, these needles are triggered"—he changed slides—"to pierce the skin so that toxins flow into the victim's bloodstream. The toxin rips mitochondria from human cells allowing the Vigo to absorb it into its body."

"How exactly is it absorbed?" Montclaire asked crisply from her seat upfront.

The boy smiled and moved to his next slide. "Through these pock-like receptors found both on the tip and the back of the tongue."

"Brings new meaning to getting tongue, huh?" Scott whispered, playfully poking Phoebe in the side.

Phoebe gave him a quick smile, but continued to clench her chair as the boy reached the end of his twenty minute presentation.

"A job well done, Cadet Bane," Montclaire said. She rose to her feet and turned on the overhead lights. "You've certainly set the bar for Cadet Pope."

Phoebe understood her cue. As she walked to the front of the class, she could feel her throat closing and sweat gathering in her armpits. Not only did she fear public speaking, but she hadn't prepared any slides. Her effort already felt painfully below the bar.

When Phoebe arrived at the lectern, she scanned the faces of her classmates; some were amused, but most, like Scott, smiled encouragingly, trying to ease her discomfort. Before she'd even assembled her notes, an impatient Montclaire prompted her.

"Sometime this moonester, Cadet Pope. I'm sure the class is eager to have you tell us about the Mark Day," Montclaire said with a smile that cut. She returned to her seat and crossed her arms.

Phoebe cleared her throat. "Newly made Vigos—cubs—are housed in crèches, which is a fancy way of saying nurseries."

A few students snickered at that.

"Next person to even hiccup will take Cadet Pope's place," Montclaire said, waving a hand at Phoebe to continue.

Phoebe nodded appreciatively, and swallowed. "The cubs," she said shakily, "are watched over to make sure they make the transition from human to Vigo. The ones that don't are killed. Those that do transition are taught to control the beast."

"Please clarify what you mean by 'control the beast'," Montclaire said.

Phoebe cleared her throat. "New cubs are unstable and prone to spontaneous morphing," she said. "Controlling the beast means learning to only morph at will." Phoebe paused, waiting for a follow up question from Montclaire. When none came, she said, "During that time, the cubs learn all things Vigo: politics, law, and hunting. At the end of two years, they receive a tattoo on the right side of their necks to signify becoming fully Vigo—almost like a graduation."

"What is this tattoo of?" Montclaire asked.

"The Mark of Wang," Phoebe replied confidently.

"And it's symbolic to Vigos because?"

Phoebe stared at Montclaire blankly. She then glanced down at her notes. She'd forgotten the significance of the Mark of Wang. She only remembered that when written, the Chinese character looked like three horizontal lines stacked one on top of each other with a vertical line running through the middle.

"Anyone?" Montclaire asked, twisting around in her seat to look at the class. A girl's hand shot up in the back. "Go ahead, Cadet Ramirez."

"Wang means 'king' in Chinese," the athletically built girl said. "It's symbolic because the stripe pattern on the forehead of Tigers looks just like the Chinese character Wang."

"Correct," Montclaire said, satisfied.

"I know this because I can speak Chinese," the girl quickly added.

"Thank you for verifying this," Montclaire said, not hiding her annoyance. Still facing the class, she added, "The tiger has been revered in Chinese culture for centuries. In fact, they consider it to be the king of all animals. Vigos take this as a sign of their superiority and feel that their human form should also bear the Mark of Wang, hence the tattoo."

For ten minutes, Montclaire continued to pepper Phoebe with questions, stopping her presentation now and then for fine detail clarifications on Beta and Alpha marks. And as Phoebe noticed the expressions on her classmates' faces slowly slide from mildly entertained to eyebrows furrowed with sympathy, Phoebe knew that she wasn't the only one in the room who thought Montclaire was being tremendously unfair. Finally, the bell rang and Phoebe made no attempt to conceal her immediate dash for the door, wishing with all of her hearts for Professor

Jones' return so that Montclaire's substitute teaching stint would come to a speedy end.

"Was it really that bad?" Hayley said as she zipped Phoebe into a hunter green, tea-length dress with a sweetheart neckline that she'd ordered online from Macy's.

"It was awful," Phoebe said. "Just a heads up for your presentation,"—she looked over her shoulder at Hayley—"go with slides 'cause—"

"This is definitely the dress!" Hayley squealed, clapping her hands as she took a step back, admiring.

Phoebe looked into her mirror, relieved. She liked it too. "So." She turned to face her bed; it held the two other dresses she'd ordered. "This one over the powder-blue?"

"No question." Hayley came to stand by Phoebe. "At first I thought the whole redhead-in-a- green-dress was going to be cliché, but this one's so dark it's almost black." She bumped Phoebe with her jean clad hip. "Besides, the ruching at the waist is flattering."

Phoebe moved her hips from side to side. "And you don't think it'll be a big deal that it's not designer?"

Hayley shrugged. "Don't sweat it. These days, lots of celebs like to gush about shopping for vintage clothes and secondhand stuff like that. Besides, the photographers will be so focused on how hot you look in that dress no one's going to care about who made it."

The door opened and closed behind them and Cyn's voice said, "Seriously, mom. Let this one go. I will out scoop you." She paused when she noticed Phoebe and Hayley. "Yes, but—" she continued. "Yes, but you forget that I have direct access!" Cyn snapped her phone shut and stripped out of her blue pea coat. "So what's the occasion, ladies?" She sat on the sofa and crossed her legs.

Hayley's lips twisted into a grin. "Didn't Phoebe tell you she got—" she started.

"Invited to the Fall Enviroball," Phoebe said, speaking over Hayley and giving her a meaningful look.

Cyn squinted at them, forehead creased with suspicion. "Who are you going with? Colten?" she asked in a tone that bordered on a sneer. When Phoebe said, "No," Cyn shot forward in her seat.

"No?" she echoed, genuinely shocked.

"No," Phoebe said, running her fingers along the ruching in her dress.

Cyn, disbelief still ruling her face, said, "So he didn't ask—I mean—" She censored herself and grabbed her coat. Then, muttering something about an editorial deadline, she bustled out of the room.

"Editorial deadline my ass," Phoebe mumbled when the door had snapped shut. "She's off to report to Karli."

"My bad," Hayley said. "Didn't mean to almost blab there."

"It's all good," Phoebe said. "Don't get me wrong. She's okay. And I respect how passionate she is about the *Gazette*. But I can't get past her friendship with Karli—"

Phoebe's phone buzzed and she darted for her desk.

"What's lover boy saying today?" Hayley said, reading the glowing expression on Phoebe's face."

"He can't wait for dinner tonight," she said, not bothering to mask her excitement. She and Colten had been exchanging text messages during his absence. It had reduced Phoebe's post study date anxiety. Ignoring the kissing noises Hayley was making, Phoebe scrolled through her phone and reread a few of her favorite messages.

Colten: "Help. Being stalked by a seven-year-old."

Colten: "Guy interviewing me must have had onions and tuna for lunch. Can't breathe!"

Colten: "80-year-old woman just gave me her underwear to sign. No joke. See pic."

Phoebe ended with today's text.
Colten: "Looking forward to dinner."
She wrote back: "Me too."

TWENTY- ONE

"I can't just do nothing!" Phoebe protested. Steam infused with tantalizing aromas of pepper and garlic rose from a sizzling frying pan and spiced the air.

From behind her, Colten tugged the spatula out of her hand. He lowered his head to her ear, his breath warming her neck. "This kitchen isn't big enough for the two of us," he said, before placing his free hand on Phoebe's hip and sliding her body to the side. "Now, sit!"

"Fine," Phoebe scowled, secretly memorizing the thrill she'd felt from having Colten's hand on her hip.

"It's almost done, anyway," he said

"What's on the menu?" Phoebe sat on his bed and grabbed one of several text books that lay on it. She had a sudden need to keep her hands occupied.

"Pad Thai and papaya salad," Colten said.

"Wow," Phoebe said, impressed. "Thai food."

"It's a great option in a gluten-free diet," he explained. He returned his attention to the frying pan.

"If you're not going to let me do anything," Phoebe said playfully. "At least let me ask you some questions."

Colten looked over his shoulder. "May I remind you of what happened the last time we went down this road?"

Phoebe scowled and Colten laughed. "Okay, shoot," he said. He removed a square plastic container from the refrigerator.

"Favorite band?" Phoebe said, running a finger along the spine of the book.

"Arcade Fire," he said.

"Cool. Favorite board game?"

"Chess. It's a thinking man's game."

"Favorite color?"

"Gray."

Phoebe said, "Really? Gray's so drab."

"Not when it's the color of your eyes," Colten said softly, turning to look at her. His gaze was almost indulgent. Phoebe swallowed. Every now and then the intensity of Colten's green eyes stunned her.

After a moment, when only the crackling sound from the frying pan filled the air, Phoebe said, "What's 'Project Cuddle'?" Her eyes had settled on the words embroidered in the black apron he was wearing over a gray henley shirt and sweatpants.

"They rescue abandoned babies," he said, resting his elbows on the small counter, "and provide women safe options for giving up newborns."

Phoebe looked up at him, stunned. "That's not what I was expecting," she admitted.

Colten smiled slowly. "What were you expecting?"

Phoebe shook her head, averting her gaze.

"No judgment," Colten said. "I swear."

"I was expecting some cute remark about some fan club of yours. . . . But," she said, looking over at the apron, "what you're talking about is intense." Phoebe eyed him closely, waiting for judgment to creep into his eyes. His expression remained even.

"It is intense," he murmured. "That's why I volunteer when I can."

That was it: the chains around Phoebe's skeptical hearts loosened, the links breaking off one by one, until there was nothing left to restrain her feelings for Colten.

"Looks like we're all set!" He turned the stove off and began to rummage through the kitchen cabinets. He swore under his breath.

"What?"

"Small technical difficulty." Colten looked almost embarrassed. "Be right back." And before Phoebe could ask if there was something she could help him with, Colten had left the room.

Phoebe found herself taking a few deep breaths. She couldn't believe all that she was feeling; a new sense of ease flowed through her. She'd been keeping herself guarded from Colten. But that seemed to be changing. He seemed to be changing around her, giving her guided access to private areas of his life. For the first time, she allowed herself to believe that Colten had a sincere interest in her. Phoebe stared down at her hands that were beginning to feel clammy. She noticed suddenly that she'd been holding an Ancient Civilization text book.

"Okay, we're back in business," Colten said, returning. He had plates and forks in his hand.

"Hey," Phoebe said, raising the book. "Is this class any good?"

"Boring as hell," he said, glimpsing the title. "But take it if you need an easy A. The prof reuses old tests."

"Nice tip," Phoebe said. She flipped to the front of the book. Pompeii was listed in the table of contents. *Of course,* she thought. Humans had varying accounts of what happened the morning of August 25, A.D. 79, and they were all wrong. An earthquake did not trigger the eruption of Mount Vesuvius. Members of the exiled Tiger clan did. A suicide mission sent thirty Tigers into the mouth of the volcano and caused the deaths of 8,000 Shapers unable to flee the volcanic ash that rained down on Pompeii. The clan, who called themselves Vigos in honor of their slain king, vowed to continue killing Shapers.

"Time to eat," Colten declared, returning Phoebe to the present. She quickly slid off the bed and went to join him in the kitchen.

Colten set a stack of paper plates on the counter and removed his apron. "I hope you don't mind sitting on the floor," he said, pointing to the coffee table, embarrassed. "I didn't plan too well."

"What?" Phoebe said, feigning elitist disgust. "No pedestal dining table set with linen and fine china?"

"You're my kind of gal," Colten laughed, relief plain in his voice.

When he reached up to hang his apron on a high wall hook, Phoebe's eyes immediately went to the bare strip of skin exposed between the edge of his shirt and the top of his sweat pants. A crazy desire to run a hand across the nicely defined contours of his abdomen hit her unexpectedly. For a moment, Phoebe let her imagination run with that thought. When she looked up, Colten was studying her. Phoebe shivered from the force of his stare.

"So . . . ready for a taste?" he said, huskily, his expression both teasing and curious. Phoebe nodded and tried to ignore the double meaning she'd heard in Colten's tone. It was all she could do to keep breathing. They both knew she'd been caught lusting.

Colten filled two plates with food and handed one to Phoebe. They settled around the coffee table, and starving, Phoebe took a bite of noodles. "Oh my God," she said, rich flavor exploding in her mouth. "This is amazing."

"Is that a matter of opinion?" Colten said with a smirk.

Phoebe laughed, remembering. "I concede. It's fact."

"The trick," Colten said, flashing a victorious smile, "is to marinade the tofu overnight. You also don't want to over-caramelize your onions."

As Colten doled out more cooking advice, Phoebe wolfed down her food without a care for etiquette. Colten watched her, openly entertained. Minutes later, he said, his tone suddenly serious, "Can I ask a personal question?"

Phoebe raised her eyes from her plate. "Sure," she said after a moment's hesitation.

"I know you live with your grandfather when he's in the country," he said cautiously. "What happened to your folks?" Phoebe stared at him, suddenly moist-eyed and nervous. She hadn't been expecting that question. "It's fine if you don't want to talk about it," he said, noticing the change in her demeanor.

Phoebe shook her head. "It's okay." She took a breath. "My father and I were in a car accident at the beginning of the summer," she said, telling the version of her story all humans got. "I survived. He didn't."

"I'm so sorry—"

"Please," Phoebe interrupted, her voice slightly strained. "Let me continue or I might not be able to finish." Colten nodded, his eyes warm as he watched her. "I don't know my mother. A few days after I was born, she simply left. No letter explaining why. No one has heard from her since. And when I say no one," Phoebe said, her voice lower, but just as bitter. "That includes her own father. It broke him. He moved us in with him to help my father raise me and also to be near a part of his daughter."

Colten reached out a tentative hand and touched Phoebe's arm. "Damn. That's heavy," he said, his voice thick. "I'm sorry." Phoebe could tell that Colten was unsure of what else to say, and she tried to show through her expression that he'd said enough. He removed his hand from her arm and gazed past her, thinking.

"I never knew my mother either," he said, returning his emerald eyes to hers, a tinge of vulnerability in his voice. Colten ran both of his hands through his hair. "She died when I was born," he explained. "There's a sense of loss. Like I wonder what could have been. But there's not that ache you get from loving someone and then losing them—" Colten stopped. "I'm sorry, Phoebe. I didn't mean to be insensitive."

Phoebe spoke at once. "Don't worry about it," she said, keeping her voice even. Colten's disclosure had sent a jolt through her. She immediately felt a strong sense of kinship. A part of her recognized that they were bonding over the most intense absence in her life, something she had never been able to fully share with anyone else, even her father. She shoved it away. "Do you know anything about her?"

A hesitant smile touched Colten's lips. "Yeah. She was an actress."

"No way!"

"No one famous," Colten said. "She was just getting started."

"Was she in anything you've seen?" Phoebe couldn't believe how much Colten's face lit up at her question.

"It took me some time, but I managed to track down the one movie she did." He sounded proud. "It's a b-grade campy flick. But it's fun to see her."

Phoebe loved seeing the glow in Colten's eyes, a vulnerable softness in his expression. "I'd love to see it sometime," she said. There was a brief silence where Phoebe saw a dark mood flit across Colten's face. Quickly she said, "I didn't mean to be presumptuous."

Colten's features relaxed. "I'd love to show you some day. About tomorrow," he said, changing subjects. "I can pick you up around two o'clock, if you don't mind missing a few afternoon classes."

Phoebe held back on a sigh. Up until that point, she hadn't been thinking of the sting. She'd been swept away by the dinner's intimate atmosphere. Feelings swirled inside her—feelings she'd never dared to entertain before. Not once had she thought to run through the things Afua had been going over with her: don't make eye contact with any of the Blackcoats while on the red carpet; focus her attention on Colten; breathe easy to keep her posture relaxed; don't search the faces of the crowd; act as though it's not a sting. She'd laughed at that last point even though it wasn't funny.

Phoebe bit her lip. "Actually," she said slowly. "There's a midterm I have to take then, so I'll just meet you at the hotel in the early evening." That was part of the Blackcoat plan. They wanted as much control over Phoebe's movements as possible and would be escorting her personally to Colten's hotel.

Colten reached across the table for her hands. "Whatever you're comfortable with is cool," he said.

Frankly, Phoebe wasn't comfortable with any of it, and if Colten hadn't gleaned this from her sudden unease, then surely he'd realize something was wrong from the hot moisture beading in her palms. A hammering at the door broke the silence.

"That's my cue that this little arrangement is over," Colten said. He stood up and offered Phoebe a hand.

"What do you mean?"

"I pulled a couple strings to have a lady in my room outside of co-study hours," he explained, smiling conspiratorially. "Don't want to push my luck."

Colten pulled Phoebe unresisting to her feet and walked her to the door. She leaned her back against it and said, "Thank you for dinner. Everything was great." If Colten heard the wavering note in Phoebe's voice he didn't show it. He closed the gap between them and Phoebe had an overwhelming sense of déjà vu. This was it. This was their "do over." She held her breath as Colten stroked her cheek with careful fingers.

"I'm glad you liked it," he said, his eyes gleaming.

Phoebe's thumping hearts almost drowned out his words. Smiling, Colten lowered his head and gave her a soft, brief kiss on the tip of her nose.

"See you at the hotel," he whispered as he took a step back.

That's it? Phoebe's mind screamed. She was a little crestfallen. Still, Phoebe couldn't budge, her breath escaping as a slow hiss. She had to admit that Colten's innocent kiss had packed enough force to pin her to the door.

"See you at the hotel," she echoed before slipping out.

By bedtime, Phoebe was a mass of nerves. And although she knew that her strength and reflexes had grown considerably over a series of stick fighting sessions with Afua, Phoebe was feeling less sure that she had the courage she needed to be Vigo bait. The idea of exposing herself to such great danger was proving to be a bit too much. Almost every evening, Phoebe would resolve to tell the Blackcoats she couldn't go through with it, but then the eyes of the Vigo astride her father's broken body would come back to her in her sleep, and by morning, her resolve would return.

By late morning the next day, Phoebe knew that all the faculty Below had received and read the email containing the list of the day's student absences. And because hers was a half-day absence, she was around in the morning to receive the curious glances and knowing smiles from Professors when she walked past them in the halls. A few, including Montclaire, couldn't help but comment.

"I hope those of us who will be busy playing celebrity for the night will find time to study for tomorrow's exam," she declared at the end of class to a room full of knowing faces. Phoebe ducked her head and bit back a scowl; she had to keep reminding herself that Montclaire had ample reason to dislike her. After all, even though she still didn't know why that feeling of hate had emanated from Montclaire in the teacher's lounge, Phoebe still didn't really have any proof or justification to call her a traitor.

That afternoon, when Phoebe met Afua for their last fighting session, she was surprised to find the Blackcoat seated behind a long trestle table that had been placed in the center of the combat room. Instead of the normal linen workout outfit, Afua was dressed in black pants and a matching form-fitting blazer. Phoebe's eyes were drawn like magnets to the elaborately embroidered royal crest on the right-hand side breast pocket: a gold lion circled by seven purple crowns.

Afua was sorting through a pile of red folders, but looked up as the door swung closed behind Phoebe. "Please have a seat, Cadet," she said, gesturing at the chair across from her.

Phoebe sat down, tense, remaining silent as Afua slid all of the folders but one to the end of the table and looked up.

"Why are you here, Cadet?" she said, surveying Phoebe.

Phoebe said, "I thought we were meeting for one last session before tonight."

"Yes. Fair enough. But what I meant was, why did you enroll at the Campus Below?"

"To gain physical toughness—"

"I'm not asking you to recite the enrollment oath."

"I—I don't know what you're expecting me to say," said Phoebe, who began to feel thoroughly flustered and nervous.

Afua removed an elastic band from around her wrist and used it to tie her hair back. "Everyone has a story behind why they choose to become an agent," she said. "Some are truly born for service. Others are pushed into it by life forces. I want to know what put you on this path."

Phoebe looked at her lap. She had not expected this line of questioning. In fact she was certain that the Blackcoat had done a background check on her so Phoebe was not at all sure what kind of answer would satisfy Afua's curiosity. Twice she opened her mouth to speak, but unable to meet Afua's gaze either time, she said nothing.

Afua picked up the folder in front of her, lifted the cover and read, "Candidate: Phoebe Elisabeth Pope." Phoebe looked up. "Age: 16. Projected time of conversion: first full moon after December 14th. Admission Status: candidate has declined offer. Notes: several follow up calls made to candidate with no success. Update: candidate has petitioned for last minute enrollment citing Legacy Courtesy. Ruling: permission granted."

Afua stared over the top of the folder at Phoebe who was twisting her hands in her lap. "It's clear that being here was not your original plan," she said. "And given the date you filed your petition, I'd say that your decision to enroll has to do with your father's—"

"Legacy," Phoebe said quickly, splotches of color appearing in her neck and creeping up her face. "I came here to follow in his footsteps."

"We both know that's not what I'm talking about."

Phoebe couldn't help the tightness in her voice when she spoke. "If you know why I'm here," she said, "then why ask?"

Afua narrowed her dark eyes and leaned forward. "Because me knowing and you coming to terms with it are two different things, Cadet," she said in an intense voice that goaded a now emotional Phoebe into saying, "I don't know!"

Afua remained unmoved. "I'll ask it again. Why are you here, Cadet?"

An overwhelming sense of frustration engulfed Phoebe. "I don't know," she repeated through clenched teeth as intense emotions roiled within her.

"I will ask one last—"

"Fine!" Phoebe blurted. "Redemption! I'm here for redemption. I—I just left him there. . . . I left him to the Vigos. God, what do you want from me?" Phoebe's voice trembled and then failed.

For a fleeting moment, Afua's face seemed to soften. But then, leaning back, the Blackcoat pressed the tips of her slender fingers together and looked at Phoebe over them with an unfaltering gaze. Phoebe, who had to grit her teeth to keep from crying, lowered her eyes to her shaky hands.

"It wasn't your fault," Afua said matter-of-factly and without emotion.

Phoebe snapped her head up so fast that strands of her hair whipped into her eyes. She glared at Afua for a second, and with tears rolling down her cheeks, said almost indignantly, "You don't know what happened. It was my fault." All the pain Phoebe had felt that night came rushing back, a burning, helpless feeling that threatened to suffocate her.

"What could you have done, Cadet?" Afua said.

Phoebe choked on a breath. Afua's voice had gotten significantly louder and sharper.

"Answer me," the Blackcoat pressed. "What could you have done? Fight them? With what skill? What power? Is that what your father would have wanted? Wouldn't his sacrifice have been wasted if you had been killed, too? Answer me, Cadet!"

Phoebe stared at Afua, her vision blurred by tears. "Yes," she whispered.

"I can't hear you, Cadet!"

"Yes!" Phoebe yelled, almost jumping out of her seat. "His sacrifice would—would have been wasted."

Afua stared at Phoebe, eyes still blazing. "It's a harsh reality of the field, Cadet. Agents face those kinds of tough decisions. And from what I know, your father was among the best SIS has ever produced. If he was willing to make such a sacrifice for a fellow agent, you better believe he would do it for his only child." Afua reached behind her chair and brought her hand forward with a tattered leather-bound book, which she slid across the table to Phoebe.

Phoebe dropped her gaze to the book, let out a breath, and bit down on her trembling lip. Feeling as if her insides were draining to the floor, Phoebe ran a finger over the faded title, *An American Dictionary of the English Language*.

"How—Where?"

"It was taken from the scene of your accident," Afua explained quietly. "Whenever an SIS agent is abducted or killed, SIS goes through any personal effects found near or at the scene in case that agent was able to leave a message or a clue behind that can help with the investigation."

As if she hadn't heard a word Afua said, Phoebe whispered, "That is a first edition copy of the dictionary Webster published in 1828. I saw an ad online that it was going up for auction at an antique store, and I convinced my father that we should go and bid. He was excited to add something that rare to our collection. Minutes after we left the store, we sensed the Vigos. If we'd stayed at home . . ."

"Your father left a message inside the dictionary," Afua said, and Phoebe felt the wind go out of her. A new rush of tears started easing their way down her stricken face. She looked at Afua with disbelief, but her face was composed. She was simply stating a fact.

Hands shaking, Phoebe opened the thick, battered cover to the first page. The words hastily scrawled there were barely legible. Her father's handwriting said: "*my phoebe LOS12.*"

Suddenly the room seemed colder to Phoebe. These were her father's last written words. Words she did not understand.

"I may be wrong," Afua said, "but I believe your father wrote that knowing the dictionary would eventually be returned to you. Do you know what it means?"

Phoebe wiped at her tears, still feeling completely overwhelmed and confused. "No," she said. To Phoebe's relief, Afua did not push the matter. "Why did you get it? Why was it given to you?"

"There isn't time to get into the details at this moment," Afua said.

And as if on cue, Yelena entered the gym. "Are you ready?" she asked Afua without looking at Phoebe.

"Yes," Afua said.

"We're done?" Phoebe asked, confused. "What about our last session?"

"We just had it," Afua said. "One of the toughest fights you can find yourself in is the one that goes on in your head. And that can be detrimental to the one on the field." When Phoebe stared at her uncomprehending, she added, "You need a clear mind for what you're about to do tonight and that means understanding that the enemy isn't you. You didn't kill your father. So focus your fight on the enemy that did."

At the sound of heavy footsteps echoing loudly in the hallway, Afua rose from her chair and gathered up her folders. Phoebe stood up as well, wobbling on her feet as she considered what Afua had just said. It was a lot to swallow.

"One more thing," Afua said. She slipped her hand into an inside pocket of her blazer and retrieved a flat, red, velvet-covered box, which she handed to Phoebe. "This is for you."

Phoebe opened the box: inside was a luminescent golden-brown stone encircled by a narrow band of silver. Teardrop in shape, it hung from a length of black silk. Phoebe held the necklace in her palm.

"It's a tiger's eye," Afua said.

"What?!" Phoebe squealed, shocked, dropping the pendant; Afua caught it just before it hit the table.

"Tiger's eye is a gemstone," Afua said, handing the necklace back to Phoebe who couldn't help feeling foolish. "It offers protection to the wearer. Roman soldiers wore them in battle, and so do we." Afua tugged on the gold chain around her neck to reveal the lustrous stone concealed beneath her top.

"Tiger's eyes providing protection from Tigers," Phoebe thought aloud. "Ironic."

Afua almost smiled. "Carry it with you tonight," she said in a tone that conveyed it as more of an order than a request.

Phoebe turned the pendant over in her hand; she saw that the other side had a flashing grayish-blue hue to it. Before she could ask Afua why that was, the door opened and Yelena and Deborah-Anna walked in, followed by fifty civilian-dressed men and women; some looked quite young, others slightly older. The group filed past Phoebe and with mesmerizing martial efficiency, they arranged themselves in five evenly spaced lines and crossed their arms in an X over their chests in formal salute. All eyes were on Afua who strode around the table toward where Yelena and Deborah-Anna stood before the group.

"At ease, agents," Afua said.

The men and women dropped their arms to their sides. Phoebe stared at them blankly. She was only dimly aware of Afua handing each agent a folder. A gut-churning thought had seized control of her mind: this sting was happening. Of course, she had been preparing with Afua for two weeks, but there was something about seeing all of these agents tasked with her safety that made the sting all the more real and terrifying. There were so many of them. All this concern for her safety was a humbling reminder of how seriously everyone was taking this prophecy. Perhaps she and the other Hyphas were truly that important.

Phoebe didn't know how long she'd been standing in a daze when Yelena's sharp voice ringing in her ear made her look up. "We'll come for you at six, Cadet," she said, staring at Phoebe in a way that suggested she'd been repeating herself.

"Okay." Phoebe could barely get the word out. She cast a quick look between the agents and Afua, then picked up the dictionary and walked toward the door. As it snapped shut behind her, Phoebe heard a man's voice ask, with a tinge of awe, "Was that one of the Hyphas, ma'am?"

"Yes, Agent Rodriguez," Afua replied. "Now if you would all open your dossiers to page . . ." the Blackcoat's words faded as Phoebe, turning a corner, took her next steps at a run.

Hayley came to see Phoebe off that evening bearing a tray of freshly baked muffins and looking as nervous as Phoebe, if not more so.

"Banana nut," Hayley said, laying the tray on the desk before grabbing one and sinking cross-legged onto Phoebe's bed.

"I'm too nervous to eat," Phoebe said, closing the door.

Hayley laughed. "I made them for me. So I've been thinking about that whole kiss-on-the-nose thing," Hayley continued, in a bright, cheery voice. "You know you're being silly, right? He hasn't parked you in the friend zone. It was sweet."

"Fine, fine," Phoebe laughed. "Maybe I was a bit melodramatic."

Phoebe had fired off a series of text messages to Hayley immediately following her dinner with Colten. She'd reviewed the dinner—great. The conversation—candid. The goodbye—"KISS ON THE NOSE. WHAT THE HELL??" But with all of the day's final preparations for the sting, Phoebe hadn't been able to meet up with Hayley to discuss.

"I just thought I gave off the right signals." Phoebe, who had been obsessively checking and re-checking her bags, finally grabbed a muffin from the tray and sat next to Hayley.

Hayley gave Phoebe a doubtful look. "Did you really?" She took another bite of her muffin. "Show me?"

"Show you what?"

"Your best come-and-kiss-me look."

Phoebe began arranging her features and Hayley fell over laughing, thumping her chest as she choked on a piece of muffin. "You look like you're constipated!" Hayley wheezed. "But you've made my point."

Phoebe shot to her feet, irritated. "Whatever—what point?"

Calmer now, Hayley said, "You can't force it. When you feel it, you feel it. You were trying too hard to make that dinner the 'do over.'"

Phoebe took a bite of her muffin, chewed, and scowled at Hayley. Perhaps Hayley was right.

"Anyway," Hayley said. "It wasn't a kiss on the cheek. Now that can be a one-way ticket to the friend zone. The nose . . . well the nose is just a slippery slope down to the lips."

"Slippery slope?" Phoebe laughed. "Really? Where do you think up such stuff?" She was grateful for Hayley's crazy chatter, as it was enough to cut through the frantic pre-sting noise in her own head.

"That color is gonna make your hair pop in photos," Hayley said as Phoebe pulled the dress they'd chosen from the closet and zipped it into its Macy's garment bag. "Speaking of photos, do you know the right way to pose for the cameras?"

Phoebe looked up from her packing. "There's a right way?"

"Oh God, yes," Hayley said, stuffing the rest of her muffin into her mouth. "There's a pose that arranges your body in a flattering position so that you look lean and curvy where it counts. I can't believe I didn't think to do this earlier."

"Do what?"

"Use my pageant experience to help make you paparazzi ready."

"Don't worry about it," Phoebe said, grabbing her brush from the desk and slipping it into the side pocket of her backpack. "I'll probably be in the background somewhere."

Hayley almost choked. "Are you kidding me right now? There's no fading into the background when you're on Colten Chase's arm. Cameras will be flashing. You will be famous—Phoebe Pope will be a name known around the world!"

Phoebe's eyes widened at those words.

"So, let's get this right." Hayley hurried forward and grabbed Phoebe by the hand. "The trick with posing," she said, after she'd dragged a reluctant Phoebe to the closet mirror, "is to angle your body. That's the secret to looking leaner—not that you need any help in that department."

"Angle my body?" Phoebe said. "You're kidding."

"Nope. Never face the camera straight on. Now, pretend the mirror is the cameraman. This is how you work it." Hayley moved behind Phoebe and angled her right shoulder away from the "cameraman", setting that arm's hand on her hip. Then Hayley's hands traveled to Phoebe's hips, shifting them slightly forward. Phoebe's eyes widened at seeing the immediate effect this had on the appearance of her frame.

"So that's it, then?" Phoebe said.

Hayley smiled in the mirror. "Almost, my friend. Let your left arm hang away from your body and allow your fingers to hold your purse in a relaxed manner."

"There's no way I'm going to remember this," Phoebe said as Hayley placed a purse in her hand, took her arm and made a minor adjustment.

"Even if you only remember a couple of things, it will make a huge difference." Hayley tapped Phoebe's foot with her own. "Now cross your left leg over your right. See how that makes those stilts you walk on look even longer? And lastly—"

A loud knocking at the door swallowed the rest of Hayley's instructions.

"I'll be right there," Phoebe answered in a voice of forced calm, while throwing a panicked look at Hayley whose complexion had suddenly paled. "Lastly what?" Phoebe whispered, now staring desperately at Hayley. The Blackcoats had arrived. She was out of time. And all she wanted to know at that moment, as if her life depended on it, was Hayley's last piece of advice.

"Don't forget to smile," Hayley said in a rush. "It can do more for your face than makeup."

Phoebe briefly studied her reflection. The pose Hayley had put her in had her looking sophisticated and confident—everything she didn't feel. Phoebe opened the closet door and got her coat. She threw it on and squeezed the tiger's eye pendant she'd put in the pocket. Then, she picked up her bags and headed for the door.

Hayley gripped Phoebe's elbow before she turned the knob. "You'll be fine," she whispered reassuringly. "Remember you're on a date!"

"Kinda rhymes with bait," Phoebe chuckled nervously, although the excitement of being with Colten was welling up again.

Hayley punched Phoebe in the arm. "You've got the easiest job— looking good." Lowering her voice she added, "They've got you covered."

Phoebe bent over and swallowed her pint-sized friend in a tight hug. "Thank you for everything," she whispered in Hayley's ear. "The company, the muffins, the tips, everything."

Hayley wriggled herself free of Phoebe's hold. "Yeah yeah. I'll be waiting for the post-premiere recap!"

❦ TWENTY-TWO

When Phoebe knocked on Colten's hotel room door, she was shocked to come face to face with his co-star, Tanya Brown, who whipped the door open with one hand resting lightly on her cocked hip. Phoebe's stomach plummeted; even the perfectly airbrushed photos she'd seen of the glamour girl had failed to do her proper justice. Her eyes, dark and piercing beneath long mascara-tinged lashes, stared inquiringly at Phoebe.

"Can I help you?" Tanya said, with luscious lips painted an enhancing shade of cherry red.

Phoebe took a moment to calm her nerves before answering, "I'm looking for Colten."

Tanya arched perfectly plucked eyebrows. "And you are?"

"Be nice to my date, Tan," Colten's voice came from inside the room.

Phoebe looked over Tanya's head to where Colten sat on a sofa, a book in his hand, gorgeous grin firmly in place.

"So you're Phoebe," Tanya said instantly breaking into a pleasant smile. "Sorry, I thought you were some crazed fan who managed to get past security. Come in." Tanya stepped aside to allow Phoebe to pass.

At first Phoebe didn't move, dumbfounded that Tanya Brown knew of her and that her name had generated a smile. And then, engaging her feet, Phoebe walked through the door, entering a suite that took her breath away all over again. With wall-to-wall windows rising from mahogany floors to a gracefully arched ceiling, it offered stunning views of the Charles River and the Boston skyline beyond it. The dark wood paneling, plush furniture, ornately woven throw rugs and two huge fireplaces burning with healthy flames all had Phoebe's senses working to absorb the splendor around her. If she weren't wound so tight with nerves, she might have rushed over to the balcony to take in the whole spectacular panorama. She could feel Colten's smile as he took in the amazement on her face.

"Well kids, I gotta go get ready." Tanya's voice snapped Phoebe out of her reverie. Phoebe turned to look at the slender star who was grabbing her bag and coat from a love seat.

"We'll see you out there," Colten said.

Tanya threw Colten a wicked grin. "I know you're happy to be rid of me," she said. And then looking at Phoebe, "I've been giving him crap for being a bore." She gestured at the coffee table stacked with books. "We have a premiere tonight and he's here reading poetry by Yeats and some other long dead English men."

Colten stood. "Tan. Go," he said in mock warning. The suite door closed and Phoebe could hear Tanya's ringing laugh in the hallway.

Colten crossed to Phoebe. "Don't mind her."

Phoebe spoke, careful to keep all jealousy out of her voice. "So were you two prepping for the premiere?"

Colten grinned. "It's been leaked to the press that Tanya and I are no longer an item." Colten laughed as Phoebe wrinkled her forehead. "And since this premiere will be our first public appearance since the 'split,'" he raised his hands to make mock quotation marks in the air, "we met to get our story straight for the reporters who will be hounding us." Colten then reached toward her and took Phoebe's hands in his. "It's really dumb and you don't have to worry about it. Let me show you your room."

Colten led Phoebe to a bedroom with thick carpeting that swallowed her feet the moment she entered. She toed off her shoes to luxuriate in the softness while Colten took her bags from her and deposited them on a silk-covered bed set with giant pillows. And then turning, he watched her quietly.

"I'm glad you're here tonight," he said softly.

Phoebe smiled. She was glad too, even though she couldn't truly relax enough to enjoy it.

"What's up with the books? Homework?"

"No. Independent research."

Phoebe gave him a quizzical look.

"Someone I know told me they couldn't have another person's mouth on theirs unless they liked the things that came out of it, their thoughts, opinions, and ideas." Phoebe blinked, shocked to hear her own words being said back to her. "So I figured," Colten continued with a hint of nervousness in his voice that Phoebe had never heard before, "if smart things are to come out of my mouth then I should brush up on some of the brilliant minds that said them."

Phoebe felt a flush flare, rising rapidly from her navel to the roots of her hair. Colten had been walking slowly toward her, and now, standing inches before her, he hooked his thumbs to the back of her jeans, lowered his face toward hers and said softly, "'Though I am old with wandering / Through hollow lands and hilly lands / I will find out where she has gone / And kiss her lips and take her hands / And walk among long dappled grass / And pluck till time and times are done / The silver apples of the moon / The golden apples of the sun.'"

"'The Song of Wandering Aengus,'" Phoebe said breathlessly, her hearts thumping in her throat.

Colten nodded. "I think a guy should give himself a fair shake at getting acquainted with your lips, Phoebe Pope."

Phoebe gasped. Colten cupped the back of her head with one gentle hand while the other hand palmed the small of her back. He gently bit her lower lip, teasing. When Phoebe didn't move, Colten stepped back, meeting her eyes with curiosity. *Is he asking permission to continue*, Phoebe wondered. Almost involuntarily, she closed the gap between them with the smallest step and wrapped her arms around his neck. *Oh this kiss is happening*, her mind screamed as she raised her lips to his. Colten kissed her softly, then deeper, letting his tongue gently caress the shape of her lips. Tiny firecrackers exploded in Phoebe's stomach as his hands slipped into the space between her jeans and her hips and pulled her even closer against him. Phoebe felt her spine curve at the touch of his fingertips to her skin. Everything about it was amazing and her head buzzed with sensation. As he pulled her, carefully walking backward toward the bed and softly kissing her ear, a voice from the living room yelled, "Colten! The pre-sale numbers are off the charts!"

They broke apart instantly. Phoebe's eyes widened in surprise, her mind swirling with what had just happened and the sudden presence of someone unknown. *Yeats. Colten Chase had memorized Yeats just so he could impress me with it.*

"Nicole," Colten mumbled.

Phoebe ran a hand through her hair, struggling for composure, and moved to sit on the edge of the bed while Colten remained on his feet.

"Oh good, you're here," Nicole said, appearing suddenly in the doorway, smiling. She leaned against it, a cell phone and sheet of paper in one hand, a designer tote bag hanging from the crease of her other elbow. She oozed sophistication in a flowing black sweater over indigo skinny jeans and pointy cowboy boots, her neck draped with strings of gold beads.

"Am I ever late?" Colten said. He walked the short distance to her, and Nicole tilted her face to receive a kiss on both cheeks.

"We're on our way to breaking all kinds of records—opening night, opening weekend." She smiled and slapped the piece of paper against Colten's chest. "Read it and . . ." At that moment, Nicole looked past Colten, meeting Phoebe's eyes with a scrutinizing brown-eyed gaze.

"I didn't know you had company," Nicole said flatly.

"I told you about Phoebe." Colten turned his head to wink at her over his shoulder.

Nicole's highly drawn ponytail swung as her head turned back to Phoebe. "This is your date? When you said Phoebe I thought you meant Phoebe Monsaria, the super model." She rolled her eyes from the top of Phoebe's head to her feet and then back, at last, to her face, with an expression that was far from flattering. "This situation,"—she waved her hands at Phoebe—"is going to take some work."

Phoebe grabbed a fistful of the silk comforter and forced herself to breathe. Frustration swelled inside her. She looked up at Colten with a hurt look on her face, as he continued grinning down at her and she realized that this was probably par for the course for Nicole. That, however, did not make Phoebe feel any less like a wart on an already misshapen nose.

"You don't like anyone I date, Nic." Colten held Nicole by the shoulders, looking into her eyes with a raised eyebrow and a hint of annoyance in his tone. "And besides, last I heard, you thought Phoebe Monsaria had a horsey smile."

Nicole narrowed her eyes at him, paused, and then let her eyes slide to Phoebe. "What did you bring to—" she started, and then stopped, her eyes having located Phoebe's Macy's garment bag. Her eyes closed involuntarily in disdain, and Phoebe felt her stomach drop. Just then, the shrill sound of Nicole's cell phone broke the tension in the room. She flipped it open and put it to her ear.

"Just the person I need to talk to," Nicole said into the phone. "Yes, we're very pleased with the numbers. . . . Yes, biggest opening yet. . . . Listen, I need you to do me a huge favor and throw in a few dresses with the Armani suit you're bringing up for Colten. Size six. Bring knee or tea-length options unless your goddess of a seamstress can do a quick hem job on a floor-length. . . . No, not Tanya, a prom-dress-toting newbie. . . . I know! That's what I said. Yes . . . glam squad, too. There's a funky streak in her hair. . . ."

Colten gave Nicole a reproving look, cocked his head at the door and mouthed "Out". Waving him off, she spun around and stalked out of the room. Phoebe stared at the door, trying to scrub the words "prom-dress-toting newbie" out of her mind.

"Don't pay attention to her antics," Colten said, turning to face Phoebe. "She thrives on drama and you'll only feed the beast if you react to it. Besides, I'm sure what you brought is beautiful. Nicole only cares about name dropping designers in magazines."

Phoebe bit her lip and said nothing. If it weren't for her need to be there for this sting operation, or the fact that Colten was looking at her with a gaze so inviting, Phoebe would have grabbed her things immediately and toted her "prom dress" out of there.

"If I remember correctly," Colten said, his tone full of gravel as he crossed to the bed, "I was in the middle of getting acquainted with that pouting mouth . . ."

Phoebe couldn't stop the salacious wink that accompanied her smile. It surprised her. But she'd gotten a taste of Colten's lips. And she wanted more. For a moment she worried about Nicole in the next room. But that was washed away by the warmth of Colten's breath pulsing on her cheek. "Relax," he said, kissing her nose and sliding down to her lips, "she won't hear a thing."

"Are you sure?" Phoebe said, stealing a breath. She couldn't believe how sexy Colten's murmuring voice sounded, how the hairs on her body prickled with heated excitement. It was official; she'd surrendered to her feelings.

"The room is sound proof . . ." Colten said in a husky whisper. Phoebe vaguely heard those words. Colten's body had melted into hers, tipping her, unresisting, onto her back. Desire claimed her. Her hands found the hem of his shirt and slipped underneath it, her fingers tracing the lines of muscles that roped up his back to thick shoulders. A gasp escaped Phoebe's lips. Colten's mouth was on her neck, gently sucking at her skin. Her toes curled back. Her body trembled as he left a trail of warm kisses from the hollow where her collar bones met, all the way down to her stomach. His tongue tickled her navel beneath her shirt. Phoebe dug her hands into Colten's hair and moaned.

"You're not like anyone I've met, Phoebe Pope," he murmured, bringing his face back up to hers. "You're—"

Phoebe silenced him by softly nibbling his lower lip before moving up to cover his entire mouth in a kiss.

When the glamour squad eventually arrived to peel Phoebe from Colten's arms, she made only two meek requests: she must wear her hair down and she'd prefer to wear the one dress they'd brought that wasn't strapless. Phoebe wanted to make sure that all of her scars were concealed. With that understood, she sat contritely and not a little disheveled in a chair in the middle of the suite's massive marble bathroom and relinquished herself to them. Soon there were hands in her face plucking at eyebrows, curling lashes, and applying mascara, eye shadow, and lipstick. She felt the bristles of a brush against her neck as it was yanked through the tangles of her hair. Lastly, Phoebe stepped into a dress that was fastened so tightly it threatened her ability to breathe.

When a full-length mirror was rolled in front of her, Phoebe made eye contact with a person she'd never met before. This girl had the radiance of models pictured in magazines, with eyes that sparkled and flawless skin. The smoky eye shadow framing her gray eyes made her stare that much more piercing. Her always wild hair had been tamed into soft curls that fell around her shoulders. Even her streak had an extra glow to it. And the Armani dress: a rose-hued lace confection that ignited the fiery tones in Phoebe's hair. The body hugging dress, with its scoop neck, and delicate cap sleeves added curves to Phoebe's figure, giving her a startling reminder that she had breasts and that they were quite lovely. Phoebe moved her hips from side to side, and watched the gown's flowing skirt swirl around her. The stylist snapped a diamond bracelet on Phoebe's wrist, placed a gold clutch purse in her hands, and sent her on her way.

Shyly, Phoebe stepped into the suite's living room, balancing precariously on a pair of stiletto pumps that were as painful as they were beautiful. Nicole's approval was immediate. Although she made no comment other than, "It's about time," Phoebe could read it in her wide, appraising eyes.

Colten emerged from his room then, expertly styled in his own Armani with the neck of a crisp white shirt open underneath a charcoal suit. When his eyes caught hold of Phoebe, his entire face broke into radiant pleasure at the sight of her. He took in everything about her in one appraising gaze: the dress, the hair, the dress. Phoebe bit her lip as Colten immediately crossed to her and took her in his warm and reassuring arms. "Beautiful," he said low and gruff, and tilted his head toward hers as Phoebe felt a quick rush of heat sweep over her, raising goosebumps on her bare arms.

"Don't you dare kiss her and ruin her lipstick!" Nicole snapped, as Colten continued to lower his head to Phoebe's. "She needs to look good for the press!" Colten abruptly took a step back and turned his palms up in a playful retreat from Phoebe who laughed.

Nicole glanced down at her watch, frowned, and then looked up at Colten. "Now that glam's done with her, go have them take care of your make-up, and let's get this show on the road."

Phoebe snapped her eyes to Colten, surprised. "You wear make-up?" She hadn't expected that.

"Oh, God yes," Nicole answered, brushing pieces of lint from Colten's jacket. "In this age of HD the cameras pick up everything. Look at those bags under his eyes"—she placed a hand under his chin and tilted his face—"a quick dab of concealer and he'll be all set." Colten pushed Nicole's hand away. And as Phoebe continued to stare incredulously, Nicole added, "All the men in Hollywood do it."

Colten shrugged with mild amusement. "Just one of the many perks of my job," he said to a still disbelieving Phoebe.

"All right," Nicole said. "Make-up now, flirting later. We've got to go."

The red carpet was some distance from the hotel. When the limousine finally cruised to a stop, Phoebe pressed her nose lightly against the glass, staring out at a daunting scene. Several streets had been closed off with police and private security personnel every few feet to direct both human and vehicular traffic. Fans, (mostly girls and their equally crazed mothers) waved posters from raised bleachers waiting for Colten's arrival, hoping to catch a glimpse of him. Only because she was in a car, could Phoebe let her eyes roam over the star-struck faces; somewhere out there was a potential threat.

The carpet itself, which was green in honor of the environment, stretched over the length of a city block, ending at the threshold of an imposing art deco theater. Throngs of beautiful people were already milling around, talking with reporters and posing for cameras. Phoebe found herself smiling, thinking it was a living picture from Hayley's *Dish* magazine.

"Ready?" Colten said, squeezing her hand.

Phoebe nodded.

The car door opened. Colten smiled and waved as he exited. The crowd went mad for him, their screams of adoration deafening. Hand firmly in Colten's, Phoebe stepped out after him, fear and excitement gripping her. From the moment they crossed onto the carpet, Afua, Yelena, Deborah-Anna and six more formally dressed agents emerged from the crowd to surround Phoebe and Colten from a small distance. Colten was unfazed by this; the six agents had gotten jobs as members of his security detail for this premiere. Phoebe knew that they were armed with diamond daggers. And she knew that a number of them walked among the fans while others surveyed the press. But even so, it did not comfort her nerves. If anything happened and Colten got hurt, it would be her fault; she'd agreed to this plan.

"Relax. You'll be fine," Colten said under his breath, misinterpreting her sudden tight grip on his hand. Phoebe smiled tightly in response.

Aside from reporters, Colten spoke with other co-stars and celebrity well-wishers, celebrities so famous Phoebe held her breath when looking at them. Phoebe listened in on conversations, losing herself in the banter of the newly famous and the veterans, at one point hearing Tanya say, "I'm fine; the break-up was amicable. He'll always have a piece of my heart."

The scenery was so surreal that it wasn't until Phoebe felt the brush of a nearby Blackcoat's physical energy that her reality crept up on her. She was a pawn in a sting. Not a princess living out a fairytale. The hairs on her arms rose as she wondered whether or not there were Vigos around, waiting to make a move. Were they watching her now?

So far, Phoebe had managed to remain such a quiet observer of the Colten love-fest that she almost didn't hear it when a reporter inquired about her dress. The voice drew her out of her thoughts.

"Who are you wearing?" the woman asked, beaming at her. Smiling widely with pride, Colten nudged Phoebe forward to where people could get a better view of her.

Phoebe stared a moment, then stepped forward and placed a hand on her hip, and remembering said, "Armani." She saw members of the assembled press smile approvingly and it suddenly hit her just how wrong her own dress would have been. Suddenly the comments started coming. A photographer yelled, "You two look great together!"

Another said, "How about you give us a sexy pose!"

At that, Colten took both of Phoebe's hands in his and brought them slowly to his face, brushing his lips against them. In that instant, Phoebe could hear the cameras clicking as wildly as her beating hearts.

"C'mon. You can do better than that!" someone shouted.

"Yeah, we've seen more heat with you and Tanya."

Phoebe felt irrational jealousy at that. She wanted very much to make the crowd forget his staged relationship. It was powerful, this need, and in a PDA move that was uncharacteristic of her, Phoebe stretched onto her toes, swept Colten's sandy hair aside and placed a kiss on his neck, just below his ear.

The response was immediate. A storm of whistles and screams.

"That's what we're talking about!" someone yelled out.

Phoebe pulled away, and satisfaction began to fill her up until she saw the lipstick she'd smeared on Colten's neck—apparently her kiss had been a sloppy one. Phoebe hastily removed a white handkerchief from her purse and reached to dab at the lipstick when to her surprise, Colten clutched her wrist, pulling her hand down.

"Leave it," he whispered firmly. "It will be cute for the cameras." He flipped his shirt collar up but not before Phoebe caught a glimpse of something that made her hearts stop. It couldn't be. It just couldn't be. Phoebe stared at her handkerchief, and saw at once what had happened: along with her red lipstick she'd also removed a layer of foundation. A layer that had been hiding a Mark of Wang tattoo.

Phoebe's hand dropped, falling limply to her side. Time seemed to slow. She stood there, horror burning through her, hardly daring to believe what she had seen. *"Vigo?"* she breathed into Colten's ears before slowly backing away from him.

Colten turned and stared at Phoebe calmly. But for one hearts-stopping moment, as something painfully like regret crept into his eyes, Phoebe read the truth in them as though his lips had said it out loud. Phoebe turned, her mind completely blank, and broke into a run. As she pushed through the crowd, the clasp on her diamond bracelet broke; the sparkling piece of jewelry slipped off her arm to the ground. Not stopping to retrieve it, Phoebe continued running, willing away the tears that beat against her eyes. For a moment, a hush hung in the air, as people tried to figure out what had just happened. She saw the Blackcoats begin to mobilize. Then cameras began clicking away madly and reporters yelled out for comments. Phoebe didn't care. All she wanted was to get as far away as possible from Colten Chase.

❧ TWENTY-THREE

Phoebe sat, hearts still thumping, in the deep backseat of a parked limousine, her body pressed against a window, her long legs stretched across the floor. Her abrupt exit from the red carpet had sent the Blackcoats scrambling to find out what could possibly have caused her to flee. Nicole, who had been trailing behind her and Colten, had started immediate damage control, herding her client into the theater, yelling "no comment" to all reporters who then turned to others for their take on the turn of events. Phoebe rubbed her temples; she had ignited chaos. Not just on the red carpet, but in her mind.

Had she really seen what she'd seen? Colten, a Vigo? Was life playing some sort of cruel joke? She tried to settle her mind to think through it clearly. How was it possible? It defied everything she knew. Her skin had never once burned in his company. She had felt heat from Colten, but just her own attraction, not the singe of a Shaper's reaction to a Vigo. Phoebe knew that burn. And she couldn't ignore the fact that they'd been surrounded by Blackcoats. How could a Vigo walk among Shapers undetected?

The door opened and the slender figure of an elegantly dressed woman was outlined by the wash of light from nearby street lamps. Phoebe drew in her legs as Afua climbed inside the limousine and sat down opposite her.

"What happened out there?" Afua asked stiffly, her expression seeming less severe in the dim light.

Phoebe kept herself in check; she'd been expecting this question. She considered her answer. Something in her gut was preventing her from disclosing the truth. Perhaps Colten liked tattoos. She considered that many peopled got inked with Asian characters. Could it merely be a coincidence? Or could the Chinese character for "king" hold a different meaning for Colten? Phoebe shook herself inwardly. There was no denying the location and the size. It had been the Mark of Wang. But still . . . Phoebe was understandably shaken, and could use that, but she still knew she had to appear in control of her lie. "There was a photographer," she started, her voice creaking. "He got too close. . . . I panicked." Phoebe found that the lie burned her throat.

Afua studied Phoebe for a moment, her arms crossed over the bodice of her stunning beaded red dress. Her gaze was so direct that Phoebe found her eyes traveling to the tattooed rings that glowed on the Blackcoat's wrists. Then Afua said something she didn't expect. "Given the amount of pressure put on you, I am impressed you lasted out there as long as you did."

Phoebe raised her head and looked into Afua's eyes. A bubble of guilt rose in her throat and she waited, hoping for Afua to say something more critical. When she didn't, the bubble burst and threatened to choke Phoebe.

Afua turned in her seat and rapped her knuckles on the dividing glass; it slid down soundlessly to reveal Deborah-Anna behind the wheel.

"You're good to go," Afua said.

"Should we debrief her when we get back?" Yelena's voice floated to Phoebe from the front passenger's seat.

"I'll handle it later," Afua said, stepping out of the limousine and closing the door.

Phoebe's stomach plummeted. Afua wasn't done with her yet. Had the Blackcoat not believed her? Or was it just protocol to follow up again?

The hum of tires on asphalt let Phoebe know that they were moving. She spun around in the seat and looked at the red carpet through the rear window; Afua's lithe figure was disappearing into the madness. As the limo entered the flow of traffic, Phoebe closed her eyes against the guilt churning inside of her.

Knowing she would draw unwanted attention in her Armani gown, Phoebe sat in the limo and waited for all the dorm lights to wink out. It had pained her to see Hayley exit the building. They'd planned to meet up and discuss everything. Now, while the rest of her dorm slept, Phoebe finally stepped into the shower and cried into the water that loosened the curls from her hair and dissolved the make-up on her face. Her body ached with a pain that radiated from her hearts to her extremities as though burrowing for a way out. She scrubbed her face, her lips, her hands, anywhere that Colten had touched her. Anywhere a Vigo had touched her. She felt contaminated.

The tears didn't stop. Steam rose and her body trembled from the unshakable questions in her mind: was Colten responsible for the abductions? And if so, was tonight the night he'd planned on taking her?

Knowing that any other Shaper would have instantly turned him over to the Blackcoats, Phoebe wondered what it said about her loyalty to her race. Why hadn't she? Perhaps she was a traitor. A traitor to her father's memory. An enemy walked among them and she had said nothing. A question from before struck Phoebe again as she reached a hand for the hot water knob to turn it off. How was a Vigo walking among Shapers undetected? Was this all her fault? Had she tapped into his emotions instead of hanging on to a romantic notion of preserving his mystery, would she have detected something sinister?

After flinging her tomato pillow to the ground, Phoebe climbed into bed numbly, still pondering the question. And that was the problem. She wasn't really sure how she felt at all, besides betrayed. Phoebe knew the oath: kill Vigos, no questions asked. But that hadn't been her impulse; she hadn't even wanted him captured. The words of the oath plagued her mind as she fell into an uneasy sleep.

When Phoebe awoke late the next morning, she had a sense of someone's eyes on her. Her roommate, Cyn sat at her desk across the room from Phoebe, dressed in her uniform, her fingers absently tapping her laptop keyboard. The first thing to occur to Phoebe, as she sat up slowly, was that this was a strange moment for her and her roommate. With her penchant for early morning photography, rarely did she cross paths with Cyn before breakfast.

"You lied to me," Cyn said rather coldly and without preamble. "And to think my good word got you the job at the paper. The least you could have done was hook me up with the scoop."

"Excuse me?" Phoebe said, sleepily rubbing her eyes. "What are you talking about?"

Cyn frowned and folded her arms. "When you and Hayley were trying on dresses, it was about Colten's movie premiere. You said it was for the Fall Enviroball."

Phoebe suddenly became conscious of the rose-colored gown thrown over her desk as the previous night came rushing back to her. "I didn't want to make it a big deal," she said to Cyn who had followed her gaze and was giving the dress a covetous look. "That's all."

"Oh, it's a big deal. A very big deal," Cyn said. Phoebe was immediately on guard. It wasn't what Cyn had said that made her uneasy; she expected Cyn to consider the premiere crucial news. It was the way she'd said it; like it was a universal fact. "They're calling you the 'Runaway Date.'"

"What? Who?"

"It's all over the internet. All of us in Colten's Cuties signed up for Google alerts for anything to do with Colten. And I got a whole bunch of alerts from half a dozen websites this morning. Do you want to see?" Cyn started to cross the room with her laptop, but at Phoebe's furious head shake, she stopped in her tracks.

"I just thought I'd give you a head's up," Cyn said, sounding almost sympathetic. She lifted her backpack to her shoulders, paused, and then quickly removed something from inside it. She looked from what she held in her hand, to Phoebe and then back to her hand, thinking something through. "By the way," she said, coming to some decision. "You accidentally included these with the pictures of Collette Nole you submitted to the paper." She placed three prints on Phoebe's desk and quickly left the room.

Phoebe swung her feet out of her bed and padded over to her desk. When her eyes settled on the slightly blurry photos of her and Colten from the Garden Café, her breath caught. His smile was broad and happy and her eyes shone with the nervous energy she'd felt around him at the time. "Flummoxed" had been her word choice for that moment. Today it was "heartache." In sheer frustration, Phoebe flung the photos against her wall.

When Phoebe walked into the barn, the dining hall instantly quieted, and all eyes seemed to mark her entrance. Phoebe knew that Cyn had given her a head's up. But she hadn't realized how difficult it would be for her to try and keep her own head up while pushing back the frown that fought with her face. Phoebe forced herself to walk, careful not to catch any eyes. Slowly, chatter resumed across all tables; many people openly speculating about why she'd fled from the red carpet and what that meant about her relationship with Colten, apparently oblivious or uncaring that she could hear every word.

"Maybe she got nervous."

"Maybe she couldn't handle the stress."

"Maybe she really had to go pee."

But it was Karli who seemed to enjoy Phoebe's spectacle the most. "When it comes down to it," she said loudly to the girls gathered at her table. "He just picked an amateur. I would have never done anything like that. They are so over." And although the opinions were many and the voices penetrating, somehow Karli's cut through the most.

"You don't need this," said a voice at Phoebe's elbow as she joined a buffet line. She turned to see Hayley, a brown paper bag in each hand. "I packed us a to-go breakfast," she said. "So, let's go."

A gust of relief rushed into Phoebe. "Thank you," she mouthed. They exited the cafeteria, leaving the low, animated sound of mindless gossip behind.

"So how bad was it?" Phoebe asked when they had settled themselves on Hayley's bed. She fixed the TV with a nervous stare.

"I'm not going to lie," Hayley said, between bites of yogurt. "It was pretty bad . . . but you don't have to watch it. I mean,"—Hayley snatched the TV remote that lay at Phoebe's feet—"I only recorded it so that we could gush about it later."

"That would have been fun," Phoebe said, mourning what could have been and toying with her bagel. "Especially since I was excited to come back and tell you that we made out—"

"You—what?" Hayley bounced on her bed like a sugar-high toddler, her loose curls swirling around her face. "Holy crap! How was it?!"

For a moment Phoebe allowed herself to get caught up in Hayley's excitement. "It was amazing," she admitted airily. She shook herself from it, remembering that she'd kissed the enemy.

"God, making out with Colten Chase must be like losing your virginity on prom night—a little overboard?" Hayley said, noting Phoebe's sharp, disapproving frown.

"A lot overboard," Phoebe said, and then laughed

"Did you lose your shirt?"

"No. But my hands went under his and that chest is all muscle!

Hayley picked up a pillow and shrieked into it. Once she'd regained her composure, Hayley flung the pillow at Phoebe. "So then what the hell happened on the carpet?"

The smile slipped from Phoebe's face. She'd decided that she couldn't tell Hayley the truth. She knew that Hayley would react in one of two ways. She'd either remind Phoebe of their sworn oath and insist that they report Colten, or she'd choose to protect the secret and help Phoebe unravel the mystery. If it were the latter, Phoebe feared the consequences. The thought of Hayley facing treason charges on account of her, made Phoebe shudder. She wanted her friend to have plausible deniability.

"I got spooked," Phoebe finally said. And then to sell it, "I've no business becoming an SIS agent."

Hayley shook her head. "You rock for even signing up to be bait. You're a Hastati-year, remember? And I'm sure if we think hard enough we can come up with a believable excuse for you to tell Colten."

Phoebe grimaced. That was the furthest thing from her mind.

The rest of the week continued to be horrible for Phoebe. Colten's conspicuous absence kept the story fresh in people's minds while Afua's attendance at each of her classes Below made Phoebe more paranoid by the day as she worried that the Blackcoat knew she was hiding something. As if that weren't enough, on Friday Montclaire raised the tank in class for a segment on Vigo physiology. Each time Phoebe gazed upon the Tiger, her stomach burned at the thought of Colten being one of them.

At the end of Bio Encryption, Phoebe muttered apologetically as she shoved her way out of the classroom and through the throngs in the hallways. In a haze of fatigue, she slumped to an overcrowded corner of the courtyard and did something she would normally never even consider. She lowered her mental gate. Completely. At once, strangers' emotions that had been gnawing at the boundary of her mind came crashing in— all the things-really-suck feelings . . . jealousy . . . happiness . . . horny-teenager frustrations. Like a furious torrent of spinning balls, they banged against the neural walkways of Phoebe's mind until they'd managed to do what she had wanted them to do: drown out the sound of her own desperate emotions.

Phoebe's mind practically rattled in her skull, but she didn't care. In that moment, she felt liberated. There were no thoughts of Colten. No confusion over whether or not to tell the Blackcoats what she knew. All of her heartache and sense of betrayal was gone. For now.

"—hit someone," a voice said in Phoebe's ear, returning her to her senses. She looked up to find Scott watching her, his white shirt half untucked from his pants. He flicked at a lock of black hair that fell across his eyes.

"Oh—hey," Phoebe said, blinking hard and working to snap her mental gate back into place. "What did you say?"

"I said you look like you need to hit someone," Scott repeated and grinned. "And I think that someone should be me." And when Phoebe looked at him baffled, he laughed. "We have a rain check on you teaching me fighting techniques, remember? So how 'bout we do it tonight—take your mind off things?"

"Oh, that . . ." Phoebe said, distracted, staring curiously around her. She couldn't help wondering where some of the strong emotions had come from. Some cadet in one of the groups nearby was harboring dark anger and pent up aggression. Phoebe brought her hands to her head and pressed her palms against her throbbing temples, the severity of her emotion-induced headache suddenly registering.

"You okay?" Scott studied Phoebe. Then he said very seriously, leaning in, "You're not looking too hot—I mean"—he ran a hand over the scars on his neck—"you're hot, but not looking great, that is—have you been sleeping—?"

Phoebe, who had suddenly spotted Afua threading through the courtyard crowd with Gabe talking at her side, cut Scott off. "Let's meet tomorrow after dinner," she said pointedly, keeping her gaze down, not wanting to catch Afua's eye as the Blackcoat and the custodian moved in their direction.

Phoebe had barely been aware of leaving Scott; all she knew was that she had shouldered her way through a few knots of students to the narthyx chamber and was now racing up a passageway. There was an edge of panic in her need to get Above. Phoebe knew that Afua was conducting her one-on-one debriefings with the agents involved in the sting, which meant the Blackcoat would be pulling her in soon for their session. Phoebe didn't want "soon" to be "now."

"So what if it made the cover of *Dish*?" Hayley said the next afternoon. She speared a piece of lettuce with her fork and made a funny face at Phoebe who was flipping through the issue that had just arrived. "People are fickle with their celebrity disasters." Hayley continued speaking around the salad in her mouth. "Trust me. Once the next thing happens they'll forget all about this one," she insisted with false conviction in her voice.

Phoebe found herself frowning; she was eager to get off the disaster roller coaster she seemed to be on. She could do without the continued whispering and the less than discreet finger pointing every time she moved through the hallways or entered a classroom. And if she heard one more snide remark from Karli, it was possible that she'd explode.

"How did you find this place anyway?" Hayley said. "It's so much better than the barn." Between it being Friday, and Phoebe wanting to avoid scrutiny, she had dragged Hayley up to the Garden Café for lunch. But she wondered about her real reason for being there as her eyes flashed around the greenhouse, stopping on any boy in a baseball cap who was even remotely tall.

Hayley put her fork down and asked the question again. Phoebe, returning her eyes to Hayley, opened her mouth to explain and then stopped, not wanting to walk a line of conversation that involved Colten. Any mention of him and Hayley would launch into her don't-worry-he's-not-avoiding-you spiel, trying to convince Phoebe that things between her and Colten would return to normal once everything blew over. At that moment as Hayley's eyes burned with impatience, Phoebe's thoughts went to Mariko and Lewis. Were they nearby? Were they hurt? Had her blunder on the red carpet sealed their fate? So ignoring Hayley's question, Phoebe instead asked, "Anything new from Liam? Any mention of the missing two?"

Hayley shook her head. "He's been quiet on the blog for the past week or so," she said, and then thinking, added, "I wonder if that means no news is good news. What do you think?" But Phoebe had stopped listening. A sickening feeling twisted her stomach. She couldn't give in to coincidence that in the week of Colten's absence, Liam had nothing new to report. Was Vigo activity related to Colten activity?

When Phoebe met up with Scott the following night, he greeted her with a mysterious smile. She looked him over and frowned at his choice in clothing. He wore a faded t-shirt, grass-stained jeans and a pair of

Converse sneakers. "You're not planning to fight in that?" said Phoebe, who'd arrived in a black jogging suit.

"Change of plans, Pope." Scott threw his arm around Phoebe and began to lead her out of the athletic wing.

"Got scared, huh?" Phoebe teased.

"Yup. Decided my ego wouldn't survive the beating."

Phoebe laughed. "So where are we going?"

"Not far," Scott said as they climbed a flight of stairs. Soon, they arrived at a door that bore the words: AUTHORIZED PERSONNEL.

Scott pushed Phoebe through the door saying, "Welcome to the best light show you'll ever see."

Phoebe came to a stutter stop. She was in a long, rectangular room, with more than fifty rows of tables draped with the purest linens, each holding locked, glass display cases full of nothing but Utaviium. The bolts of lightning bouncing around within their blue, crystal cylinders were almost blinding.

"How do you know about this place?" Phoebe said, her face breaking into a look of astonishment and pleasure, she turned to look at Scott who beamed at her.

"I had to polish those cases as part of my doghouse punishment," he said. "Sit down, I want to show you the best part."

Phoebe settled herself comfortably on the ground, pressing her back against the wall. Grinning, Scott switched off the lights. A loud gasp immediately fell from Phoebe's lips. The darkness had made the display cases invisible, creating the illusion of fiery lightning bolts floating in the center of the room.

"Wow," Phoebe said.

"Thought you'd dig it," Scott said, sliding down the wall beside Phoebe's outstretched legs.

A warm feeling of contentment burgeoned in Phoebe's chest, one that she wouldn't have expected Scott to stir in her. She was stressed, she hadn't been sleeping, her thoughts were conflicted beyond measure, and with this field trip, Scott had managed to do what she didn't think was possible—take her mind off of things. Gratefulness washed over her like a warm bath.

Phoebe's eyesight adjusted to the dark, giving her a better look at Scott; she was surprised to see a frown on his face.

"Hey," she said, nudging him with a foot. "What's wrong?"

Scott turned his face to Phoebe, and it held frustration and a morose expression. "I bailed on fighting tonight 'cause you shouldn't have to teach me," he said. "It's been weeks. I don't get why they haven't bothered to show me a few things. I mean, hell, I'm still on that hit list. . . ."

Phoebe looked away; she drew her knees up to her chest, watching the brilliant lights dance against the darkness. She thought over whether or not to tell Scott about the sting and decided that discretion was no longer necessary now that the field operation was over.

"Listen," Phoebe said, looking at him. "Don't feel slighted. There was a very specific reason they had to train me when they did."

"What are you talking about?"

Phoebe took a breath to assemble her thoughts. "Contrary to what you might think, I didn't go to that premiere for fun," she said. "The Blackcoats asked me to go—"

"They what?" Scott turned to face her fully. "Why the hell would they do that?"

"Because they think the abductions are an inside job," Phoebe explained. "The point of my going was to set up a sting. The Blackcoats were trying to flush the traitor out." Scott said nothing, his face darkening with each word Phoebe spoke. "But I was protected the entire time. They pulled in extra agents for the event. Afua just gave me a head start in fighting just in case—"

"They shouldn't have dangled you out like that!" Scott said cutting her off, sounding livid. "You could have been killed."

"But I wasn't."

"You should have told me all this was going down." His eyes were liquid with hurt and obvious fear for her.

"I couldn't," she said softly, her voice laced with regret. "I wanted to."

"I know, I know," Scott said, patting his pockets nervously for a cigarette and finding none. "Information containment." Then, sounding a good deal calmer, "You've got some balls on you, Pope. Don't think I would have done it."

Phoebe shrugged off the comment. "I didn't quite complete the mission."

They sat in silence for awhile, then Scott said, "I don't even know why I bother caring, anyway. I'm not planning on enrolling in SIS when I'm done here."

"What?" Phoebe said, shocked. She couldn't imagine why anyone would go through the double course load if it wasn't a career path.

"I want to play pro soccer. Got my eyes set on the Shaper World Cup, Pope," Scott said. "But my old man's not cool with it, so he sent me here." Scott chuckled darkly. "He thinks three years of discipline will set my head straight, but I'm just doing things his way now so I can do it my way later."

"Three years is a long time to work toward something you don't want to do," Phoebe said.

"I have to wait that long anyway until I'm eligible to try out for teams." Scott patted himself again for cigarettes as though he still couldn't believe he didn't have any. "How about you, Pope? What would you do other than SIS?"

Phoebe shrugged.

"C'mon. There's gotta be something?"

"I've thought about photography," Phoebe said at last. "But sometimes I think I'd hate it if I was getting paid to do it."

"Personally," Scott said, briefly meeting her gaze, his eyes unreadable. "I think you're on the wrong side of the camera."

Because she couldn't stop her flush, Phoebe bit her lip and changed the subject. "Are you sure we can be in here?" she asked with a wavering voice.

"No," Scott said, laughing. "Don't rat me out to Yelena." He stood and helped Phoebe to her feet. Almost simultaneously, they both reached for the light switch, their faces barely inches apart. A brief flicker of a smile started on Scott's lips and he leaned forward. Phoebe was startled by the intent she saw in his eyes, and took a hasty step back.

Scott bit his lip and crossed one leg over the other, "I'm sorry," he said, scrubbing the back of his neck with his hands as Phoebe put more distance between them and averted her eyes. "I wasn't—I shouldn't—" Scott was interrupted by the sound of the door opening.

"This place is not a hangout," said a male Blackcoat, poking his head into the room and turning on the light.

"We were just leaving," Phoebe said, pushing past the broad-shouldered agent who was her shadow. Scott may have followed, but she didn't wait or look back to see. As she picked up her pace, now fairly jogging down the hallway, Phoebe realized that it wasn't Scott's attempt to kiss her that she'd found most upsetting; it was the fact that somewhere deep inside, she knew there was a part of her that would have been happy to let him.

❦ TWENTY-FOUR

"I hope you haven't been waiting for me, lass?"

Phoebe looked up. A berobed Gabe stood smiling at the end of her pew. Behind him, the logs in the chapel fireplace crackled with hearty flames.

"No," she said smiling back. "I just needed a really quiet place to get some work done."

"Your father used to do his homework in the chapel, too." The custodian gave a soft chuckle. "Said it was the one place he could count on being empty during the week. Please don't let me interrupt you," he quickly added as Phoebe closed her laptop.

"My French essay isn't due until next week," she said, slipping her computer into her backpack.

Gabe sat on the pew in front of Phoebe and turned to face her. "How are you finding your Above classes?"

Phoebe shifted on the velvet cushion and shrugged. "Fine, I suppose," she said. "It's hard to focus on them—or anything really—with everything that's going on."

Gabe stared down at his lap. "I can only imagine what you're going through," he said, his pensive voice barely audible.

"Can I ask you something?" Phoebe said, leaning forward.

Gabe looked up. There was a flash of hesitation in his eyes. Then he said, "Sure, lass."

"How'd you get to know my father?"

A smile crinkled the skin around Gabe's eyes. "He was my intern at the Eye."

"Huh?"

"In your Triarii year, you'll be given an opportunity to intern with an instructor of your choosing. Your father chose to intern with me. He was fascinated with the Eye and surveillance in general. It was an unusual request since I'm not faculty, but the school allowed it. Your father," he added with a warm smile, "was a star student. If he'd wanted to intern with the janitor, the school would have let him."

Phoebe laughed, trying to picture that. Then solemnly, "I didn't know any of this."

"Did your father not talk about his time here?" Gabe said, furrowing his brow.

"Sometimes. But only when I pressed him." Phoebe sighed and leaned back against the pew. "Even then, he wasn't that forthcoming. He didn't want me to—"

"Get too excited about this place," Gabe finished quietly.

Phoebe tipped her head sideways and studied Gabe's fatherly expression. "Yeah. That's how it was."

"SIS is not an easy life, lass" Gabe said, breathing deeply. For a moment he stared at Phoebe, his blue-eyed gaze piercing. "Perhaps your father wanted a safer option for you. Like any parent would."

"Maybe . . ." she said. In fact Gabe was right. Her father had wanted her to follow a human curriculum and pursue a human career.

He'd even hidden the SIS application from her when it had first arrived.

As though reading her mind, Gabe said, "If you knew your father didn't want you here, why did you enroll?"

Phoebe didn't answer. She tried to smile, not wanting her anxiety to show itself. Her intense session with Afua on this very subject remained fresh in her mind and the emotions it stirred were difficult ones. In the stillness of the chapel, Phoebe heard the sound of tittering voices approaching from outside. Gabe heard them as well.

"Looks like my new flock of interns are right on time," he said, glancing down at his watch.

"Interns?" Phoebe turned her head and looked back. Behind her a group of four students entered the chapel.

Gabe smiled and drew himself up. "Your father helped make interning at the Eye an official option for third-years. Listen," he said, as he stepped out of his pew. "Concentrate on the reason you decided to enroll here and it will make everything worthwhile." Gabe gave Phoebe's shoulder a gentle squeeze before sweeping down the aisle to greet his interns.

"Stop me if I get too philosophical for you," Hayley said to Phoebe later that night as they sat in the Above library basement, their backs against the wall, a batch of Hayley's I'm-worried-about-midterms cinnamon rolls between them. "I think that almost-kiss happened because you and Scott are two confused people flung into a metaphorical darkness together, both reaching out, wanting to touch the only other person who understands the abyss. To feel less alone—"

"Stop," Phoebe interjected quickly.

"What?" Hayley threw up her palms.

"You said to stop you if you got too nutty, Dr. Phil."

"C'mon, it makes sense," Hayley said, examining the leaf in her hand before adding a few more dots with her Decomp Pen. "You hear about people developing deep feelings for each other after surviving intense situations together. And," she quickly added when Phoebe opened her mouth. "Hypothetically, he hasn't told a soul what's going on, so you're the only person experiencing it with him."

Phoebe frowned as she considered Hayley's words, then said, "God, what does that say about me? I mean, I talk to you."

"You, my friend, are a whole different situation." Hayley bit into a cinnamon roll. "I mean, you're currently avoiding one boy by hiding out in the basement where you attacked another boy. I'm not qualified to assess what's going on with you."

Phoebe stretched an arm to take a swipe at Hayley. As she did, the book she'd been reading fell out of her hands and Hayley grabbed it.

"What are you doing with a Body Linguistics and Deception textbook?" she asked, surprised. "That's second year reading."

"I thought I'd see what's coming," Phoebe said evasively. And what was coming was a debriefing with Afua. Phoebe had checked out the book in the hopes of learning basic techniques for veiling her emotional state.

"Okay, overachiever,"—Hayley's fingers leafed through the book— "learn anything I can use on the parentals?"

"It's all in the eyes," Phoebe said.

"What is?" Hayley asked.

"Lying. Deception," Phoebe said. "They say you can control your voice and your facial muscles, but eyes give people away all the time. So if you can control that . . ."

"How the hell do you do that?" Hayley said, blinking.

"Years of practice," came a woman's rich voice from somewhere in the semi-darkness. Afua, black duffel bag slung over her shoulders, emerged from the shadows of the stacks as both girls shot to their feet, preparing to show their respect.

"Cadets Corman, Pope," Afua said, nodding alternately at both of them.

"Good evening, ma'am," the girls said in unison, nodding back.

Afua, her gaze trained on Hayley, said, "Mind if I borrow Cadet Pope?" She spoke in a tone that made it was clear that it wasn't a question.

"Yes, ma'am—I mean, no, ma'am," Hayley said as a hint of a smile played at the corner of Afua's pressed lips.

Phoebe picked up her belongings and threw them hastily into her backpack, shaking her head ever so slightly when Hayley attempted to give back the Body Linguistics book. Phoebe followed Afua out of the library basement, brushing cinnamon roll crumbs from her clothes.

When Phoebe stepped outside, the wind that whipped her hair across her face made her feel as though she'd entered the heart of a frozen tundra. She walked in silence beside the Blackcoat, the dark, jagged outline of the Campus forest getting closer. In minutes, they reached the expanse of tall trees and began making their way through, avoiding the tangled underbrush and fallen branches. As they walked, Phoebe found herself grateful to have the symphonic hum of nocturnal insects intrude upon what had become nerve-wracking silence.

Afua came to an abrupt halt.

"We're here," she said, getting to her knees. Grabbing two fistfuls of earth, Afua pressed her palms together—her hands crackling with electricity—before flinging the dirt out into the trees. The floating particles formed a thin, glowing rope that stretched and tied itself around the trunks of a long line of trees. Then, as if yanked by some invisible hand, it pulled the trees sideways.

Phoebe gasped, her mouth gaping, her bulging eyes fixed on Afua who rose to her full height and dusted off her dirt-caked hands. A cluster of trees roped to one side, they were now standing in a semi-circle-shaped clearing, brightly lit by the low-squatting moon that had previously been blocked. A feeling of nervous anticipation rushed in to replace Phoebe's shock, and she brought a hand to her neck, absentmindedly stroking the pendant on her silk necklace.

"That blue-gray side is called falcon's eye," Afua said.

Phoebe snapped up from looking at her pendant. She should not have been surprised that the Blackcoat had been watching her closely. "Is it another form of protection?" she asked.

"No," Afua said, opening her black bag. "It's believed to free the wearer of the emotional turmoil that cripples rational thought."

Phoebe tensed. "Do you believe it works?" she asked cautiously, watching Afua strap a quiver to her thigh.

"I believe overwhelming feelings can force us into a maze of confusion." Afua unsheathed a beautifully polished recurve bow engraved with gold symbols, and strung it. "As to whether or not the falcon's eye provides a path out of that maze," she continued, "it may depend on the wearer being open to receiving help."

Phoebe stood motionless, absorbing the impact of those words. She almost opened her mouth to ask Afua if falcon's eye had ever helped her, but stopped when she noticed a gold arrow, with a single perpendicular line just above the bottom embroidered into the side of the Blackcoat's quiver; she recognized it as her Zodiac sign.

"Are you a Sagittarius?" Phoebe asked as Afua filled her quiver with dark wood arrows.

"Yes, but not in the way you're thinking." At Phoebe's confused look, Afua said, "How is your Latin, Cadet?"

"Not good," Phoebe admitted, sheepishly. Cadets were encouraged to learn Latin on their own time, as a way to connect more with their history, but Phoebe hadn't taken to it. "But I do know that Sagittarius is Latin for archer and the plural is Sagittarii."

"Well, that's a start," Afua said. "In ancient times, Roman armies were accompanied by auxiliary—support—regiments. A good number of those regiments were called Sagittariorums, which meant they contained archers. After the fall of Pompeii, the Royal Court decided to have its own Sagittariorum for added protection. Archers have remained a part of the royal security detail ever since."

"So you're a Sagittarius and a Blackcoat?"

"I'm a Sagittarius who was recruited to become a Blackcoat," Afua said, slipping on a fire-red arm guard. "Blackcoats are pulled from various disciplines. I don't do as much archery now, but I like to get some practice in. That's where you come in, Cadet." Afua threw an object at Phoebe, which she caught against her chest. "You'll assist in my target practice while I debrief you."

Phoebe stared down at her hands; she was holding a thin black disc with about twenty numbered buttons on it.

"This area has been wired with targets that are buried beneath us," Afua said, answering Phoebe's unasked question. "You'll use the remote to launch them from the blast-free zone." She pointed to a black X drawn at the base of a pine in the north end of the clearing. Phoebe moved over to it at once, fearing the undetectable targets as if they were landmines.

"This debriefing," Afua said, "by the way, is not about your recalling the events of the previous week's sting." She reached into her jacket pocket, withdrew a black silk cloth and tied it around her eyes. "It's what we call a 'psychological debriefing' that we use to check in on your state of mind."

At that, Phoebe accidentally pushed a button. A clay ball the size of a fist exploded from the ground in a towering spray of dirt and rocks. Without a sound, the ball shot upward and hovered between two pines. Before Phoebe had even processed what she'd done, Afua had nocked an arrow, drawn the string to her cheek and hit the target with a ringing *thunk*. Clay chunks rained to the ground.

"Sorry," Phoebe said, and began to scold herself internally. She found herself rather grateful for Afua's blindfold because she did not want the Blackcoat to see her shaky hands.

Afua had a second arrow nocked and ready. "That's the idea. Fire at will," she said before adding, "Tell me how you are."

"I'm fine," Phoebe said, sending another ball sizzling upward. Unlike the first one, this target moved in a zig-zag motion. In seconds, it too lay in pieces.

"We both know that isn't true," Afua said, bringing the bowstring to her cheek. "You look like you haven't slept for days. And although your class attendance has been one hundred percent, your focus hasn't."

"I . . ."

Afua spoke over Phoebe. "There's no shame in feeling what you're feeling. You're a Hastati-year trainee. Most SIS agents go their entire careers without having to be bait in a field mission. And the impact of the operation has been made worse by the fact that you can't share it with your peers."

Phoebe said nothing, but launched another target.

Turning in place, Afua shot it down.

"How do you remain so unaffected?" Phoebe blurted, pressing several buttons at once before she could stop herself.

Afua's hands were a blur as, one shot after another, her arrows impaled each swirling target with precision and speed. "Don't mistake my focus and sense of duty for lack of emotion, Cadet," she said with a softer tone, lowering her bow. "I choose to connect with feelings I find productive: pride, loyalty, triumph, and courage. It's simply what works for me."

Phoebe thought about that for a moment, then cleared her throat. "Permission to speak freely, ma'am," she said.

"Proceed."

"You told me that everyone comes to the service for a reason. What was yours, ma'am?"

Afua slipped off her blindfold and fixed her intense gaze on Phoebe. Several seconds passed before she answered. "Survival," she finally replied. "Joining the service gave me a sense of purpose and allowed me to change my circumstances." She began unstrapping her quiver. "I grew up in a Shaper orphanage in Cape Town, South Africa. One day a woman came by and handed us older kids a bow and some arrows and taught us how to shoot. I took to it like breathing.

"The woman was impressed with my skill and offered me wonderful things—opportunity to see the world, a better home, and a chance to hone my shooting skill. It turned out that she was a recruiter for the Sagittarii and orphans fit the NET profile they looked for."

"NET?"

"No Emotional Ties, Cadet," Afua said. "It's a sacrifice made by those of us who guard the Crowns. Some make that tough choice willingly. Others, like me, come in having none."

Phoebe lowered her eyes to the ground; she felt an overwhelming need to say something to Afua. But what to say, or how to say it, eluded her.

"Listen," Afua said, removing the string from her bow. "I am well aware that I am not the most approachable person. But should you need to discuss anything regarding the sting operation, I can make myself available to you."

"Okay," Phoebe said weakly. She couldn't meet Afua's eyes. Instead, Phoebe glanced around at the broken clay, trying to bring herself to tell the Blackcoat about Colten. She was frustrated. This wasn't her. She knew right from wrong and everything about her behavior was wrong. Withholding such information was treasonous. But every time she thought of turning Colten in, the image of the Vigo in the glass case came to her in a rush; Colten would not be allowed to live. It was law. *Kill Vigos no questions asked.*

Something within Phoebe clamped her tongue; a voice that kept screaming that there was a contradiction between the boy she'd come to know and the monster he was supposed to be. Or had it all been one brilliantly acted role on his part? She thought back to dinner in his room. Their connection had felt real. Raw. Didn't she owe it to herself to find out what was behind her hesitation before making an irreversible decision? On the other hand, the potential consequences of her inaction could be too frightening for words. It wasn't just about her own death. A frantic part of her mind wondered if Colten was just a small part of a bigger plan? Perhaps a massive attack on the school? Was her silence dooming her fellow cadets and the future of the SIS program?

Phoebe began retrieving Afua's arrows from the ground. A gust of wind swirled from behind her, sending her a waft of a smoky cinnamon scent. Phoebe took a breath and halted all movement. *Has Colten returned to campus? Has he been watching us this whole time?* In panic, Phoebe scanned the stretch of trees looking for shadows in the darkness, seeing nothing, hearing nothing.

"Something wrong, Cadet?" Afua said.

Phoebe was startled, realizing suddenly that Afua was right beside her. She felt a hollowness in her throat. "I thought I heard something," she said, grateful for the words that came.

"I'm sure you did," Afua said. "There are four agents wandering around on guard duty."

Phoebe exhaled in nervous surprise. "There are?" she said.

"I wouldn't have brought you into these woods without precautionary measures," Afua confirmed, her mild offense implicit in her tone. "But our debriefing"—Afua indicated the Privaque on her collar—"was confidential."

A minute or so later, after returning all of her arrows to her quiver, Afua walked over to the particle rope while Phoebe's penetrating gaze once again darted around. Phoebe inhaled deeply. The smoky cinnamon musk was now barely discernible, but it was there. Colten was somewhere close by, that she was sure of. But so were agents. She still didn't understand how his presence continued to raise no alarms.

"I suggest you start moving," Afua called out to Phoebe, who had just barely dodged a tree that had snapped back into place; she didn't need to be told twice. Phoebe broke into a run following Afua closely. The particle rope began to disintegrate, and trees returned to where they belonged, leaving no trace of the clearing.

When they broke free of the final line of trees, the security foursome at their flanks, Phoebe's thoughts returned to Colten. Where had he been all of this time? What about his classes? Didn't he have assignments he was required to do regardless of his star status? Phoebe glanced over her shoulder on instinct. Her hearts rammed against her ribs, as a silhouetted figure with Colten's build stood at the edge of the tree line, unseen by Afua or the others. Before Phoebe could completely trust her eyes, the figure pulled the bill of his baseball cap over his face and faded into the darkness.

Phoebe returned to her room and she dropped onto her bed in a heavy heap. Before the thought of undressing even crossed her mind, she fell into a deep, tormented sleep. In her dream, she was on the red carpet again. This time, instead of running, she pointed a finger at Colten's neck and screamed "Vigo!"

The weekend's dreary overcast weather made most everyone into hermits. Eager to be by herself, Phoebe seized the opportunity to wander the campus freely. Her camera bobbed against her chest in its case, where it would remain until inspiration hit—something that was increasingly hard to come by. Before long, however, an unexpected downpour forced her to seek cover in the nearest shelter. Phoebe found herself running a short distance to the chapel. And if it weren't for the gale force winds that had begun to blow, she would have paused to capture the image of the steeple spearing a thick, hovering cloud like a sentinel in battle.

Soaked and cold, Phoebe stood in the entryway, surprised to find the pews filled. *Of course*, she thought. It was Sunday and some students had gathered for the nondenominational service that was optional for Green Lane. Out of respect, Phoebe moved to sit at the back of the chapel, scanning for familiar faces as she went. Gabe stood in the shadows, leaning against the wall, eyes firmly fixed on the pulpit. He wore a vaguely tortured look on his face and Phoebe wondered if his concern lay with the priest who moved energetically and far too close to the narthyx. But then she noticed that Gabe's hands were clutched around the red picture frame that held a photo of his daughter. Phoebe's hearts went out to him.

As she continued to look around, she saw focused Blackcoats standing along the walls, too many to be there just for her. Phoebe spotted Scott sitting on the opposite side of the aisle, his arm around the girl she only knew as "Gorgeous." She couldn't help but stare at them. She'd been wondering a lot about how she'd feel the next time she saw Scott. And she had her answer. Seeing Scott with Gorgeous evoked no sense of jealousy, hurt, or pain. Instead she felt happiness for him. Perhaps Hayley had been right: Whatever she may have thought she'd felt for Scott had just been a byproduct of one of those intense moments.

"Please bow your heads for the Lord's prayer." The priest's request pulled Phoebe's gaze from Scott. She closed her eyes and listened to the congregation recite the words her grandfather had taught her as a child.

"And give us this day our daily bread," Phoebe said, joining at the part she remembered. "And forgive us our trespasses as we forgive those who trespass against us. And lead us not into temptation . . ." Phoebe let her voice trail off for a moment, her mind having momentarily tortured her with visions of Colten with another girl. But then she returned to echo "Amen."

"In the Lord's Prayer," the priest was saying, tugging at Phoebe's attention. "We say 'Forgive us our trespasses as we forgive those who trespass against us.' It's because we all need to be forgiven for some of our decisions and our actions."

We all need to be forgiven, Phoebe repeated to herself. Would she be forgiven if the truth about Colten were to surface? Would they understand that she sometimes found herself wondering how he was doing? That she wondered what gluten-free meal he was cooking up. That she pictured him playing chess with an old man in a park or pumping out a painful tune on an accordion. It made sense to have these thoughts about the human Colten, not the Vigo.

We all need to be forgiven, Phoebe repeated. But could her decisions and actions—or lack thereof—be dismissed as a rookie mistake made under the influence of misguided emotion? Would they listen if she were to list his altruistic endeavors and argue that no true Vigo would live his life that way? Or would she be sent straight to a traitor's hell?

"—and yes, the internal struggle with forgiveness is a difficult one," Phoebe heard the priest continue. "But I ask you to consider this closing verse from 1 Peter 4:8. 'Above all, love each other deeply, because love covers a multitude of sins.'"

Phoebe put a hand on her chest. She struggled to breathe; it was as though the priest had known exactly where to punch her to inflict the most pain. The priest wished everyone peace and sent the congregation on its way, but Phoebe was frozen to the spot, unable to move a muscle. Those words he had chosen had broken the seal on the root of her conflict: whether he had betrayed her trust or not, she was in love with Colten. Really, truly, head over heels. But could love really compensate for the sins of generations of Vigos killing Shapers . . . of a Vigo killing her father? How could she have anything to do with him, trust him, forgive him? And did he even want her, or was he just using her? . . . Or even hunting her? Distantly, Phoebe was aware of her pew creaking under the weight of someone who spoke a soft "Hello." Gabe.

She looked at him for just a moment, and then stared down at her hands. "Do you think it's true?" she said softly.

"Is what true?"

"What the priest just said . . . about love covering over a multitude of sins?"

Gabe leaned forward, his elbows on his knees, his bony hands tightly clasped. "I hope it is, lass. I hope it is."

When Phoebe looked over at Gabe, she found that his eyes were closed.

I hope it is, she mouthed to herself.

❦ TWENTY-FIVE

When Phoebe walked into the Gazette office, she found Cyn perched on a table, flirting with Miles, the sports photographer, a lean boy with a gelled mohawk.

"You out-scooped *the Globe?* That's awesome," he was saying. Phoebe rolled her eyes; Miles only had eyes for Cyn's chest, something Cyn was clearly aware of. Phoebe moved past a shelf laden with plaques and trophies and settled at her corner workstation.

"I know," Cyn giggled. "It just happened. My mom's so pissed. But I told her I'd—" she broke off having just noticed Phoebe.

"Just the person I'm looking for." Cyn pulled up a chair next to Phoebe. "I know I said you were done, but I need one last portrait for this feature."

"Really?" Phoebe tried to keep the eagerness from her voice. When Cyn had first told Phoebe about the seven part *Gazette* feature, Phoebe had never imagined that she'd come to depend on the assignments to ease her mental limbo. She had become grateful for the distraction that kept her Above, grateful for something that made her feel more like herself. Reaching the end of the list had brought her a mild, unexpected sense of loss.

"Yeah. They're actually waiting in the portrait studio," Cyn said cheerfully.

"Right now?" Phoebe was surprised; she didn't have her camera on her.

Cyn observed Phoebe for a moment. "I'll understand if you don't want to do it though," she said softly after a moment. "I can always put Miles on it."

"Why wouldn't I want to do it?" Phoebe asked, confused.

Cyn and Miles exchanged looks.

Phoebe spoke quickly. "I'll do it." Without asking for further details, she took off before Cyn could reassign the shoot.

She burst into the photo studio apologizing for running late—she'd made a quick stop at the dorm to pick up her camera and one of her favorite lenses—and stopped dead in her tracks. Her hands went to her face, and her stomach constricted and seemed to form a block of steel in her gut. Colten was hunched over on a swivel stool, arms hugging his own chest, his gaze intent on her. His eyebrows were drawn down, his expression tired and pained. A few days' growth of a patchy beard covered his jaw, a rough look that clashed with the stylish dark jeans and black sports blazer he was wearing.

Next to Colten, Nicole was reading a magazine, perfectly coiffed as the first time they had met, and completely unaware of Phoebe. But then, upon hearing Colten say, "Hi," in an uncertain tone, she glanced up, went immediately rigid, and said slowly, "You have got to be kidding me." She looked between Phoebe and Colten. "She's the one taking the photos?" She turned to Colten whose eyes had not left Phoebe's face. "You knew she'd be involved in this, didn't you?"

Phoebe ignored Nicole. At that moment, only Colten existed. She stared at him and he held her scrutinizing gaze. Phoebe fought against the pressure building behind her eyes, wrestled the pain threatening to become fury, and forced herself to breathe. There he was, finally, the reason for her torment, the reason she found herself questioning what it meant to be Shaper, what it meant to love a Vigo. After weeks of silence, it had all been a mental exercise. And, now here he was, making it all real.

"I can't do this," Phoebe said, speaking softly.

Nicole snapped. "You can't do this? Thanks to your 'Runaway Date' stunt I've been doing nothing but constant damage control. People want to know why any girl in her right mind would bail on Colten Chase. They want to know if he's losing his appeal!" She paused for a moment, looking ready to burst. "We have too much of a full schedule, Colten, to waste time on this one."

"I'm staying," Colten said, his voice calm, eyes never leaving Phoebe's stricken face. "You can go ahead and leave if you want."

Nicole threw her hands up in the air, which Colten ignored. "Fine," she said, pulling a pair of dark sunglasses from her purse and making a show of putting them on. "I'll be in the car when you're done." Looking as though she would like nothing better than to grab Phoebe's camera and smash it over her head, Nicole left the studio in a huff.

"How've you been?" Colten asked softly, with caution in his voice.

"*How've I been?*" Phoebe knew she was laughing, but it sounded like someone else, dark and humorless. "Oh, I've been great Colten," she said, sarcastically. "How 'bout you?"

Hurt flashed through Colten's eyes. A moment passed and he said, "Sorry about Nicole. She's just—"

"Nicole? That's what you're sorry about?" Again, Phoebe heard that stranger's laugh erupt from her chest. "No love lost there. It's not as if she approved of me from the beginning, anyway. And how convenient for you that I look like the bad person in all of this," she said with a vicious edge in her voice. "But I guess you can't tell Nicole the reason I left, can you? Can't tell her that her golden boy is actually a monster." Phoebe watched Colten cringe at her words and finally lower his eyes, and she took a savage delight in his confidence faltering. He took a deep breath and raised his head again, seeming to gather himself.

"Am I a monster, Phoebe?" he asked earnestly, searching her face. "Have I ever been monster-like to you?"

Phoebe found herself shaking, and for a split second, Colten's forlorn expression seemed genuine. It made her want to let go of her anger and her doubts. *Maybe I should hear him out*, she thought for a moment, pausing, *but he's an actor*, she mused, snapping out of it. *Could this all be part of some elaborate performance to make me trust him?*

"I'm not going to play some twisted mind game," Phoebe said out loud. She had to guard her hearts. She stared at her feet, her rein on her emotions threatening to fail. She brought a hand to the pendant around her neck and squeezed it.

"Look at me, Phoebe," Colten pleaded. Phoebe looked at him then, held his gaze briefly, and then looked away, staring at the shelves of equipment. "If you're so sure I'm the enemy," he said, his voice low, "why haven't you turned me in?"

Phoebe stood frozen, as if struck. Colten's question, one that she'd forced down within herself, had now sprung into her chest and burned. She still had no answer. And now Colten knew it too.

Taking a step backward, she drew herself up and forced out the most professional tone she could muster, "I'll arrange for someone else to take your photo."

Colten was on his feet and began to move toward her, eyes flashing, head slightly lowered as though he didn't want to spook her. "I don't care about the stupid article." And then he was in front of her. "I came to talk to you." He grabbed Phoebe's hand and tightened his fingers around her wrist, then loosened his grip, as if fearful he was hurting her. "Give me a chance to explain so that you can understand—"

"Understand?" Phoebe said, breathing heavily. She took several little gasps, trying not to hyperventilate. The situation had escalated so quickly, and his effect on her had never been more dramatic. She simultaneously longed to run her fingers through his hair and to tear it out at the roots. "Here's what I understand: Vigos killed my father."

Colten dropped Phoebe's hand like a hot iron and his face became stone. "I didn't know," he said, not meeting her eyes.

Without waiting to hear more, Phoebe ran out the studio. In her confusion-hazed mind, she ran blindly, the students in front of her jumping out of her way. All but one, and Phoebe crashed right into him. Head lowered like a charging steed, the top of Phoebe's crown smacked Scott under the jaw, and finally drew her to a faltering halt. Scott winced, dazed as Phoebe fought for her balance.

"Whoa. Where's the fire, Pope?" Scott dropped the soccer ball he'd been holding and seized Phoebe's shoulders to keep her from falling back.

Dazed, Phoebe looked up and took in his concerned expression. "Sorry I—" Phoebe started, breaking off at the sound of Colten's voice behind her.

"Phoebe, wait a sec," Colten called, pleadingly.

"Ah," Scott said, looking over Phoebe's shoulder and frowning. "Romeo's back."

Phoebe turned on the spot to face Colten. "Leave me alone," she said through gritted teeth. "Please."

Colten took another step toward Phoebe, but stopped when Scott inserted himself between them. "I think she just asked you to take a hike, friend," Scott said, raising a hand mildly in a traffic signal "stop".

Anger flashed in Colten's eyes, but then it cooled and one side of his mouth curled up in an almost sheepish look. "Fine," he said, trying to catch Phoebe's gaze before turning and heading off down the hall, seemingly dejected. Phoebe rested her head lightly on Scott's back, inhaling the outdoor scent that clung to his blue and white Green Lane varsity soccer windbreaker. She kept her gaze to the side until Colten was out of view. She could feel Scott's quick breaths against her ear.

As soon as Colten had disappeared around a corner, Phoebe pivoted, turned on Scott and glared. "That wasn't necessary," she said. "I was handling it."

"Didn't look like it." Scott's eyes were kind, and looked into Phoebe's searchingly.

"I'm sorry," Phoebe said. "Didn't mean to snap at you."

"I can take it." He play-punched her chin. "Now tell me," he said, his voice serious. "Did he violate my one toe policy?"

"One toe?" Phoebe asked, arching a brow. Then remembering, she shrugged. "Don't worry about it."

"Sure? 'Cause we can settle it like grown men."

Phoebe opened her mouth to argue, and then closed it, noticing the snickering group of girls that had gathered in the hallway, a self-satisfied Karli among them. Karli smirked at Phoebe when their eyes met.

"That's right," Karli said with dramatic flair, "all you doubters pay up!" A few girls made a show of pulling out designer wallets and began handing her wads of cash. Waving the cash in the air Karli added, smugly, "I told you they were over."

"Hey," Scott said, waving a hand in front of Phoebe's hardened face. "Don't pay attention to that. How 'bout we go somewhere quiet and talk?"

"I—I can't," she said, shrugging off the arm Scott had protectively thrown around her shoulders. Phoebe knew she couldn't handle getting into the kind of conversation Scott probably wanted to have. She shot him a vaguely apologetic look, and took off in the opposite direction from Colten.

"That's right, Phoebe," Karli's voice rang shrilly from behind her. "Do what you're famous for and run!"

Phoebe came to a halt. She dug her nails into her palms and exhaled air through her teeth. She turned and stormed over to Karli, passing Scott who was slowly shaking his head. Phoebe understood his message: *leave it alone.* But enough was enough.

"You know what?" Phoebe said, her eyes wet with fury. She stepped to Karli, who stunned, took an involuntary step back. "I did make a fool of myself on the red carpet but at least I got invited to a movie premiere. And so what if the story got splashed in a lot of magazine? Haven't you heard? All press is good press. At least people know who I am. Who the hell are you, other than some opportunistic celebrity-chasing bitch?" Karli began to make incoherent garbles, which were silenced by Phoebe's seething stare. "So say what you want to say about me," Phoebe barreled on. "I don't care what you think. No wait, I lied," she said, grinning wickedly. "I do care what you think about one thing: I made out with Colten Chase and it was hot, steamy, and spectacular!"

A chorus of whoops and "hell yeah!"s erupted around them. For a moment, Phoebe was thrown by the noise. But she continued to stare daggers at Karli who had lost her grasp on the dollar bills that now floated to the ground like autumn leaves. Karli had also lost the admiration of a few of her followers who now stared at Phoebe, awed.

Phoebe was still shaking as she turned to leave. She paused for a moment, taken aback by the size of the crowd that had gathered. She scanned the faces looking for Scott. He was no longer there. She wondered if he'd witnessed her tirade. The press of students parted as Phoebe started walking. Soon her pace became a jog, then a sprint out of the school building. Phoebe's mind was reeling. She'd never stood up for herself like that before. It had felt good. Everything about her life made her want to scream. And the dam of pent-up frustration had finally burst, claiming Karli as its first casualty.

❦ TWENTY-SIX

When a translucent moonlight rose over the campus, bathing the buildings in shimmering light, Phoebe finally returned to her room to find both Afua and Yelena sitting on her sofa.

Startled, she dropped her backpack. "What's wrong?" Phoebe asked, quickly closing the door behind her.

"Scott's been taken," Afua said.

The news hit Phoebe like an avalanche. Her body began to sway. If it hadn't been for Yelena, who moved fast enough to catch Phoebe, she would have hit the ground.

"I'm okay," Phoebe stammered, regaining her balance. "How? When? I saw him a few hours ago!"

"Sometime this evening," Afua said. "His Blackcoat lost track of him after he returned to his dorm."

Phoebe screwed up her face. "You think he was taken from his dorm?"

Afua frowned. "Other than the usual pizza deliveries and courier services—all of which were observed by Blackcoats—only students came in and out of the guarded exits."

Phoebe felt a growing madness whirling in her mind; a student entering and leaving would raise no alarms. A student by the name of Colten Chase. The thought that he might be responsible pressed heavily against her chest and she began to suffocate in the guilt. The week he had been absent had seen no incidents. Now, within hours of his confrontation with her, Scott had gone missing. And Phoebe had not missed the darkness flashing in Colten's eyes when Scott had intervened earlier. Cold. Calculating.

"We would like for you to remain in your room for the remainder of the night," Afua said, barreling through Phoebe's thoughts. "Four guards will be stationed right outside your door—"

"Is it okay if I spend the night at a friend's dorm?" Phoebe said, tugging at her white streak, an idea dawning on her. "I could use the distraction and you can guard me there."

Afua and Yelena exchanged quick looks.

"It could actually be a good idea for her not to be in her own room tonight," the blond Blackcoat said in a low voice to Afua who nodded.

It is a good idea, Phoebe thought. *But not for the reason that they're thinking.* There was something Phoebe needed to do, and she needed to be in Hayley's room to do it.

"Dude's chasing you with a knife and you head for the basement?" Hayley screamed. "Go outside!"

Phoebe sat on Hayley's bed with her arms around her shins, her head resting on her knees. At her request, they were not discussing Scott's disappearance and Hayley had put on a movie instead. But Phoebe wasn't watching. She couldn't bear the thought of what she was about to do. It involved manipulating her friend, and the very thought was filling her up with guilt. She glanced at the clock on the wall. Hayley's roommate would be returning soon, so if Phoebe was going to go through with it, it would have to be now. Closing her eyes, Phoebe *pushed*.

Phoebe had only once *pushed* the feeling of fatigue. It had been on a night her father had fallen into a sadness so deep that sleep could not reach its fingers down to him. And now, watching Hayley rub her chest uncomfortably before reaching for a pillow, Phoebe saw that it was something she could still do. She was careful not to *push* too much, fearing that the lingering effect on herself would be a detriment to her plan.

The moment Phoebe saw Hayley curl into herself and succumb to the *push*, she shot to her feet. She grabbed her backpack, crossed over to the window and released the locks. It swung open, and for once Phoebe didn't pause to reconsider. She climbed through the window, pulled herself into the tree that hugged the building, paused a moment to catch her breath and then jumped.

There were two ways to get to the boys' dorms: one path would take Phoebe through lighted walkways heavy with the traffic of students. The second would lead her through the dark and tangled tree line. Upon hearing the distant voices of students heading home from their various Friday night social events, Phoebe made her choice. Mind racing, she ran through a thicket, feeling the sting of the cold air that raised goosebumps on her skin. It distracted her momentarily from the fright edging into her mind: she was about to confront a Vigo without a plan, and she could think of nothing more dangerous. All Phoebe knew was that, no matter what happened next, one way or the other, she needed to know what part Colten played in her nightmare.

When Phoebe broke through the trees into the clearing in front of the boys' dorms, warning drops of rain dripped from the black sky. By the time she arrived at Clay House, a wind had picked up, whipping the ice-cold water into her eyes. She stopped at the back of Colten's dorm and her eyes instantly found his corner room, windows up, lights on. Something like relief moved through her at the sight of his form in the room. He was still on campus. Perhaps Scott's disappearance had nothing to do with him.

Suddenly, Colten appeared at his window. He poked his head out and scanned the courtyard before moving to another window. Phoebe wondered if he was somehow aware of her presence; she stepped into the shadow of a pine tree and crouched. After a number of calming breaths she looked up again and shot to her feet. Colten's windows had been pulled shut. The lights were off.

In Phoebe's mind, thoughts began to whirl. Colten was leaving. An impulsive anger swept over her. Was he running? The very notion put Phoebe into action. She rounded a corner to the front of the dorm and saw Colten push through the doors. As she took in his outline, whatever hope she'd been holding onto dissolved. He was moving in the direction of the parking lot, baseball cap pulled low over his eyes, and an oversized duffel bag in his arms—the kind of bag large enough to transport a body—a bag he carried as if it were heavy.

Phoebe swallowed hard and made a split decision. Shoving all of her misgivings aside, she began to follow him at a distance. If Colten was taking Scott somewhere, she would be the one to stop him. Phoebe passed a knot of students who were smoking and talking outside the dorm.

"Hey, where's the emergency?" a girl in the group called out to Phoebe as she flew past them while the others laughed.

Phoebe knew she was radiating the tension she felt. In the back of her mind, a voice yelled at her to stop and think for a minute. She knew that she was acting on emotion, and that this was probably the time to turn things over to the Blackcoats. Ignoring that voice, Phoebe gritted her teeth and kept racing after Colten.

She could not believe the speed at which he moved. By the time she arrived at the parking lot, he had already jumped into his car and was driving away. Phoebe was determined not to lose him that easily. She glanced about the lot, looking for a car she wouldn't feel too badly about hot wiring. The trouble was, Green Lane students drove high-end vehicles, and finding one she could hot wire among them would be difficult. Then Phoebe spotted one that would do just fine. Four minutes later, Phoebe peeled out of the campus in Karli's vintage VW Beetle.

Luckily, there weren't that many Smart Cars on the road, and although Colten had a head start, Phoebe soon spotted him waiting at a red light just outside the campus. The light changed. Careful to keep another car between them, Phoebe followed Colten past the outskirts of town and onto the freeway.

After what seemed like an hour of driving, Colten made a sharp exit that Phoebe almost missed. The longer they drove, the scarcer the streetlights and the buildings became. At every traffic light, Phoebe expected Colten to notice her and stop, but he continued on. Phoebe gripped the steering wheel with sweaty palms, her eyes wide. No longer having any idea where she was or where Colten was going, Phoebe began to feel the weight of her impulse to follow him. As the darkness pressed in on her, she reached for the car's high beam controls, catching herself just before she turned them on—she smacked her own forehead. *Could I give myself away any easier?* she scolded herself. Phoebe hadn't taken her eyes away from Colten for more than a second, but when she looked up again, he was gone.

Phoebe eased on the brake and brought the car to a stop. Then she leaned against the steering wheel, her eyes flashing about nervously; she was in a dark, long, and narrow alleyway between two rows of concrete commercial buildings. Broken beer bottles, newspaper pages, plastic shopping bags, and empty take-out boxes lay scattered over dark, wet stones. Phoebe stared ahead for a moment, hoping Colten's car would reappear. But it only took a minute of sitting in that isolation before instinct spurred her to get out of there.

A small shower of pebbles from above made Phoebe look up at the rooftops. The next thing she knew, something dropped down and hit the hood of the car with enough weight to make it shudder. Phoebe shrieked, staring through the windshield at a woman who had landed in a crouch and stared back at her without flinching a muscle. Dressed from head to foot in black, her shiny gold locks spilled from underneath a beret. A dull heat began to spread all over Phoebe's body as the woman's fuchsia-colored lips twisted into a nasty sneer.

Phoebe threw the shifter into reverse, slammed the accelerator and shot the car backward. Seconds later, the VW Beetle came to a complete abrupt stop. Phoebe spun around in her seat to see a man with both palms of his large pale hands planted into deep dents in the back of the car. He too was dressed in black, a baseball cap on his head, his lips set in a thin line below icy blue eyes.

"Looks like you're having some car trouble," Phoebe heard the woman say from the front.

"Yeah, let's have a look," the man said. He ripped off the Beetle's back engine hood and let it drop hard onto the ground. Then, smiling, he pulled out several wires. The engine sputtered and then died.

The woman laughed. And when Phoebe sat stunned, gripping the steering wheel with both hands, the woman studied her with more interest. Excitement flashed in her crazed eyes.

"Do you know how long we've been waiting for one of you Hyphas to wander off without protection?" the woman said frostily, rubbing a crease in her pants in mock exasperation. She thrust a manicured hand into the pocket of the blazer she'd buttoned at the waist and produced a cell phone.

"Guess it's true what folks say 'bout patience." She looked over at the man. "You see who we got?"

"Yeah," he said in a syrupy voice that dripped with distaste. "Stop your yapping and call it in already." The man slid around the car, carrying a large stone. Phoebe's stomach lurched. What more did he plan to do? The fingers she'd clenched around the steering wheel shook as she watched the man leap onto the hood of the car and crouch next to the woman who was yelling into her phone, "Yes, I'm sure it's her! Just tell the Padrone! Uh huh ... okay ..."

The man raised his hands and Phoebe watched him, her eyes on his eyes as he looked from the stone to the windshield, his intention plain on his smooth, angular face.

"No more games," the woman said, knocking the stone out of his hands. "Our orders are to—"

Phoebe didn't wait for the end of that sentence. She flung open the car door and bolted. She sprinted as hard as she had ever run straight down the littered alleyway, stumbling and tripping on her shaky feet. Phoebe could hear the car groan as the weight of the two Vigos came off of it. She snuck an anxious peek behind her and saw the woman a short distance away, her legs pumping as hard as Phoebe's hearts. Phoebe couldn't believe anyone could run that fast in stiletto-heeled boots. The man, on the other hand, seemed to be taking a more leisurely approach. Phoebe didn't even want to know what he had up his sleeve.

"There's nowhere to run, cousin," he said with a laugh, his voice echoing off the building walls.

Frantic, Phoebe moved from steel door to steel door, jerking cold handles ineffectively as she did. To her intense relief, she found one that opened. Phoebe entered the building and locked the deadbolts. Pausing to catch her breath, she inhaled deeply and choked on a lungful of sawdust that hung like river mist in the cold air. It clung to her hair.

Lungs burning, eyes watering, Phoebe squinted around at her surroundings: a long, open space under renovation. Light from streetlamps slivered through the fanlights and illuminated another door. Phoebe sped toward it, avoiding the metal tools and stacks of empty paint cans that littered the cracked tile floor. Phoebe felt her hearts trying to hammer through her chest as she almost tripped on a thickly cobwebbed chair. She was halfway across the room when the door banged open and the blond woman walked in.

"You really need to stop wasting our time," she said, standing in the doorway, boredom legible in her eyes. Her lips stretched to form a cruel line in a smug face.

Phoebe began moving backward, her mind racing. She was stuck between the Vigo in front of her and the one she could hear whistling out in the alleyway. There were no alternate exits other than the windows on either side of the woman. Getting to either one of them would be impossible. Then, from the corner of her eye, Phoebe spotted the next best thing: construction rebar tucked beneath an unfinished west-facing wall with exposed insulation. She shot toward them.

The woman leaped agilely after Phoebe, but not before Phoebe had snatched a rod in each hand. Charged with improved reflexes and dexterity gained from hours of stick fighting practice, Phoebe deftly connected a blow to the woman's chest. Her strike was powerful enough to pitch the woman across the room, where she landed in a noiseless crouch, looking both surprised and vaguely amused.

"Impressive," she said, standing and beginning to clap condescendingly. "And here I thought you were a dumb girl—too cute for the red carpet—I was wrong to underestimate you. That Armani gown was wasted on you, though. I would have rocked it way better." The woman's voice oozed sarcasm and she grinned wickedly.

A sudden surge of irritation shot through Phoebe then, and she failed to react fast enough to block the swift kick the woman delivered to her right knee. *Frivolous emotions can give your opponent an advantage over you.* . . . Phoebe could hear Afua's words echoing in her ears as she teetered off balance and dropped the rods with a ringing crash.

Phoebe made a mad scramble for her lost weapons, managing to curl her fingers around one just as the woman barreled down on her. She raised the rod and struck the woman across the head with all her might. For a moment, Phoebe stared at the woman, who had crumpled to the ground from the impact. She was motionless. Then, realizing she'd only rendered the woman unconscious, Phoebe snapped out of her torpor. She staggered to her feet and flinched as the syrupy male voice bellowed behind her.

"What's the hold up? Thought we had to get her to the crèche before—" Phoebe spun around. From the door, the man stood stock still looking between the woman and Phoebe. He removed his ball cap and tossed it. Then he scrubbed claw-like fingers through his sweaty shock of blond hair. The crazed fury boiling in his eyes made Phoebe's stomach jolt with fear. Her rod was halfway in the air already when the man morphed into a Tiger and charged.

Phoebe's scream wouldn't have been audible even if she had expelled it. An explosion of glass from a breaking window came right before she could get it out, and a bone-chilling growl seemed to fill the entire warehouse. The Vigo charging Phoebe swung his head to the side in confusion just as a streak of black crashed headlong into him. Phoebe stood paralyzed as the blur of struggling forms rolled toward the back of the room in a vicious battle of tangled fur and teeth. A horrendous crunching of breaking bones pierced the air with a sharp intake of breath and was followed by a gut-ripping wail of pain. And then silence spread over them like quilted feathers, smothering Phoebe's senses.

Phoebe had no sense of how long she stood there motionless. Her eyes were transfixed on the body emerging from the shadows. Silver spikes glowing down its back, the Vigo inched cautiously toward Phoebe in a submissive posture, holding her gaze all the while. It came closer. Hardly daring to breathe, Phoebe could smell the odor of its coat, blood mingled with a scent of something smoky, something vaguely like cinnamon. . . .

A wave of disorientation swept over Phoebe, sending sparks of color flashing about her peripheral vision. The room began to spin. And then she felt her feet go from under her as someone cradled her in strong arms and began to run.

❦ TWENTY-SEVEN

Phoebe woke to find her knees throbbing with intense pain and a pair of jewel-green eyes with acute concern in them just inches from her face. She jerked backward in sudden alarm, banging her head against something hard. It was the window of a car.

"Easy there," Colten said gently. He reached a hand toward Phoebe who recoiled, hitting her head again.

"Ouch."

Colten's soft demeanor hardened, his worried expression replaced by a bitter scowl. "What were you doing out there?"

"Following you," Phoebe snapped. She rubbed the back of her head.

"Why?"

"Scott got taken—"

"And you thought I took him?" Colten interrupted. He looked at Phoebe, his eyes blazing. Phoebe felt her stomach turn at the sound of Colten's dark laugh.

"I saw the body bag," she said, her tone indignant.

"What?" Colten laughed again. "That was just my stuff. Clothes, books. I packed up my room. Let me guess," he said frowning. "Your big plan was to follow me to where I was going to stash Scott with the others."

Phoebe said nothing. Her attention had been drawn to something burning on the far end of the parking lot and she heard the distant sound of sirens. It had just dawned on Phoebe that the fire was coming from the building she'd been in, when she turned her head sharply as Colten turned the key in the ignition.

Startled out of her daze she asked, "Where are we going?"

Colten's face hardened. "I'm taking you back to campus."

"I don't believe you." Phoebe yanked at the door handle.

"You're wasting your energy," Colten said. "It won't open."

Phoebe glared at him. "You've locked me in?"

"It's for your own good." Colten stared at her then, his face taking on a sad smile. "How many times do I need to save you Phoebe, before you start to believe that I'm not a threat?"

Phoebe froze, her eyes widening in disbelief.

"Who do you think just stopped that—" Colten let his voice trail, bringing the car to a stop at a light and shaking his head dejectedly. He then turned to look at Phoebe with a look both gentle and intense, pleading with his eyes. But Phoebe didn't see him. What she saw was the memory of one Tiger flinging a larger Tiger against a tree in the clearing, and that smaller Tiger holding her gaze. . . .

Phoebe swallowed hard. "It was you in the woods that night." Colten's gaze intensified. "Y—you were—"

"Trying to keep that Vigo from taking you," he said simply, lowering his gaze to the faint scars on her arm.

Just then, the light changed and they were moving again. Phoebe drew her knees to her chest and hugged them.

"What are you?" she said, keeping her gaze ahead.

Colten glanced at Phoebe as though she were crazy. A hard edge entered his voice. "You know what I am."

"But I don't understand how you could be . . . when I've never felt—never felt—"

"—the burn?"

Phoebe nodded confused. "And not just me. An entire campus with Shapers didn't sense you. I don't understand."

"That's because I was born this way," Colten said after a minute, his hand gripping the steering wheel tightly.

That made Phoebe laugh, even though it wasn't funny. "Vigos aren't born."

"I know that."

"Then how is what you're saying even possible?" Phoebe couldn't keep a sliver of animosity out of her voice.

"I'm one of a kind," Colten sighed. "My mother was bitten while pregnant and the venom got passed on to me through the umbilical cord," he said softly. "She went into early labor when the change started happening with her."

Phoebe gasped, her head whirling with questions. "How early?"

"I was born at five months and survived." He added bitterly, "The ironic thing is that the change killed my mother, but it's what saved me." Colten measured Phoebe's expression and frowned. Phoebe had looked away too late to hide her horror.

"God . . ." she said, bringing a hand to her chest. "So that's what happened to your mother."

"I couldn't exactly tell you the truth earlier," Colten said his voice full of regret.

"So you're half-Vigo, half-human?" Phoebe asked, trying not to focus on the fact that both she and Colten had lost a parent to Vigos.

Colten shrugged. "I really don't know how much of either I am. . . . I just know I have enough Vigo in me to be able to change."

"And enough human to go undetected by Shapers?" Phoebe said, putting it together.

"Something like that." His voice was low and intense.

Phoebe couldn't make sense of his answer. "Then what is it exactly?"

Colten kept his narrowed eyes on the road. "I can manipulate my physical presence to emit the energy of a Vigo, human—even a Shaper. . . ."

"What? How's that even—" Phoebe broke off and brought a hand to her throat; she could feel her skin getting hotter, almost to the point of scalding.

"Can you feel me now?" Colten said, his voice tight.

Phoebe choked. "Yes." Slowly, her skin began to cool and her breathing steadied.

Cars slipped by faster now than they had before and Phoebe saw that Colten had merged onto the freeway. They drove in silence. Demonstrating his ability upset Colten, Phoebe realized. He was staring ahead, eyebrows furrowed, his lips and jaw tight.

"I didn't hurt you just now, did I?" Colten asked, his voice soft and apologetic. Phoebe shook her head; Colten's jaw seemed to slacken slightly.

"How does that work?" Phoebe said shakily.

"Think of it like a volume dial with Vigo physical energy being at the highest setting. I'm mentally able to dial the energy I radiate down to the cold point where to you I feel—"

"Human," Phoebe finished.

Colten nodded.

"And if you wanted to feel Shaper you'd dial the energy up to some middle point?"

"Yeah, something like that. But it's a bit harder. The warmth of Shaper physical energy comes from the fact that you have two hearts operating two circulatory systems—one regular for your human appearance and the other one mystical. It's hard to mimic. It takes me being around a Shaper for a while to get it right. . . ."

Almost at once, Phoebe felt a warm tingling energy move through her body, then it was gone.

"That's crazy. . . . Which energy is most natural to you?"

"Vigo," Colten said, anger vibrating his voice. "I have to keep a strong mental guard up to prevent it from flaring. I almost slipped around you a few times, and when I yanked it back in place, I noticed that you'd get dizzy."

"That was you?" Phoebe said, stunned.

Colten's jaw tightened again. "I don't know why it affected you like that, but I'm sorry."

They lapsed into a silence. Phoebe reached for the radio and turned it on. The dial had been set to a talk radio station and she was happy to listen to other voices for a change. After ten minutes of scholars debating the state of the economy, Phoebe asked, slowly, "After you were born, what happened?" Her eyes were fastened on his face, and she fought her impulse to read him.

"I was born in a crèche." Colten paused, then glanced sideways at her. "Do you know what that is?" Phoebe nodded. Colten focused on the road and continued. "Given my situation, I stayed at the crèche for thirteen years until they thought I was ready to receive my—"

"—mark," Phoebe finished.

"What do you know about our Mark Days?" Colten asked, looking genuinely confused.

"Cubs get the Mark of Wang to signify learning all things Vigo. We learn it in class."

"It's a bit more involved than that," Colten said.

Phoebe turned to gaze out of the window, waiting for Colten to explain.

"Crèches mark cubs in a private ceremony," he said. "After that, it becomes a big lavish event thrown for the Consiglio dei Alfa to attend and bid for new graduates for their packs."

Phoebe hadn't expected this at all. "What's the Consig—Consig—?"

"Consiglio dei Alfa," Colten said in a false Italian accent. Then, shaking his head, "You'd think as much as Vigos hate the Old Country, they'd lose the Italian terms. It's basically a council of all the local Alphas. From what I know, they meet a few times during the year for various reasons. One of those times is the Mark Day, which can turn into a crazy bidding war when the Alphas compete for the best of the new recruits."

"Which pack did you end up with?"

"I didn't go to a pack." Colten raised an amused eyebrow. Phoebe knew she was missing something important—something Colten had expected her to glean from his words. What was he getting at?

"No one bid on you?"

"I was actually predicted to go high in auction," Colten said, chuckling. "But every marked cub can choose to enter the pack bid or select to be a loner. I chose to be a loner. It's rare, and it's frowned on by the crèches, but . . ." he threw his hands up.

"Why?"

"Because it's a source of pride for them to have a one hundred percent 'graduation rate'—it means more bids and more money. They line the walls with the photos of their graduates and the names of which pack they went to."

"What I meant," Phoebe said, a tiny smile forming on her lips at his continued disregard for status, "is why did you choose to be a loner?"

"Following nature, I suppose," Colten said. At Phoebe's questioning look he chuckled, and added, "In the wild, tigers are solitary animals. They don't form packs. It's unnatural." He tapped a finger against the steering wheel and then after almost a full minute, he fixed Phoebe with a serious gaze. "The truth is, over the years, whatever humanity—soul—I have within me started fighting the Vigo soullessness and started winning. I don't have the same thirst for—"

"Then why didn't you leave earlier?" Phoebe broke in, her eyes wide, her mind invigorated by the idea of his fledgling soul.

Colten's eyes went distant. "I have no mother," he said. "There's no record of my father. So, it isn't that easy to get up and leave the only family you've ever known. The crèche indoctrinates you with what it is to be in a pack. Growing up in that environment, I came to depend on it. But after years of seeing cubs enter and graduate, I began to question what it meant to just be me. That's when I knew something else within me was overpowering the Vigo. By the time they considered me ready for my mark, I had my mind made up that I would be a loner."

Phoebe frowned. Something was still gnawing at her. "Then why get marked at all?"

"Because you have to," Colten said, his tone serious. "If I hadn't gotten marked it would have raised suspicion to a level where I could have been killed."

Phoebe shivered.

"Besides," Colten continued. "Your mark is your calling card among Vigos. Even a loner is given the respect and courtesies of the mark. I needed that to be able to move among them. It was the only way I could collect information to undermine Vigo activity."

Phoebe stared at Colten, eyes wide. "To turn against your own?"

Colten's breathing got heavier for a moment, then ragged, and when it steadied, he said with effort, "Do you know what it's like to walk around knowing that much of the blood in you belongs to a race that is responsible for killing your mother? Responsible for killing all kinds of innocent people? It's a nightmare. I've spent the last few years loathing my Vigo side—everything to do with it.

"One night I came across a triad taunting a human woman before a kill and something came over me. Before I knew it, I lost myself and had killed them all. That was the night I found my new purpose. Triad by triad, plot by plot, I work against Vigos. I know it won't change what I am, or redeem anything I've done, but it helps me sleep a bit better at night."

Something that had been lurking in the back of Phoebe's mind finally formed and she swallowed hard. She found her voice enough to ask a question she wasn't sure she wanted the answer for. "What do you do to survive?"

"Are you asking me what I eat?"

"Yes." Phoebe turned her face from his and gazed out the window.

Colten hesitated for a moment and then spoke carefully. "My human side allows me to process some regular food. Mostly vegetables . . . but, I need mito to—" Colten broke off, his eyes locked on Phoebe who was now staring at him openly, devastation marching across her face.

Phoebe was unable to feel her own expression, but whatever her face held was enough for Colten to make a sharp turn, pull over, and stop the car. Then she felt what Colten must have seen. Her chest hurt, her back ached. All at once, something bitter rose from the pit of her stomach and Phoebe's need for air was immediate. Pushing her way through a door that was now thankfully unlocked, she vomited.

Colten jumped out of the car and went to Phoebe's side. He held out his hand, but Phoebe turned from him and stumbled toward a bench in the corner of the small park they were now in. She sat under the creamy glimmer of a quarter moon perched high in the clear night sky and found relief in the cold breeze that blew against her skin like the gentlest kiss. Forehead resting on her fist, Phoebe stared at her feet for a moment, wishing the ground would stop moving. *What was I expecting,* she thought to herself, *when I asked him that question?* Avoiding answers she didn't want meant not asking those questions in the first place; Phoebe knew that.

A few feet away, Colten stood with his face raised to the sky, his thoughts as distant as the horizon. Watching him now, Phoebe couldn't help but picture him hunting and her stomach clenched, violently threatening a repeat performance. It was a few minutes before Phoebe felt that she could breathe again.

As if sensing this, Colten came to Phoebe and knelt on the ground in front of her. "I promise you," he said softly. "I'm not a monster." A pleading note in his voice tugged at Phoebe. He reached a hand out, hesitantly, placed it under her chin and raised her face to meet his eyes. "I'm not—"

Phoebe looked away. "But you hunt."

"I only take what I need to repair my wounds and I only take it from people who wouldn't even notice," he said.

Phoebe forced down another upward movement of bile.

"Who would never notice?" she said in a hoarse whisper. Phoebe hugged herself, waiting for an answer in the heavy silence that followed.

"City drunks mostly," Colten said, sighing. "I find them passed out on street corners or park benches like this one late at night. They wake up in the morning with a more intense hangover than they would have otherwise. That's about all."

"How are you able to control yourself from not killing them—turning them? I thought mito was an intense need for Vigos. An addiction." Phoebe hugged herself even tighter.

Colten's green eyes clouded. "It is. But I wasn't created from a human drained of mitochondria, so I don't thirst for it as intensely as other Vigos do. And, I try and stay off mito for as long as I can, and only hunt when my bruises start to show. As for turning someone"—Colten scrubbed his hands on his jeans—"Vigos do that one of two ways. The first way is a reflex response to being mito drunk—our venom is released into a victim's blood stream once we feel the high of being full. Because I only take what I need, I've never let myself feel that high."

"And the second way?"

"An intentional release of venom that has nothing to do with feeding." His voice was flat, emotionless; Phoebe could sense that the interrogation was beginning to wear on his patience. He seemed desperate to win back her trust, but the effort was clearly costing him. Still, Phoebe had another question to ask.

This question was the painful one she'd been turning over in her head since the day she'd found out what Colten was. But judging by how she'd handled the question about mito, she was uncertain of this one, the knowledge she was asking for could ruin her. Still, Phoebe couldn't turn away from it. If she was to find a way to accept what she'd learned about Colten, not turn him into the Blackcoats, and get on with her life—with or without him—she needed to know. "Have you ever killed a Shaper?" Phoebe finally asked, trembling from head to toe as she waited for his response.

Colten bent forward involuntarily as though the wind had been knocked out of him with an invisible punch. He walked away from her and Phoebe drew a deep shuddering breath.

"I spent thirteen years in a crèche," he said, facing a cluster of round picnic tables. "And from about the age of ten I trained with each group of cubs that came through. By twelve I was an expert in every one of the triad positions. I've hunted. I've done many things"—his voice hardened—"that I wish I hadn't done, but I have never killed a Shaper." And turning to look at Phoebe, his gaze was fierce, his eyes clear and deadly serious, "I swear it."

Phoebe let the breath she'd been holding rush out of her, hardly believing the surge of relief that came to her like a storm. The release brought with it the sting of tears, and she let them flow freely. She shivered. Colten went to her, took her hands, and blew warm air onto them. For a moment, the gentleness of the gesture released Phoebe from her thoughts. She looked up into his face, tentatively.

"It's another reason I didn't join a pack," he said softly. "You earn the mark of your pack after you make your first Shaper kill. And it's not something you can fake—the Alpha joins the hunt to verify the kill himself."

Colten stood, dropped Phoebe's hands, and scrubbed his face with his fists. "I should get you back."

"Not yet." Phoebe blurted, "How does this whole movie star thing fit in?" She couldn't help herself. She thought she had been done, but now, in her relief, her curiosity was taking on a life of its own. Colten closed his eyes and smiled tiredly. "It's nice to be able to step into someone else's life and deal with their choices and conflicts, and not think about what I am or what I've done. . . ."

"And the other reasons?" Phoebe asked, her stubborn streak at full blast now. "There's more to it than that. I can tell."

"Like I told you before. My mother was an aspiring actress. I thought I'd try my hand at the family business," he chuckled bitterly. "And do what she wasn't able to. And it doesn't hurt that Hollywood is a hotbed of Vigo activity. It keeps me tapped in."

Phoebe grappled, trying to comprehend what Colten had just said. She wrapped a few strands of hair around her finger, thinking it over. "There are . . . Vigos in Hollywood?"

Colten frowned. "Why is that so surprising? You're talking to one right now."

"You mean, other actors that I know of?"

"It's mostly the folks behind the scenes like producers and top execs. But there are other actors and rock stars and pop stars, too." He chuckled. "It's why a lot of them look so good for so long. Vigo venom is a great preservative. There's even a long-standing joke that it's the secret ingredient in Botox."

As much as Phoebe wanted to play the 'Who in Hollywood is a Vigo' game, she held her tongue as Colten continued.

"Other Vigos," he said, "don't really think highly of Hollywood Vigos as part of the race. They call them the lazy ones."

"Why?"

"Because they don't have to hunt. Fan clubs, backstage passes, and after parties exist for the sole purpose of bringing the prey to them. . . . That's how my mother was taken. At some after party. They can blame it on drugs—overdosing—so easily." Phoebe cringed as Colten stared into his hands. "As a loner, I don't get the daily benefit of the pack filling me in on what's going on within Vigo circles. So I stay in the loop by attending functions and parties in L.A. It's how I learned that the New England

Padrone had put a hit on four Hyphas with the promise of a big reward to anyone who got the job done."

"How much money?" Phoebe's fury seeped from her pores as she thought of Scott and the others.

"Not money. A title. The position of Alpha of a new pack. You have to understand," he said, when Phoebe raised a brow. "It's a very big deal."

"Why?" she tossed her head scornfully. Even as a Shaper cadet, she had a hard time feigning interest in Vigo hierarchy. It just reinforced to her how they managed to be both cold and calculated and completely ruled by mito lust.

"Anyone who wants to make a bid for starting a new pack must present their case to their regional Consiglio dei Alfa. It's a very political and sometimes a dangerous process. A Padrone's blessing trumps the Consiglio."

Phoebe sucked in a breath and Colten came to sit by her.

"At first, I wasn't going to bother trying to disrupt their plan. There were too many unknowns—like the location of the school. Then . . ." Colten let the unfinished thought hang in the air.

"Then what?" Phoebe said, hearing the desperation in her voice.

Colten, whose gaze had drifted, snapped back to Phoebe. "Do you know who the Anzaini are?"

Phoebe's breath quickened and her eyes went wide. If there was one Italian word all Shapers knew and feared, it was the one for "Elders." Comprised of the original surviving members of the exiled clan from Pompeii, the Anzaini were the Vigos' governing body.

"What about them?" she asked, thinking with a shiver about how many centuries those immortals had seen.

Colten said, "I found out that Alexori's orders had come from them,"—Phoebe gasped, trembling—"it's why I decided to pursue this plot. Everything I've done 'til now has been small time. But this—I couldn't pass up a chance to disrupt an Anzaini sanctioned operation."

Phoebe couldn't believe that what Colten was saying might be true. It had been one thing to learn that a Padrone was after her, but to now find out that the Anzaini—a group that was shrouded in mystery—were involved . . . the thought chilled her to the bone.

Were the Blackcoats aware of this fact? And if so, why had they not disclosed it? Phoebe listened as well as she could in her agitated state while Colten explained how he'd gotten the names of the four Hypha targets through working sources, located the school, and learned that Alexori had found a way to breach campus security.

"—I enrolled to see how I could foil the plan," Colten finished, exhaling with a small cough.

Phoebe mulled over all she'd heard, until something clicked "So that's how you knew who I was . . ." her mind drifted to when they'd met on a bench similar to the one they were sitting on now.

"I knew your name, but I didn't know what you looked like." Colten smiled to himself. "When I approached you at the bench it was for entirely different reasons . . . then I sensed your physical energy as not being . . . wholly Shaper or human. I realized you must be a Hypha, and then by process of elimination figured that you had to be Phoebe Pope."

Phoebe raised an eyebrow. "Process of elimination?"

"Well, it seemed unlikely that you were Mariko Higashi, but I guess I had a fifty-fifty chance of being right." He winked at her, and his eyes glittered, a bit of the ferocious intensity from before having died down since their conversation moved past his hunting. And killing.

"So hanging out with me was about getting information on my school?" Phoebe couldn't believe how disappointed she sounded. She needed to pull it together.

"I told you," Colten said. "I first approached you for other reasons, but once I knew what you were, I tried to discard those thoughts and focus on how I could protect you from whatever Alexori had planned."

"What did you think you could do?" Phoebe said bitterly, knowing her attitude was misdirected. He had genuinely meant to protect her; she should be grateful.

Colten shrugged. "I figured I'd patrol the campus at night and try and figure out how a Vigo could get around a security system that was specifically set to detect Vigo physical energy. For obvious reasons, I knew that my own movements would go unnoticed. During my first night of patrolling I saw a group of you entering the forest. So I followed you to the game . . ." He broke off and scrubbed his face again. When he continued speaking, his voice had hardened. "I let myself get so distracted with watching you that I didn't sense the triad in time to stop the arrow."

Phoebe gasped and thought of the girl who had gone home to recover. It had never occurred to her that it was even possible that someone could have prevented the whole thing.

"In the chaos of everyone running off," Colten continued, "I lost track of you and the other three. At the risk of exposing myself to the Vigos I couldn't see, I took my Tiger form and broke into the clearing just as that Closer was pulling you toward the forest."

Phoebe shuddered and the memory in all its horrid detail assaulted her mind. She had tried so hard to put that night behind her, and had genuinely been so caught up in everything that had happened since—the kidnappings, and Colten himself—that she'd all but expelled it from her mind. Until now. She clasped her shaking hands in her lap. "What happened when you left the clearing?"

Colten's voice was tight. "I tracked and killed the others."

Phoebe's throat closed. "Others?"

"The triad. They'd seen me try to rescue you and Tiger stripe patterns are unique to each Vigo. I couldn't let what happened in the clearing get around . . . I waited a few days after that to see if there would be another attack, and then when nothing happened I went down to L.A."

"The audition?"

Colten nodded. "I planned on also seeing if I could get any details on what Alexori was up to while I was in town. But when I heard that he'd successfully acquired two of the four Hyphas, it made me sick. I was so angry, I couldn't see straight. I chartered a plane and came back right away. I wouldn't have been able to forgive myself if anything had happened to you because I'd left. And, Phoebe, it was a relief to see you, but I was still so frustrated because I couldn't tell how he'd done it. It was almost as if . . ."

"—he had help from the inside?" Phoebe finished, her voice cracking.

Colten glanced at her sideways, caught off guard. "Did he?"

"That's what the Blackcoats think. That's why they let me go to the premiere. They thought they could flush the traitor out."

"Ahh, so they are Blackcoats," Colten said with a knowing smile.

Phoebe looked at him surprised. "You mean you didn't know?"

"I had my suspicions at the premiere, but I wasn't sure how far up the food chain your security went." Phoebe narrowed her eyes at Colten, a thought coming to mind. "If you knew I was in danger, then why did you invite me at all? I mean, if your whole purpose was to protect me and thwart them . . ."

Colten looked away. "When none of my efforts to foil the plan were working, I realized I needed something more public. If I could get you to the premiere, I could monitor any Vigo attempts to approach you, make note of their faces, and seek them out later. Get them to lead me to Alexori."

"You were using me?" This was a new thought to Phoebe. She had almost reconciled the idea that she was just another victim to Colten, someone to protect. But the idea that she had been "bait" in his eyes, just as the Blackcoats had seen her—it was too much.

"I wasn't doing anything different from what the Blackcoats were doing," Colten said quietly. In fact, he and the Blackcoats had shared a very similar plan; still, she was hurt. Phoebe opened her mouth to say something, but Colten spoke over her. "It was a dangerous gamble. I know. But I also figured when you changed your mind about going that the Blackcoats wouldn't have allowed it unless they had a plan in place to ensure your safety. And it seems like my guess was right. I just didn't anticipate you finding out the truth about me that very night. Or that way. . . .

"After the premiere, I just sat in my hotel suite and waited. I figured if you'd turned me in it was only a matter of time before the Blackcoats came for me. Secretly, I think I even wanted them to come and take me— not for being Vigo, but for what I'd done to you. The look in your eyes before you ran was . . ." he shuddered, "It was almost unbearable. But then the Blackcoats never came." Hesitation crept into his tone and he paused.

"I tried to convince myself that maybe you didn't turn me in because you . . ." His voice got thin, and then trailed off, as he looked at Phoebe with the most unbelievably tender eyes that she'd ever seen. Finally, he lowered them and scuffed at the ground. Phoebe was relieved that he didn't say it.

"Not seeing you was driving me crazy, so I finally came back to campus. I thought that maybe I could make you hear me if we were somewhere private, that if at least you understood what I'd been doing then maybe you'd forgive me. . . . But when you told me that a Vigo had killed your father . . . I realized there was no hope."

Colten lifted his gaze to the sky, watching clouds drift toward the moon. He looked as though he was suffering from the weight of all Vigo sins, and Phoebe found herself beginning to feel empathy for him.

"I fought hard not to fall for you, Phoebe, I really did. I knew what my being a Vigo would mean to you. But I needed to see you all the time, be with you. And then there was that day you laughed so freely and uncontrollably at my miserable tomatoes . . . I know it sounds silly, like infatuation or a kid's crush, but the truth is, even though I was still just getting to know you, I couldn't fight it anymore. You had this moment of unguarded openness that was . . . so delicate and I just had to love you, protect you. I had to."

Shocked, Phoebe sat back dumbfounded and stared at Colten anew. And then Phoebe decided to break her own rule: She had told herself again and again that she would never trespass into Colten's emotions, but now, more than ever, she simply had to know. She needed to understand what he felt and know whether his words were true. Phoebe could never have imagined all that she'd heard in the last few hours, and she was still having a hard time taking it all in. She needed an assurance that this was not just his actor's skills fooling her into believing some invented madness. She couldn't subject her hearts to another beating, and if she found out later that he'd been toying with her, she knew it would break her.

Ever so slowly, Phoebe bowed her head and opened her mental gate. The immediate strength of Colten's love pouring into Phoebe almost choked her, for it mirrored a certainty she'd suppressed in herself. She allowed herself to absorb the intensely sweet emotion. To find peace in its promise of comfort and support. It overwhelmed her.

Phoebe realized, with a torrent of relief, part of what had been exhausting her all these weeks— it wasn't just the Vigos and her fear she had been fighting all this while. She hadn't imagined that it was possible that Colten could feel for her so deeply, or that a Vigo could feel at all. She hadn't wished for this, to love a Vigo who loved her back more furiously than she'd even thought it was possible to love. The balance of things she knew had slipped away, and she gripped the edge of the bench to steady herself. Unable to look at him just yet, she kept her gaze down, for she knew what she'd see in his eyes. Hope. She'd felt it laced in his love.

"Are you okay?" Colten asked, surveying Phoebe with concern. "You kinda zoned out for a moment there."

"No, I'm not okay," Phoebe said. "But I believe you. . . . It's a lot to process."

Phoebe felt the touch of Colten's fingertips against her cheeks as he cupped her face, raising it to meet his eyes. He leaned in, close and then closer still, stopping just short of touching his nose to Phoebe's and she could hear the staccato of his breathing. His lips brushed against hers ever so gently and Phoebe took a breath as she felt them tremble against hers and pulled back.

"I'm sorry." His eyes were soft and a little guarded as they watched hers.

"Too soon," she said. It was all too much for her at once. In Phoebe's mind she knew that her hearts belonged to Colten, but at that moment she couldn't bring herself to express it in that particular way. Not yet. Resolving within herself never to tell anyone what he really was would have to suffice for now.

"I understand," Colten said sadly, his hands dropping from her face.

And then Phoebe began to sob and Colten's hands were back on her face, wiping away the tears that dropped to her cheeks. He searched her with those gentle green eyes, eyes that had never been so beautiful, so completely honest and genuine before. "What's wrong, Phoebe?" The way he said her name just about undid her. She had never heard anyone give it such fullness, such a complete sound before.

But Phoebe couldn't tell him what was wrong, for at that moment she was thinking of her father, and hoping that Colten's love for her was enough to push the memory of that night away.

Colten wrapped his arms around Phoebe and she felt a splinter of joy that she couldn't quite revel in. It wasn't the right moment, but just knowing that there might be a right moment was enough for right now. "We should go," he said brusquely, bringing Phoebe back from her thoughts.

They didn't speak the rest of the ride back to campus. But even as he kept his eyes on the road, Colten kept finding Phoebe's cheek with his hand and brushing it softly with his fingertips.

"Can I ask another question?" Phoebe said with a curious twist to her lips as the car made a silent stop near Hayley's dorm.

"You can ask any question, always," Colten said, a wan version of his usually effortless smile having returned for the first time Phoebe could recall in a long while. His teeth almost lit the dark.

"I guess I don't understand how you're getting away with it. Wouldn't the Vigos you trained with growing up recognize you?"

Colten shook his head. "Not even if I shook their hands."

"Why not?" Phoebe said.

"Let's just say I've evolved." Colten flushed and gave a sheepish grin. "I sort of went through puberty late and look nothing like the short scrawny kid I was when I left the crèche at thirteen."

Phoebe stared at Colten, unable to picture that version of him. Another thought came to her. "What about now? I mean you have one of the most famous faces in the world." Phoebe stuck her tongue out at Colten then, her own playfulness returning for an instant.

Colten smiled wider. "Hollywood Vigos don't know I'm Vigo because I keep my mark covered up and my physical energy human. But when they talk to each other in code at parties, unbeknownst to them, I understand what's being said. And whenever I do need to show my mark in situations that require it, I never go as myself. I'm an actor, remember?" Colten said with a trace of sarcasm when Phoebe furrowed her brows. "I get paid to change my appearance. I have a skilled prosthetics makeup artist who asks no questions."

Phoebe shuddered. "It still sounds dangerous. How can you do that day-in, day-out?"

"Deception is in the details," Colten said. "I take all the necessary precautions. Besides, you're the one in training to become SIS. And you're lecturing me about taking chances?"

"Fine, fine," Phoebe said nodding. Then, seriously, "So what are you going to do now?"

"There's a lead I'm following about Vigo-owned warehouses that I'm hoping will take me to the others. It's what I was doing when you followed me," Colten said.

Then, with a start, Phoebe remembered what she'd heard back at the warehouse. "They're at a crèche!" she gasped. "That's where those Vigos were planning on taking me."

Colten leaned toward her abruptly and grabbed Phoebe by the shoulders. He looked into her with a piercing, nervous gaze. "Are you sure?"

Phoebe nodded fearfully.

"Did they mention a name? A location?"

Phoebe shook her head.

"Think!" Colten urged, running his hands through the back of his hair, and growing more disheveled by the second.

"That's all I heard!" Phoebe's eyes crinkled and she looked down, feeling useless.

"I'm sorry," Colten said, loosening his grip and sweeping Phoebe's white streak out of her eyes. "It's still helpful. . . ."

"You think they might still be alive?" Phoebe bit her lip.

Colten's expression was grim. "I don't know. If they're at a crèche . . . I don't know, but I promise to keep looking. If I find them at one of the crèches, I'll leave an anonymous tip with the Blackcoats. In the meantime, my priority is for you to stay alive." He cupped her cheek with one hand, and turned back to the car.

Feeling terrified, electric, and overwhelmed by everything she had heard and felt with Colten over the last few hours, Phoebe tried to keep it together as she watched him leave. Slowly, she made her way over to the tree outside of Hayley's window. The notion of being with Colten again and all she'd learned burned in Phoebe's mind. She was consumed with such emotion that she didn't hear a sound as a figure crept up behind her and struck her across the base of her skull. She collapsed into unconsciousness without a single thought.

❦ Twenty-Eight

Phoebe's eyes flew open to complete darkness. Her wrists and ankles had been so securely strapped to a chair that she was sure it hindered her circulation. Anxiously, Phoebe rocked her chair back and forth, trying to loosen the bonds that cleaved into her extremities.

"You only exhaust yourself doing that," said a man's oily, Italian-accented voice from speakers somewhere overhead. The noise saturated the room like surround sound in a theater. Shocked by the sudden sensory input, Phoebe became still.

"You respond well to advice, I see," the man said. "This may go *molto facile* for you." He laughed. "Excuse me. I meant to say very easy for you."

"Who are you? And where am I?" Phoebe yelled, tossing her head about, hair whipping around her.

"I'm Alexori and I'm—"

"—a maniac!" Phoebe blurted, rancor in her voice.

"I'll try not to take that personally." Alexori released an easy chuckle that belied a venomous undertone. "In the interest of time," he said, "let me tell you how I operate. I'll ask questions and only because I'm feeling generous, you'll get the benefit of up to two lies." Phoebe could hear his words slither between his vocal chords. "After that, things will start to get entertaining—for me only. Are we clear?"

"Where are my friends?!" Phoebe shouted, her anger rising and her hearts palpitating crazily.

"You're a bit emotional, no?" Alexori said icily. "A calmer mind would allow you to process that I'm the one asking the questions and what I want to know is all about your secret."

"I don't have a secret," Phoebe said through gritted teeth.

A pause. "That's lie number one, Phoebe."

"I'm not—"

"Careful now. Remember, you only have one more chance." The oil in his voice seemed to thicken.

"What secret do you think I have?" A violent shiver ran through Phoebe. The room's temperature had dropped significantly and the darkness around her seemed to be pressing in.

"Tell me who's been protecting you," Alexori said, a knowing edge to his voice that caused Phoebe's chest to tighten and her mouth to go dry. Of course she knew what Alexori was getting at, but it couldn't be possible. How could he possibly know? *Calm down*, Phoebe told herself. Telling a lie would only work if she sounded confident.

"I've had Blackcoat protection," Phoebe said matter-of-factly.

Alexori warned in a rougher tone, "That's lie number two, *ragazza*."

"That's the truth!" Phoebe screamed.

Alexori spoke slowly, enunciating every word. "Perhaps you need a bit of convincing."

Over the speakers came another man's growling voice. "Don't try anything stupid," this man warned. Phoebe opened her mouth to speak, but stopped when she heard the distinct sound of tape being ripped from skin. A hoarse voice squeaked, "Phoebe?"

"Mariko!" Phoebe yelled, eyes rolling around crazily in her head as she sought Mariko's image in the darkness, of course finding nothing. *She's not in the same room as me. Stop it. Get a hold of yourself,* Phoebe commanded herself.

A harsh slap, followed by a guttural wail of terror sounded over the speakers.

"Convince her," the man's growling voice commanded again.

"Please, Phoebe," Mariko cried in clear terror. "Tell them whatever they want to know!"

"I don't—" A few more slaps in rapid succession clenched Phoebe's gut. "Where are you?" she yelled.

"First—" Mariko was cut off with a static click.

Alexori's lethal voice returned. "Since that didn't seem to loosen your tongue, let's have you listen to something new. Perhaps this will move you."

A speaker crackled behind Phoebe. "Don't give them what they want, Pope," Scott's voice blared. "You hear me! Don't—" Phoebe heard the crack of a whip in motion. Leather on flesh. Scott's howl amplified around her.

"Scott!" Tears streamed down Phoebe's face. With the effort of a full body motion, she thrashed in her seat, scooting it forward, her head moving wildly about. "Scott!"

Another crack of the whip. Scott screamed again.

"This is madness. Make it stop!" Phoebe yelled at the top of her lungs. Never in her life had she heard a scream like the one that had erupted from Scott's throat.

"You're the one in control here, Phoebe," Alexori said in the darkness. "It's all music to my ears, so I can do this all night. Tell me what I want to know and I'll make it stop."

"I don't understand what you're getting at," Phoebe said, her voice rising in exasperation despite her sickening fear.

"Curiously, there's a disturbing Vigo body count that seems to be linked to you," Alexori said. "Allow me to give you the highlight reel. We had you at the soccer game until there was interference. The members of that triad were each stalked and killed. We had eyes on you at the red carpet, and they later turned up dead. Earlier this evening, two of my finest managed to track you to an abandoned warehouse—I think you get the picture. Someone in my organization must be behind it. No Blackcoat could have such success."

"What gives you that idea?" Phoebe said mockingly.

"How I know what I know is no concern of yours. I must know who the traitor is. My patience draws to an end, *ragazza*." The words were spoken in quiet fury. "Perhaps you'd like to hear from Lewis next? I understand his lung power is impressive—him being a singer and all."

Phoebe couldn't bear to hear any more screaming, but she had no idea how to make it stop without sending them all to their deaths. Giving up what Alexori wanted would only make it easier for him to dispense with them all. "I have nothing to tell you," she blurted. And her desperation overruling caution, Phoebe added sarcastically, "It's not my fault if you don't have control over your organization!"

Suddenly, a bright light flashed on. Delivered from darkness, Phoebe saw that she faced a thick, glass wall. Behind it, a heavy-shouldered man with dark, wavy hair sat in an armchair, stroking the white silk tie that hung over the white shirt he wore under his finely-tailored white suit. Next to him, a side table held a silver tray containing a decanter of brandy and a short glass.

Phoebe dug her fingernails into her palms, unable to keep her eyes off the deep, rope-like scar that ran along the length of his forehead, marring his sharp, impossibly handsome face. And as Phoebe's gaze moved to his unusual eyes—pale blue irises that seemed almost colorless—she unconsciously began to shake. An aura of danger hung about the man in front of her, an aura that was intensely magnified by the silence.

Alexori reached for the decanter and poured himself a drink. Revolving his glass slowly, he sat forward in the chair, his thick arms straining the sleeves of his jacket.

"You should know, *ragazza*," he said, his voice slippery and just a touch shrill, "that I don't take kindly to insult." The Padrone breathed deeply, then added crisply, "I have killed people for much lesser insults than yours." He paused and took a few swallows from his glass, his eyes never once leaving Phoebe's face. "Unfortunately, I have to let this one slide since there are people way above me whose interests lie in keeping you alive. For now."

Alexori leaned back in the chair, gripping the empty brandy glass tighter in his hand as if in an effort to control himself. Phoebe knew he was talking about the Anzaini. Her shaking worsened. Alexori noticed. His thin lips formed a sinister half-smile just before his hand crushed the brandy glass into small shards—it seemed as though his fingers had done it of their own volition. Phoebe choked on a gasp, her tired eyes widening. She saw no sign of blood as the glass particles seeped through Alexori's fingers and onto the silver tray. It was as if his hand was made of granite. Without another word spoken between them, the light went out, returning Phoebe to a darkness filled with the echo of her own heavy breathing.

The beep of a security code unlocked a door behind Phoebe and heavy footsteps stomped toward her. As strong hands grabbed her by the shoulders, Phoebe felt the sharp prick of a needle in her left arm. Unconsciousness rushed in, but not before she heard Alexori say to someone, "I'll be back by morning. I trust you'll have gotten results by then."

Phoebe woke to pain and the sound of voices above her. Dark figures encased in white lab coats weaved in and out of focus. Hands wrote furious notes on clipboards. Pain surged within Phoebe from a source she couldn't identify. A scream tore from her chest and she dimly heard someone suggest lowering the voltage. A rough voice barked instructions to increase it instead. The pain burgeoned to an unfathomable point, then ceased with unconsciousness.

Phoebe woke again without the foggiest idea how much time had passed. She quickly took stock of the room, aware of the restraints that bound her to a narrow raised bed. Fifty or so wires covered her chest. She twisted her head to the left, following the silvery trail they made across a hardwood floor and up to a black machine with a panel of blinking LED lights and buttons. A glass cylindrical tube rose from the center of the machine's steel top up through a hole in the ceiling. Phoebe pulled her eyes away from the machine and looked around, taking in her surroundings. It was a large bedroom, empty but for two armchairs at the end of the bed. On a far wall, diaphanous drapes revealed French doors behind them.

Phoebe began struggling against her bonds. The sound of a key turning made her pause. When the door opened, Phoebe lifted her head and saw Scott walk in. Though his soccer jersey was torn in several places, he didn't appear gravely hurt. Relief rocketed through Phoebe.

"You're okay," she said, choking up. "How'd you get away? Nevermind. Tell me later."

Scott pressed the door closed with his back and spoke quietly. "Nice to see you too, Pope."

"Can you unchain me?" she asked, hope and desperation in her voice.

In answer, Scott raised a hand to show a ring of keys dangling from his index finger. Phoebe exhaled and relaxed somewhat. She had many questions, but there would be time for that. But then, just as Scott began to walk toward her, he changed direction and headed for the left wall.

As Phoebe twisted to look at him, her eyes narrowed with confusion. "What are you doing?"

Scott turned to face Phoebe with a blank expression and continued walking backward toward the machine. "I wish I could let you go Pope, but I can't."

Phoebe stared at him, puzzled. "What do you mean, you can't?" she asked slowly. Somewhere in her mind a sickening thought began to form, but she dismissed it at once. They were a team.

Scott's eyes began to flash, his face stripped of his signature teasing look. He now appeared almost unrecognizable, and eerily sinister as he began to speak low and seriously. "I went through a lot of trouble to get you here and"—he drummed his fingers on the top of the machine—"this thing hasn't done what it's supposed to do yet."

Phoebe glanced from the machine back to Scott in abject horror. Before she could process what he'd said, he inserted a key into a hole at its side and turned it. A shaft of blinding light flared in the glass tube half a second before a sharp heat seared through Phoebe. In reflex, her upper body snapped up, then fell back, her scream echoing off the bedroom walls.

"You truly are a sight to behold, Pope," Scott said, sarcasm and awe competing in his voice. He gestured at her. "Look at yourself."

Painfully, Phoebe raised her head and looked down at her body. Sparks of brilliant light seemed to shoot out from every one of her sweat-slicked pores, encasing her in a powdery, gold halo. Phoebe stared in wonder.

She was a star in the dimly lit room. For a brief moment she didn't feel the spasm of pain in her chest or her arms and legs bucking against the pressure of her restraints. Then the hypnotizing awe splintered into terror. Was she about to explode into iridescent pieces?

"You—?" Phoebe said without breathing, turning her attention to Scott.

A flicker of apology crossed his face, a scant trace of the friend she knew. Then he smiled a sickening smile. "Yes, me."

"Traitor . . ." Phoebe choked, briefly closing her eyes, then opening them to release hot tears that spilled down the side of her face and into her ears. That burning suspicion within her, the one she'd suppressed on reflex, had exploded into undeniable fact: Scott was under the employ of Vigos.

"Traitor," repeated Scott, as if trying the word on for size; his eyes seemed to dance at hearing himself say it. "I guess that depends on who you're asking."

Phoebe could barely breathe from the pain. Grappling for understanding, she asked, "What—what did they p—promise you to b—betray?"

"Alpha of my own pack, if you must know," Scott answered, his lips curling into a sneer as he savored the intense distress his words had caused Phoebe. "You see," he added, mock-conversationally, "I hate being Beta to an Alpha that lacks imagination and drive. I need to break from his suffocating shadow. To emerge a warrior. When this opportunity came along, I seized it."

Phoebe stared at him, terror in the shimmer of her eyes. "You're a—" Phoebe stopped herself, unwilling to believe it.

"I think Vigo is the word you're looking for." Scott scrubbed a hand over the side of his neck. "Removing my marks was a small sacrifice, but I'll get them redone when I have the Alpha one added."

Suddenly, Phoebe's pain receded. She fixed her watery gaze on the machine. Scott had turned the key counterclockwise. "It's been recommended," he said, sounding rather put out, "that we take breaks between jolts since killing you now would defeat our purposes."

Phoebe wasn't listening. Spared from the mind-blistering pain for the moment, she began thinking many hurried thoughts. In all her time with

Scott she had only sensed the warm physical energy of a Shaper. Even now, he radiated warmth. Phoebe's breaths came faster as a new and frightening possibility snaked its way to the front of her mind: Colten had been wrong. He wasn't the only born Vigo. Scott could also manipulate his physical energy.

"You filthy cretin . . ." she said, bringing her attention back to his smug face.

"Are we resorting to name calling, Pope? I thought we had a better relationship than that." Scott walked to the French doors and stared out into the night.

"Lies," Phoebe said hoarsely, watching his face in the white glow of moonlight that filtered through the curtains.

"I prefer artistic deception," Scott said vacantly, still looking outside.

"So how did you do it?" *Keep talking*, she thought, *Stay the hell away from that key.*

Scott whipped his head toward her, grinning. "Do what? Get you?"

"I mean how did you get past the Vigo sensors?" Phoebe clarified, though she was quite confident that she already knew. However, hearing Scott say it would make it real.

"Let's just call it a special talent of mine, which unfortunately, is not part of today's lesson plan." Now Scott's grin widened. "But speaking of lesson plans," he said, glancing down at his watch, "I have to thank you for helping me fit in a bit more than I would have, Below."

"What are you talking about?" Phoebe spat, fighting against the new surge of tears burning behind her eyes; she hated showing how scared and helpless she felt.

"If you hadn't struggled as much as you did during that sorry academic boot camp, then my lack of skill would have been more apparent." Scott tilted his head toward her, sniggering at her discomfort.

Because Vigos can't wield elements, Phoebe thought.

"I failed to accomplish even one simple task, but the Blackcoats didn't think twice about it." Scott laughed. "I was just a Hypha struggling to connect with his elements. . . ." Scott shook his head with a "tsk" and sidled around Phoebe, pausing to run a finger over her bite marks.

Phoebe stiffened. "Don't touch me," she said, her voice roughened like never before, sandpaper grit rubbing between her syllables. Even Scott cocked his head at her tone.

"Don't beat yourself up," he said, making his way back to the machine. "It's not as if you did it on purpose. I mean you were actually so bad I started to think you were a Vigo too."

"Wait!" Phoebe shouted, her voice on the edge of desperation as Scott reached for the key. "Why shoot Katie Banks with an arrow? She wasn't Hypha."

Scott paused, puzzled, then smiled with dawning comprehension. "Oh. Was that her name? She was incidental. Something to create chaos so that we could grab at least one of you without anyone noticing." A frowning pause. "My plans got screwy after that when it turned out that the mentors were actually Blackcoats sent to protect us." He rolled his eyes.

"Don't you dare say 'us,'" Phoebe growled, furious.

Suddenly Scott was crouching near Phoebe's head, a nasty grin on his face. He traced a finger along her chin and his voice rumbled. "Trust me, it gave me no pleasure to be lumped among you Shapers. To play my part as a Hypha. It was torture. But," he said, speaking softer now, his voice tinged with regret. "Shaper or not, there's something pleasant about you. It's almost magnetic. I couldn't help myself even though I hated myself for wanting . . . wanting just a little taste—" Scott leaned toward Phoebe until their lips were almost touching. Then, he stopped, stood up, and shook himself. "But in the end I had to focus, Pope. Keep my eye on the goal and get to work faking my own kidnapping."

Phoebe couldn't stop her next words from tumbling from her mouth with bitter distaste. "So what did you do for mito?"

"I found a source I could tap." Scott moistened his lower lip with the tip of his tongue. A dark laugh burst out of him at seeing the horror of comprehension on Phoebe's face.

"Gorgeous," she said barely above a whisper.

"I only took what I needed from her, not that any minor damage would've been noticed, considering I chose someone who was already— let's say, dim." He gave a short laugh and walked back to the machine, grinning again as he turned the key. "Our little break is over."

The white-hot heat pounded through Phoebe and once again her glowing body lit up the room. An explosion of colors danced before her eyes and her back arched from the excruciating impact of the current. This time, if possible, felt much worse, as her muscles already ached intensely. When Scott returned to Phoebe's side, he studied her twitching body dispassionately.

"I—I told Alexori," Phoebe said between strained breaths, "that I don't know anything."

"I believe you, Pope," Scott said with a shrug. "Any doubts I had were erased at seeing your reaction to my staged whipping. I knew you would've broken then if you had something of value to say." Scott lowered his face to her ear. "Between you and me," he said with a confidential tone. "I tried to tell Alexori that no Vigo would be insane enough to cross him, but he wanted to question you himself. I suppose he hasn't remained Padrone without being a little paranoid." Scott rose to his full height. "But that's not what this is about."

"What—then?" Phoebe closed her eyes, the pain inhibiting clear thought.

"Shhh. Don't fight it." Scott moved to the foot of the bed and grazed the back of his hand along Phoebe's leg. "The sooner you surrender to the energy, the sooner your second heart awakens and the sooner the pain will stop."

Phoebe's eyes flashed open. "C—conversion?" she said, watching a grin spread on Scott's face, her mind racing, wondering if forcing that was even possible.

"Yes, Pope. Some of the brightest minds in physics helped to—well they were forced to—create what we're calling an artificial Utaviium. That"—Scott proudly swept his hands toward the glass tube—"is where we store the lightning we've been collecting. The lightning that's now running through you. We couldn't wait for you to naturally come into your powers. And it's easier to control you this way."

Phoebe panted, feeling as though her body was going boneless. "W—why didn't you steal—"

"Steal the Utaviium?" Scott laughed. "I guess I should expect such a naive question from a Hypha. Vigos can't touch Utaviium, Pope. It won't kill us, but it will come close. Your Utaviiumsmiths made sure of it. But we digress."

"Machine—won't—work . . ."

"You see, Pope, once conversion happens," Scott continued, as if he had not heard Phoebe, "we can harvest your mito."

A choked laugh came from Phoebe's throat.

"What's so funny?"

"You're wasting your time," she gasped through the pain, "Shapers don't have mito."

Something like excitement flashed behind Scott's eyes. "That's correct. Shapers don't have mito but Hyphas do. You have it from your human side."

Phoebe's chest iced over, the truth more electric than the current running through her. She did have mito; somehow, the thought had never once crossed her mind.

"You have a large supply in humans," Phoebe said warily, not believing she was saying it. "So why—"

"Your mito?" Scott finished, his voice high, sounding like a petulant child.

"Yes," Phoebe said, watching him closely. "Why my mito and what are you going to do with it?"

Scott's face took on an expression of mingled pride and insanity. "The Anzaini's plan is genius really—" he broke off as chaos sounded up from below. Men yelled in terror. Tiger roars shook the walls.

In milliseconds, Scott had switched off the machine, crossed over to a wall intercom and pushed a button. "What the hell is going on?" he bellowed.

A voice crackled back. "We got trouble, boss."

"What—"

"But we got him under control," the voice hurriedly added.

"Him who?" Scott fumed.

"You won't believe this, boss. We're bringing him up."

Minutes later, the door opened and two lean men in dark pants and black t-shirts burst in holding a limp body between them. Wrists zip-tied behind his back and head slumped forward, the man was shirtless, covered in bloody claw marks. Some looked superficial, while others cut through to bone. Phoebe could hear his labored breathing and an odd feeling of dread moved through her.

Scott moved toward them, and then took an involuntary step back. "What the—?"

"That's what we said, boss," said one of the men.

"Put him over there." Scott pointed to one of the chairs in front of the bed.

Blood dripped on the hardwood floor as the guards carried the man in. As they dumped him onto a chair, the man's head snapped back, then fell forward, his face having been visible for a split second. Colten. Phoebe couldn't stop an agonized cry from escaping her lips. Scott swung his head toward her and gave her a vicious look as her eyes began to water. He raised a hand, signaling the guards to leave. Barely masking their confusion, the two men did as they'd been told. Scott lowered himself, bringing his eyes level with Colten's. He reached for Colten's head, turning it side to side, stopping to examine the now-visible Mark of Wang on his neck.

"Impossible," Scott said with a genuine note of wonder in his voice, walking his hands down to Colten's throat. "I thought I was the only one."

"I know about your talent," Phoebe sneered, hoping to recapture Scott's attention. His hands looked dangerously close to vising a grip around Colten's neck. "I know you can manipulate your physical energy. I know that's how you got past the sensors."

Scott shifted his eyes to Phoebe, then released Colten's head, letting it fall forward. "Ah, that's much better," Scott said with clear relief, standing. Phoebe didn't have to wonder what he'd meant by that. With no current running through her, she felt it; Scott was radiating his Vigo energy now, but a milder heat since he was human in form. "I guess you know what I can do, after all. What a relief."

"What I don't know," Phoebe said quickly, in her frantic attempt to keep Scott talking, "is how you managed to kidnap Mariko and Lewis and still be present for roll call during the drill—" Suddenly Phoebe broke off, the answer having been clear all along. "You had help," she said flatly, answering her own question. "Oh my God. Another traitor?" Had she been right about Montclaire?

"Like I said before, Pope," Scott said, his amusement obvious, "it depends on who you're asking. And by the look of things, you've earned that title yourself." He glanced over at Colten. "How long have you known the truth about him?"

Phoebe didn't answer.

"Couldn't bring yourself to turn him in to the Blackcoats?" Scott said, his voice rising. "What's that part in the oath again? Yes ... kill Vigos, no questions asked. Tsk, tsk, tsk—"

At that precise moment, an unconscious Colten made a violent convulsive movement.

"What's wrong with him?!" Phoebe screamed.

Scott stared briefly at Colten's flailing limbs. "He's suffering from withdrawal," he said, his voice and his face conveying his disgust. "And if you tell me he abstained out of some twisted desire to prove himself to you, I'll vomit."

"Is he going to die?" Phoebe's words were a breathy whisper, an attempt to hide her panic.

"The withdrawal won't kill him," Scott said disinterestedly, looking at Colten whose movements had stopped. "But I will."

Phoebe's lips trembled. She moved her tearful gaze from Colten and stared up at the recessed lights in the ceiling, trying not to think about his pain. She shut her eyes, blocking out thoughts of how powerless Colten was to defend himself should Scott make good on his threat.

Scott called for a guard. The door opened and a stocky, blond, tattooed man walked in.

"I'm assuming there were casualties," Scott said.

The guard nodded.

"How many of you are left?"

"'Cluding me, boss, two."

"He took four of you down?" Scott sounded incredulous, his rage barely contained.

"Caught us a bit off guard, boss. Obviously knew who 'e was, but thought 'e was human."

"He's like me!" Scott said, his anger exploding.

The guard stuttered, "Oh 'ell, we should call the Padro—"

Scott's hand shot forward, cutting the man off with a strike to his throat. "Nobody talks to the Padrone but me," Scott said, hitting every syllable like a hammer. "Are we clear?"

"Yes, boss," the man said, bringing a hand to his throat.

"When does the next rotation get here?"

"Two hours."

Scott frowned. "We've got cubs in the basement?"

The guard stood motionless, alarm in his eyes. "Yes, boss, but they're no' ready for—" the guard stopped before his thought was completed, recoiling at the expression on Scott's face.

"Finish what you were going to say," Scott said.

The guard didn't meet Scott's eyes. "They haven't had a hunt yet. They're weak."

"You forget we have the scientists to dispose of," Scott said. Comprehending, the guard's eyes widened. "Stay here. I'll handle it." Scott pointed to the machine. "She's due for another jolt in five minutes. Turn that key clockwise to start the power and leave it on for only three minutes. You understand?"

The guard nodded. Then, jabbing a finger in Colten's direction, "What 'bout 'im?"

"If he moves, kill him." With that, Scott left the room, slamming the door behind him. Scott's command echoed in Phoebe's ears and she stared at the guard wondering if he would follow it.

"Wha' you lookin' at?" The guard massaged his throat as he dropped his heavy frame onto the chair closest to the bed.

Phoebe diverted her gaze to Colten, but not before seeing the guard glance down at his watch. The countdown had begun. Her hearts pounded somewhere in the region of her throat. Five minutes. That's all she had to come up with a plan. But what? Phoebe took several deep breaths. She knew she needed to settle her emotions in order to think past her sense of helplessness. *Emotions.* In a burst of clarity Phoebe had her answer. But would it work? Could she do it in her weakened state?

"Time ta git you going, sweets," the guard said, jerking Phoebe's attention back to him.

Had it been five minutes? The guard got to his feet and crossed to the machine. *You are not helpless,* Phoebe told herself furiously. *You are not helpless.* And with that, she opened up her senses, reached for Colten's mind and *pushed.* Then prayed.

 TWENTY-NINE

Phoebe's hearts fluttered as Colten began to stir. His head lolled at first, but then it snapped up and he shook his hair out of his eyes. Phoebe couldn't believe *pushing* the rage in Colten was working. She'd sensed it simmering hot in his mind. Even so, she hadn't been sure that stoking it would draw him out of his unconscious state. But there was no doubt now, as the eyes that took in her bound body were ablaze, fury raging within them.

"Wha' the 'ell?" the guard said, noticing Colten stagger to his feet.

Her breathing erratic, Phoebe ignored the guard; she concentrated on *pushing* more rage in Colten, trying to give him as much emotional adrenaline as she could. Colten looked at her; their eyes locked, and somehow the tilt of his head told Phoebe that he'd felt the *push*, that he knew what she'd done. Phoebe's lips parted in surprise.

"Don't touch that key," Colten said to the guard in a choked voice, his sweaty chest heaving with uneven breaths, his eyes riveted on the machine.

The guard laughed. "From where I'm standin', you in no position to make demands, ol' boy." To illustrate his point, the guard reached for the key and turned it.

Flooded with pain, Phoebe screamed.

"Don't you worry, luv," the guard said to Phoebe. "I'll be done wit' 'im in three minutes, tops."

Phoebe kept her misting eyes on Colten. He released a deep growl as he watched the guard sidestep his way around the bed toward him.

"Now, to take care of—what the 'ell . . ." The guard broke off. Phoebe gasped, not believing her eyes. It had happened so quickly, so suddenly that she couldn't process it. Before them, stood Colten, free of his restraints, and in Tiger form from the neck up.

"No one can split forms," the guard said in a hollow tone, disbelief, bewilderment, and fear all flashing in his eyes at once. Colten took advantage of his would-be-assailant's distraction and lunged at him, his body an uncoiling spring. The strike was fast and precise. Colten's foot plunged into the guard's chest, propelling him toward the wall by the door. With one smooth motion, Colten sprang between the guard and the wall and rammed his Tiger head into the stocky man's shoulder. The guard arched backward, but did not fall. Instead, he regained his footing, and began to shudder into his own Tiger form. But he wasn't quick enough, as Colten's right foot struck his midsection and the guard expelled air. His body doubled over. Colten hurled himself at his back, forcing the guard down, one knee pressing into his neck. The struggle on the ground was quick. The guard went limp in no time, silenced by the decapitating power of Colten's Tiger jaw around his throat.

A moment later, Colten returned to normal, looking paler than before. He wiped the blood from his eyes and from his mouth and searched the guard's clothes; he pulled out a ring of keys from the pants pocket, and then rushed limping and wincing to the machine.

Seconds later, Phoebe's relief came. Only an intense ache in her bones and a current of rage remained, a feeling that had been overshadowed before by the excruciating pain. Phoebe knew it was a side effect of her *push* and not her true feelings, but for a moment, she couldn't help embracing the rage. Had she been in her right mind, its intensity would have frightened her. Only the touch of Colten's gentle hand brushing back her hair returned Phoebe to herself.

"You okay?" Colten asked.

Phoebe, whose body was still shaking involuntarily, managed a small nod. "Scott . . ." she whispered.

"I know."

"About what just happened," Phoebe heard herself say slowly as though it came from someone else, the full realization of what she'd done to Colten beginning to fully register in her mind.

Colten pressed a finger over her lips and spoke in a rush. "Later. Not now." It took several tries before he found the key that unlocked Phoebe's restraints. She exhaled at the sight of the last chain slipping off her ankle. A minute after, he'd removed all the wires from her chest. Phoebe tried to raise herself, but found it difficult; needles of pain continued to shoot through her limbs, and her spine seemed to want to curl in on itself.

"Careful." Colten slid his hands beneath her shoulder blades and propped her up carefully.

With his help, Phoebe sat up painfully and swung her legs over the side of the bed. "Where are we?" she asked, rubbing circulation into her wrists.

"A crèche on the outskirts of town. The others are in rooms on the first floor. I heard them when the guards dragged me up here."

"How many floors?"

"Three. We're at the top."

Phoebe was silent for a moment. Tears came to her eyes. Then an irrational urge to hit Colten overpowered her, and Phoebe pushed her hands against his chest roughly. "Why, Colten? Why are you here?" she asked, and then in the same sobbing breath added, "You've exposed yourself."

Colten gripped Phoebe's hands to stop them from trembling and looked at her tired, tear-streaked face. "I sent the Blackcoats a tip about this place. . . . I only came to watch from a distance to make sure they got here. That you were okay. But then I heard a scream and I knew it was you, that you were in pain—" Colten broke off, cupped Phoebe's face and looked into her eyes. "There's no time for this. We should get moving." He released her and looked over at the guard sprawled on the floor. "With him out there's only Scott and one other guy to deal with."

Phoebe shook her head, wearily. "Scott went to get the cubs," she said, her voice scratchy and fearful.

Colten frowned. "How many?"

"I don't know—but the guard said they're not ready."

"Doesn't matter. Let's move."

Phoebe tried to stand, immediately growing dizzy from the effort. Colten placed steadying hands on her shoulders. She stood, tentatively shifting weight from one foot to another, testing her legs, her balance. It was still there. Her muscles could still function. But then, just as Phoebe took her first steps forward, Colten's hands slipped from her shoulders and he collapsed, writhing on the floor.

"Oh, God." Phoebe fell to her knees; she knelt beside him, touching his face, his chest. Sweat beaded across his forehead and blood oozed freely from his wounds. His body felt cold. The fight had drained him of what little energy he had. With labored effort, Phoebe pulled a semiconscious Colten to his feet. She fought for balance under his weight. Once steady, she gently grabbed one of Colten's arms and wrapped it around her neck. She moved them slowly and carefully toward the door, her senses on high alert. With each step, it became increasingly difficult for Phoebe to keep her focus and support Colten's weight at the same time, and she took in little puffs of breath, eyes darting everywhere.

"Leave me here," Colten mumbled, his consciousness returning. "There's a staircase at the end of the hallway. It'll be impossible for you to drag us both down."

Colten was right; he was too battered and weak to move any further. Phoebe lowered him to the ground and cupped his face. "What are we going to do?"

"You," Colten said wryly, prying her hands from his face, "are going to get out and call for help. I parked a block away from here. There's a disposable cell phone on the front seat. Keys are in the ignition." Colten grabbed Phoebe's arm as she scrambled to her feet. "I didn't drive my car. Look for a black SUV."

He looked up at Phoebe, his face twisted with pain. "Don't come back unless there are Blackcoats here, Phoebe," he said, his eyes now pleading. "No matter what happens, don't come back without help."

"I'm coming back for . . ." Phoebe stopped, knowing she wasn't heard; Colten had passed out again. She leaned down, brushed her lips against his cold cheeks, then made for the door. She was coming back.

Phoebe opened the door and edged her face around the frame. She looked up and down the short hallway, but her senses picked up no noise, no physical energy. Her breath short, her body aching, Phoebe ran as quietly as she could manage to the top of the dark staircase where she glanced over the railing. The foyer below was dimly lit by shafts of moonlight streaming down from a row of beveled-glass windows perched high in the white walls.

The percussive din of Phoebe's hearts echoed in her ears as she raced down the stairs, sliding her grip along the railing for balance. She reached the last step and paused. Directly in front of her, two doors stood open; one led to a dark, narrow hallway, the other into what remained of a sort of living room. The latter was a war zone of upturned furniture, broken lamps, and splintered wood strewn across the floor from Colten's brawl. There was a frosted glass door at the far end of this room. Careful not to trip on anything, Phoebe gunned toward it.

Phoebe was so focused on escaping that she almost didn't sense the bodies that emerged from the shadows of thick drapes: two men, one muscular and tall, the other of medium height, converged on the door. Phoebe stopped in her tracks, her breath stolen, her skin tensing against the mild prickling heat from the men who were no more than thirty feet away. Cubs. There would be no getting past them.

The men separated as the door opened and Scott walked in. Cold air blasted Phoebe in the face. Scott stared at her for a moment, shocked speechless. Then regaining himself, he shook his head and said smiling, "Nothing hurts more than being almost there, right Pope?"

Scott snapped his fingers. At once the two cubs flanked him. Phoebe took several cautious steps back.

"I'm really impressed, Pope," Scott said casually, as though they were back in the hallways of Green Lane, conversing like friends. "None of the others have come close to escape, so I guess it's safe to bet you're the powerful Hypha. How'd you do it?" He paused, suddenly remembering something important. He glanced over Phoebe's shoulder. "Where's Colten?"

Phoebe, who had begun a backward retreat toward the foyer, jerked her chin in the direction of the stairs.

"You left him?"

"Deadweight," she said, feigning dispassion as best she could.

"I like how you work." A wicked grin appeared on Scott's face, but quickly dropped when he asked, "And my guard?"

"Him?" she affected an innocent tone, "Why, he's just plain dead."

"I see."

Scott barely suppressed a shudder. Phoebe noticed it. She realized that if she could keep Scott thinking that she'd killed the guard, she could buy time to figure out an alternate avenue of escape.

Phoebe raised her hands and pointed her palms toward Scott and the cubs. "Let me go," she said, forcing a false control on her voice and adopting a tone of authority. "Or it could be 'bye-bye cousin' for you too."

Scott stabbed a hand through his hair and slowly grinned. Then his whole body convulsed. Phoebe watched in terror as Scott morphed into his Vigo form, the heat from the change scorching her skin. Knowing he could do it was one thing. But actually seeing him do it caused dread to move through Phoebe's veins like a glacier. Her eyes never left him as he stretched his front paws and whipped his tail in a slow circle. The growl in the back of his throat rooted her to her spot. Seconds later, Scott was back to his human form.

"Meet the rest of the cubs," he said, his voice dangerously calm. He gestured at three women and a man who had just emerged from the side hallway. Phoebe stared at the new arrivals and swallowed. "You seriously think you can take on all seven of us single-handed?" Scott made a show of sniffing the air. Sweat rolled down Phoebe's back. She understood his message. No smoke. No fire. "I think I'm going to call your bluff, cousin," he said, smiling a smile so evil that it sliced across both of Phoebe's hearts.

Phoebe dug her fingernails into her palms, channeling her fear into physical pain. She'd lost her leverage. Besides, there was no way she could fight seven Vigos. Before Phoebe could blink, Scott leaped away from the cubs and raced toward her. In a matter of seconds he'd plunged his heavy boot into her chest with the force of a swung bat. Phoebe flew backward, bouncing off a side wall to the ground. She rolled over twice and sat up, gagging and coughing up dry air. Breathless with pain, her mind burned with the fact that her weakened body was no match for Scott.

Phoebe picked herself up painfully, placing a hand on the wall for balance as Scott started toward her again.

"So where's the fire, Pope? he said, pausing inches from her face, his voice crisp with acidic revulsion. "I was hoping for a good pyro show."

Terror-stricken, Phoebe simultaneously spat in Scott's face and swung an arm at him. To her surprise, he did not deflect the blow that struck his chest. Instead, his hand reached for his face and touched the saliva trailing down his right cheek.

Their eyes locked.

"Not cool," Scott said, his eyes wide in lethal hatred. "Not cool at all," he repeated, spinning Phoebe by the shoulder and slamming her face against the wall so hard that blood poured out of her nose. She could feel her lips begin to swell.

"I've tried to keep our relationship in mind when dealing with you," he said, breathing heavily in her ear, his elbow rammed into the back of her neck. "But now you've gone and ruined that show of courtesy."

Phoebe gave a muffled response.

"What did you say?" Scott yanked Phoebe by her hair, pulling her face from the wall.

"I said." Phoebe spat blood onto the floor and wiped at her nose. "That you can kiss my Hypha ass." Her voice was hoarse but she'd laced it with as much venom as she could muster.

"You really don't want to live, do you?" Scott said, his eyes glaring, his voice full of contempt.

"I thought that wasn't up to you," Phoebe spat back, finding vicious satisfaction in the flush rapidly rising in Scott's face.

"No. It isn't," he said, his voice quietly dangerous. "But how much you suffer is." Scott gripped the collar of Phoebe's blood-stained shirt and pulled her across the foyer to where the cubs stood watching by the staircase. Twisting, turning, and with fitful jerks, Phoebe struggled to break free, hindering Scott's progress. A hundred feet from the cubs, Scott crashed his knee up into Phoebe's ribcage, forcing her back down to the cold, marble floor. Paralyzing pain swept through her and she coughed uncontrollably.

Scott drew out an ottoman from the living room and sat down as Phoebe dragged herself backward with all of her strength, still coughing from the blow. He glanced at her, and then said to the cubs, boredom in his voice, "Have at her. And when you're done take her back upstairs." Scott's command had the effect of a sharp whip jolting the cubs into action. Grins spread across their faces as they moved as one line toward Phoebe. To her surprise, they moved slowly, taunting her with each step forward.

With a surge of adrenaline, Phoebe rose to her feet. Panic assaulted her chest like a physical pain. *Panic is both an enemy and a friend,* Phoebe thought, suddenly recalling Afua's words from an earlier time. But how to befriend this torturous emotion was the question. In a moment of insight, Phoebe remembered the night of the soccer game; a night when she had *pushed* the mood of multiple people at once. Could she do on purpose what had happened by accident? Phoebe realized that for once in her life she'd have to stop fighting her emotions and surrender herself to them. Give them release.

Phoebe was only vaguely aware of her surroundings now; an emotional tempest had taken over her. Guided by an instinct beyond her understanding, she smashed her palms together. A scream exploded from Phoebe's chest and she felt waves of electric energy pulsing out from her.

The cubs lurched to a halt ten feet away from Phoebe; it was as though they'd slammed into an invisible wall, their faces contorted with panic, their bodies convulsing from it. They moved about in confusion, colliding with one another. Drained, Phoebe's shoulders slumped as Scott shot to his feet. His eyes darted between her and the disoriented cubs.

"What—what the hell did you—" Scott's words ended when an arrow struck him just below the ribs. Stunned, he went motionless. Then, sagging to one knee, he stared dumbly at the arrow as if in disbelief; a ring of blood grew out from the embedded shaft like an unfurling crimson rose. Scott looked up, and Phoebe followed his burning gaze, looking for the archer; a shadowy silhouette darted across one of the high windows.

An instant later, cries of pain erupted from the cubs as a fusillade of arrows riddled them. One by one they fell over dead. Phoebe gasped at

Scott's labored attempt to rise to his feet. Another arrow plunged into his chest, ending his effort. He crumpled face forward on the ground, blood spreading like a small carpet underneath him. Her whole body trembling, Phoebe stared at the bloodied Vigos lying several feet away from her. She couldn't believe her nightmare had come to an end.

The front door crashed open and Phoebe spun to face it. Afua walked in, her bow in hand, an arrow nocked in its bowstring. A midnight blue lion and a gray-spotted white leopard followed in her wake, their strides long and powerful, their flashing eyes staring about. Afua surveyed the scene, her gaze roaming over Scott and the cubs before meeting Phoebe's.

"It's a good thing you helped me dust off my archery skills, Cadet," she said, removing the arrow from the bow and returning it to her thigh quiver. "Came in handy."

Phoebe stood motionless, barely registering Afua's words or the fact that the two great cats behind the Blackcoat had converted into Yelena and Deborah-Anna. Suddenly, Phoebe had a constricted sensation in her throat. Scott had jumped to his feet and wrapped an arm around her neck. Phoebe gasped in fear.

"I'm walking out of here," Scott hissed, his ragged voice just above a whisper.

Surprise flickered briefly across Afua's face before her steely self-control returned "Not happening," she said, nocking an arrow to her bow and taking a step forward.

"Try and stop me and I'll shed prophecy blood," Scott said, breathing heavily. His arm tightened around Phoebe's neck. Phoebe found herself digging her fingernails into his forearm, but it was no use.

When Afua took another step forward, Scott pulled a thin dagger from his boot with his free hand. He pressed its smooth, cold blade against Phoebe's skin.

"I'll do it," Scott said.

Phoebe had no doubt that he would. Her lips trembled in fear, but Afua gave her a reassuring look before nodding in Yelena and Deborah-Anna's direction. Phoebe watched apprehensively as the two Blackcoats began rubbing their palms together. Scott's gaze shot to them and he gave a deranged laugh. "Whatever you do to me will kill her, too," he said, watching thick silver ribbons of mist coil around their hands and slither to the ground ominously. He took a step back, pulling Phoebe along with him.

A whooshing roar filled the foyer as the mist billowed between Yelena and Deborah-Anna, becoming two luminous towers of swirling air. With a snap of their wrists, the Blackcoats pushed their respective five-foot rotating columns toward each other, merging them into a bigger, more violent vortex.

"I said I'd kill her!" Scott yelled, pressing the blade even harder against Phoebe's throat. Something warm trickled down her neck. Phoebe couldn't help herself. She started hyperventilating. Tears rolled down her cheeks.

"Stay calm," Afua said with a pointed look at Phoebe. "He won't kill you. You're his only leverage here so stay calm."

Stay calm? Phoebe's mind screamed. *How in the hell am I supposed to do that?!*

With sharp flick of their outstretched palms, Yelena and Deborah-Anna sent the whirlwind on a rapid collision course with Phoebe and Scott. Phoebe watched the advancing cyclone with disbelief. Were the Blackcoats really prepared to sacrifice her life in their effort to kill Scott?

"You're insane—" he started. The powerful winds swept up Phoebe and Scott and lifted them ten feet in the air as if they were specks of pollen. Phoebe tried to keep her eyes open even though they stung from the wind ripping every bit of moisture out of them. *If I don't vomit now, it will be a miracle,* Phoebe found herself thinking desperately, while Scott yelled obscenities only she could hear.

The whirlwind's wild rotational force intensified. After a nausea-inducing minute, which felt like an eternity to Phoebe, Scott's grip on her neck began to loosen. It was as though strong, icy, invisible fingers were prying their bodies apart. They spun faster and faster, and faster still, the wind turning them head over heels.

Scott's hold broke. Afua converted into a golden falcon and shot upward, scooping Phoebe, who had been ejected from the whirlwind, under her massive wing. Phoebe took several gulping breaths. It had been a drill the last time she'd been caught by an enormous bird. Now, tucked between Afua's golden chest and wing, she didn't want to leave the protective hold.

Afua landed and Phoebe felt her feet touch the ground. She expected to be dizzy, but she was not. She ran a finger along her neck; the thin wound had started healing. Phoebe released a long exhale as Afua spread her lustrous wings before returning to human form.

"Bring him down, Yelena," she commanded, sending Phoebe's gaze up to Scott who still remained in the whirlwind. He was spinning horizontally now, mouth wide open, hair blown into his eyes.

Phoebe asked, "How is he still in there when I got tossed out?"

"Yelena kept a wind hold on him—" Afua broke off. Scott's arms and legs were jerking about. Then he stopped moving; his body hung limp.

"Now!" Afua added, a note of urgency in her tone.

The wailing winds calmed to a soft whir. Scott was floating downward. Phoebe watched as Yelena moved her hands in front of her chest in an alternating fashion; it looked as though the Blackcoat was tugging at a length of rope that only she could see. When the winds dissipated and Scott lay on the ground, it was clear that he was dead.

Afua swore under her breath.

"He was as good as dead when your arrows went through him," Yelena said matter-of-factly, a mild defensive edge to her voice.

"I know," Afua said. "But when he sprung up again, I was hoping he'd last long enough for us to question him."

Phoebe was staring at the arrows embedded in Scott's chest when, suddenly, the entire house shook. A deafening explosion of glass followed as a tornado of falcons, hawks, and eagles rushed in from the windows overhead. Phoebe flung her arms up to shield her face from the sharp fragments raining down in all directions. She felt pin pricks of pain as smaller shards lodged into her skin. A swirling sea of gleaming feathers surrounded Phoebe as the birds, landing as one, encircled her. With their chests puffed up, they lifted and lowered their immense wings in a graceful, almost choreographed motion that belied their shrill battle cries. A wall of wings had formed around Phoebe.

"Break formation," Afua said, her voice, cutting through the noise. "She's fine."

At those words, bright light pulsed all around Phoebe like giant flashbulbs as one by one the birds changed forms. Phoebe shivered in place. Tears filled her eyes. It was over. As Afua shouted, "Sweep the entire place for anything or anyone that will help lead us to Alexori," and agents dispersed throughout the house, one thought broke Phoebe from her daze. Colten.

Phoebe glanced over her shoulder at the mansion whose beautiful exterior had encased terror and fear. She was happy to be leaving. As she walked toward the van waiting to take her back to campus, she inhaled deeply, still unable to detect Colten. When Phoebe had finally been able to make her way up to the room where she'd left him, she'd found the French doors open, the curtains swaying inward, and Colten gone. And as much as she worried about his physical state, at that moment, Phoebe had felt relief in equal measure; Colten's presence was one less thing for her to have to explain. And his absence also meant that he hadn't succumbed to his mito withdrawal.

The wind had grown colder with the dawn, and so when Phoebe climbed into the van, the warmth that met her was almost as welcome as what she saw inside. Leaning against the left side, Mariko sat with her head pillowed on Lewis's shoulder, her hand laced with his, both of their eyes closed. Phoebe could only imagine the kind of bond that must have formed between them through their shared ordeal. She smiled softly at their slack faces, contented. In the row behind them, a woman with wild black hair sat staring back at Phoebe, tiredly. Something in the shape of her eyes caused Phoebe's hearts to plummet. And as Phoebe imagined the woman years younger, she came to realize who the real traitor was. The thought of it stung her, causing her hands to clench into fists. Phoebe ached so much for it not to be true that she almost didn't notice the raven-haired boy at the back, gazing blankly out of the window.

❧ THIRTY

hoebe sat in the back of the chapel, pouring over everything she'd learned in the van ride to campus. At first, she had been entirely shocked to find out that Gabe's daughter was still alive. Especially considering how the custodian had told her, "*Vigos took her from me.*" But then Phoebe realized that she'd automatically assumed that Gabe's daughter had been killed. Even more surprising was the fact that his daughter was Professor Jones, the Understanding Vigos instructor who was believed to be tending to an urgent family matter. "She used to be close enough for me to see her every day," Gabe had said. Phoebe still couldn't believe it.

Now, Phoebe found herself gripping the edge of the pew, watching the bittersweet reunion between father and daughter. Tears were flowing and desperate hugs and kisses being exchanged under careful Blackcoat watch.

Phoebe wasn't quite sure why she had come. Perhaps to witness the truth for herself? Or maybe to torture herself. After all, the scene before her eyes reflected a private pain, an unspoken wish she could never realize herself. She froze as Gabe was carted off by a couple of Blackcoats, his sobbing daughter trailing after them. His eyes met Phoebe's only briefly as he passed and he stopped, said something to a Blackcoat who looked over at Phoebe and nodded. Next thing Phoebe knew, Gabe was seated next to her.

"She's the only family I've got," he said quietly with a hint of desperation as he stared down at his bound hands. Phoebe didn't say anything. "They took her and told me to disable one narthyx entry if I had any hope of seeing her alive."

"The one to the Above library."

Gabe nodded miserably.

"It was the next one scheduled for maintenance, so I knew it wouldn't raise eyebrows if the sensors and cameras were down for a few days. But they wanted more time. When I refused, I received a picture of my daughter, with a message that her freedom would require some sort of big distraction."

"The drill was your idea?"

Gabe squeezed his eyes shut for a moment. "It was an easy sell to Professor Yori. He was already on edge because of the soccer game attack and there hadn't been a drill in a while." The old man sighed heavily. "I was told that an inside man would contact me with further instructions when the time was right. I was shocked when I was approached by Cadet Roland."

"Why didn't you tell anyone?" Phoebe's voice was low and held a scathing edge. She felt for him, but was wracked with resentment for her pain, for Mariko and Lewis. How could he just give them up—the very kids he was there to protect?

"He gave me a sob story about Vigos kidnapping his parents. He had pictures like mine. Pictures of his loved ones in chains. As far as I was concerned, we were in the same boat. Together we came up with a plan. He would isolate Mariko and Lewis, and I would get them ready for pick up."

"Pick up?" Phoebe turned the words over in her mouth, hating their business-like tone.

"There were three large trunks stored in the library narthyx. After the drill, I transported Mariko and Lewis—who Scott had rendered unconscious in a classroom—and put them each in a trunk."

"Then what?" Phoebe said, feeling her anger sizzle.

"I erased the footage from the Eye."

"I meant, what did you do with them?" she gritted her teeth.

"Nothing," Gabe said. "I was told a courier would pick them up, which actually surprised me because there were no labels of any kind on the trunks—nothing to indicate where they were going."

Concierge Courier, Phoebe thought, remembering the guy who had asked for directions to the library. *Could I have inadvertently aided in the kidnappings?* Phoebe's stomach churned at the thought.

"I'm sorry, lass," Gabe said, softly. "I had no idea this involved you. At least not until they brought you to the Eye. And by then I was in too deep."

"Would it have mattered if you'd known?" she lowered her eyes, unable to look at him; the feeling of camaraderie she had felt for Gabe fell through her fingers like sand.

Gabe was silent. And in that silence, Phoebe knew his answer.

"I guess I don't understand," Phoebe said slowly. "Why didn't you tell Professor Yori or the Blackcoats about your daughter. You had resources to help find her."

Gabe sighed heavily. "My initial instinct was to seek help. But I got a warning note that my every move was being watched, that if I alerted the officials, my daughter would be killed." He brought his hands to his face and rubbed his eyebrows. "I let my fear for her life trump seeking help."

"So what are they going to do to you?" Phoebe asked, calmly nodding toward the Blackcoats.

Gabe shrugged. "Nothing they do will torture me more than knowing my daughter was with those monsters."

A Blackcoat gestured at Gabe, indicating that his time was up.

When Gabe made to rise, Phoebe said suddenly, "But now you're going to sit in jail for the rest of your life."

"Yes," Gabe said, smiling weakly. "But my daughter is alive to visit me. I'm an old man, Phoebe. What do I have to live for if I don't have her?" Looking up at Gabe's face, reading the peace in his eyes, Phoebe felt she understood his motivation. In fact, she didn't think anyone could have witnessed his recent display of desperate love for his daughter without feeling empathy. But it didn't mean that she had to forgive him.

🍁 THIRTY- ONE

"And this torture went on for how long?" Afua asked the boy who sat staring at his hands; obvious curiosity was etched on Afua's face as she sat across from the real Scott Roland in an armchair in Professor Yori's office.

"I don't know," he said, his voice stiff. "Maybe hours."

Phoebe watched from her seat on the sofa, feeling a double pang of both sympathy and curiosity. It had been a shock to meet the real Scott Roland, a Hypha whose electric blue eyes held both intense anger and profound relief. His dark hair was closely cropped instead of wildly disheveled. But the build—tall and athletic—was eerily the same. And then there was the soccer jersey. . . . What he'd been through, all this time a prisoner, Phoebe did not want to know. But here she was, listening to the real Scott's debriefing at Afua's request. The Blackcoat had explained that listening to Scott's debriefing could help make better sense of her experience in the crèche.

"What kind of things did they want to know?" Afua asked, watching him closely.

"Everything about my life. My likes and dislikes. My passions and future ambitions." Scott growled. "He wrote everything down."

"The impostor?" Afua asked, clarifying.

"Yes." Scott clenched his jaw. "I didn't think he could pull it off. But he knew everything about Shaper history and customs. He knew everything about my family. That's how he . . ." Scott's voice trailed off as he clenched his hands into fists.

Afua prompted him, gently. "That's how he what?"

"That's how he could threaten their safety. They knew where my parents were."

"And your parents had no clue of your abduction?" This was Professor Yori speaking.

"He sent them weekly emails from my account. My parents,"—Scott looked around at those gathered—"know that I can get absorbed in camp so to hear from me at all is a big deal."

"Camp?" Phoebe spoke louder than she'd meant to. Scott met her gaze briefly, his blue eyes appraising. He looked away when Afua explained, "Cadet Roland was scheduled to be on campus two weeks before the start of classes to take part in a soccer camp Green Lane holds for its varsity players."

"Only I didn't get to participate," he said bitterly. "I got snagged at the airport."

"Oh," Phoebe said, feeling bad for having opened her mouth.

"I have a question." Scott sat forward in his seat. "How did he physically pass as me??"

The headmaster cleared his throat and spoke. "All of your admission documents came with the impostor's photo."

"We're in the process of investigating how that happened." Scott didn't hear Afua's words. His face had taken on a color of fury that Phoebe recognized. He felt violated.

After a few more questions, Scott was dismissed. Phoebe watched him go, finding it strange that she knew a lot about a boy she didn't know.

"Did the impostor tell you how he was able to move among us undetected?" Afua asked, pacing in front of Phoebe's sofa. It was Phoebe's turn for a debriefing.

"He said he could mentally dampen the heat of his physical energy to feel like the warmth of a Shaper, so that we would sense him as one of our own," Phoebe said, guiltily relaying what she'd actually learned from Colten.

"And he told you that he was the only born Vigo?"

"Yes," Phoebe lied. Even though her hearts thundered against her chest, Phoebe met Afua's gaze with an equally intense one of her own.

Within half an hour Phoebe had told them everything about her time in the crèche: the artificial Utaviium, the dead scientists, Scott's potential promotion to Alpha for his services, and a full description of Alexori—something that had previously been unknown. And when Afua had asked about the dead guard upstairs, Phoebe had held her breath while saying tersely, "The impostor killed him for his insubordination."

Afua continued. "Did the impostor mention how they had acquired Professor Jones?"

"No." Phoebe had learned in the van ride that Professor Jones didn't know who had kidnapped her; like Phoebe, she had been hit from behind at night. The only reason she felt certain that it hadn't been a Vigo was that Jones hadn't felt the warning burn.

There was a moment's silence, and then Yelena, who had been quietly leaning against a bookcase with Deborah-Anna at her side, addressed Professor Yori. "Was there any sign of distress in Professor Jones's note? Anything that sounded unlike her?"

"No," Professor Yori said. "And when I mentioned her leave of absence to Gabe, he never let on that he had a problem. I didn't pursue it. To tell the truth," the headmaster raised his hands in a helpless gesture, "at that time, I was preoccupied with how to fill the position, given the short notice. But I caught a break when Montclaire called me for old time's sake. She told me she'd retired, and when I brought up my situation, she offered to sub until Professor Jones got back."

Phoebe stopped staring at her hands. She'd heard a distinct break in the headmaster's voice when he'd said "old time's sake." She was unable to stop the words from leaving her mouth. "You already knew Montclaire?"

Professor Yori looked past Phoebe, sweat beading on his bald head. "We were friends—co-agents in SIS before she was tapped to become a Blackcoat."

Again, Phoebe heard the headmaster's voice break. It had wavered when he'd said "friends." Quickly lowering her mental guard for just a moment, Phoebe sensed an emotion from him that made her eyes widen. It was faint, but it was there. *Love.* In the moment that Phoebe registered that feeling and flashed her eyes to meet the headmaster's, his words came flooding back to her: *I know for a fact that Montclaire's loyalty is immutable. It transcends work, love . . . and unless you can give me proof stronger than that. . . .*

"—what you are saying is that Montclaire called you the same day you received Professor Jones' note informing you of her absence." Afua's words brought Phoebe back from the memory.

"Is there a problem?" The headmaster's eyes flicked to Phoebe when he spoke.

Afua brought a finger to her lips. She then pointed between Deborah-Anna and the door. Deborah-Anna nodded, quickly sweeping out of the room. Both Phoebe and Professor Yori stared in puzzlement as Afua and Yelena began to methodically lift objects in the office and examine them.

Three minutes later, Deborah-Anna returned, her face fixed in a frown. "She's gone," she said.

"What?" Professor Yori and Afua said in unison.

"Everything in her office has been cleared out," Deborah-Anna added.

Phoebe could tell that Afua was becoming increasingly incensed. "Does everything in your office belong to you?" she demanded, her eyes boring into Professor Yori.

"Yes—why wouldn't it?"

"No recent deliveries? Gifts?"

"Why?" his eyes narrowed slightly before taking on a slightly hurt and distinctly puzzled expression.

Yelena said, "Have you forgotten Montclaire's expertise was in collecting intel? Think."

Professor Yori paled, his eyes darting to the tall white orchid on his book shelf. Deborah-Anna swept over to it at once, placing her palms inside the pot. Phoebe caught her breath as the plant slowly wilted and then disintegrated, leaving in its place two hair-strand-thin wires.

"I don't believe it," Deborah-Anna said, openly shocked for the first time since Phoebe had met her. She stepped back from the desk, her expression awe-filled.

"What is that?" Professor Yori sputtered.

"It's a PLANT," Deborah-Anna said softly.

"Of course, it was a plant." Professor Yori sounded insulted.

"P.L.A.N.T.," Deborah-Anna said shaking her head, "stands for Plant Laced Acoustic Nano Technology." She leaned in, giving the wires a closer look, studying them. "It's a listening device grown from seeds that are engineered to develop with the technology inside. I've only seen seedling prototypes," she added. "Never anything this big. . . . Montclaire launched this program before her retirement."

Afua glared at the headmaster who kneaded the back of his neck, trying to relieve tension. "When did Montclaire give you the plant?" she asked.

"She brought it on her first day here. It was a thank you gift to me for giving her something to do while she sorted out her next steps after retirement."

Afua was suddenly agitated. "She was aware of our every move and—"

Phoebe, who had been quietly watching the exchange, blurted. "Why did Montclaire retire? She's not much older than you three. Please. At least tell me that much."

The Blackcoats exchanged glances and then Yelena began, "Earlier this year, the Royal Court ordered a classified mission. Apparently, Montclaire advised against it claiming that according to her intel, it would be too dangerous, but she was ignored by the Court.

"The mission went forward and Montclaire lost several members of her unit. When she returned to the Court, Montclaire stormed into a royal meeting and with a few choice words expressed what she thought of them. Shortly after receiving her remembrance tattoos she was asked to take an early retirement."

"She told me she left on her own. . . ." Professor Yori gazed blankly at the wires shooting from the clay pot and then added, "Why didn't any of you say something to me?"

"Our main focus has been this investigation. As far as we were concerned, Montclaire had found a new vocation. And because of our awareness of your history with her, we didn't think it strange that she would end up here."

Professor Yori looked up, surprised. "You knew?"

"We made it our business to run a background check on you," Yelena said. "It's completely standard."

"Why? My record speaks for itself."

"So does Montclaire's," Afua said.

Professor Yori said nothing, as Afua's words sank in. Fingering the Privaque on his lapel he said, "I knew Montclaire years before she was selected for the Royal Security Corps. My trusting her was based on what I knew then. Had I been aware,"—his eyes flicked to Phoebe's—"well, had I been aware. . . . Do you actually think she could she have been behind this whole thing?" his eyes were incredulous and Phoebe could feel guilt emanating from him even with her mental guard firmly in place.

Afua removed the plant from the shelf and bent the wires. "At this juncture, we can only speculate what role she played. Cadet Pope," she said, turning her attention to Phoebe. "Unless there is anything else, you are free to go."

Phoebe paused on her way to the door. Another thing Colten had mentioned flashed into her mind.

"What is it?" Afua said, when Phoebe turned on the spot and looked around at her, hesitation writ all over her.

"The Anzaini," Phoebe said.

Afua narrowed her dark eyes. "What about them?"

"Alexori was following their orders. To capture us." She bowed her head.

Everyone in the room stilled. Yelena and Deborah-Anna looked at each other while the headmaster colored and loosened the tie around his neck.

"Are you sure?" Afua asked, a little more forceful than usual. "It's very important that you are."

Phoebe swallowed. "Yes."

"And Alexori told you this?" Afua said, expectantly.

Phoebe nodded. Colten had said it. Alexori had alluded to it. Either way, it was the truth.

"Thank you," Afua said. Phoebe left the headmaster's office wondering about the strange look of satisfaction that had subtly spread across the Blackcoat's face.

🍁 THIRTY-TWO

"So Vampire Weekend, huh?" Colten said, running his fingertips through Phoebe's white streak. "That's another new thing I've learned about you." It was evening, and Phoebe was comfortably curled up in Colten's arms on the sofa in her room. The privacy they enjoyed came courtesy of Cyn who had left half an hour ago after grabbing a few dresses from her closet and mumbling something about having a date. As Colten continued to caress Phoebe's head, she knew he was only trying to distract her from the questions she'd just asked him. She'd give him some more time.

"Yes, I'm a fan," Phoebe said, gazing adoringly at her wall. "You object?"

"No." Colten made an effort not to grin. "I can get behind your taste in music."

"You better!" Phoebe said, play-slugging Colten in the chest. She couldn't help the shiver that came with each of Colten's caresses.

"I even dig some of Adele's stuff," he said, waving a hand at the singer's poster.

"Oh, God," Phoebe said, a thought coming to her mind. "Please don't tell me she's Vigo." She raised her head to get a better look at Colten's reaction.

"She's not, but I can't vouch for Vampire Weekend." Phoebe paled and Colten, laughing, pulled her back down to him. "I kid. I kid. Remember it's mostly behind the scenes execs." Colten leaned in for a kiss and Phoebe's hearts fluttered. She welcomed it like the soft feel of a wonderfully worn-in sweater. She twisted her fingers in his hair as she enjoyed the warmth of his lips pressed against hers. Every nerve in her body sizzled, as they brought their bodies closer together and their kisses grew more desperate and intense. The heat from Colten's chest permeated her clothes warming her down to her toes.

"Look," Colten said, pulling away and sighing heavily. "I know you're waiting for answers but you're not going to like one of them."

"There are a lot of things I haven't liked about this whole thing," Phoebe said, fingering the Privaque she'd clipped to her sweater.

A moment of serious silence followed.

"I've never done it before—split forms," Colten said, finally. "I don't even know how it happened. I'm still trying to figure it out myself."

"You were weak," Phoebe said. "Maybe that's all you could manage to morph."

Colten shook his head. "I've been around weak Vigos. It's not something that's normally possible. Ever possible." Then frowning, "Guess there's stuff I'm still learning about my Vigo-human condition."

"And my other question?" Phoebe said, stopping Colten before he started kissing her ear.

Colten clenched his fist. "You have to understand, I was desperate. I wouldn't have done it otherwise. . . ."

Phoebe looked into his darkened eyes and braced herself.

"When I heard the Blackcoats coming, I knew I only had minutes before they searched the mansion," Colten said apologetically. "The balcony had a fire escape. I barely made it down. I kept to the shadows and found my way to the road. I was delirious. . . . There was a woman walking a dog and . . . I couldn't stop myself. I needed the mito."

Colten's words hung in the air for a moment before Phoebe could say, "Did you—?"

"I didn't kill her," Colten said at once. "I took what I needed. But I won't lie, Phoebe. I needed a lot."

Phoebe let out a breath. "And she's okay?"

"Yes," he said. "I called an ambulance for her. Look—"

Phoebe brought a finger to his lips, cutting him off. "You were desperate," she said. "End of topic. Now tell me how you found us."

"You were right about the crèches," Colten said. "I narrowed my search to the only two that had gone up within the last year. I went to the wrong one first . . ." Phoebe felt his body tense beneath her. "If I hadn't reached you in time to stop . . ." his voice broke and he nuzzled his face in her hair for a moment. Phoebe felt tiny electric shocks all over her body.

"But you did," she said in a whisper and then louder, "How did you know about the fake Scott?"

"At the first crèche, the photos of the recent Mark Day graduates were up."

"And you saw Scott," Phoebe said, guessing. Colten nodded, his face lost in a dark thought. "Were you shocked to learn there was another Vigo like you?"

Colten didn't answer her question. Instead he slid his hand between her hairline and the back of her neck and carefully traced her scar with his thumb. Phoebe was too distracted by his silence and his unexplained mood change to register what he was doing.

"Tell me what you did to me at the crèche," Colten said cautiously, after a while, yanking Phoebe out of her daze.

She looked into his brilliant green eyes, carefully considering what it meant to answer this question, to trust someone other than herself with an ability that she was still growing into, still understanding. Colten's hands had slid underneath her shirt now, and he traced the pattern of the scar along her stomach with an almost unbearable tenderness. She admitted to herself that she felt safe in a way she never had before. And she was allowing herself to love and feel love in a way she'd never felt she had the freedom to explore before either. The intensity of it was all so strange for Phoebe, but knowing that she knew Colten's secret, she decided she could tell him hers. Just as she was about to respond, another question flashed across her thoughts.

"Wait. Why didn't you tell me about the Vigos at the red carpet? Phoebe asked, sitting upright.

"What are you talking about? I told you there were other Vigos in Hollywood," Colten said at once.

Phoebe explained that when Alexori had listed his Vigo casualties he'd mentioned having eyes and ears at the movie premiere.

"But you didn't tell me about killing them," Phoebe said, finishing.

"Because I didn't," Colten said, his voice tight, his eyes suddenly unfocused.

"You didn't?" Phoebe asked, looking at him with a confused expression on her face as his gaze drifted to something on her desk.

"Do you not want to answer my question? Even after I told you everything?" Colten asked, slowly returning his gaze to Phoebe, a pained look on his face.

"No, that's not it—I mean, I still don't understand it." Phoebe paused and gathered herself. "For as long as I can remember I've been able to sense people's emotions. It used to drive me crazy. One moment I'm walking down the street, minding my own business. Then, all of a sudden I'm crying because I just passed someone who's suffering."

Colten looked at her awed. "So you're feeling what everyone is feeling all the time?"

"Oh, God no," Phoebe said. "At least not anymore. . . ." Phoebe's let her voice trail as she remembered the day she'd learned how to block out other people's emotions.

Her father had run a gentle hand through her hair as they sat side by side on a wooden bench in the middle of a public playground.

"I—I can't do it," she'd whimpered, retreating into the bulkiness of her heavy coat. "They're so strong."

"Yes they are," her father said. He stared around at the excited children and the watchful adults moving about the play equipment. "People's emotions are living things that want to be acknowledged and understood," he said softly. "Many—especially the unpleasant ones, are often repressed by those who own them. So they're drawn to us because we sense them. We validate their existence by allowing them to be felt."

Phoebe turned her blazing gray eyes on him. "Why is it our job to validate them?" she said, her tone resentful.

"It's not, honey. It's just something that you and I can do. I want you to see it as a gift and not a curse, so it's important to learn how to raise a mental shield against them. Once you can do that, you can grant them audience on your terms." He gently rubbed her chin with his calloused thumb and gave an encouraging smile. "Now, try again. Picture that gate shutting them out."

Phoebe curled her hands into fists to keep them from shaking from the strain of her effort. A tear rolled down her cheek. Desperate to succeed, Phoebe fought against her own emotional melting pot of frustration, anxiety, and fear. And then it happened, very fast, very intense. The mental gate was iron-thick, and it bulldozed all the strangers' emotions from her mind before locking into place with a satisfying bang. Slowly, Phoebe raised both hands to her once throbbing temples, as if to see whether or not they would collapse from the instant relief.

"I did it," she said slowly. Then, bouncing up and down on the bench, "I did it!"

Her father savored her excitement. "And do you know exactly what you did?"

Phoebe stilled and gave him a blank stare. Almost shamefully, she said, "No."

"You mastered your own emotions," he said, beaming down at her. "You have to be able to do that before you can do other things." He leaned over and kissed the top of her head. "That's it for today. You did good."

The sound of Colten's voice returned Phoebe to their conversation. "That must be crazy," he said, laying back. "Knowing what people are feeling." He sat up with a jolt. "So . . . have you been tapping into my feelings?"

Phoebe gave a guilty smile. "In the beginning I wanted to because it was hard being around you without knowing how you felt about me. But then I decided against it."

"So you never tried?" Colten sounded shocked.

"I did eventually. That night at the warehouse. I needed to know . . ." Phoebe left the rest unsaid.

"I understand," Colten said.

"What I did at the crèche was different. I physically manipulated your emotions." Colten stared at Phoebe, following every word she spoke. "The only way I can explain it is that I *pushed* you to feel your rage more strongly. But doing that has an effect on me."

Colten was fascinated. "It drains you?" he said, guessing.

"No. I end up feeling whatever emotion I *push*." When Colten raised an eyebrow, Phoebe explained, "I have to find the emotion inside of myself that mirrors the one I see in the other person. It's that connection that allows me to *push*. And that connection causes me to feel the manipulation. Like I said, it's hard to explain."

"Well," Colten said, his eyes wide with wonder. "I've been on the receiving end and it was intense. Also a bit scary since I didn't know what was happening to me."

For the next few minutes, Phoebe told Colten a few stories from her childhood when her father had her practice her skill on him. When she'd finished, he pulled her back to him, and she rested her head in the crook of his arm.

"And no one else knows?" Colten said after Phoebe had closed her eyes a moment, relieved to have finally unburdened herself of that, her deepest secret. She shook her head. "Good," he said, quite serious. "Your father was right; trust no one."

"But I just told you," Phoebe said, half teasing while nervously wrapping strands of her hair around a thumb.

The corners of Colten's mouth turned up in a teasing smile. "Well, I believe it would be covered under some kind of boyfriend-girlfriend privilege."

"Uh huh," Phoebe said, sticking her tongue out, her hearts beating at Colten's use of the word "boyfriend." She worked to control herself; Colten's tone had been teasing.

He said, "But seriously—"

An insistent knock on the door cut Colten off, and reluctantly, Phoebe untangled herself from him and went to answer it. Hayley stood in the doorway dressed in a knee-length sequined blue dress, her hair and make-up perfectly done. Her eyes roamed over Phoebe's appearance and she frowned.

"Why are you not ready?" Hayley said, pushing her way in. "I've been calling your cell and you haven't been picking up—" Hayley stopped talking when her eyes fell on Colten laid out on the sofa.

"Hi, Hayley," Colten waved. "You look nice."

Hayley's ears went red.

"Yeah, what's the occasion?" Phoebe asked, making her way back to Colten.

Hayley narrowed her eyes at Phoebe. "Are you kidding me right now? Tonight's the Enviroball and you and I are going, remember?!"

Phoebe stared at Hayley blankly. "Me at Karli's thing? No thanks."

Hayley spoke through tight teeth. "I think you're forgetting about two young men that helped us out with a problem in exchange for us being their dates." Hayley stared meaningfully at Phoebe who stared back confused until understanding hit her just as Hayley said in exasperation, "I actually had a feeling you'd forget, so I have a dress ready to go."

Phoebe turned to Colten and bit her lip. "I kinda have an obligation to fulfill," she said.

"Sounds like it," Colten said, laughter in his eyes. "Should I be worried about the gentleman?"

"No," Phoebe said, grinning. "I don't even know his name."

Colten arched a brow. "Really?"

"Trust me," Hayley said, "it's no competition unless you're intimidated by a guy who's a foot shorter than you and still going through puberty."

Colten chuckled at this. "I've learned never to underestimate the competition."

Impatiently, Hayley grabbed Phoebe's hand and began dragging her toward the door.

"Where are you taking me?"

"We're getting dressed in my dorm," Hayley said. "I know you had access to a glam squad at the premiere and all, but here I'm still your fashion guru."

"Okay, okay," Phoebe said flustered. "Give me five minutes."

Hayley glanced at her watch. "Three minutes."

"Sure."

Hayley left and Phoebe returned to Colten who pulled her back into him.

"How come you're not going to this stupid dance?" Phoebe said, pouting. "Isn't it in your honor?"

Colten laughed. "I said they could use my name, but I didn't say I'd go. Besides, I'm heading to L.A. for one last stop on Nicole's Damage Control Tour."

"One minute!" Hayley's voice rang from the hallway.

"What's your last stop?"

"The Kamron Hyack Show."

"Wow—You're coming back after, though?" Phoebe asked. A sliver of insecurity came creeping into her even though the look in Colten's eyes said she was crazy to doubt him.

"Of course. I still have to graduate! And, besides, we have a few more important things to talk about. . . ."

Phoebe agreed. They hadn't discussed how Alexori believed that there was a saboteur within his organization. Although Colten had assured Phoebe that his tracks had been well covered, she now worried about his safety. And given what they now knew about each other, there was still a conversation they needed to have about the risks involved with being together. Could their love for each other trump the danger? For now, she'd revel in the idea of being his girlfriend.

"What are we doing down here?" Phoebe asked Hayley, four hours later. Her feet were throbbing. She'd danced all night with a boy who apparently believed toe-stepping was the name of a dance. And what she needed now was her bed, and not a midnight trip Below.

"Now that the four of you are safe and sound,"—Hayley pushed through the library doors—"I'm curious to see what our friend Liam is saying."

Phoebe couldn't believe it. "You realize that you're now becoming almost as obsessed as your father."

"I know." Hayley laughed. "I know."

"I'll humor you on two conditions," Phoebe said blithely.

"Name them."

"First, no more spontaneous plans that involve me and a blind date."

"Done." Hayley grinned mischievously. Phoebe raised her eyebrows to indicate her seriousness and Hayley laughed again.

"And second, can I watch Colten's Kamron Hyack interview on your TV tomorrow?" This time it was Hayley who spiked an eyebrow and Phoebe laughed. "It's the last stop on his manager's 'Damage Control Tour.'"

"I love that woman's show! Done."

They sat behind a computer and Hayley quickly typed in the URL. Shortly, *Circle of Awareness* flashed on the screen.

Vigo Elders
Posted by **Liam Corten** on October 2nd at **1 PM**

I have it on good authority that the Anzaini have surfaced. I've got word that they are behind the Hypha hunt. . . . Believe me, I hear the questions exploding in all of your minds. All of us history buffs know that the Anzaini swore only to surface when they had a sure way of defeating the Crowns. So what does that have to do with the Hyphas? For now, show-and-tell is over as I take a much-needed break. But rest assured, I will be back to keep you informed when the news is worthy.

Posted in: history

"Is that true?" Hayley said, her voice suddenly hoarse. She looked at Phoebe with bulging eyes. "Why didn't you tell me about the Anzaini?"

Phoebe stared unseeingly at the computer screen. For the first time, she stopped to seriously wonder how it was that Liam always seemed to know things. She couldn't put her finger on it, but something about his post was really bothering her.

"I didn't get a chance to bring it up," Phoebe said, shaking her hair and returning to Hayley's question, "because I got dragged to some dance!"

Hayley had the grace to look sheepish. "Right." She closed the browser and in a hushed voice said, "Well, pull out that Privaque and start talking—wait," she said. "Before you start, I have a confession." A scandalous expression flickered across her face.

"What?" Phoebe said slowly, eying her friend suspiciously.

Bursting with excitement, Hayley said, "I might have made out with my date tonight—"

"What? Soccer Paul?" Phoebe screamed as Hayley giggled senselessly. Putting on her best Hayley expression, Phoebe said, "Now, dish!"

Later, arms wrapped around her tomato pillow, Phoebe couldn't sleep. For some reason, her mind kept returning to Liam Corten's last post. It was almost as though he'd been excited about the Anzaini. *But what would their reappearance mean to him?* Phoebe bolted upright, her hearts pounding. *Show-and-tell is over*, Liam Corten had said. No. It couldn't be. Phoebe reached for her bedside table lamp, turned it on, and grabbed a pen. Unable to breathe, she scribbled in her palm. She couldn't believe it. But it made sense. The only reason everything had been reported with such authority: the letters in Liam Corten, when rearranged, spelled Montclaire.

At the sound of the door opening and closing behind Phoebe, she almost expected to hear the words *Sorry to keep you waiting, Gorgeous.* The view of the sunset from the boathouse balcony was radiant. Phoebe had come back to the lake to try and let go of the sense of sadness that lingered from Scott's betrayal. Yes, he had been a Vigo, but a small part of her had been holding on to the belief that their friendship hadn't all been an act. That perhaps something within him—his humanity—had been the reason she'd been able to bond with him. "Being near water helps clear my mind," he'd said the day after the kidnappings. Whether that had been an honest statement or not, it rang true for Phoebe as well.

"I got your note," said a soft voice in Phoebe's ear.

Phoebe turned and saw Afua standing next to her, her dark eyes trained on some distant point on the lake. Her wavy hair fluttered in the gentle breeze.

"It's just a theory—" Phoebe started.

"And a good one," Afua said. "You have strong sleuthing instincts, Cadet."

Phoebe blinked a few times at the Blackcoat's compliment. "So you think it's Montclaire's blog?"

The Blackcoat nodded. "Liam Corten was her grandfather's name." Afua paused. "Not only that, her text included some of her key phrases. How did you find it?"

Phoebe wrapped her arms around herself. She knew she couldn't mention Hayley's involvement. "It's something I stumbled across when I did a web search on the prophecy," she said. "I didn't think twice about it until Montclaire disappeared. Will she get in trouble for it?"

"She reported what she knew, but never disclosed the location of The Four," Afua said. "But it is something I'll bring up next week at Court."

"You're leaving?" Phoebe said, shocked.

Bringing her gaze to Phoebe's, Afua nodded once sharply.

"But we still need protection!" Phoebe said, trying to keep the whine out of her voice, not wanting to sound as upset as she suddenly felt.

"And you'll have it," Afua said, calmly. "Your protection has now become a priority with the Royal Court. You'll have their utmost attention and service."

A frown creased Phoebe's eyebrows. "Hasn't it always been a priority?" she asked, confused.

"No," Afua said, raising a hand to forestall the question forming on Phoebe's lips. "Every Blackcoat meeting begins with a look at the Threat Grid—geographic-based intel on Vigo activity that may impact the Crowns. A representative of the Royal Court sits in on these meetings as we discuss which intel is actionable and which should be dismissed.

"When the intel about you Hyphas initially appeared on the Grid, it was immediately dismissed."

"What? But—"

Afua's intense look silenced Phoebe again. "You have to understand the reasoning behind it, Cadet. First, it involved a prophecy —not exactly reliable sourcing. Second, Hyphas are still not fully understood or accepted by some in the Court," Afua said. "Put those pieces together and that intel becomes a non-priority."

"Then why were you sent?" Phoebe said, keeping her voice controlled; it stung to hear that Hyphas were not accepted among the Crowns.

"In my ten-year career, nothing on the Threat Grid has ever involved Hyphas," Afua said. "For Vigos suddenly to be interested in them rang an alarm for me. I specifically asked to lead a team to investigate it further. When the request fell on deaf ears, I threatened to resign."

Phoebe, shocked, stared at Afua blankly for several pin-drop silent moments. "And that worked?"

Afua offered her the first real smile that Phoebe had ever seen on her face. "My service record has given me some leverage that I chose to—let's just say—exploit."

"You risked your career on us?" Phoebe said, disbelieving.

"I've risked my life for the Crowns," Afua said. "So why not a career for our entire race? The chance that one of you Hyphas could be the answer to defeating Vigos was worth looking into.

"I came here with the understanding that this case was a non-priority. Even when Cadets Higashi and Baker were taken, my request for back up was denied."

"But two men followed me all the time, and—" Phoebe stopped herself from saying Scott. "I was often shadowed," she said. "And all those guards for the red carpet sting—"

"Were local SIS agents I used my weight as a Blackcoat to secure," Afua said. "For them, it was an opportunity to impress someone who could potentially advance their careers." Afua looked briefly at Phoebe, then stared at the lake. "I let you think they were Blackcoats in order to continue selling the idea that your protection was a Royal Court priority—to help ease your anxiety about the sting."

Phoebe's mouth fell open; it was becoming quite clear that she had no idea who to trust or what to believe anymore.

"I know you must feel misled," Afua said. "But it was a deception necessary for the greater good."

"Why the high priority now?" Phoebe asked, tightening her grip on the railing.

"Your intel about the Anzaini," Afua said, a hint of pride in her voice. "It has shaken the Crowns. They've already convened the Royal Court to discuss this matter."

"So it's true what Lia—Montclaire's blog said about the Anzaini?"

Afua nodded. "The Anzaini have historically been silent leaders. Their mystery adds to their power. They went underground centuries ago promising to make their presence known only when they could crush the Royal Court. So if they want you Hyphas, the Royal Court wants to know why."

"Then why take you off the case? When you've brought them something they consider . . . valuable." She almost choked on the word, knowing that for the Crowns, it didn't apply to her, just to the information she represented.

"I'm still involved. I've been recalled to the Court." Afua gave a dark chuckle. "Apparently my 'expertise' has been requested at some meetings. Not to worry," Afua quickly added at seeing the look of disappointment on Phoebe's face. "I'll be seeing you there."

"What?" None of this made sense anymore, as far as Phoebe was concerned.

"The Crowns want to meet the four of you before your Conversion. After you've all had time to recover from the trauma, of course," Afua added. "This is a big deal. For all Hyphas."

Phoebe stared out at the lake, thinking about everything Afua had risked for her safety. She felt a pang of guilt over her own deception. "A deception necessary for the greater good," the Blackcoat had said. Phoebe decided that would be how she was going to justify keeping Colten's secret. After all, not turning him in had ultimately saved her life. And it was his intel about the Anzaini that now had the Royal Court on high alert. But Phoebe knew that it wasn't only Colten's secret she was sheltering. At a few points during their talks, she had been tempted to tell Afua about her ability, but held back. There was still a chance that the prophecy had nothing to do with her, and in a way, she was hanging onto that notion. Lewis could be right. Maybe one of them would be able to wield the missing elements. Their December birthdays were coming. Conversion was around the corner. They'd know soon enough. And in the meantime, Phoebe needed to have that one thing that was just her own, separate from her other abilities as a Shaper, as part of the Shaper community. Not everyone valued her like Afua did, and those people were still in command of Afua, on some level.

"Thank you for—" Phoebe swallowed, twisted strands of her white streak around a finger and turned to face Afua, thoughtfully. "Thank you for my life," she said.

Afua nodded. "Until later, Phoebe," she said with a small smile.

Phoebe remained at the boathouse long after Afua had left, watching moonlight seep into the horizon like pale translucent tentacles reaching up to embrace the darkening sky around them.

❦ Thirty-Three

"He's the biggest teen sensation to hit the movie screens in years," Kamron Hyack gushed to her audience. "And frankly, I have a big crush. I know you've been waiting patiently for him to come out, so please give a big Hyack Studio welcome to Colten Chase!"

The audience erupted in screams as the DJ played music and Colten entered the studio bobbing his head and dancing along. When he reached Kamron Hyack, the host stood and joined him in a short dance routine. The screams got louder.

Hayley pinched Phoebe's arm. "Damn! Your boyfriend has some moves!"

"Ow! He's not—"

"Yeah, yeah. Zip it!" Hayley said.

After a few minutes of talking about Colten's new movie, Kamron Hyack said, "So the question on everyone's mind Colten: what was going on with your date?"

"Well, Ms. Hyack . . ."

Kamron Hyack tapped Colten's knee. "Clearly you were raised well," she said. "But after that hot dance we shared, you can call me Kamron. In fact call me, anytime."

Colten laughed with the crowd. "Okay, Kamron," he said. "Well, the first time I met my date, she ran away from me. Then, when I tried to walk her to her dorm, she ran away from me again." A flush spread through Phoebe's cheeks as she remembered, and she was embarrassed as if both Colten and Kamron Hyack could see her. "At least," Colten continued, "when she ran this time, she left something behind. So I'm getting closer." He broke into a grin.

A swell of "oohs" and laughter came from the audience as Colten produced a diamond bracelet and dangled it from his index finger.

"You lost a diamond bracelet?" Hayley squealed at the same time a visibly excited Kamron Hyack leaned toward Colten gushing, "Is Colten Chase letting the world know that he's found his Cinderella?"

"She's getting too excited," said Phoebe, who suddenly became nervous.

"Shhh, diamond girl," Hayley hissed, waving Phoebe off. "I want to hear what he says."

A few seconds passed and Colten said nothing. Phoebe's hearts hammered in her chest. She bit her lower lip. Colten looked directly into the camera then, leaned in and gave a smile that could be interpreted either way. And Phoebe understood.

THE END

For more information on Phoebe Pope and the sequel, please visit:
Web: www.PhoebePope.com
Facebook: www.facebook.com/PhoebePopeBooks
Twitter: @TheNyaJade

ACKNOWLEDGMENTS

It takes the time and support of a small village of enthusiasts to get a novel published. First off, I must give love and thanks to my husband, Al, who read every single version of this book, and without whom Phoebe Pope's adventure would never have made it out of my head; my family and my in-laws, for cheering me on. And to Mrs. Coon, my high school English teacher, who asked my fifteen-year-old self to consider the idea of one day becoming a writer.

Thanks to Jenn for our Inner Sunset critique sessions over crepes and coffee. To Sam and Hayley for giving my story-telling imagination a workout when you were young kids. Big warm hugs to my early draft readers: Mom, Al, Mrs. Coon, Afua, Nancy, Jenn and Ernest.

In addition, I'd like to thank the professionals who brought technical and creative expertise to this novel: for editing, Jaimee Garbacik; for copyediting, Carin Siegfried; for cover art, Damonza.com; and for illustrations, Coby L. Cyr.

And to the global village of readers, thank you for choosing to spend your time with my novel.

Made in the USA
Columbia, SC
28 March 2018